What people are saying about

Her Morning Shadow

Buckle down for a wild saga in history that starts in the Great War and charges through the three-way battle for the Crimea and the Ukraine to reach its beacon, the torch of Liberty. A superb alloy of genuine history and vivid imagination. Even better than Semple's *Black Tom*.

Leslie Wilbur, Emeritus Professor, University of Southern California

World War One shattered the world. It swept people off the streets of Europe and America, a fearsome new force that reached into quiet parlors and shops and alleys, butchering the old world and its ideals. Ronald Semple has written a rich and piercing novel about how that European war caught working people and quiet families in Jersey City, and hurled them into life and death. Here is a story of armies marching in the night and people trapped in unimaginable events. It is Mr. Semple's genius to depict the war's impact on blue collar American citizens, some of them first-generation Americans, an ocean away from the battlegrounds. Read this haunting story, and you will be introduced to modern times.

Richard S. Wheeler, Historical novelist and writer

Her Morning Shadow

Ron Semple

TOP HAT

Winchester, UK
Washington, USA

First published by Top Hat Books, 2018
Top Hat Books is an imprint of John Hunt Publishing Ltd., No. 3 East St., Alresford,
Hampshire SO24 9EE, UK
office1@jhpbooks.net
www.johnhuntpublishing.com
www.tophat-books.com

For distributor details and how to order please visit the 'Ordering' section on our website.

Text copyright: Ron Semple 2017

ISBN: 978 1 84694 493 2
978 1 84694 990 6 (ebook)
Library of Congress Control Number: 2017957126

A CIP catalogue record for this book is available from the British Library.

Design: Stuart Davies

Printed and bound by CPI Group (UK) Ltd, Croydon, CR0 4YY, UK

We operate a distinctive and ethical publishing philosophy in
all areas of our business, from our global network of authors to
production and worldwide distribution.

Also by the Author

Black Tom: Terror on the Hudson, ISBN: 976-1-78535-110-5
Winner of the J. Owen Grundy History Award offered by the
Jersey City Landmarks Conservancy.

Miss Bidwell's Spirit (with Warren Murphy),
ISBN: 0-972-63406-1

Dedicated, as always, to Jane Guarascio Semple and in memory of Bob Gallagher, Warren Murphy and Bob Waldron.

Black Tom

No one saw them. A new moon gave off little light and there were no street lamps at Black Tom.

The three German saboteurs moved quietly through the midnight darkness into the unfenced railroad munitions depot on the Jersey City waterfront.

They planted their chemical firebombs in a freight car loaded with ammunition, in a warehouse full of war material and in the hold of a lighter crammed with high explosives.

Then they vanished into the night. Unseen.

A quarter of an hour later, the chemicals touched off intense fires which doubled in size every five minutes. At first, no one saw the fires either.

The fires ate away at wooden crates, red tongues licking at the explosives within. A half hour after that an automatic alarm in the warehouse sounded. That brought the fire department's engines and ladder trucks rolling across the causeway onto Black Tom.

Men began to fight the fires, pull the barges farther into the Hudson River and move the boxcars away from the flames.

It was too late.

Rounds began to cook off lighting up the sky and peppering the Statue of Liberty and Ellis Island with shrapnel.

Then came the explosions shaking the earth, obliterating Black Tom, killing five people and injuring hundreds.

New York City's millions were awakened and took to the streets in panic. Much of the plate glass south of Thirty-Third Street was shattered. The explosions were felt as far away as Maryland.

It was July 30, 1916, and America was not yet at war.

President Woodrow Wilson had been on the tight rope of neutrality for more than two years balancing British provocations against German outrages. America didn't want to join the slaughter in Europe. She was getting rich selling war material to the Allies. She would have sold to the Germans too, but the Royal Navy's blockade scotched that.

So the Germans turned to sabotage trying to stop American ammunition from getting to Allied guns.

The spectacular death and destruction at the Lehigh Valley Railroad's munitions terminal at Black Tom should have caused Wilson to demand a declaration of war. But it didn't.

Local, state and federal investigations into Black Tom came up with the politically convenient conclusion that the devastation was caused by some sort of never explained accident.

People talked about Black Tom for days or weeks, or even years, but most Americans quickly forgot about it.

A few would never forget. The families of the dead. People like Frank Hague, the ambitious and ruthless Jersey City commissioner of public safety who couldn't persuade Congress to forbid the shipment of munitions through Black Tom. Lieutenant Mickey McGurk, the policeman who suspected the Germans did it but wasn't allowed to try and prove it.

Or Detective Sergeant Tony Aiello, Detective Hans Mannstein, Hannah Ganz, Kathy McCann, Fat Jack Lynch, and Abram Ashansky, all of whom did their best to protect Black Tom.

But their story did not end with Black Tom. Like all of us, these immigrants or children of immigrants found that the ordinary lives we yearn to lead are upended by great events beyond our control but which demand our attention and, sometimes, even our very lives.

This is their story. The story of ordinary people in a place called Jersey City who less than nine months later found themselves coping with a world at war, here and beyond the seas, and with its chaotic aftermath.

It is the story of a cobbled together American family. Perhaps, much like yours.

Abie Goes to War

"Can any of you clowns speak French?"

The bored company first sergeant clearly didn't expect a positive answer from these recruits who had been in the Army a bit more than a month.

The men, standing at ease, looked at each other. Then a single arm was slowly raised.

It belonged to Private Abram Aaron Ashansky.

"Ashcans? You speak French?"

"I do, Sergeant."

The first sergeant gestured to his right with his thumb and said, "Fair enough. When you are dismissed, get rid of that rifle and cartridge belt and report to the lieutenant there at company headquarters."

Ashansky looked at the lieutenant who nodded.

"Yes, Sergeant," said Ashansky.

The first sergeant called the company to attention and dismissed them.

"Now you've done it, Ashcans. I thought a smart guy like you knew better than to volunteer," said one of his tent mates as they put their rifles in a rack.

"You'll be lucky if all they make you do is peel potatoes for French fries tonight. Where'd you learn French anyway? I thought you were Russian."

"I'm from the Ukraine. Look, I'd love to discuss the Russian educational system with you, Billy, but I better go see that lieutenant."

"Right. Good luck, pal." They never saw each other again.

Abie removed his campaign hat, stood at attention and saluted. "Private Ashansky reporting as ordered, sir."

The lieutenant returned the salute and said, "Stand at ease, private... Comment avez-vous parlez francais?"

Ashansky smiled, noted the harsh American accent, and said, "Problement, mieux que vous, monsieur."

The lieutenant laughed and said, "Sans aucun doute."

The first sergeant looked up from his desk on the far side of the headquarters tent and shook his head as the conversation continued in French.

"Are you from France, Ashansky?'

"No, sir. From the Ukraine, in Russia."

"Where did you learn to speak French then?"

"At the university, sir. In Kiev."

'Truly? You went to the university? What did you study?"

"Law, sir. I was trained as an advocate—a lawyer."

"Is Russian law based on the Napoleonic Code like most of the countries in Europe?"

Ashansky was impressed. The lieutenant was no dolt.

"No, sir. Russia and the Scandinavian countries are exceptions."

The lieutenant looked at him for a few seconds and then asked, "What happened, Ashansky?"

Ashansky sighed. "War was breaking out, sir. I didn't want to get conscripted into the Russian Army so I ran away—without my diploma and my papers. I worked as a stoker on ships and made my way to America and since then I have been working as a laborer. I couldn't get anything else."

"Really?"

"Well, I didn't want anything else. I like being a worker." Abie didn't tell the lieutenant that he took his fiancée's dowry with him to America and it was now in a safe deposit box in Jersey City.

The lieutenant asked, "Do you speak other languages, private?"

"Russian, Ukrainian and I can get along in German... and Yiddish, of course." Ashansky looked directly into the lieutenant's eyes as he spoke. The lieutenant didn't blink.

"Is Russian that different from Ukrainian?" he asked.

"Some," said Ashansky.

"I'll take your word for it, private. Can you type?"

"With two fingers, sir." *If the keyboard is in Cyrillic,* thought Abie.

"That will have to do for now."

The lieutenant switched back to English as Ashansky and the first sergeant listened attentively. "Go back to your tent and pack all your uniforms in your duffel bag. All of them. Leave your rifle, your cartridge belt and the rest of your field equipment right where they are, the supply sergeant will take care of it. Report back to me as quickly as you can. Just you and your uniforms. Understand?"

"Yes, sir," said a totally puzzled Ashansky who came to attention, saluted, did an about face, and hurried out of the tent.

The first sergeant thought, *What the hell?* "Where's Ashcans headed, sir?'

"Ashcans?"

The first sergeant laughed. "That's his nickname. His platoon sergeant kept messing up his last name. Not many Russians in Kentucky, sir."

"Well, Ashcans is going with me."

"What unit is the lieutenant with," asked the first sergeant.

"Statistics, sergeant. I'm in the statistics section at headquarters."

"Sounds like an interesting job, sir." *What the hell do they want with a Russian who can speak French in the statistics section? Things were a hell of a lot simpler back in the Spanish War.*

Ashansky was back in less than ten minutes, his duffel bag over his shoulder. The lieutenant was waiting for him, standing next to a touring car and smoking a cigarette. He looked at Ashansky as he got closer. Average height, muscular, fair skin, brown hair, blue eyes. He thought, *I wonder how many Jews have blue eyes.*

He said, "Put your duffel in the front with the driver. Sit in the back with me."

"Yes, sir."

Ashansky was uncomfortable. He didn't feel it was his place to start a conversation with the lieutenant although he was bursting with curiosity about where he was going and what he would do. They rode in salience for more than five minutes.

Good. He knows how to keep his mouth shut, thought the lieutenant.

He spoke in French. "We are headed for Hoboken and a troopship to France."

"France? My God. I don't even know how to fire a rifle. I haven't even been to the range. I've only been in the Army a few weeks."

"You won't need a rifle where we're going, Ashansky. We are going to the headquarters of the American Expeditionary Force in Chaumont. We're assigned to the Intelligence Section. You'll probably be working for me as a translator, clerk and runner."

"Intelligence? You mean like the Deuxième Bureau, sir?"

"Exactly."

Ashansky laughed. "The last Jew I heard of that worked in intelligence was named Dreyfus."

"Let's hope you end up better than he did,' said the lieutenant. "As for knowing what you are doing, none of us are trained in intelligence but our boss, General Nolan, is a whiz. We're all going to learn from him and from the Brits and the French. And we're going to learn quickly. We have to."

"Yes, sir."

"Forget that rifle, you're done with that. You'll be issued a .45 pistol but I doubt that you'll ever have to use it. It's not much good unless you're really up close to the enemy and if you're that close you're really in deep shit."

The lieutenant reached into his briefcase on the car floor and took out a pack of chevrons and handed them to Ashansky.

"By the way, you're a corporal now. Get these sewed on your uniforms as quickly as you can. They'll make life a little easier for you aboard the ship. Rank has its privileges even there."

"Will we have any time in Hoboken before we sail? I have a friend that I would really like to say goodbye to, sir."

The lieutenant thought for a second. "Well, the troops will be staging nearby before they board so I probably can get you a twenty-four hour pass. But I've got to warn you. If you miss that troop movement and the ship sails without you, that's desertion in the face of the enemy. They'll hang you."

"Don't worry, sir. I won't miss the ship. I love the thought of a sea voyage where I don't have to shovel coal."

The men fell silent again and the lieutenant asked, "Did that nickname 'Ashcans' bother you?"

"Not at all, sir. It's better than the one I had when I worked in the junkyard back in Kearny."

"Which was?"

"Abie the Jew."

It took a couple of hours to drive from Camp Dix to Hoboken and the scenery wasn't much to look at. The men remained silent.

The auto stopped at the foot of a pier in Hoboken. It was one of twelve the Army had commandeered from the Hamburg-American and North German Lloyd Lines after war broke out.

Abie jumped out and opened the door for the lieutenant who said, "Wait here. I'll be right back."

Abie pulled out a bag of loose tobacco, rolled a cigarette and looked around as he smoked. He saw a small tailor shop in a row of buildings across the street.

The lieutenant emerged from the pier and Abie ground out his cigarette on the pavement.

"Here's your pass. I'm sorry; it's only good for twelve hours. You have to be back by ten tonight. I guess we're sailing on the tide. For God's sake, don't be late. Report right here. Someone will give you instructions then. Good luck, corporal. I'll see you in France."

He extended his hand and Abie shook it. Then Ashansky came to attention and saluted. The lieutenant returned the salute and said, "Don't get drunk and miss the ship. There would be hell to pay."

Ashansky smiled and said, "Don't worry, sir. I'll be here." Ashansky drank nothing but a glass of wine on the Sabbath and he hadn't celebrated the Sabbath since he left the Ukraine in 1914. Tea was his drink and that was hard enough to get in the United States Army which operated on coffee.

"Sir," Abie called out. The lieutenant turned around. "Sir, I don't know the lieutenant's name."

"Lynch. Lieutenant Terrence Lynch."

"Thank you, sir."

Another Irisher, thought Abie.

Ashansky retrieved his duffel bag from the front seat and walked across the street to the tailor.

A small bell above the door rang as he entered the shop. The tailor looked up from his work. He was a small, thin man, wearing a black skullcap. He was seated at a sewing machine putting chevrons on a uniform blouse.

Good, thought Abie, *he knows where they go.*

"*Sholem Aleikum,*" said Abie.

Grinning broadly, the tailor replied, "*Sholem Aleikum.*"

The men switched to English. "I see you know how to sew stripes on a uniform," said Abie.

"That's true," said the tailor. "You're not the first soldier I've met although I don't meet many Jewish ones."

"You will. What time do you close your shop?"

"What time am I done with my work?" Both men laughed.

"Of course. Can you sew chevrons on this jacket right now and then sew them on the rest of my uniforms before, say, six o'clock this evening."

The tailor rolled his eyes. "Yes, Captain."

"Corporal. I'm a corporal," said Abie.

"Who knows? Maybe someday you'll be a captain—like Dreyfus."

"Oy!" said Abie pressing his fingers to his temples and drawing a laugh from the tailor. He took off his uniform blouse and handed it to the tailor along with his stack of chevrons. The man immediately started to sew while Abie rooted in his duffel bag for his other jacket and his shirts.

By the time Abie had found them, the tailor was biting off the last thread on the second chevron.

He handed the blouse to Abie who donned it. "Perfect," he said.

"You're surprised?"

"Not at all," said Abie. "I hope I'll be as good a soldier as you are a tailor."

"Then you'll be a captain for sure," said the tailor.

Abie put on his overseas cap and said, "*A dank.* I'll see you at six o'clock, my friend."

"I'll be here."

Abie put his duffel bag in a corner and left.

A cab was easy to find. They were constantly pulling up to the pier and disgorging officers. Abie hopped in one.

"Take me to Police Headquarters in Jersey City, please."

"You got it, General," said the cabbie.

Aha! Another promotion, thought Abie who had already decided to give the man a decent tip.

The ride was short and it took Abie less than fifteen minutes to track down Detective Sergeant Tony Aiello with whom he had worked in 1916 keeping an eye on anarchists and other crazies who might want to drag America into a bloody war.

Well, America was in the World War now and Abram

Aaronovich Ashansky, who had fled the Ukraine rather than serve in the ranks of the Czar, had surprised himself by enlisting in the American Army.

This is my country now, he had thought. *Not a bad country for Jews. She needs us now.*

The policemen he had queried had treated him, or least his uniform, with respect and now he was knocking on a door marked with Aiello's name.

"C'mon in," said Aiello who jumped up as soon as Ashansky crossed the threshold and rushed to embrace him.

"Abie! Abie! Hot damn! Look at you. A corporal, no less," said Tony excitedly. "What are you doing here? Are you on leave? How long can you stay?"

He gestured to a chair. "Sit down, Abie. Sit down and tell me what's going on with you."

Abie removed his cap and sat. "I don't really know, Tony. All I know is I'm leaving for France, probably tomorrow. From Hoboken."

"Wow," said Tony, "that was quick. I thought it took a lot longer than that to train an infantryman."

"It does, Tony. I've never even fired a rifle. Thank God, I'm going to work in…" Abie hesitated. "I'm going to be working in 'statistics' at headquarters, way behind the front lines."

Aiello was an excellent detective and had noticed the pause. "Statistics is it? Wonderful work for a junkyard strongman."

Abie smiled and said, "Tony, if you think about 'statistics' and come up with one plus one equals two, please keep it to yourself."

"Abie, I have no head for 'statistics,' I'm just a dumb cop. Don't worry about me, my friend. I'm worried about you."

Tony reached into his vest pocket and took out a safe deposit box key attached to a pocket watch chain. "What do you want me to do with this?"

The box this key opened contained his fiancée Rachel's

dowry, mostly gems, some gold and platinum. Abie smuggled it out of the Ukraine and entrusted it to Tony when he enlisted. The dowry was worth a small fortune.

"Nothing, my friend. Keep it safe for me. But I'd feel better if it wasn't dangling from a watch chain tempting every *goniff* in sight."

Tony smiled and said, "I'll have my wife hide it at home. Believe me, it will be safe."

He frowned. "What should I do if you're not as far from the front line as you think and something happens?"

Abie put his hand on Tony's shoulder. "I've listed you as my next-of-kin. If the kaiser gets lucky, the Army will tell you I'm not coming back."

"What then?" asked Tony?

"Then your daughter—when you have a daughter—will have a much nicer dowry than any honest cop can come up with."

Tony shook his head. "My daughter doesn't want Rachel's dowry. She wants to grow up with you and her Aunt Rachel."

Abie choked up and bit his lip. Now he grabbed Tony by both shoulders. "My friend. My American brother. Please God, we both live to see that day."

Tony jumped up and said, "Enough silly talk. We got to get you fed. You look like the Army is trying to starve you to death."

Abie said, "Not really, Tony. The Army gives us plenty to eat but we sweat it off between meals."

"Well, I know a couple of nice ladies who will remedy that, my friend. Let's go."

Abie and Tony climbed the stairs to his flat just across the hall from his parents. His father, a master bricklayer, had bought the four-family building. Two daughters presumably would live in the downstairs flats once they married. Tony's mother, Carmella, was a happy woman.

"I'm home," cried Tony, "and guess who's with me!"

His wife, Peggy, a very tall, beautiful strawberry blonde, was setting the table. She dropped a plate and came rushing, her arms outstretched, past her husband and hugged Abie tight. Taller than him, she kissed him on the forehead first.

"My God, Abie! It's you! I can't believe it. You're home."

Abie stood on his tiptoes and she kissed both cheeks.

"Whoa! Whoa!" said Tony, "Let the poor man sit down, woman."

Abie, smeared with lipstick, sat down.

"Tony, pour Abie a glass of wine and I'll see if I can get this poor man something to eat. Abie, you know, my lout of a husband didn't let me know you were coming."

"Your lout of a husband didn't know I was coming," said Abie. "Don't go to any trouble, Peggy."

"Ha!" said Tony as he poured three glasses of homemade red wine.

Tony picked up his glass and said, *"Salute!"* Abie answered with *"L'Chaim!"* and Peggy finished with *"Slainte!"*

Peggy disappeared into her mother-in-law's flat and came back with a big bowl of antipasto. "Here. This should hold the two of you until we can make lunch. It shouldn't take long."

Peggy left and, what seemed like just minutes later, a procession of smiling women came through the door. Peggy carried a huge bowl of pasta topped with tomato gravy. Her mother-in-law trailed her bearing bowls of sausage and meatballs, Carmella's elder daughter had bracioles and more gravy and the younger one bore bread and grated cheese.

Controlled chaos ensued amidst shouts, kisses, while all the food was put on the big wooden kitchen table. Tony finished setting the table for six.

Abie grabbed Carmella's hand—delicate as a piece of granite—bent to kiss it and said, "Signora Aiello, I am delighted to see you again."

Carmella grunted with pleasure and said, *"Infine, un*

gentiluomo." The girls squealed with delight and rained kisses on a laughing Abie.

It was a typical Sicilian meal. Six people with a minimum of three conversations going on at the same time.

Carmella sat on one side of Abie, Peggy on the other.

When Carmella spoke, the others fell silent, "Thank God you got here before you starved to death. You're all skin and bones, Abie."

"Signora, no one leaves your table hungry."

"Peggy helped make the gravy," said Tony proudly.

Carmella raised her hand for silence. "I've had enough of this 'signora' stuff, Abie. I'm no signora. You're family. I'm your aunt. I'm your Aunt Carmella."

Then, pointing both of her index fingers at her daughters across the table, she said, "And you two are his cousins."

"Cousin Abie," they cried pushing past Carmella and Peggy to kiss him again.

Once they were back in their chairs, Carmella continued, "We're your family, Abie. We love you and you will love us."

"I already do, Aunt Carmella. It doesn't bother you that I'm Jewish?'

Carmella shrugged. "So was Jesus Christ. Besides this is America. We're an American family. Sicilians, Irish, Jews, Germans."

Tony couldn't resist. "Maybe, some day, even Italians."

Carmella frowned. "Watch your mouth," she said. "Now let's talk family. Your fiancée, what's her name— Rachel? She's still in Russia or Rumania or someplace like that?"

"Yes, Aunt Carmella. She's in the Ukraine. Or least I hope so. I don't know whether she is alive or dead."

"She's alive," said Carmella. "I'd know if she was dead. Family always knows. Is this Ukraine near where you are going in France?"

"No, Aunt Carmella. It's a thousand miles away."

"Too bad. Well, you'll just have to come back after the war, pack a bag and go to Ukrainia and find her. Tony could go with you and help you look."

Both men and Peggy were startled.

"She belongs here with us," said Carmella Aiello. "We'll find you someplace nice to live. Maybe across the street." No one laughed.

"I'll find her," said Abie.

"Of course you will," said Carmella as the others nodded.

Abie warmed to the occasion. "Maybe at our wedding, Uncle Antonio, can give the bride away. Tony will be the best man and Peggy the matron of honor. The girls can be bridesmaids and you, of course, would be mother-of-the-bride."

Carmella gave him a slow, dignified nod and said, "We'd be honored, nephew."

The meal finally ended and the women cleared the table and did the dishes. The men sat on the stoop in the late October sunshine sipping black coffee and smoking cigars.

Abie turned to Tony and gripped his shoulder, "I can't tell you how much your family—my family—means to me. I've been alone since I came to America and I hated it. No family. No one I loved within my reach. No Rachel, no mother, no father, no aunts and uncles and no cousins. Now, in hours, that is all changed thanks to you, my American brother. I will cherish the memory of this afternoon until the day I die."

"There will be lots more of them when you get back, Abie. Maybe one of my sisters will become a nun and you and Rachel can live downstairs from us." Both men laughed.

"They say the war will be over and you boys will be home for Christmas," said Tony.

Abie puffed on his cigar. "They said that in 1914 too. I don't think so. I think it will be a hard slog." It was.

Abie was back at the tailor's at quarter to six. His blouse and shirts were hanging, neatly pressed, on a rack. He took them down, folded them, and put them in his duffel bag.

"How much do I owe you, my friend?" asked Ashansky.

"How can I overcharge somebody that calls me his friend? Fifty cents should do it."

Abie handed him a two dollar bill. "Here, send your son to college."

He walked onto the pier and soon found a sign tacked to the wall. "Statistics Unit: Report Here." There were two other corporals standing there.

Abie asked, "Who's in charge?"

"Not me," they answered in unison.

The three of them sat against the wall making small talk but being careful to avoid any mention of their assignments when a sergeant walked up to them.

"Are you men assigned to statistics?"

"Yes, Sergeant." Again in unison.

"Okay. I'm Sergeant Talbot. My job is to get you aboard ship, see that you don't die on the way to France and then deliver you to a Lieutenant Lynch when we get there. Obey my orders and we'll get along. There'll be seven of you, all corporals, and I'll try to keep you off any shit details that come up. Do you understand me?"

"Yes, sir."

"Don't call me 'sir,' goddamn it. I'm a Sergeant."

Abie asked, "When will we board, sergeant."

"When all seven of you are here."

That moment didn't arrive until 9:45 pm when a somewhat disheveled corporal staggered onto the pier. "Statistics! Where the hell is statistics," he bellowed.

The sergeant, who had been checking his pocket watch every few minutes for the past hour, called out, "Over here, asshole."

Over There

The sergeant led his seven men up the gangplank and checked in with another sergeant standing next to the ship's officer of the deck.

"Statistics? What division are you people with?"

"No division, pal, just Statistics. I don't know shit about it so don't bother to ask," said Sergeant Talbot.

"Right," said the check-in sergeant recognizing another regular. He started to thumb through a thick sheaf of paper and some minutes later said. "Got it. Sergeant Talbot and seven corporals?"

"That's me and that's them."

The naval officer spoke. "This man will take your unit down to your berths, Sergeant."

"Thank you, sir," said Sergeant Talbot who saluted.

A sailor said, "This way, chum."

The USS *America* was a big ship at 669 feet long with a beam of 75 feet. At 41,500 tons she was a lot heavier than when she was launched in 1905 as the SS *Amerika* for the Hamburg-America Line. She had been a well-appointed passenger liner.

When war broke out, the SS *Amerika* was interned in Boston. Years later when the United States declared war on Germany, the Navy seized her.

The Navy had converted her into a troopship, changed the spelling of her name, and had armed her with four six-inch guns, two one-pound guns, three machine guns and nine depth charges.

She could do 17.5 knots, much faster than any U-boat. She was manned by almost a thousand sailors and would take 4,000 soldiers to France. There were 4,000 tons of cargo and equipment in her holds too.

Any ship is a complex of confusing passage ways and what

the Navy calls "ladders." The *America* was no different and in less than a minute six of the corporals were helplessly lost. Abie and the sergeant had been on ships before and were mentally mapping their way.

The sailor looked at his scrap of paper and said, "Okay. Here we are. Pick a rack. The head is over there. To starboard." He pointed to his right and vanished.

The sergeant took over. "We'll stick together. Five of you take the racks on that side. Three of us will be on this side." With that the sergeant climbed to the highest rack as Abie did on the other side while the others quibbled over who would get the racks closest to the steel deck.

As they settled their duffel bags onto the end of the racks where there was no pillow and blanket, the sergeant looked over at Abie and said flatly, "You've been to sea before."

"Yes, Sergeant. The *Baltic* and the *Atlantic*."

Talbot nodded. "I sailed to the Philippines and back across the Pacific. It took forever. This should be a shorter run."

"But maybe just as rough," said Abie.

Talbot laughed. "Then some of these people will find out gravity is not your friend in rough seas."

The troop compartments filled up fast.

One corporal stood up and addressed Talbot. "Hey, Sarge, where do you think the latrine is? I got to piss."

"That's what the Navy calls a 'head' and it's right over there. Don't lose your way back. Better yet. We'll all go together. . .I said now, people."

Grousing, his seven men formed a ragged line behind him and followed him into the head.

There was a long line of metal sinks topped with mirrors on one side and on the other, metal toilets hovering over a trough of running water. There were no showers.

"Now, pay attention when you are taking a crap. It won't take long before some imbecile amuses himself by floating wads of flaming toilet paper down that trough. If you don't want your ass singed, pay attention."

They made it back to their racks without incident. Several card games were already underway as was a crap game with the dice bouncing off a steel bulkhead.

Ashansky approached the sergeant. "We're going to be working with French soldiers in the statistics section, Sergeant. Would you mind if we practice our French?"

"Hell, no. Help yourselves. I know a little oxcart Spanish myself so I'll probably know what you are talking about." He didn't understand a word but he wouldn't admit it to these pretend corporals.

They didn't sail on the tide. In fact, they didn't sail for two days although they couldn't leave the ship. Most of their time was spent standing in line waiting to get fed. The sergeant introduced them to an old joke. "There's only two things wrong with the food on this ship. It's lousy and there ain't enough of it."

You could always gamble if you trusted that the game was honest. Some soldiers weren't and arrived in France with a duffel bag stuffed with currency. One cheater was caught and beaten badly enough that he had to go to sick bay.

The lights were dimmed at 2200 but if you had anything to read you could always go into the head where the lights were always on.

The only duty Talbot's squad had was cleanup around its own area. As Talbot said to a senior sergeant, his men were non-coms and shouldn't do any dirty work as long as a private was still breathing.

The corporals practiced their French and gleefully corrected each other's use and pronunciation. They were becoming a unit. Beginning to trust one another. No one spoke about intelligence work or even asked questions about it.

The sergeant was happy. *These people aren't going to give me any trouble, thank God. I wonder what they're actually going to do in France.* He noticed that they never talked about "statistics" whatever that was.

The word buzzed about the ship. They were sailing. Virtually all of the soldiers rushed to the open deck.

The wives, girlfriends and families of the officers were on the pier waving goodbye. Thousands of men waved back. Tugs nudged the big ship into the Hudson River. Any vessel in earshot sounded its whistle. The soldiers waved madly.

This was it. They were going off to war. They were wildly happy just like their kin on both sides who marched off in 1914 singing songs, with flowers in their rifle barrels. Then they were blown to bits and died by the millions in the mud of France and Belgium.

The USS *America* quickly passed by the Statue of Liberty. They could see the scars she had suffered from shrapnel when the munitions depot at Black Tom, just behind her right shoulder, had blown up the year before.

The ship slipped through the Narrows. The tugs disengaged and tooted their goodbyes as the local pilot took her through the Lower Bay.

Other ships were joining her. By the time she reached Sandy Hook, the convoy was complete.

There were other troopships, the USS *Von Steuben*, USS *Agamemnon* and the USS *Mount Vernon* with her distinctive four stacks. All had been German ships interned in US waters because of the war. They were escorted by an armored cruiser, the USS *North Carolina*, and two destroyers, the USS *Duncan* and the USS *Terry*.

The soldiers were impressed by the small armada that was on its way to join the ever growing American Expeditionary Force in France. By the following June there would be a million American soldiers in France. But these were among the first to go.

"Those heinies don't stand a chance," said one.

Some men—and a few sailors—onboard the USS *America* began to get seasick long before the vessel reached the open ocean.

"I don't feel so good," said one corporal. "Me neither," said another. A third said, "What's the matter? You guys seasick already? Wait till it gets rough out there."

That was not helpful.

Sergeant Talbot nodded to Abie who nodded back. "All right, people. We're going on deck. Let's move."

"I really don't want to go on deck, Sergeant. I think I'll just close my eyes and see if I can sleep it off," said the first man.

"Wrong," said Sergeant Talbot. "You close your eyes and you're going to end up puking your guts out. Off your dead ass, my lad. We're going topside. That way if you really do get sick, you can throw up over the side and not make a mess for the rest of us."

That's exactly what the corporal did, as did the second. Two others were a bit queasy but Abie told them to look at the horizon and that seemed to help. Scores, maybe hundreds, of soldiers were bent over the lifelines vomiting.

"Dear God," said the ashen-faced corporal. "How long before we get to France?"

"Don't worry, son, you'll get your sea legs long before we tie up." By the mercy of God, he did.

Others did not. In the troop compartments hundreds of men took to their racks as the seas grew and the ship rolled and pitched.

Soon the contents of their stomachs spewed from their mouths. Vomit rained down from the fourth, third, second of the stacked racks. Rarely from the fifth where all the men experienced in the ways of the sea had taken up residence.

Every toilet and most of the sinks had soldiers in sorrowful attendance.

The stench in the compartments was awful. Cleanup was continuous as non-coms insisted that resentful soldiers wield mops and buckets. Compassion for the sick was conspicuously lacking. Most men remained on deck coming in only to eat—if they could.

"I'd tell you to avoid greasy food," said Sergeant Talbot. "Except that's all the Navy serves." More casualties were taken before, during and after meals. That meant "seconds" for those hardy men who had complained they weren't getting enough to eat. Indeed, it's an ill wind that blows no good.

Day-by-day fewer men were getting or staying sick although the weather was typical for early November in the North Atlantic. The moans and groans at night were diminishing too.

A new fear gripped the soldiers on the seventh day out. The ships had been zigzagging in unison as a routine defense against a German U-boat that might draw a bead on them.

The USS *Von Steuben* zigged while the USS *Agamemnon* zagged. The troopships collided panicking the soldiers on every ship in sight. "Do you think those boats are going to sink? That'd be worse than the goddamn *Titanic*."

What was worse, the *Von Steuben* then signaled that she had seen a submarine. The ships scattered like a covey of quail.

In nanoseconds every soldier on every transport had heard the word *submarine*. "Don't worry," said one. "We can outrun any submarine."

Another answered, "Sure, just like the *Lusitania*."

Hours went by with no further alarms and the ships, somewhat sheepishly, fell back into their assigned positions and started to zigzag again.

The badly damaged *Von Steuben*, its bow open to the sea, managed to rejoin the convoy the next afternoon. The convoy had slowed down to accommodate her, which did nothing to improve the soldiers' anxiety about U-boats.

The twelve-day voyage finally ended when the USS *America* pulled into its slip in the port of Brest. Silent prayers of thanksgiving were uttered by many, if not most.

Sergeant Talbot constantly shouted, "Stick together! Stick together!" as he shepherded his squad off the ship and to the right of the gangway.

"There's Lieutenant Lynch. Over there," said Abie. They headed for him.

"Sergeant Talbot, reporting as ordered, sir, with the detail all present."

"Very good. At ease, Sergeant," said Lynch, returning the salute.

Lynch reached into his briefcase and produced a one-page order and some vouchers.

Sergeant Talbot interrupted him. "Begging the lieutenant's pardon, but does he know where the Signal Corps people are supposed to report?"

"You report right here, Sergeant."

"Statistics? I don't know nothing about statistics. I'm not even that good at long division," said Talbot. The lieutenant and all the corporals laughed.

"That was just a cover name for what we are going to be doing, Sergeant. You're going to be the senior non-com in the Intelligence Section."

One corporal said, *sotto voce*, "I'll bet he doesn't know what that is either." That earned him a laugh from his peers and a dirty look from the sergeant.

"You're also going to be Brigadier General Nolan's driver and bodyguard."

"General Dennis Nolan?"

"Yep," said the lieutenant. "That's our boss man."

"I heard of him," said the sergeant. "He was one nasty son-of-a-bitch during the Spanish war."

Ashansky sucked in his breath but the lieutenant was

nonplussed. "Well, heroics are not in our future. We'll be miles and miles behind the lines."

"Suits me, "said the sergeant. "I got shot at enough in the Philippines and Mexico. No sense giving Fritz a turn."

Lieutenant Lynch handed the papers to Talbot. "Here are your orders, train tickets and vouchers for the train station restaurants. Get the men fed and take the train to Chaumont. You'll have to walk from there. Ashansky can translate for you. Report to the headquarters battalion sergeant major. He'll tell you what to do next. Good luck, men."

With that, Lieutenant Lynch and his briefcase strolled away.

"Okay, Ashansky. Let's find out where the train station is and how we get there." The first French dockworker they saw had that information.

Their train to Gare Montparmasse in Paris was due to leave in two hours which gave them time to eat breakfast.

"Don't the Frogs eat bacon and eggs?" asked one corporal.

"Eat what they give you. You're a long ways from Hoboken," said the sergeant.

The train was filled with officers from several different countries, many French civilians and a few French enlisted men. "Sit down and shut up," said Sergeant Talbot. "Look out the window and don't make eye contact with the officers. Ashansky, sit next to me."

The train made many stops along the ten-hour, 350-mile route to Paris but no one spoke to them except a French sergeant who asked where they were going. Ashansky said, "We don't know, sergeant. I guess they'll tell us when we get there."

The Frenchman laughed and said, "All armies are the same. I'm glad you're here. It's been a long war. Good luck, my American friend."

All the corporals said, "Merci, mon ami." That drew a puzzled look from a French officer seated across the aisle, but he remained silent.

The train pulled into the huge railroad station and the men retrieved their duffel bags from a porter unloading them from a baggage car.

"What now?" asked Talbot. Ashansky read the tickets and said, "We change trains here. Terminals too, we have to go to Gare D'Est."

"Where in the hell is that," asked Talbot.

It was about three and a half miles away. Too far to walk, in the dead of night, carrying heavy duffel bags.

"We'll grab a bite to eat and then we'll take taxis," said Talbot.

"I'll bet we can change American money into French money here at the station," said Ashansky. They could and did.

It took two taxis, four men in each with their duffels riding in racks on top. The cabs moved along at a leisurely fifteen miles per hour. Traffic was light.

They started off on the Boulevard de Sebastopol, but when they crossed the Boulevard St. Denis the road morphed into the Boulevard de Strasbourg.

Ashansky was crammed in up front with the cabbie, an elderly man who pointed to the signpost and said, "We never forget. I was there when Sedan fell. We lost almost all Alsace and much of Lorraine to the Boche. You'll help get them back, eh?"

"You'll get them back," said Ashansky.

The cabbie grimaced. "I am too old for this war. I've been out of the reserves for twenty years." He turned toward Ashansky and smiled. He pointed his thumb at his chest.

"But I helped save Paris. Me and my cab. Hundreds of cabs. We took thousands of *poilus* to the front. Along the Marne. They stopped the Boche. They did. We did. We saved Paris"

"Good for you," said Ashansky as the cabs pulled up to Gare D'Est.

24

The train ride to Chaumont was only 150 miles but it took six hours. The Americans slept. One of the first things one learns in the military is how to fall asleep whenever you are given the chance.

A camion was waiting there to shuttle them and a few other American enlisted men to the headquarters of the American Expeditionary Force in France.

A sign pointed the way to the regimental sergeant major's office in the enormous stone building. "You men wait here. Ashansky's in charge."

The sergeant-major said, "Here are the assignments for you and your men and a copy of the daily routine. You all will be billeted together. Stow your duffle bags in your squad room and then go to the quartermaster sergeant and get your gear and winter clothing. It gets goddamn cold in sunny France."

The quartermaster sergeant was another regular. The intelligence squad drew heavy wool winter overcoats, canvas leggings, hobnailed trench boots, a steel helmet, a gas mask, a first-aid pouch, a canteen and cup, a mess kit, a pistol belt with a pouch for two extra magazines, a leather pistol holster with US engraved on it and a pouch containing a set of wire cutters.

"What are we going to use the wire cutters for?" asked one corporal. The sergeants looked at each other and shook their heads.

Then they got two blankets, two sheets, a pillowcase and a laundry bag.

"We change sheets and pillowcases every week," said the quartermaster sergeant. "Put your dirty clothes in the laundry bag and it will be returned with the clean sheets. Make sure everything you own is marked with your name and section number, which in your case is G-2.

"You won't need rifles, bayonets, shelter halves, tent poles or entrenching tools here. But we do have them if you do need them later on." That sounded ominous.

"Okay. Now go next door to the armorer and draw your pistols."

Each of them received an unloaded Model 1911 Colt .45 pistol which they handled as gingerly as rattlesnakes except for Talbot who pulled the slide back, checked the chamber, released the slide, pointed the pistol at the ceiling and pulled the trigger. *Click!*

"You will be issued ammunition when you are in the field or at the pistol range. You will sign for it and you have to account for every round when you get back. We don't want you shooting up the place."

"Can we shoot at the Germans?" asked one corporal.

The armorer looked at him like he was a schoolchild. "With luck, you won't get a chance to shoot anybody. With even more luck, you won't shoot yourself or me."

"Right on," said Talbot who intended to take them to the range as soon as possible and teach them how to use a .45. Talbot was first introduced to the .45 in the Philippines where Moro insurgents were responsible for its development. The Moros, Muslims who inhabited the southern islands and who had no intention of becoming America's "little brown brothers," were fierce fighters. So fierce that bullets from the standard .38 caliber revolver rarely stopped them.

Hence the .45 with its big, slow moving slug that would knock a man down even if it only clipped his pinky. But the .45 was an automatic pistol that could be as dangerous to its shooter as to its target. Talbot knew, loved and respected the .45. So would they all, in time.

The intelligence squad settled in, made their bunks, stowed their gear in footlockers or on wall pegs and stared at their .45s.

"Wrap those pistols in handkerchiefs and lock them up in your footlockers. We're off to meet our bosses." Talbot and Ashansky quickly found Lieutenant Lynch who was seated behind a desk browsing through a record book, Ashansky's.

"Sergeant Talbot," he said. "The general wants to see you." With that he cranked a telephone on his desk. "Sir, Sergeant Talbot is here... Yes, sir."

"Walk right in, Sergeant. No need to knock." Lieutenant Lynch was General Nolan's gatekeeper, a task he had performed for Frank Hague, now the mayor of Jersey City.

He looked at Ashansky and pointed to his record book. "I didn't realize you are from Jersey City, Corporal. So am I. When we were in Hoboken, you said you wanted to visit a friend. Who was that?"

"Tony Aiello, sir. He's a policeman."

"Detective Sergeant Aiello. I know him. He was one of Hague's Zeppelins. Did you know I was Frank Hague's secretary?"

"No, sir." *So that makes you Fat Jack Lynch's brother. Interesting.*

"Say, were you one of those, what did they call them, confidantes?" Lynch asked.

He's fishing for information that's none of his business.

"Hardly, sir. We were just friends," Abie lied.

"Never mind," said Lynch who dismissed Ashansky as not being of much use in what he hoped would be a brilliant, political future once the war was over.

"The general will see you now."

The Ukraine

Rachel lay stiffly under her mother's bed, the sides of the cover concealing her. She could see the rough rope springs an inch or so from her eyes. Her fists were tightly clenched.

She heard her mother who was standing a few feet away from the bed.

"You don't want me. I'm an old hag. I'm fifty years old."

"You don't look like a hag to me, *koxaha*," said the heavyset, bearded Ukrainian ataman. "Besides, I'm fifty-one. At least you know what you're doing. If you don't want your underwear ripped off, take it off yourself."

"No."

"Yes," he said moving towards her, opening the buttons on his fly.

She sobbed. "Why are you doing this to me?"

"Why did you kill Christ? Don't make me kill you. You know I will. Don't be stupid. Let the sun rise in the morning."

Her mother sat on the bed and Rachel heard a rustle of a skirt and then she heard rather than felt movement on the bed. The rope spring drooped closer to Rachel's nose. She turned her head to the side and bit her lips.

Now she felt the movement of the bed too.

"Show a little life. Do you want to end up dead? No? That's better."

Rachel felt her tears and was panic-stricken. She was sure she had made a sound.

Oh my God! What have I done? The movement continued more quickly and then, minutes later, came to an abrupt stop.

"Agggh!" It was the ataman.

All was still for a few moments and then she sensed him getting off the bed. The rope spring lifted a fraction.

"Now that wasn't too bad, was it, Mama?" said the ataman.

Rachel's mother was silent.

The ataman buttoned his fly and looked around the sparsely furnished room. It was illuminated by a kerosene lantern on a table and the embers of a wood fire that gave off both heat and light.

"Where do you Jew bastards hide all your good stuff? You can't bury furniture too, can you?" He walked over to the fireplace and took a pair of brass candlesticks off the mantle.

Rachel's mother remained silent, now sitting on the edge of the bed.

"Well, I don't have time to dig up your whole yard so it looks like you're going to get away with it this time, *koxaha*. I'm going to find me some rich Jews."

He walked to the front door, his hand upon the handle and said, "Goodbye, *koxaha*. You'll never see me again. And tell whoever is hiding under that bed to keep quiet if she doesn't want to be next. I'm fifty-one so there is no next until tomorrow." He laughed. The women did not.

He opened the door and stepped out into the night. Several of his men came running.

"Did you find a Jewess, Ataman?"

"I did and it was like fucking a dead cow."

"You should know, Piter," said an older man to loud laughter.

The ataman grabbed his shoulder and said, "Come on, old friend, let's find us some rich Jews." A younger man pointing to the house asked, "Should we burn it down?"

"Don't bother," said the ataman, "It's not worth the match. Saddle up, boys." He handed the candlesticks to the young man who grinned.

Rachel's mother went to the door, cracked it a bit and watched the men ride away.

"You can come out now, Rachel."

Rachel ran to her mother, arms outstretched. "Oh, Mama!" They embraced with Rachel burying her head into her mother's hair, crying uncontrollably.

"Shh! Shh!" said the mother caressing Rachel's hair. "It's all right. It's all over. It will be all right."

Rachel's head bobbed up and she said, "It will never be all right. That bastard! That pig! If Papa was here, he would kill that bastard."

The mother took Rachel's face between her hands and said, "Thank God, your father wasn't here. He would have done something stupid and now I would be a widow too.

"That pig was right. The sun will rise tomorrow and so will you and I."

Rachel had stopped sobbing.

"Do you know why we Jews have survived over thousands of years while other tribes and peoples have vanished?" her mother asked.

"Because we are the Chosen People?"

"Yes, my darling daughter. We are that and our creator has given us the gift of eternal endurance. No matter what happens, we endure. No matter what our enemies do to us, we endure. And despite what happened here tonight, you and I will endure. We are Jews."

"Yes, Mama."

Her mother kissed her and stepped back. She pointed her finger at Rachel. "But we won't tell your father what happened here tonight." She smiled. "Jewish men aren't as good at enduring as Jewish women."

"But what if...?" asked Rachel. Her mother waved her hands in dismissal.

"Don't worry about that. I'm too old... I think. But even so, any child born of a Jewish mother is a Jew. Our enemies forget that and go out of their way to help us survive.

"Now, go heat some water. I have to wash the smell of that pig off my body."

"Yes, Mama."

The hetman that had violated her and his band were in full gallop in pursuit of the loot that would be their only compensation for helping to drive a Russian army out of Kiev. They were wearing red armbands.

They were 'soldiers," so to speak, of the Kiev Bolshevik Committee that had fought forces loyal to both the Ukrainian Central Rada and the Kiev Military District that still supported the Russian Provisional Government.

Violence had broken out on November 10 and fierce firefights erupted throughout the city. Three days later, the Military District leaders had enough and signed a ceasefire. They then withdrew their 10,000 troops from Kiev leaving it to the Reds.

Of course, the hetman and his band were not communists. Ignorant men, they had never heard of Karl Marx, let alone Vladimir Lenin. They would change armbands more than once in the wake of the Russian revolution. They were out for loot and adventure. They intuitively knew that no politician of any stripe cared whether they lived or died. Mostly, they died.

Days later, there was an urgent knock on the door. Rachel stiffened and said, "Don't answer it, Momma."

Her mother said, "Get under the bed and don't move. And be quiet this time."

Her mother hesitated. The knocks became more urgent. With a sigh, she unbolted the door. It was her husband and a tall, young man in ill-fitting civilian clothes. Her son, Shemuel.

She pushed past her husband and embraced her son. "My boy. My boy! You're alive!" He leaned down and she covered his face with kisses as the men laughed.

Rachel heard what was happening and scrambled out from under the bed. She threw her arms around both her mother and her brother.

"Easy! Easy!" said her brother. "I love you too. I'm home for good but let's get inside before anyone asks who I am."

Shemuel was a deserter. When the Kerensky Offensive in Galicia collapsed, he walked away and went home as did thousands of Russian soldiers. Morale was shattered. Bolshevik agitators urged the men to desert. Many did and murdered their officers as they went.

It took him months and he suffered much, staving off starvation once by eating rotting turnips he found in a picked over field. He did things along the way that he would never speak of to anyone.

The women were fussing over him in the big room when his father, with a smile on his face, asked, "Does anyone care that I'm alive too?"

His wife answered, "Who would bother to kill an old fool like you? But since you're alive, I'll bet you're hungry."

"I know I am," said her son. "I'm always hungry."

The meal Rachel and her mother cobbled together was very heavy on potatoes and stale bread and almost devoid of meat but the men ate as though at a banquet.

The table was alive with a babble of happy talk until the father asked, "Have you heard from your brother? Do you know where he is?"

Shemuel swallowed a chunk of bread. "No, I don't, Papa. You know we were in the same battalion, so we would get to see one another once in a while. He was fine the last time I saw him." *As well as any Jew is in the hands of a shit kicking peasant sergeant,* he thought.

"He was healthy and hadn't lost much weight although he couldn't stomach the pork we got once in a while."

"Did you eat pork?" asked Rachel.

"Yes." It was the least of my sins, dear sister.

"Anyway, when we retreated—it really wasn't a retreat, it was a rout—men just threw away their rifles and ran. The battalion just melted. I never saw my brother again. I don't know where he is. I'm sorry."

"Don't be sorry," said his mother. "It's not your fault. He'll turn up just like you did."

A third son was killed in the first month of the war in 1914 when the Russians pushed into East Prussia only to be pole-axed by the Germans at Tannenberg where two Russian armies virtually were destroyed. The family was still grieving.

Now the father said with some satisfaction, "Well, anyway, my plan worked. You are safe and sound here. Things were terrible in Kiev."

Rachel and her mother looked at each other but said nothing.

The father continued. "I was a bit worried when I saw that some other houses along the road were burned down but they must have missed this one in the dark, eh?"

"We heard horsemen," said his wife," but we didn't see anyone."

Her husband had hustled them off to the small house in the countryside he had bought from a widow when tensions began to bubble in Kiev. No one was to know they were there.

"I knew it would be safer here," he said. "But I think it will be all right to go back to Kiev now. The Bolsheviks have the city under control and our apartment was untouched."

"Can they be trusted?" asked his wife.

"I think so. Some of their leaders are Jews, if you can believe that."

"What?"

"Yes. People we know. Oleksandr Horwits, Issac Kreysburg. Hell, even their commissar of foreign affairs is a Jew. Leon Trotsky."

"I think I'll throw in with them," said his son, quietly.

"You'll do no such thing," said his mother." You'll stay in our apartment until this stupid war is over."

"And when will that be, Momma?"

"Maybe sooner that you think," said his father. "I've heard rumors that Trotsky is trying to negotiate peace with the

Germans."

"Why would the Germans bother to make peace? They're winning," said Shemuel.

"Could be the Germans would like to take their troops out of Russia and send them to France now that the Americans are coming."

Rachel's heart skipped. "Does that mean the fighting will stop in the Ukraine?"

"Hardly, sister. Lots of people want the Ukraine. There will be fighting here for years. They are choosing up sides right now."

"I hate it," said his mother.

"Speaking of Americans, have you heard from that beau of yours, sister?"

"Not a word since he ran off with your sister's dowry more than three years ago," said his father.

I have no idea how I am going to marry her off without a dowry, he thought, not for the first time.

Rachel was firm. "Don't you worry. My Abram will come back from America to get me just as soon as the war is over. We'll get married and settle down and he will be a successful—and rich—advocate. You'll see." Her father rolled his eyes as his wife kicked him under the table.

"So you don't know whether he is alive or dead?" asked her brother.

"Of course he's alive," said his mother. "I'd know if he wasn't."

But has he spent that dowry? If he has, why would he come back? thought her father.

The family made the trip back to Kiev in a horse-drawn carriage. There was little baggage. The family's valuables had not been buried in the yard.

"This place is a disgrace," said Rachel's mother. "Dirty dishes. Beds unmade. Rings on my good table. I don't think it would have been much worse if the Cossacks had used the place for a stable. Men!"

"Now, *koxaha*."

"Don't ever call me that," she snapped.

Her husband was puzzled. "Why not? I've always called you that."

"No longer. I hate it."

Her husband shrugged his shoulders. "All right, *moja*. I live to please you."

"And enough with the sarcasm too."

Her son changed into clothes he left behind when he was conscripted. They hung loosely on him but most men in Kiev had lost weight. Food wasn't easy to come by and prices were high. One by one valuables were sold off. Farmers whose crops had not been destroyed grew wealthy.

It was a long walk from the apartment to the Bolshevik headquarters but Shemuel, like all infantrymen, was used to walking. His eye picked out the places that had changed since he left and those that hadn't. Debris from the firefights still littered the streets but the people seemed to be going briskly about their business.

One or two smiled at him as if they might know him but weren't quite sure. Shemuel smiled back but kept walking. This was no place for casual conversation. He was a deserter and if most folks weren't wary, he was.

He climbed stairs, entered the building and walked up to a desk.

"I'd like to see Gospodin Horwits, please."

"Comrade Horwits."

"Of course, Comrade Horwits."

The functionary at the desk pointed to his left. "That's him, right over there, comrade."

"Thank you...comrade."

Horwits was talking to an older man, his back to Shemuel,

who didn't want to interrupt so he stood there until Horwits turned around.

"I know you. You're Nicolay Zeidman's son," said Horwits trying to remember his name.

"Shemuel, sir."

"Of course, Shemuel. You should call me 'comrade' now. How is your father? I haven't seen him in weeks."

"He's fine, Comrade. He just got back to Kiev. He went to fetch my mother from the country."

"Good. Tell him I want to see him. We could use a man who understands money. All we know how to do is spend it. Now, what can I do for you, my young comrade?"

"I have left the army."

Horwits chuckled. *I'll bet you have.*

"And I would like to serve the Ukrainian People's Republic in any way I can."

"Good for you. What were you trained to do?"

"Not much, Comrade. I was still in school when I was conscripted. I'm just an infantryman. I'm pretty good with a rifle and I know how to use a bayonet but that's about it."

"Believe me, Shemuel; we need infantrymen now more than we need scholars. I take it you weren't a non-commissioned officer, what being a Jew."

"No, sir...Comrade."

"Still, you're obviously bright. If I gave you a squad of men could you lead them and turn them into infantrymen who will obey orders?"

"Yes, Comrade. I think so. It can't be much harder than studying the Talmud."

"We don't study the Talmud anymore. As Marx said, 'Religion is the opiate of the people.'"

"Yes, Comrade."

"Do you have any field equipment?"

"No, Comrade. I left it behind."

"Too bad. Well, I'm sure we can scrape up some for you. Report back here tomorrow at 0700 and we'll see what we can do.'

Shemuel grinned. "My mother is not going to like this."

"Well, she better get used to the idea of Jews fighting. We're going to do a lot of it."

Shemuel found Horwits waiting for him when he returned. They walked down a flight of stairs and into a storeroom where a man handed Shemuel a rifle, a bayonet, a bandolier full of 7.62 millimeter bullets and a red armband.

"I'm sorry," said Horwits. "That's all we have. You'll have to come up with the rest yourself."

No problem, thought Shemuel who would put most of what he needed into a bedroll.

"What am I going to do, Comrade?"

Horwits clamped his hand on Shemuel's shoulder, "You are going to lead a squad of men who are going to guard the coal pile at the power station down by the river."

Shemuel was crestfallen. "What's the matter?" asked Horwits.

"I had been hoping for something...more military."

Horwits took his hand off Shemuel's shoulder. "This is an important assignment, boy. Without coal, they can't make electricity. Without electricity, the trams will stop, the lights will go out and Kiev will cease to be a modern city. Coal is important. Vital.

"We never know when we are going to get another coal shipment, so you must guard what we have.

"It will be a cold winter and when people have burned all the wood they can find, they are going to look at all that coal behind that fence. They will want it and you and your men must stop them from taking it."

"How will we do that, sir?"

Horwits glanced at Shemuel's rifle and nodded. "If nothing

else will stop them, a bullet will."

"Yes, Comrade." *If you think I am going to shoot someone over a lump of coal, you're crazy.*

Horwits's hand was back on his shoulder. "Good. Now let me give you some more instructions and then we'll go meet your men. They're waiting for you outside."

Seven men were sitting against a wall. They stood when Horwits approached.

"Stand easy, men," he said. "This is Shemuel Zeidman, your squad leader."

"Another Jew," whispered one man to his neighbor.

"Now, Comrades, you know we are all equal but when your comrade squad leader gives you an order he gives it in the name of the Ukrainian people."

Jesus! What bullshit, thought all eight.

"Now I am going to leave you to it. Go home and get blankets and anything else you need but be back here by noon. A truck will take you to the power station."

All made it back and when they got to the power station they found a large shack where they would live. There was a big, stone cold, potbellied stove.

They were inside smoking when Shemuel addressed them.

"All right, guys, we are going to do our job guarding this coal but we are going to make ourselves as comfortable as possible." That was greeted by appreciative murmurs.

"A truck will deliver our rations every day but we have to cook ourselves. Is anybody a cook?" Blank stares.

"I have an idea," said Sasha, the oldest among them, a man who had fought the Japanese more than a decade earlier. "My wife had seven kids. She wouldn't have any trouble cooking for a mob like this and she could go home at night."

And if there is anything left over she could feed it to her kids. A good deal for everybody, thought Shemuel. All agreed it was a good idea.

"That's settled," said Shemuel. "Now, here's how I propose to organize the squad. Three two-man teams working two hours at a time patrolling the perimeter. And a supernumerary who fills in for each man who takes a day off each week and goes home. When you aren't on perimeter patrol, you can sleep, clean your gear or do what you like but you are still on duty. That means we would have seven men to handle any emergency and we have a field phone to call for help if we need it."

"That sounds fair," said Sasha. "Who's the supernumerary?"

"You," said Shemuel. "That way you and the cook can have the same day off." That day soon became known as "Starvation Sunday" when the men fended for themselves.

Their rations turned out to be exclusively black bread, potatoes, turnips and beets but they were guarding their own treasure chest. They bartered coal for meat, green vegetables and tobacco but not alcohol. Shemuel had said, "Get drunk on your day off." They did.

One day, sitting around, one man had asked, "How do they make electricity?"

Sasha answered, "It's like a steamboat really. You burn coal to heat up water in a boiler. The steam turns a turbine which, instead of turning a propeller, turns a generator which produces electricity. A condenser sends what's now just warm water back into the river."

"How do you know this stuff?"

"I used to run a small steamer on the river before they called me up. The principle is the same."

Fish liked the warm water that flowed from the power plant and the men liked to eat the fish.

So it went for months, without serious incident, until Commissar Trotsky finally accepted the harsh terms the Germans demanded and signed a peace treaty that sent hundreds of thousands of German troops to the Western Front. The Ukraine was "independent" but under German tutelage.

Seeing some official-looking strangers walking up to the power station, Shemuel told his men, "Take your armbands off, guys, and put them away. I think we're about to get new bosses."

They did but they still guarded the coal. The ordeal in the Ukraine was not over.

G-2

Brigadier General Dennis Nolan was a well-liked man. He was genial, brilliant and he looked, spoke and acted like a scholar except in combat. Then he was a terror. Nolan had been cited twice for gallantry during the Spanish-American War.

It had always been thus. At West Point, Nolan ranked high academically but he was a bruiser on the football team in an era when the game was played without protective equipment.

Now he was General John "Blackjack" Pershing's intelligence chief, the G-2 of the American Expeditionary Force in France.

Pershing knew Nolan well. He had been Blackjack's adjutant in the Philippines.

The United States Army did not have an organized intelligence staff before the start of World War I. It was up to General Nolan to create it. He did and became known as "the father of Army intelligence."

In the past, if a commander needed intelligence—information about where the enemy was, what he was doing and was likely to do—he sent out the cavalry to look for them or an infantry patrol. World War I had changed that. Cavalry couldn't face machine guns.

Now the AEF—and Nolan—were up against the German General Staff, men who had all but perfected the arts and sciences of administration, intelligence, operations and logistics.

Nolan knew he could lean on the French and the British for intelligence. The Americans would learn from them but they had to learn fast, very fast.

Pershing intended to keep the AEF intact rather than parcel it out as replacement units as the French and British wanted. The near spent Allies were in no position to win the argument.

Nolan intended to have G-2 people at the division level at least. Intelligence and information would filter up from them to be passed on to Nolan. Refined intelligence would be passed back to the divisions to filter back down.

Nolan's first move was to pull seven lieutenants from the Statistics Section of the Judge Advocate Corps as trainees. These men were selected for their smarts, for their ability to handle French or German and for their innate aptitude to handle intelligence. They proved to be excellent choices and were amply rewarded with swift promotion.

General Nolan produced two summaries every day for Pershing that would also be circulated to the other general staff chiefs for their use.

The first was information of a diplomatic and economic nature. The second was intelligence, a snapshot of what was known about the enemy and his intentions at that moment.

The summaries were as concise as possible. If Pershing or any staff member wanted more, it would be provided but Nolan knew that the longer the summaries were, the less they would be read and digested.

Nolan worried constantly about tunnel vision. The tendency of each section of the general staff was to concentrate on its responsibilities and ignore what the others were doing. Nolan insisted on having one of his people sit in on every conference held by the other sections.

He was invaluable to Pershing.

Nolan worked long hours. He was often in his office until 2100 and back at 0730. He also frequently left to visit the divisions on the line.

That meant that life was as taxing for his small personal staff as it was for him. To a man, they were devoted to him.

Sergeant Talbot was his driver and bodyguard. But the seasoned regular soldier was more than that. Since Nolan refused to have an orderly, it was Talbot who pressed his uniforms, shined his boots and brewed the tea that the son of Irish immigrants favored.

Corporal Ashansky was a translator—fluent in French, fair in German— and a runner. He also would help out with typing the daily summaries as needed. He had progressed from two to ten fingers.

Lieutenant Lynch was his gatekeeper, a job he was good at since he had performed the same duties for Frank Hague, the ruthless mayor of Jersey City.

Nolan did not like to be needlessly interrupted when he was working and Lynch saw that he wasn't. Lynch's French was also good— especially when he read it.

But Nolan's French liaison officer was flummoxed by Lynch's accent when he first heard it.

"And where did you learn your French, my friend?" asked Commandant Xavier Roche.

"In Jersey City, Commandant. At college."

"I see," said the Frenchman. *Where, in the name of God, is Jersey City?*

Commandant Roche's job was to help Nolan extract information from the French—and the British—and to make sure the French knew everything the Americans did. A French courier picked up a report from him daily.

A commandant was the French equivalent of a major and it was unlikely that the middle-aged Frenchman would climb much higher in rank. He was both a reservist and a Catholic, the latter being viewed with suspicion by the French Army which revered its secular origins.

At any moment, day or night, Nolan would say, "I want to go the —th Division Headquarters. Do you know where it is, Talbot?"

The sergeant's invariable answer was, "I do, sir." He studied the big map every morning and noted where each divisional headquarters was and the best way to get there.

If the weather was good and the roads dry, the four of them would pile into an Army automobile, Ashansky in the front with

Talbot. Roche in back with the general.

If the weather was bad or the roads too muddy, they would take two motorcycles with sidecars. It was easier to unglue a motorcycle from the mud but it was frequently heavy work nonetheless.

Ashansky knew the front lines as well as Talbot. He was a runner and as such he took frequent communiqués from G-2 to the divisions, usually alone on his motorcycle. Sometimes Roche accompanied him. It gave the commandant a chance to talk to— and gossip with—the other French liaison officers. They would pass on appraisals of American commanders that otherwise would never have made their way into official papers.

Lynch never went into the field with them and that suited him fine. He didn't intend to get shot at, even by accident.

Despite all the activity, there were long hours at headquarters when the out baskets were empty.

A friendship—within limits—sprang up between Roche and Ashansky when the former learned that the later was trained as a lawyer in the Ukraine before the war.

"Incredible," Roche said. "What a coincidence, I am an advocate too. I was practicing law—and making a good living— when war broke out and my regiment was called up. I chased the Boche, the Boche chased me and, finally— too old and too fat— I ended up here."

During downtime—often at night—Roche and Ashansky played chess. They were good but not expert players which meant they were content to chat and drink coffee while they played.

They were evenly matched. Whoever was "white" usually won although "black" tied or won enough games to keep it interesting.

Sergeant Talbot watched, at first seeing no relationship to checkers despite using the same board. But little by little, Talbot began to pick up the fundamentals of the game. He also began to pick up some French. A word here, a word there. A phrase here and there. Then simple sentences.

Talbot found that he could use what he knew during his infrequent visits to the town of Chaumont. He even felt that his use of French so delighted the merchants that they cheated him a bit less than other Doughboys.

Moving a pawn forward, Ashansky asked, "So where are you from, Commandant?"

"The Vendee," answered Roche countering with his own pawn.

"Aha! Do we have a monarchist in our midst?"

The Vendee was famous for its resistance to revolutionary France. Its peasants revolted in 1793 because the Jacobin regime had clamped down on the Roman Catholic Church. The region refused to recognize Napoleon in 1815 when he returned from Elba and in 1832 rose up again championing a doomed Bourbon against the Orleanist king.

"That's probably what my superiors think. But, alas, I think the day of the monarch is just about over. It's a pity in a way. The idea of a monarch representing the people was a nice check against the expedient excesses of a parliament."

"Is your family still there, Commandant?"

"Yes. In St. Jean de Monts, by the coast. My wife, four grown children. One of my daughters is pregnant. I haven't seen any of them in almost two years. What about you, my friend. Is your family in America or the Ukraine?"

"In the Ukraine, I hope. I haven't heard from them since war broke out in 1914."

"My God."

Abie then told him the story of escaping the Czar's clutches with his fiancée Rachel's dowry safely tucked away in a money belt.

"I'm going back for her as soon as I can. When the war is over.

I'm not a religious man, but I pray every day that she's still alive. If she is, I'll find her and I'll take her to America."

"So the New World is to your liking, eh?"

"Yes," said Abie Ashansky, surprising himself as he realized it was true.

"We'll make a life there. A good life. And our children will have an even better one."

"Ah, that famous Yankee optimism. I hope your dream comes true, my friend," said Commandant Roche.

"How did you manage to get into the university anyway? I thought that was impossible for a Jew in Russia."

"It usually is. But my father had a patron. A very powerful gentile and it was he that got me a place at the university. My father wouldn't tell me his name. All he would say is 'the debt is repaid in full now.' I don't know what the debt was."

Abie's father, in true Horatio Alger style, had plucked a toddler out of the path of a streetcar. The toddler's father was grateful in the extreme. The toddler's governess was fired.

Abie's father cosseted that debt until his son was ready and then called it in. His Russian benefactor never hesitated. Abie matriculated at a university where Jews were otherwise despised. Abie studied unmolested in the penumbra of his unknown protector.

The Russian Revolution shook the world and the Bolshevik takeover in November, 1917, electrified AEF Headquarters. Would the Reds stay in the fight? Who were they? What did it mean for Europe, if anything?

Corporal Abram Ashansky soon found himself as the resident expert on things Russian despite his protests that anything he knew was three years old. He found he was the one-eyed man in the kingdom of the blind. But not the king.

He translated Russian documents and told General Nolan what he thought they meant. He also conveyed some sense of the importance that the Ukraine was to all sides.

"The Ukraine is a place, not a country," he said. He told Nolan that Russia had completely dominated most of it.

"All of the government officials and the important people are ethnic Russians. The Ukrainians are peasants who till the fields and dig the coal. And, of course, Austro-Hungary has ruled the southwest chunk of the Ukraine since 1815. The people there are Catholic, not Orthodox. So civil war is the natural state of the Ukraine."

Abie said, "Everyone wants the Ukraine. It is Europe's biggest breadbasket." Most of the nations of Europe were on the brink of starvation.

"What do you know of the Bolsheviks?" asked General Nolan.

"Almost nothing, sir. They were just another Marxist faction among scores of such factions when I left. But there is one obvious difference between them and the other Marxist daydreamers, sir."

"How so?"

"They're ruthless, sir. If you don't go along with them, they'll kill you. Even if you do go along, they still might kill you."

"Well, they don't seem to be killing many Germans, do they?" said General Nolan.

AEF Headquarters was alarmed but not surprised when the Communists, facing total devastation, capitulated to the Germans and signed a very harsh peace treaty. The Baltic states—Lithuania, Latvia and Estonia—were sliced off and became duchies ruled by Prussian princes.

The Ukraine was declared independent but under German tutelage. The wheat crop had already been planted.

General Pershing called General Nolan into his office.

"Dennis, you've done a wonderful job. I really wonder whether anyone else could have accomplished what you did. But I think this war is actually winding down. You need some combat time if you are going to get another star and I am going to see that you get it."

"Thank you, sir. Thank you very much," said Nolan much gratified and relieved. He knew his career would quickly grind to a halt if he didn't see combat on the Western Front. His work at headquarters and his stellar performance in the Spanish war would count for little.

"I'm going to give you the 55th Brigade of the 28th Division."

"That's a Pennsylvania National Guard outfit, isn't it, sir?"

"Yes, it is. Does that trouble you, Dennis?"

"Not at all, sir. Thank you very much," said Nolan who was a rare general officer who didn't care whether a man was a regular, a reservist, a National Guardsman or even a draftee as long as he was good at his job.

Nolan broke the news to his small personal staff. "We're going to the front, boys. Go to the quartermaster sergeant and draw field gear. We're off to the 28th in the morning. Do you know where that is, Talbot."

"I do, sir."

"Lieutenant Lynch, I'm sorry to tell you that you will have to stay behind. Colonel Conger will be taking over G-2 and I depend on you to make the transition a smooth one."

An elated Lynch managed to look downcast. "I'd rather be with you, sir," he said.

Nolan said, "I'm sure you would, Lieutenant."

Talbot and Ashansky smiled.

An hour later, the armorer tried to give Abie a rifle.

"No! No! No! You keep it. I don't have the faintest idea of how to use it. I'd probably shoot myself."

The armorer was incredulous. "Didn't you go through basic training?"

"Sort of," said Abie.

Sergeant Talbot said, "The corporal is famous for his intellect, not his marksmanship. Give him two extra magazines for his .45

and a box of cartridges."

Talbot was senior to the armorer and that ended the discussion.

It was September 28, 1918, as an Army car with two officers and their gear, followed by two motorcycles with packed sidecars, pulled up to the field headquarters of the 28th Division.

General Nolan conferred with the division commander while Commandant Roche talked with the French divisional liaison officer

Ashansky and Talbot nosed around the field headquarters.

One sergeant asked Ashansky, "Where are you from, Corporal?"

"Jersey City," said Abie.

"Is that near Camden?" asked the Philadelphian.

Abie grunted and the Pennsylvanian asked, "How about you, Sergeant."

"I guess I'm from here now."

"Oh, a regular, huh?"

Brigade headquarters was in a big French farmhouse on the outskirts of Apremont. The enlisted men were amused to see the usual pile of manure near the front door.

"A natural by-product of headquarters people," said Talbot.

The general was greeted with salutes but little ceremony. His second-in-command, a colonel, walked Nolan over to a big map and briefed him on the situation.

The 55th was fighting for the ruined town of Apremont and the Germans were resisting with their usual Teutonic stubbornness.

They had arrived only minutes before but Nolan seemed happier than they had ever seen him. It was immediately apparent that Nolan did not intend to lead from the rear.

"I've got to get up front and see what's going on myself, then this map will make more sense," he told the colonel.

"Let's take the motorcycles," he said to Talbot and Ashansky who had already dumped their gear into a nearby shed.

The Germans greeted Nolan noisily with an artillery barrage which he ignored. He also ignored the small arms fire being exchanged near the spot in the ruins where he stopped to get his bearings.

Any infantryman will tell you that urban warfare is the worst kind. The enemy could be, and usually was, anywhere. Granted, the ruins provided lots of cover but that was of little use if the enemy was behind you or right next to you. You had to fight in teams, each man covering the other's back. And your commander best have plenty of replacements ready.

"There's a gap," said Nolan to Roche. "We need the tanks to fill it." He could hear them idling off to his left.

"Ashansky! Do you know Colonel Patton when you see him?"

"Yes, sir." He had seen Patton many times when that officer was headquarters company commander and when they practiced on the pistol range. The then captain favored a pair of pistols with distinctive ivory grips.

Nolan wrote hurriedly on a piece of paper and gave it to Ashansky. It read: "George, move forward a half-mile and then pivot to your right and advance until you meet the enemy. Hit him hard. Nolan."

Just then a German soldier came out of a building and sprinted across the street. The general drew his pistol, cocked it, and fired. He missed. Talbot did not.

"Get going," said Nolan, pointing to his left.

"I'll go with you," said Roche. He wanted to see how Lieutenant Colonel George Patton handled the light Renault tanks. His bosses would be interested in that.

Ashansky found Patton, who was hard to miss, and gave him the orders. Minutes later the tanks were off in a cloud of exhaust.

"We better get back," said Roche as he climbed back into the sidecar.

A nearly spent bullet penetrated the sidecar's door, pierced his leg and came to rest next to Roche's thigh bone nicking his femoral artery on its way.

"My God! I'm hit," said Roche. Ashansky jumped off, ran around to the door and opened it. He cut the cloth of Roche's trouser and saw the small wound, blood pumping out with every beat of the Frenchman's heart. The American knew what to do.

"You need a tourniquet," he said whipping the web belt off his trousers and tying it very tight around the commandant's thigh above the wound. He handed the Frenchman a field dressing and said, "Press down hard with this and don't let up. We passed a field hospital on the way. I'll have you there in no time."

The commandant pointing, with the dressing still in his hand, yelled, "A votre droite!"

Pulling out and cocking his .45 in one practiced motion, Ashansky aimed straight at the two German soldiers just yards away, their bayonets glinting in the now bright sunshine.

His first bullet hit the man in the chest. The pistol jumped with the recoil but Abie adjusted and shot the second man in the face. His heart was pumping hard now.

"I think they were after the motorcycle, my friend," said Roche who was fumbling with his left hand trying to un-holster his pistol while he pressed down on his wound with his right.

"So are they," said Ashansky, turning to the rear of the motorcycle to meet two more Germans aiming their rifles as they ran.

He dropped the first man but the second and Ashansky fired at the same moment.

The German's 7.62 millimeter bullet tore through Abie's left sleeve and creased his bicep before continuing on its way.

Abie's big, fat .45 slug blew the German backwards, his rifle clattering on the cobblestones. The man didn't move.

The Frenchman now had his pistol in his right hand and his left pressing the wound.

Ashansky's hands trembled slightly. He had just killed four

men. Workers. He hadn't thought this was how life would turn out.

"Let's get the hell out of here," said Ashansky.

"D'accord," said Commandant Roche, a bit paler than usual.

General Pershing read the report from the 38th Division and shook his head. "Get him out of there," he told his adjutant. "Get Nolan out of there before that lunatic gets himself killed."

"Do you know he went right up to the front lines with bullets whizzing all around and directed Patton's tanks like a traffic cop? That crazy Irishman was taking potshots at Germans as the Germans ran by. Get him back now. I want to pin a DSC on him while I still can. Besides, I need him. Conger is good, but he is not Nolan."

Pershing had to move four divisions west to help the French in the center. They were not moving forward but the Americans and the British were. Pershing feared that the French reluctance to advance could prolong the war.

"Get Nolan now," he ordered.

General Dennis Nolan reluctantly obeyed his orders and was back in Chaumont with his personal staff.

Ashansky's arm was bandaged and not noticeable under his new tunic. Talbot told him to get a wound stripe sewed on the sleeve.

"But it wasn't much more than a scratch, Sergeant."

"For once, will you do as you are told without arguing? I've been shot at by assholes from three different countries and if I had been hit, I sure as hell would want a wound stripe to show for it."

Nolan called both of them into his office. Both men came to attention in front of the general and saluted. Commandant Roche was there leaning on a cane.

Nolan was wearing the ribbon of the Distinguished Service Cross on his chest. It was the nation's second-highest decoration.

He handed a set of chevrons to Talbot and said, "You are being promoted to first sergeant and we mentioned you in dispatches for your bravery at Apremont. Congratulations, First Sergeant Talbot." He shook his bodyguard's hand.

He handed Ashansky a set of chevrons. "And you are being promoted to sergeant and we mentioned you in dispatches for your bravery as well. Congratulations, Sergeant Ashansky." Nolan shook his runner's hand.

Commander Roche limped forward a couple of steps and said, "Sergeant Ashansky, it is my honor, on behalf of the Republic of France, to present you with the Croix de Guerre for your heroism at Apremont."

He pinned the medal on Ashansky's uniform and kissed him on both cheeks. "Thank you for saving my life, my friend."

Later, Ashansky said to Talbot, "I'm sorry you didn't get a medal too, First Sergeant."

"Just as well," Talbot answered. "If that Frog had tried to kiss me, I would've belted him."

Blanc Mont Ridge

Months earlier, the Kaiser lifted the field glasses to his eyes using his good right arm. His withered left arm, mangled at birth, was hidden beneath the fur-collared field cape that flowed down to his calves.

Wilhelm II, Emperor of Germany and King of Prussia, was wearing a pickelhaube, the obsolete spiked helmet that was replaced two years earlier since it couldn't protect against shrapnel. The move to the steel "coal scuttle" helmet had reduced head wound deaths among German front line soldiers by almost three-quarters.

The "All Highest" was in no danger of being hit by shrapnel or any other deadly missile as he stood with General Erich Ludendorff atop Blanc Mont Ridge in occupied Champagne. It was a quiet sector.

The Germans had been there since 1914 and had strongly fortified the ridge and the surrounding area. They had repulsed two strong French counterattacks in 1915 and the French decided they had enough. They would not attack Blanc Mont Ridge again.

Their new generalissimo, Phillip Petain, had ruled that they would wait for the Americans and the tanks. The Americans were coming but they weren't there in great numbers yet which was why the Kaiser was perusing an empty landscape.

Ludendorff spoke. "From here we will launch the Kaiserschlact, All Highest. The principal attack will be farther west. We will attack the British and crush them. They will flee to the channel ports and we will flank the French armies."

"Then what?" asked the Kaiser who was pleased since "Kaiserschlact" meant "Kaiser's Battle" and he was still susceptible to flattery even though he had been reduced to a figurehead. Germany was now ruled by a military dictatorship headed by Field Marshal Paul von Hindenburg and Ludendorff.

"Then, All Highest, we believe the French, who are exhausted, will ask for an armistice before America can get its divisions into the line."

"Good. I approve," said the Kaiser. Ludendorff smiled. *As if we need your approval anymore.*

He looked at the Kaiser's chest which displayed a number of dazzling decorations, none of them for combat. "Thank you, All Highest," he said.

This was Germany's last great gamble to win the war which had dragged on for four years and brought every nation involved to the brink of collapse except the United States of America.

The German effort was reinforced by fifty divisions and a hundred aircraft freed and moved west when the Communist regime capitulated at Brest-Litovisk.

The Ludendorff Offensive, as the world would term it, commenced when the general gave a signal to a staff officer atop the chalky precipice that was Blanc Mont Ridge.

The four main thrusts were spearheaded by small storm trooper units— tough, well armed and well organized. They broke through the Allied lines leaving pockets of the enemy behind to be mopped up by regular infantry.

The Germans gobbled up much French territory, panicking Paris once again. But the Germans failed to crush the British or flank the French armies. The offensive petered out and then stalled. The Germans simply couldn't get enough food or ammunition to their front lines.

The counterattack came in August. There were now a million American troops in France organized into their own divisions and spoiling for a fight.

The Germans gave up all the territory they had won and were now back on Blanc Mont Ridge where they started. It remained heavily fortified. The French remained inert in front of it.

The Allies' General John "Black Jack" Pershing, commander of the American Expeditionary Force, loaned four divisions to the French to shore up their line. The problem was that the British and its Commonwealth allies on the left and the Americans on the right were forging ahead while the French in the center were not moving.

The French 4th Army commander intended to break up these American divisions into brigades and attach them to his own divisions. The Americans did not cotton to that.

Major General John Lejeune, the Marine commanding the 2nd Division, told the French commander that if he would leave his division intact, he would take Blanc Mont Ridge.

That was very enticing to the Frenchman who agreed.

The 2nd was one of the strongest in the American Expeditionary Force. Its 3rd Brigade consisted of regular Army troops of the 9th and 23rd Infantry Regiments and its 4th Brigade was formed by the 5th and 6th Marine Regiments.

So the 2nd Division was to be hurled against Blanc Mont Ridge with the 36th Division in reserve. If the soldiers and Marines of the 2nd Division were among the most disciplined in France the same could not be said of the untested 36th, a National Guard unit from Texas and Oklahoma.

But its cowboys, Indians and Texicans would prove to be fighters, albeit of the barroom brawl variety. One Marine was to describe their combat style as "reckless innocence."

The Marines moved into the French trenches during the night of October 1.

The platoon leader spoke to one of his section leaders, Sergeant Michael McGurk. "Okay, Mike. We're here. Now let's find out who's in front of us. Look at the map."

The map, provided by a French predecessor who was glad to get rid of it, was large scale showing the area centered on Blanc Mont Ridge.

The lieutenant pointed to a blue line. "There's a little creek here upstream of their positions. Looks like a great place to fill canteens on a quiet night. What do you think?"

"That's where I'd go, sir," said McGurk who had served a hitch with the Marines in Central America before the war. He was older but no less fit than the men he commanded.

"Good. Pick a couple of good men and go get us a prisoner. The password is 'Fighting' and the counter sign is 'Quaker.' Be careful not to get captured yourself. We don't want the Heinies to know we're here just yet."

McGurk almost snorted. It was notoriously difficult to capture Marines. The Germans only managed to grab twenty-five of them during the entire war. It was said that the best way to capture a Marine was to knock him senseless first.

"Aye, aye, sir," said McGurk who saluted and left the makeshift platoon command post.

He picked a corporal and two solid privates. They had been on a dozen similar raids before. Getting a prisoner was a good way to find out what unit was in front of you, what they were doing and, perhaps, what they were going to do.

The captured Germans, who were fierce fighters, were perfectly willing to tell the Americans these things and more especially after they were loosened up with a cigarette and a cup of coffee. The Marines had learned in the Philippines that torture doesn't work but showing some empathy to your foe does.

McGurk said, "You know the drill. Just pistols. Keep them in your holsters. No round up the spout. No helmets. Nothing that makes a sound. And strap your pistol to your leg."

He showed them on the map the rough route they would take through the torn-up terrain of No Man's Land to the stream.

"If we are lucky, some Krauts should be filling their canteens right about now and we can peel one off. No shooting unless things go bad and it looks like we're going to be the prisoners. Then we shoot and hightail it the hell out of there. You know the password. We'll leave in five minutes."

They snaked their way over the shell pocked ground praying that the enemy wouldn't send up a Very flare and light up the night. It was very quiet and so were they. McGurk spotted the brook shimmering in the moonlight and waved his men into some bushes that would screen them.

McGurk often led prisoner raids since he could speak some German thanks to the Jesuits at St. Peter's in Jersey City. A German-American from Yorkville in upper Manhattan led even more since he learned to speak it at his mother's knee.

They squatted there for fifteen minutes neither speaking nor moving and then they got lucky.

A party of six Germans, two with rifles and four carrying batches of clanking canteens, slowly came into sight.

Too many, thought McGurk. *We don't want a firefight. Maybe one or two will straggle down later.*

It didn't take long for them to fill the canteens while their sentries looked around and saw nothing. They began to leave when a young voice called out softly but loud enough for McGurk to hear.

"Corporal. I've got to take a shit. Now."

The exasperated corporal, who did not intend to spend one more moment than necessary beyond the relative safety of the trench, sighed and answered.

"Do what you have to, boy. Don't shit in the water. Use those bushes. You know the way back. You know the password. Use it or you're going to get a bullet up that filthy asshole of yours." With that he turned and the five of them left.

The young soldier undid his trousers and squatted not three feet from the Marines. He felt a hand cover his mouth; others seize his arms and then a pistol put to his head. He started shaking.

He heard a whisper, in German, in his ear. "If you scream, I'll kill you. If you make a noise, I'll kill you. If you try to run, I'll kill you. Do you understand?"

The German nodded his head rapidly as the last of his excrement hit the ground.

No one moved for a minute or so.

Then McGurk said, "Stand up." The German did and his trousers dropped to his ankles. One Marine gave a subdued snicker and drew a hard look from the corporal.

As the German hurried to pull up his underwear and pants, McGurk said, "Off we go." Everyone understood him.

The way back took less time. The German was in the middle moving as quietly as the Marines. Passwords were exchanged and they were safely in the trench. The lieutenant, the company commander and the Marine from Yorkville joined them.

The New Yorker questioned the German while McGurk softly translated for the officers.

"Relax, youngster. You are safe now. The war for you is over and you get to go home to your mother in one piece." The German brightened.

The Marine said, "Would you like a cigarette, comrade?"

"No. Thank you. My mother doesn't let me smoke."

"How about a cup of coffee?"

"Oh, yes. Thank you." A steaming cup of coffee magically appeared.

"Sit down. We can talk a bit while we're waiting for guards to take you to the rear. Are you hungry?"

"Yes, sir."

A plate of canned corned beef was produced which the young German devoured as though it was caviar. The British naval blockade was slowly starving Germany and even front line soldiers were forced to skip a skimpy meal too often. The boy burped.

"How old are you, son?"

"Eighteen," he lied. He would celebrate his seventeenth birthday in a few weeks. Germany was desperate for men—or boys. The Americans smiled.

"So, are you in one of those reserve units with the old men and young boys?"

The German looked as indigent as only an almost seventeen-year-old could.

"I am not. I'm in the 200th Infantry Division." His chin jutted out just a bit. "No doubt, you've heard of us. We're the ones that started the Italian running at Caparetto."

"Wow," said the Marine. "Were you there?"

"No," said the German boy. "But I know men who were."

"So all the divisions hereabouts are all first class, eh?"

The blond boy took another sip of coffee and said, "No. Not really. There are a lot of old men over in the Essen Trench. You know, Landsturm. If you are going to attack, you should do it there."

The French would do that and the old men from Cologne in the 100th Landsturm Battalion would stop them dead, much to the Marines' peril.

The Marine took a drag on his cigarette. "I guess what we should worry about is your people attacking us."

The boy was feeling expansive and grateful. "Don't worry, my friend. The 200th is not going to attack anybody. We're dug in and we're going to stay that way. You stay in your trenches and we'll stay in ours."

The Marines and soldiers were set to attack in the morning.

The order was to come at 0550, October 3, 1918. The men grabbed what sleep they could but it wasn't easy just before an assault. The Marines and soldiers knew what was coming and dreaded it. Only a fool didn't taste fear in the face of the Spandau machine guns that they knew were less a half-mile away.

It was true that more men were killed and wounded by artillery than anything else but whether you were hit was usually a matter of chance. Unseen guns, firing on unseen targets.

But machine gun fire was personal. Firing from concealed, protected positions, the machine guns cut down the men running towards them. Deliberately, mercilessly.

Machine guns were ghastly in defense, worthless on the offense.

The British lost 21,000 men on the first day of the Battle of the Somme. Most of them to machine guns.

The troops hated the machine guns — and the gunners.

Precisely on time, American artillery bombarded the German positions for fifteen minutes. Enough time to hopefully soften them up but not long enough for the Germans to bring up reserves from the rear.

Then the platoon leader blew his whistle.

McGurk shouted, "Okay, men, over the top! Over the top!"

The Marines clambered over the top of their trench shouting, bayoneted rifles at high port. There was no one to shoot at yet.

They moved at a walk, a rolling barrage a hundred yards ahead of them. "Don't bunch up," shouted McGurk. The men were walking in groups around soggy shell holes.

"Goddamnit! Don't bunch up." That would make it easier for the enemy machine gunners. The Marines spread out. They would jump in and out of those shell holes once the shooting started in earnest. That was the only cover available.

Every four minutes the artillery barrage would move forward another hundred yards.

Twelve French tanks were supposed to lead the Marine battalion's attack. Tanks were a formidable weapon against machine gun nests. If they didn't blow them up, the tanks simply crushed them with their treads while bullets pinged harmlessly off their armor.

But tanks were cranky things, prone to mechanical breakdowns, with their crews more than half-blind to what was going on outside.

Things went bad today. By the time the barrage lifted, the tanks had fallen behind the infantry and when the Marines began to surge against heavy enemy fire, they found some of the tanks were firing on them not the Germans. The tanks were swiftly removed from the battle.

The artillery was now firing 1,400 yards beyond the German defenses. The idea was to stop the reserves moving forward.

The *put-put-put* of a Spandau was loud in the Marines' ears. The German-American from Yorkville was cut almost in half. He dropped without a sound. Two other Marines in the section were wounded and lay there waiting for the Navy corpsman that they knew would come regardless of the danger.

McGurk yelled to his two squad leaders, pointing at the machine gun nest, "We can take that fucking gun from the right flank. Carter! You people cover us. Hamill, start moving to your right."

"Aye, aye, Sarge.

The first squad dropped into two shell holes and started firing their Springfield '03 rifles. The Marine Corps put a premium on marksmanship and this is when it paid off.

The squad was not aiming at the two man gun crew. They were too well protected. They were shooting at the riflemen who were both ammunition carriers and defenders of the nest.

The Marines' job was to kill them or least to make them keep their heads down. Two Germans on the right were hit and stopped firing.

The second squad made it to grenade-throwing range without taking casualties. Two of them pulled the pins, counted to three, and hurled their pineapple grenades at the nest. One overshot and took out the riflemen on the left side. The other grenade stunned the gunners. The Marines charged.

The German gunners jumped up, hands in the air, yelling "Kamerad! Kamerad!"

The squad leader looked around. No officers nearby.

"That's not how it works, Fritz, you son-of-a-bitch." he said as he shot the gunner in the chest. Others shot the second gunner who lay on the ground groaning. A bayonet finished him.

A wounded German rifleman looked on in horror. McGurk looked at him. "Move him to the rear," he said. He was just a rifleman, like them. They hated machine gunners.

The 6th Marine battalions were grinding it out steadily as was the 9th infantry on the right. Inevitably a gap formed between the units.

But the French on both flanks had failed to keep pace. The Americans were taking fire from three sides as their salient extended.

The 5th Marines, just behind their sister regiment, found themselves almost perpendicular to the attack, fighting off Germans on their flank. The soldiers were in the same lethal predicament.

Three hours of hard fighting found the Marines atop the chalky massif of Blanc Mont Ridge with the Germans clinging stubbornly to their front and flank. The Regulars reached their objective too but the French did not budge.

The generals feared that a German counterattack would pinch off the salient and trap the 2nd Division.

The Marines and soldiers spent the night in what had been German trenches. The Americans moved their artillery forward and prepared for the dawn. Food and ammunition came up to the line. The wounded and the dead were moved back.

McGurk's men, like all the other Americans—or Germans for that matter—were filthy with no real way to get clean.

Dried mud caked their uniforms. They tried to brush it off as best they could. They poured water from their canteens onto handkerchiefs or rags and tried to wash their faces first and then their hands.

They removed their socks and wiped their feet with the filthy cloths and then luxuriated in new, clean, warm socks.

But worst of all were the lice. Cooties. "Goddamn little bloodsuckers," they said as they plucked them from the linings of their uniform jackets, trousers and underwear. They crushed them between the thumb and forefinger. They ran combs through the hair both on their heads and in their pubic regions. They rubbed gasoline, when they could get it, onto their scalps.

And still the little bastards thrived.

They knew when they finally got out of the line, they would shower, be disinfected and would be issued new clothing but that was a long time off — an eternity — and until then, they suffered.

They didn't expect good food nor did they get any. They ate what they got. But they did expect good, hot, strong, black coffee and the cooks made herculean efforts to make sure they got it.

"Ah!" said McGurk sipping some from his canteen cup.

"So, what should we expect tomorrow?" asked Hamill.

"More of the same," said McGurk," Lots of counterattacks. The Germans are going to try to push us off this goddamn hill."

"They can try," said Carter.

"Right," said McGurk. "But we have to do something about that left flank. Get the Frogs moving. The gap between us and the 3rd Brigade is getting wider too. Next thing you know we're going to find Huns on our right too. We'll have to pull back."

"Bullshit," said Hamill.

"Maybe," said McGurk "But they got to do something about that gap."

Dawn came and with it the usual artillery barrage. The American artillery wasn't as accurate this day as the Germans would be.

The Germans owned the air. Their fighters hovered overhead, occasionally dropping down to strafe the infantry. Six observation balloons spotted targets for the German artillery.

No American fighters showed up until the afternoon, their arrival heralded by a furious winching down of the balloons. But the Americans soon left and the Germans returned.

The problem was the air commander, Brigadier General Billy Mitchell, who didn't want to waste his men and planes on something as trivial as air reconnaissance. Constant complaints by his earthbound brother generals didn't move him.

The Americans attacked. The Germans counterattacked but the 2nd Division kept moving forward taking heavy casualties.

The 5th Marines pivoted to their left and cleaned out the Essen hook at great expense. Now the French could move forward. So it went through October 6.

The village of St. Etienne was next.

The Germans were dug in at the cemetery where the tombstones gave them extra cover. Trenches fanned out from there to carefully placed machine gun nests. A ravine formed by a brook was a concealed pathway to move troops. It wasn't as strong a position as their original line but it was strong enough.

What the men facing each other and death did not know was that another man, far to the rear, had different plans for them.

Crown Prince Wilhelm, the onetime wastrel son of the Kaiser turned soldier, had decided to move his entire Army group back to the Meuse River, a natural defensive position. It would be an orderly, fighting retreat—not a rout.

The wild and wooly National Guardsmen of the 36th division relieved the 2nd Division, dead tired and much thinned by casualties. But prudence demanded a battalion of Marines anchor the left flank and a battalion of Army regulars protect the 36st's right. The 2nd Division's artillery remained in support of the 36th.

The exuberant National Guardsmen tore into the Germans like they were cleaning out saloons in El Paso. No matter that their units disintegrated and reformed, more like vengeful posses. No matter that the German professionals' *tsk-tsked* at their amateur tactics. No matter. The Westerners were beating them hands down.

The Germans gave way grudgingly but on October 27 the 36th devastated a German stronghold called Forrest Farm. The entire garrison was either killed or captured.

Soon the well-rested 2nd Division was on the south bank of the Aisne River. The Champagne region was cleansed of the Hun.

The Home Front

Fat Jack Lynch had lost ten pounds although it was not very noticeable since some of his hard muscle had turned soft once he stopped working on the docks and became a politician.

"What's for dinner, Maureen?"

"I got a nice piece of cod at the fish market. It should be ready in a few minutes."

"Fish? It isn't Friday. What's with the fish?"

Maureen Lynch wiped her hands on her apron. "John Lynch, you know very well, it's Meatless Tuesday." She looked at her husband with well-deserved suspicion.

"You didn't eat meat for lunch, did you?

"No," he lied.

His wife, Maureen, cooked much the same as she always had but now there was less meat, less wheat, less sugar and less fat than before America entered the war. Meatless Tuesday was followed by Wheatless Wednesday and, of course for Catholics, there was no meat on Friday either.

Her nine-year-old daughter, Grace, didn't miss the butter on her bread. She relished a new popular substitute, peanut butter, and was almost rapturous when it joined jelly on a sandwich.

Americans were getting slimmer but America's European allies were malnourished and their enemies were staring starvation in its emaciated face. The United States and Canada were shipping as much food overseas as possible.

There was no food rationing here, unlike Great Britain which was groaning under it, but Americans heeded their government's constant prodding and patriotically ate less. A lot less.

Fat Jack, a secret leader of the Clan na Gael, tried not to think about American food going to the English. The tribal memory was still strong of landlords shipping food to England while a million Irishmen died of starvation and its attendant diseases during the Great Famine a little more than seventy years earlier. His grandparents had escaped to the United States with hundreds of thousands of other Irish men and women.

He had opposed America joining in the war that he wanted England to lose. The British had ruthlessly put down an Irish rebellion two years earlier, executing its leaders and jailing thousands. Fat Jack hated the English.

Too old for the draft that, at first, took only men twenty-one to thirty-one; Fat Jack was an American patriot nonetheless and did everything he could for the war effort. Revenge on England could wait.

His job as Hudson County's superintendent of weights and measures wasn't very taxing although the merchants' thumbs on their scales seemed to be heavier now in 1918. Fat Jack had diligent people who kept that in check.

It was his political duties that kept him busy every day and most nights. Fat Jack Lynch was a very important man in the powerful organization headed by Frank Hague, the mayor of Jersey City and the de facto leader of the Democratic Party in New Jersey.

Fat Jack was one of Hague's twelve ward leaders, succeeding his father-in-law when the old man died six months earlier. Nepotism had nothing to do with it. Fat Jack had soldiered for Hague as building captain, block captain, precinct captain and as ward, city, and county Democratic committeeman. He had cajoled voters and cracked heads as needed.

Lynch's loyalty to Hague was absolute. And he had been rewarded with a well-paying county job and promotions. He now lived with his wife and stepdaughter in a nice row house with, as Fat Jack had once dreamed, its own bathroom.

He was in a position to do people valuable favors or cause them unlimited trouble. It would depend on how they voted. It was a good life.

Carmella Aiello saw to it that her family always had enough food. Her best friend's husband owned a grocery store so she never went without.

The problem was that she did not want what she could get.

She was Sicilian and the war had cut off commerce with that island, indeed with all of Italy. No real cheese, no real olive oil, no real pasta, no real salami, no real wine, no real olives, no real figs.

Carmella had always bought her ricotta and mozzarella cheeses locally. They were perishable. But she deemed all other American cheeses "inedible" and American wine "too sweet." Fortunately, many older Italian men had taken to making their own wine from California grapes and were happy to sell a gallon or two to their neighbors.

She found the spaghettis and elbow macaroni made at the Mueller plant on Baldwin Avenue "pasty and hard to digest" and all the substitute products of California's farms "inferior."

"It's a wonder I can get a meal on the table," she said. However, everyone who ate at Carmella's pronounced her food "delicious." She expected no less.

Her son, Anthony, had it worse. His wife, Peggy McCann Aiello, was tutored in fine Sicilian cooking by her mother-in-law but had converted Wheatless Wednesday into an opportunity to cook the food she grew up with. Her cousin and his old boss, Mickey McGurk, had warned him: "The apex of Irish cuisine is reached when the water comes to a boil. From there, it's all downhill."

"Ah!" Tony said, "Corned beef and cabbage. And boiled potatoes!" He considered dinner on Wednesday as punishment for his sins.

War brought other problems to Jersey City.

The Jesuit who was president of St. Peter's College was conferring with his superior, the head of the New York Province of the Society of Jesus.

"Father Provincial, I'm afraid that I have to recommend that we close the college."

"So it's come to that, has it? Is there no way, we can save it? We've been there almost fifty years."

"I don't see how, Father. Virtually all of the college's students have enlisted. Many of them are already in officer training camps. We have no one to teach."

Father Provincial asked, "What about the high school program?" St. Peter's offered a six-year program that began with high school and ended with a baccalaureate degree.

"There's no problem there. The boys are too young to enlist although a couple of them lied about their age and got in."

The priests were silent for a few moments, and then Father Provincial spoke. "I knew you were losing enrollment and I was worried about what might happen so I have given the problem some thought.

"Here's what we will do. We'll keep the high school. In fact, we'll expand it since you already have the space and the faculty but we'll change the name. We'll call it St. Peter's College High School. That way, if we get the chance to bring back the college, the name will still be there." That chance lay twelve years in the future.

So many of the young men were enlisting or, much more frequently, being drafted that a nationwide labor shortage was inevitable.

Twice as many women were now in the workforce than before the war. Many were doing jobs, and doing them well, that were exclusively male in the past. Of course, they were being paid less than the men. Blacks too were moving north looking for a better life.

The nation was as close to full employment as it had ever been. But not everyone wanted work.

There was Bozo Fitzpatrick. No one would claim Bozo was hard-working.

Most would agree with his brother-in-law who said, "He's a lazy, useless bastard. For the life of me, I can't see why you married him."

To which his sister answered, "Why? I'll tell you why. He's the only one who asked me. That's why. For Christ's sake, I was almost twenty-four." She was two years older than Bozo.

Bozo Fitzpatrick was eligible for the draft but he had no intention of serving. He didn't object to the war, Bozo objected to work. Period.

He went to the library and sat reading a book that described in detail what symptoms a person with a malfunctioning back would display. Then he went home and practiced grimacing, wincing and moaning in front of his bathroom mirror.

When he was called to take his physical for the draft, his wife said to her brother, "I hope they take him."

"I don't know, I don't think Bozo would make a good soldier."

"Him? He's good for nothing but at least I wouldn't have to feed that slob," said the wife.

The busy doctors had little time to spend with individual men and Bozo put on a good act.

"This one couldn't carry a pack ten feet," said the doctor who examined him and with that Bozo was on his way home.

"I told you I had a bad back," he said to his wife. "The doctor said I shouldn't lift more than five pounds. Maybe I can find some part-time work. Be a watchman, maybe, like I was at Black Tom."

"Oh, yeah. That's going to keep us in groceries. I'll tell you what. I'll go get a job. You stay home and try not to exert yourself."

Bozo didn't smile but he thought of those wonderful, long afternoons to come with him sitting on the stoop drinking coffee and smoking cigarettes. He'd tell the neighbors how he tried to get in the Army but they wouldn't take him because of his bad back.

"Okay. But you still have to do the cooking and cleaning. I got a bum back."

"You got the 'bum' part right," she said. She found a job in a factory making Army uniforms within walking distance of her flat. She would earn more than twice what Bozo did at Black Tom.

Hannah Ganz McGurk went back to her old job too. Mickey McGurk was a Marine in France and the allotment she got was just a fraction of his pay as a police lieutenant.

So she gave up her flat and moved back into her parents' house with her five-year-old son, Francis. Her furniture was stored in the cellar.

She was back as a clerk at Colgate which was now making soap and toothpaste for the military. She had more secretarial duties now and the company had brought in an expert to teach her and several other clerks shorthand.

Her mother, Sophia Ganz, took care of Francis all day and went to Christ Hospital two nights a week to roll bandages. She had tried to volunteer with the Red Cross early in the war but was rebuffed because she was German-born.

The old German *kultur* that had thrived in Jersey City and much of America was fast disappearing. All things German were sneered at and one rarely heard it spoken in public, even in The Heights.

German citizens, many of who had been in America for years, were required to register with the U.S. government and carry their alien registration card on them at all times.

The Pohlman Club on Ogden Avenue was all but shuttered and Otto Ganz missed the pinochle games and his occasional stein of beer. Not that he had much free time. He was a tool and die maker at Koven's, at the foot of the Palisades in Hoboken, which was producing all but indestructible field stoves for the Army.

Germania Avenue was renamed Liberty Avenue and no one was shooting anymore at Schuetzen Park.

Sophia and little Otto, as she called her grandson, would chatter away in German but would swiftly switch to English when her sixteen-year-old son, Billy, entered the room. The teenager suffered more than anyone in the family from anti-German harassment. His peers were relentless.

"Wilhelm," his mother started.

"Don't call me that," he said. "That's a German name. That's the Kaiser's name. I'm an American. Call me William or better yet, Billy."

His mother, sensitive to her son's feelings began again, "Billy." But she was hurt.

Billy was a Boy Scout. His troop at Grace Lutheran Church was fortunate. Its scoutmaster hadn't been drafted. Many troops folded when their scoutmaster was called up.

He was in his Scout uniform except when it was being washed. Khaki shirt and short pants, tan wool knee socks, kerchief and campaign hat. He sold war bonds. He sold stamps for nickels, dimes and quarters which, when a book was filled, could be converted into a war bond. He collected peach pits that would be turned into the charcoal for gas masks. He even prowled the streets looking for illegal radio antennae. Those he never found.

But mostly, he prayed for the war to last long enough for him to get into a real uniform like his brother-in-law, Mickey. These prayers, undoubtedly, were drowned out by the more fervent ones of his mother.

Heidi Mannheim went back to work too. Her husband Hans, one of the three cops on the old Bomb Squad, was now a corporal working for the Provost Marshal at Camp Upton on Long Island. He even got home once in a while and as he said, "Army life isn't that bad. I'm sort of doing the same job as usual, only for a lot less money."

Hans liked to sing "Oh, How I Hate to Get Up in the Morning," a song written for a camp musical by a private named Irving Berlin.

All in all, morale was very high on the Home Front now as autumn approached in 1918. The war seemed to be nearing its end. The newspapers were full of Allied victories in France.

Then came the pale horseman bringing pestilence to a world already bedeviled by war and famine.

The doctors called it influenza, many people complained of the grippe. All of mankind would revile it as the Spanish Flu.

Before it had ended its horrifying year-long gallop around the world, it would sicken a third of the global population and kill as many as 100 million people. That was more than would die in the Great War itself and many times more than the Black Death had claimed in the 14th century. It would be the worst, most lethal pandemic the world had ever seen.

It started harmlessly enough in the spring, albeit early for the annual flu season.

Both Hannah McGurk and her brother, Billy Ganz, came down with the flu as did lots of people they knew. That was normal. Their mother made them comfortable, kept them warm and got them to drink lots of fluids. Hannah was back at work in three days.

The usual handful died. Folks over seventy and infants younger than two. Save for those specific family tragedies, the flu was just the usual annual annoyance.

Then, sometime around August, it mutated as strains of influenza do. It became a killer.

Bozo Fitzpatrick was getting a light from a neighbor on his stoop when the man sneezed. A half-million tidbits of the influenza virus enveloped Bozo's head, many flying into his nose and partially open mouth.

"God bless you," said Bozo.

He complained to his wife when she got home from work. Though she still had dinner to cook, she said, "I'll get you a toddy. That'll make you feel better."

This was the usual elixir the Irish turned to when faced with any ailment: hot water, honey, lemon and a generous portion of Irish whiskey.

Indeed, it did make Bozo feel a little better. "Can I have another?" he asked.

"After dinner," she said.

Bozo lay in his bed. He wasn't faking this time. He had developed bacterial pneumonia, a common secondary infection to influenza.

Almost paralyzed, Bozo gasped for air. "I can't breathe! I can't breathe!" His lungs had filled with fluid. He died quickly then. He was twenty-nine. His sneezing neighbor, thirty-two, had died the day before. Pneumonia killed more people than the virus itself.

After the funeral, the widow sat with her brother in the parlor and said, "At least I don't have kids to worry about." Decades later she too would die—childless and bitter.

Bozo was lucky to get buried. Bodies were stacking up in Jersey City's cemeteries and all over the world. The gravediggers were sick too. In Bayview Cemetery, they finally used a steam shovel to carve out a long, six-foot deep ditch. A line of coffins was laid in it and covered up.

People then were sadly familiar with infectious diseases and they knew crowds help spread them. People took what precautions they could but they were rarely enough.

Mayor Frank Hague, the city's tribal leader, took the most drastic step. He closed the saloons.

That was too much. He had a revolt on his hands and an angry delegation of saloonkeepers came close to threatening him. "Mister Mayor, be reasonable. This will bankrupt us. Why things will be so bad, I don't see how we will be able to contribute what we should to your election campaigns," said their spokesman.

Hague, who neither drank nor smoked, relented. "Okay. But it's on your head. Don't come complaining to me if people start dropping dead in your bars," he said.

The saloonkeepers agreed. They didn't think anything could kill the old rummies that opened and closed their joints. They were right. The Spanish Flu killed young adults. People in their twenties and thirties. Old people and the youngsters were, in the main, spared.

Jimmy Cribbins, the fireman who had been Mickey and Hannah's best man, was on the nozzle of a two-and-a-half-inch hose pouring water on a burning shed when he almost fainted.

"Jesus, Cap. I'm as weak as a kitten. I don't know what happened."

His captain had Jimmy's backup take over the hose. "Get back to the firehouse, Jimmy, maybe you got the flu."

The firemen were a close-knit group that made their own meals and they nursed Jimmy.

They had never heard of a cytokine storm but that was what would kill their friend. Jimmy's body recognized that the influenza virus was a dangerous invader so it marshaled his immune system to fight the enemy. His doom came when his immune system, overstimulated by his cytokines, turned on the body it was designed to protect and ravaged it.

Peggy Aiello was near term when she came down with the flu, her mother-in-law who lived across the hall, knew of the dangers of contagion. She said, "I'll move in and take care of you. Tony can stay with his father and sisters. Me, I don't get the grippe."

She was right. She, like many older people, had contacted the

Russian flu in 1890 and was immune to this current strain.

Peggy seemed to be recovering when she said, "Mama. I don't feel the baby moving anymore."

Two weeks later, in St. Francis Hospital, Peggy's baby was stillborn. Weeping, she held her on her chest. A nun, knowing the hospital's priest was busy and probably sick himself, poured warm water over the baby's head and intoned, "I baptize thee in the name of the Father and of the Son and of the Holy Ghost."

"Thank you, Sister. Thank you. I was afraid my baby was going to Limbo."

"Who believes in that nonsense?" asked the nun who most certainly did believe in it.

Hans Mannheim was in the hospital at Camp Upton on an aspirin treatment recommended by the Army surgeon general and the American Medical Association. He was choking down 25 grams of aspirin a day, the equivalent of seventy modern-day tablets. It killed him.

As Hans lay dying, thousands of soldiers were leaving Camp Upton for Hoboken and the USS *America* which had just pulled in from Boston, the early epicenter of the influenza pandemic in America.

The ship sailed on September 7. By the time it reached Brest, 997 soldiers and 56 crewmen were felled by the flu. Fifty-five of them died, almost all while the ship was anchored awaiting a berth. Other troopships were hit worse.

The AEF would have 300,000 men infected and it counted 25,000 dead from the Spanish Flu which caused even more deaths among their enemies who were malnourished. Even the Kaiser was afflicted. But he recovered, not that it mattered.

Both the Allies and the Central Powers suppressed news of the pandemic because they didn't want the other side to know how bad it was. It was called the Spanish Flu because Spain was neutral and its press was free to accurately report on the plague that had swept its country.

And then it was gone. Just like that.

In mid-October, one large American city reported more than four thousand deaths and three weeks later there was virtually none. The pale horseman had retreated to his hellish lair.

Life returned to some approximation of normal. The dead were buried and people moved on.

Carmella Aiello's goddaughter was wailing to her, "I've lost my Vinnie. I'll never love another. I will never marry. Never."

"Of course, you won't, my sweet one," said Carmella.

Within six months, Carmella would find her a suitable husband. Of course it helped that her goddaughter was comely and the girl's store owner father had no sons.

The 11th Hour of the 11th Day of the 11th Month

No one wanted to be the last man to die.

That inchoate fear gripped the men manning trenches from the North Sea to the Swiss border.

Millions were already dead, millions more wounded, still more millions uprooted, empires destroyed and dozens of countries sagging to their knees. Yet each of these men, on both sides, could think only of himself— if only fleetingly and often unwillingly. The Great War was ending and no one wanted to be the last man to die.

The almost audible buzz, like flies in the presence of death, circled around the word "Armistice." Their hearts had leaped just days earlier when that word, traveling at the speed of sound across the continent, shouted that an armistice had been declared. But that was the "False Armistice" and the word died in leaden disappointment.

Still, the Great War was about to end. If not now, an hour from now, or a day from now, or just days from now, surely not as long as a week from now.

The men would have just sat in their trenches waiting and the last man to die would have already been on a drawn-up casualty list. But that was not to be.

Other men, generals and colonels, were chewing on a different fear. The Great War was about to end. There were just hours— or, with luck, days—left. One more chance to make a reputation or enhance a reputation or retrieve a reputation. Just one more chance.

The generals and the colonels made their plans and the men were expected to do their duty.

Some wondered if the men would still fight. They remembered the incredible Christmas Truce of 1915 with German and British soldiers mingling, singing carols and exchanging little gifts. They remembered the French Army mutinies in 1917 and they remembered the Russian Army abandoning the front lines just months ago and walking home to chaos.

Germany was collapsing behind its front lines. The sailors of the High Seas Fleet had mutinied on October 29 in Kiel rather than sail off to a last forlorn battle with the Royal Navy. The sailors had quickly taken over the city. From there revolution spread throughout Germany.

The Kaiser had abdicated on November 9 and fled to neutral Holland. A German republic was declared and its leaders asked the Allies for terms of an armistice. Those terms were already down on paper, all that was needed were the signatures.

"So what do you think, Sarge? Are we going to sit it out here until the Krauts call it quits?" asked one of Sergeant McGurk's corporals.

"We've got Fritz on the ropes," McGurk said. "I don't think we are going to stop punching until he drops to the canvas."

"Shit," said the corporal.

Sergeant McGurk's battalion was in reserve not far from the Meuse River. They were in old trenches dug by others. The French had imported 95,000 Chinese laborers to do just that.

The Americans attacked.

On November 10, 1918, the 143rd birthday of the United States Marine Corps, the 5th Marines massed for a night attack across the Meuse River. The Marines dashed, under heavy fire, across pontoon bridges jury-rigged by Army engineers who ducked bullets and shell fire as they worked.

The Germans fought fiercely trying to stop the Marines but when midnight tolled two assault battalions were on the other side. By the next morning, the Marines had a strong foothold on the enemy bank. Some Marines were wounded, others were killed, but they were not to be the last to die.

Sergeant McGurk told his section, "All right, get ready, people. We should be moving up soon." The sun was already up but the 6th Marines didn't move. No one did.

They didn't know it but the Armistice actually had been signed at 5 a.m. but would not go into effect until eleven o'clock.

As the minutes moved like a glacier towards the eleventh hour of the eleventh day of the eleventh month, the firing and shelling along the front line intensified. Some of it, no doubt, celebratory but some cruelly aimed to kill the enemy, any enemy.

In the front line was Private Henry Nicholas Gunter of Company A, 313th Regiment. He was the twenty-three-year-old son of German immigrants living in Baltimore. He had been a supply sergeant until he complained of "miserable conditions" at the front in a letter that was read by a postal censor. That was enough to get him busted to private.

At 10:59 a.m., Private Gunter was killed by a German bullet. He was the last man to die in the Great War.

Then there was silence.

There was little celebration at the front. The men were too wary and too weary after more than four years of bloody combat. They even kept careful watch through the ensuing night although they relaxed enough to warm themselves at log fires hitherto unthinkable.

Not so throughout the Allied world where joyous delirium reigned.

The crowds gathered first in the cities and towns of France and Great Britain. In their millions, they sang, laughed, drank, shouted, paraded, waved flags and danced in the streets. They climbed aboard trucks and draped themselves over lampposts. Strangers kissed. Conversation was impossible. The crowd actually roared.

The giddy celebration followed the sun. When the Armistice took hold, it was 5 a.m. and pitch black in New York City and the only people about were working in the wholesale fish, produce, meat and poultry markets in lower Manhattan. The milkmen were making their rounds and the policemen were walking their beats. Slowly the word spread and the crowds grew.

With daylight, Times Square was packed and repeating the pandemonium of her sister squares across the Atlantic. A cacophony of sound came from church bells, steam whistles, sirens, chimes, car horns and thousands upon thousands of throats.

Across the Hudson, in Jersey City, the crowds were very much smaller but no less enthusiastic. They gathered to cavort at Journal Square and in front of City Hall. Early morning masses were packed with grateful and relieved women and not a few men.

Along the Hudson and East Rivers, shipyard workers coming off shift met their mates coming on and exploded with prideful exuberance. They thronged the saloons, black and white men together for one day of camaraderie. That would end on the morrow.

The world celebrated as if the Spanish Flu did not exist.

There was no joy in Germany, just relief, sorrow and bitterness.

A highly decorated Austrian who served with a Bavarian regiment was recuperating in a hospital in Germany from temporary blindness caused by mustard gas.

The man in the next bed asked him, "What the hell happened? How did we lose? We were fighting in France, not Germany."

"We were stabbed in the back."

"By who?"

"By those accursed revolutionaries. You know—the Jews," said Gefreiter Adolf Hitler.

Germany and her allies were racked with inflation, a horrible housing shortage, an influx of refugees, unemployment, and the lack of food and coal to go along with riots, revolution and the millions of disgruntled, armed men coming home to a Fatherland they did not recognize.

But Pershing's staff had a lot more to worry about than just Germany.

The Russian Revolution was an earthshaking event and the Soviets' capitulation to the Germans in April had been sobering if not unexpected.

The Soviet Union was not content to consolidate within its own borders, it was exporting revolution and strong forces were marshalling in reaction to that.

Germany turned to the Social Democrats, a minority party, and gave it power so as to forestall the Bolsheviks who were fermenting revolution in the cities.

The Austro-Hungarian Empire was collapsing faster than Germany. The dual monarchy had always between an uneasy gaggle of ethnic groups joined only by their mutual hatred.

Emperor Charles I, in essence, abdicated on November 11, Armistice Day. The next day the German-speaking areas formed the German Austria Republic, immediately agitating to be absorbed by a defeated Germany. They wanted protection from their erstwhile countrymen.

Not surprisingly, the Hungarians refused to sell them food and the Czechoslovaks denied them coal.

Hungary was in worst shape. On November 4, a onetime leftist journalist and flamboyant duelist named Bela Kun formed the Hungarian Communist Party in Budapest. He had been captured by the Russians in war, converted to communism and now had returned with a large amount of Soviet money.

Soon there were strikes, riots, protests, marches and rallies throughout the country. The republican government of Hungary was shaky at best.

Ironically, it was a Serbian nationalist who had touched off the World War in 1914 when he assassinated the heir to the Austro-Hungarian throne.

Now the south Slavs were in a position to get what they wanted—a kingdom of Serbs, Croats and Slovenes. It was proclaimed on December 1. This was the beginning of Yugoslavia which would add Montenegro, Bosnia and Herzegovina to its mix of indigestible religions and ethnic groups.

Poland had been partitioned 123 years earlier and parceled out to Russia, Germany and Austro-Hungary. Now it was her hour. Independence, at last.

On November 1, Poles had peacefully disarmed the German and Austro-Hungarian troops there. Days later, Marshal Jozef Pilsudski, who had led the Polish Legion against the Russians during the war, was named commander-in-chief of all Polish armed forces.

He was wildly popular and Poland avoided the fierce internal struggles plaguing other central European countries.

Poland was free. But that didn't mean that this nation, once carved up like a melon, didn't have territorial ambitions of its own. There lay Eastern Galicia, part of the Ukraine, but land that historically Poland considered her own.

Poland was ready to go to war to get it and there already had been a Polish uprising in Lviv.

The problem with Europe, of course, was that it had much, too much, history. Land and peoples moved back and forth with the regularity of tides. Bloody tides.

There was no armistice—let alone peace—in the Ukraine.

The hetman of the Ukrainian State, faced with the withdrawal of his German masters, made a deal with monarchists who wanted to restore the Russian Empire.

On November 13, the Bolsheviks renounced their treaty with Germany and refused to recognize the independence of the Ukraine. A day later, the Ukraine's socialists announced they had formed a new revolutionary government. The Bolsheviks prepared to push into the Ukraine again.

Civil war was inevitable. In fact, it would be difficult to keep track of the different warring factions.

In Kiev, Shemuel said to his squad, "Nothing has changed for us. Whoever shows up here is going to want this coal pile guarded and that's what we are going to do."

"What color armbands do we wear now?" asked one of his men.

"Damned if I know," said Shemuel.

The signing of the Armistice brought no letup in activity at AEF Headquarters in Chaumont. Sure, the officers toasted themselves in their mess and the men celebrated with the French in town but there was no letup. Activity increased.

The war, in a way, had been simple. Offense or defense. These were the good guys, those were the bad guys. General Pershing's staff knew what their mission was and they got better at addressing it as the months went by.

Now the daily intelligence sheet was very short, simply keeping track of the retreating German armies and the advance of the Allies. But the information summary bulged with fast-changing material gleaned mostly from French and British intelligence.

The Bolsheviks were the big worry. Where would they strike next? Who could stop them? What should America do?

General Pershing had already diverted two regiments to Northern Russia. The 332th Infantry was supported by the 337th Field Artillery and its attendant field hospital and ambulance company.

"I thought we were going to France," said one doughboy.

"You'll goddamn well go where I tell you to go," explained his first sergeant.

The Americans of the Polar Bear Expedition were joining the British and French in Archangel. At first, they were to protect stockpiled war supplies from being captured by the Germans and then, after the Armistice, to make sure they were safe from the Bolsheviks.

That was the sole American mission but her Allies were fast forming more ambitious plans. Their ultimate aim was to support the White anti-communist forces now gaining strength to defeat the Bolshevik army and destroy communism along with it. The capitalists of the West, who detested socialism, abhorred Bolshevism. They would try to kill it in its cradle.

America wanted no part of that.

The American people wanted their boys home. There was no taste for more European adventures.

One problem Pershing's staff was confident of solving was sending occupation troops to Germany where they would stay until a peace treaty replaced the Armistice. They had to be prepared to fight God knows who.

Sergeant Mike McGurk was sitting on the edge of a German trench, a suicidal position just days before.

He was smoking a cigarette and chatting with the platoon corpsman sitting beside him.

"So, Doc, how does it feel not to have perfect strangers trying to kill you?"

"Pleasant, thank you. You know those stupid fuckers shouldn't have been shooting at me in the first place. I'm a non-combatant."

The corpsman was still wearing his pistol belt with its .45 caliber automatic, a pouch with two extra magazines and a wicked looking trench knife obviously unhappy in its scabbard.

The corpsman was well respected by his Marines. They remembered him at the battle of Blanc Mont Ridge when he screamed, "Get that machine gun, you sons-of-bitches. I'm here to take care of you!" They did and he had.

"How come you don't wear your Red Cross armband?" asked McGurk.

The corpsman snorted. "And give those bastards something to aim at? It's still in my pack, but I might start wearing it now. It might get me out of some working parties."

"Good luck with that, Doc. Say, are you going to stay in the Navy?"

"Hell, no. I joined the Navy because I thought I'd be between clean sheets on a battleship eating ice cream every night. Instead, I found myself up to my neck in shit with you—you, *teufelhunden*."

The corpsman used the title the Germans had bestowed on the Marines after Belleau Wood. The Marines quickly and proudly adopted it as their own— "Devil Dogs."

"I'm through with the Navy, Sarge."

"What will you do?" asked McGurk.

"Go home to Indiana and try to get into college. I'd like to become a doctor."

"You'd be a good one," said McGurk.

The corpsman reached across and with his index finger traced the small scar on McGurk's forehead where a bullet fragment had dug a furrow after it shattered on the lip of his helmet. The corpsman had stitched the wound once the firing had died down.

"Yeah, I do good work."

"Really? I'm lucky I don't look like something in a freak show. You hurt me more than the Germans."

"Bitch. Bitch."

Both men laughed.

"Seriously, what's your plan, Sarge?

McGurk slapped the corpsman on the back and said, "Boyo, it's back to my incredibly beautiful wife and my incredibly intelligent little boy in Jersey City."

"What do you do there?"

"I'm a cop. A lieutenant actually."

"Should I be impressed?" asked the corpsman.

McGurk turned and looked straight at him. "You would be if you lived in Jersey City."

Mike sighed. "But I think it will be some time before we get back home, Doc."

"How come? The war is over, isn't it?"

"Yes and no," said Mike. "That's just an armistice they signed. A truce for the time being. A real peace treaty is a long ways off."

"Nah. It's over and we won it. It was the war to end all wars so you don't have to worry about that little boy of yours ever digging trenches."

"Please, God," said Mike.

A tall Marine stood upright on the top of other side of the trench. It was their platoon sergeant. He was a commanding figure and so was his voice.

"Okay, people, listen up. We're going to be re-supplied. Clean yourselves up. We're going to stay right here for a while. Then, when the skipper tells us, we're moving out."

"Where are we going?" asked Mike.

"To the Rhine. A Place called Colbenz. In Germany."

"It'll be a while, Doc," said Sergeant Mike McGurk.

As the Marines moved forward, they realized the Germans had left in full retreat, days ahead of them. The Devil Dogs reached the German border on December 1, the Rhine about a week later.

There new challenges faced the Marines and soldiers. There was to be no fraternization with the enemy although the Marines couldn't resist giving food to children who hung around their camp hoping for something. Anything.

Their corpsmen faced a different challenge. The 2nd Division surgeon, in an order sent to his battalion surgeons, said, "Copulation is not fraternization."

To little avail, Doc told his Marines, "Go ahead, you imbeciles, but remember, if you spend fifteen minutes with Venus, you better be ready to spend three years with Mercury." The latter being the basis for the torturously slow and painful treatment of venereal disease.

Rubber prophylactics, known to the troops as "French Letters," provided some protection but the Marines and soldiers were not fond of them.

Thus some revenge was exacted by the Germans for their defeat.

While Sergeant McGurk was hiking to Germany, the man he knew as "Abie the Jew" was working just as hard at AEF Headquarters. Sergeant Ashansky had delivered many dispatches to 2nd Division Headquarters but he and McGurk had not crossed paths.

There was less time now for those leisurely chess games with Commandant Roche although Abie and the Frenchman spent many hours talking—mostly about the Ukraine.

The American kept saying that everything and everybody he knew went back four years. He even quoted General Nolan, "Nothing is outdated as quickly as military intelligence."

"I am not interested in military intelligence, my friend," said Roche. "I want to get a feel for the Ukraine and its people."

"Peoples," said Ashansky.

The French officer would bring in a small-scale map of the entire Ukraine and they would discuss railroads, waterways, roads, bridges. The next day, he would arrive with a large-scale map of a certain region or city and the questions and the conversation would get more specific.

They talked about politics and personalities and the stark differences between Ukrainians, Russians and Jews. Where they lived, where they worked, where they went to school, their different customs, their deep and ancient hatreds.

Ashansky, thanks to his university education, knew much about all three groups. Roche made copious notes.

"You don't seem to know much about this western part of the Ukraine," Roche said one day.

"No, I don't. That part of the Ukraine has been ruled by Austro-Hungary for a hundred years. I do know this. They are, for the most part, Uniate Catholics."

"What is that?" asked the very Catholic Roche.

"They follow the Eastern liturgy but they are in union with the Pope. Some of their customs are different too. Their priests can marry, for example. But not their bishops."

"What?"

"Yes, it's true. They got some concessions when they went back to Rome. The Orthodox churches hate them," said Ashansky.

"I don't know," said Roche," I think the idea of married priests might be a good one. At least it would make honest women out of a lot of housekeepers."

Ashansky laughed. "Maybe. Personally, I had never met a Roman Catholic until I got to America. Jersey City is full of them. They don't seem any worse than anyone else."

"Thank you," said Roche with a smile.

"The peasants in the west are Ukrainians or Poles. The ruling class are Teutons or Magyars. You can bet on that. You can also bet that Poland looks at the western Ukraine and drools. All that farmland. But let's get back to the central and eastern parts of the Ukraine before I have to make up stuff."

"All right, Sergeant. As you command."

One day the commandant came in without his maps. He sat down and they drank coffee making military small talk but Ashansky sensed something different.

"Sir," he said. "You are not yourself. What up?"

Roche sighed. "You are right, my friend. I have something to ask you and I don't know quite how to go about it."

"Americans tend to be blunt, sir. We like that."

Roche sighed again. "Very well. I am going to the Ukraine with a French expedition and I want you to come with me as a translator and local expert."

Ashansky's body pumped adrenalin as if he were back in combat. *Rachel!*

"When are you leaving, sir?"

"In a few weeks."

Ashansky's heart skipped. "I'm an American soldier, not a French one. How could we pull that off?"

"I'm already working on that," said Commandant Xavier Roche.

Getting There

"Sit down, Sergeant," said Brigadier General Dennis Nolan, the AEF's intelligence chief.

"Thank you, sir," said Abram Ashansky.

"Commandant Roche tells me he wants you to accompany him on a French expedition to the Ukraine. He wants a translator and he said you would go if I agreed. Is that so?"

"Yes, sir."

"Why?"

Abe thought for a minute and decided to tell the truth. It would be hard to fool the general.

"Well, sir. When I fled the Ukraine in 1914, I had to leave my fiancée behind. Now I want to go find her and take her back to the United States with me."

Nolan smiled. "Now I've heard everything. You know that the United States Army is totally uninterested in your love life?"

"I do, sir."

"Good, then let's talk about why we—the Army—might want you to go to the Ukraine. I know you've had many conversations with Roche. Do you know what the French are up to going to the Ukraine?"

"I don't, sir. All he said was they were going and he wanted me to come as a translator and local expert."

"Are you a local expert?"

"There are those that would say I was—four years ago. A lot has changed, many people are dead, the political situation is an ever changing kaleidoscope but I probably still know, or at least can remember, more than most, sir."

Nolan didn't speak for a few moments and then he said, "I believe you. We'd like to learn more about the Ukraine and what the French are doing there. Especially since the war between the Whites and Reds is heating up. Would you be willing to observe and report back to me?"

"Certainly, sir," said Ashansky who felt a glimmer of hope.

"You're a good soldier, Ashansky. You're smart and you handle yourself well under fire. But it would be a gamble sending you into the Ukraine. It's not hard to conceive of just how much trouble you could get yourself—and us—into. It's a gamble I'm willing to take, but I'm not sure General Pershing will. And he's the boss. If he says no, it's no and there is no appeal. Do you understand me, Sergeant?"

"Yes, sir," said Abie, his heart soaring.

General Nolan asked for an audience with the commanding general of the American Expeditionary Force that afternoon.

He made the case for Ashansky as an American observer with the French expedition to the Ukraine.

Pershing was blunt, "Not a bad idea. We're not risking much. One man. And if it doesn't work out, we won't know any less than we do now. If you are right about his capabilities, we might learn a great deal. All right, Dennis, you can detail your sergeant to that Frenchman Roche."

Nolan stood and said, "Yes, sir. But there is one small problem."

"What's that?"

"Roche pointed out that as an enlisted man, Ashansky would have very limited freedom of movement. The French are sticklers for rank. He'd have to eat and sleep with the enlisted men. He'd miss out on all that juicy gossip in the officers' mess, sir," Nolan said, without irony.

"Hmm. What do you suggest, Dennis?"

"If we give Ashansky a temporary Reserve commission as a second lieutenant that will satisfy the French amour proper. We can certainly disavow a very junior officer if we are forced to."

"Isn't your sergeant Jewish?" asked Pershing.

"I believe so, sir. He certainly has a Hebrew name."

"That might help. They have a reputation for being devious,"

Pershing paused. "Although I am beginning to suspect that the Irish may be their equals."

"Thank you for the compliment, sir," said Nolan pleased with the outcome.

Pershing hesitated. "What if your man decides to go charging off looking for his girlfriend as soon as he lands?"

"As you say, sir, then all we've lost is one man and we are no worse off for it," said Nolan.

Two days later, Ashansky was sitting in Nolan's outer officer when the general said, "General Pershing wants to see you and me in his office an hour from now." He pointed to the sergeant's arm. "Cut off those chevrons before we go. And give those shoes a shine."

Ashansky choked down the impulse to ask "Why?" Instead, he said, "Yes, sir." The general entered his office and shut the door.

Sergeant Talbot, sitting nearby, was shocked. "What in the hell have you done, Abe?" he asked. "They're busting you to private. Jesus, I can't let any of you people out of my sight."

"I don't know, First Sergeant," said Ashansky.

"All right, what's done is done. You cut off the chevrons. Take your shoes off and give them to me. I'll put a regular Army shine on them. Maybe that will help."

Ashansky was as puzzled as Talbot. He was careful not to cut the fabric while removing his chevrons. *I don't deserve them anyway,* he thought.

Ashansky held the door to Pershing's office open for Nolan to walk through. Then he entered and came to attention in front of the four star general's desk.

He had mastered the soldier's skill of using his peripheral vision without moving his eyes. Besides Pershing and Nolan, he spotted the regimental sergeant major, the adjutant, some junior intelligence officers, Talbot and Terry Lynch, who had been promoted to captain just weeks before.

Pershing walked up to him. Ashansky saluted and the general returned the salute.

The general spoke, "Sergeant Ashansky, you have an excellent record as a soldier. Your bravery at the Battle of Apremont has been cited by both us and the French. You contributions to our intelligence operations have been commendable. Your linguistic skills are remarkable. And your superior education and breadth of intellect does you much credit.

"Therefore, by the power invested in me as commander-in-chief of the American Expeditionary Force, I am conveying upon you a battlefield commission as second lieutenant in the United States Army Reserve."

Now both Ashansky and Talbot were shocked.

Pershing pinned one gold bar on his right epaulet, Nolan pinned one on his left.

"Congratulations, Lieutenant," said Pershing who shook his hand.

"I believe General Nolan has arranged a bit of a reception for you back in his office," said Pershing. "But if you will excuse me, I must get back to my duties."

"Thank you, sir," said Ashansky who saluted.

The procession of officers reversed themselves, this time with Talbot holding the door.

Champagne corks were popped and French pastries were devoured. The reception was cheerful and welcoming. Most of the young intelligence officers were reservists too. Talbot, an enlisted man, was not invited.

After about a half hour, Nolan said, "Lieutenant, I think you better get down to the regimental supply sergeant and draw an officer's uniform and equipment. You can turn in your enlisted uniforms to the supply sergeant. Then report back to me."

"Yes, sir," said Ashansky. "And I thank you from the bottom of my heart. My first son will be named 'Dennis,' sir."

"Well, well," said a pleased Nolan. "Is Dennis a Jewish name?"

"It will be, sir," said Ashansky who saluted and left.

Talbot was waiting outside. He saluted and said, "If the lieutenant will follow me, I will escort him down to the regimental supply sergeant." Ashansky laughed and said, "Let's go, First Sergeant."

On the way, Talbot said, "By the way, sir, the lieutenant owes me a silver dollar."

"Why is that?" asked Ashansky.

"It is the custom in the United States Army for a brand-new second lieutenant to give a silver dollar to the first enlisted man who salutes him, sir."

"I owe you a lot more than that, First Sergeant."

"That the lieutenant does, considering that the lieutenant didn't know his ass from a hole in the ground when I first met him." Both men laughed.

When Ashansky returned to Nolan's office, he was kitted out as a second lieutenant. His high collared tunic glistened with the gold initials USR for a reserve officer inside a gold wreath on one side, the gold initials INT for interpreter on the other.

A Sam Brown belt encircled his jacket. The green and red ribbon of the French Croix de Guerre was on his chest, a small inverted gold wound stripe on his sleeve. His brown boots came calf high on his cavalry style trousers. Gold bars gleamed on his shoulders. He held his barracks cap with the gold officer's insignia under his left arm as he saluted.

"Well, that's one hell of a transformation," said the general. "You certainly look like a lieutenant, Ashansky."

"Thank you, sir. But I don't feel like one."

"That will come, trust me. As soon as you chew out a senior non-com."

"I doubt that day will ever come, sir," said Ashansky.

"It will but let's get down to work. I presume you have read our daily information summaries?"

"I have typed up many of them and I read the rest. Yes, sir."

"Good," said the general. "Then you know what kind of information we want. Keep it factual. Don't bother to make suppositions. We'll do that based on the facts. But do give us your opinions on the reliability of your sources. If they are French, don't name them. You'll be sending your reports through the French at first and you can be sure they will open and read them. Don't compromise your sources. We can read between the lines."

"Yes, sir."

"Do you intend to return to France with your fiancée?"

"No, sir. Once I find her, we're heading right back to America."

If you find her, son. I hope you're not going to be disappointed, thought Nolan.

"Very well. Once you leave French jurisdiction, it will be difficult to get reports back to us. We don't have a consulate in the Ukraine and it's likely to stay that way.

"We will have a military mission in Constantinople if you come back through Turkey. You'll also find a military attaché at our embassy in any friendly country you happen to be in.

"Your reports can be forwarded from there.

"When you get back to the United States, check in at the nearest Army unit. Make your report and await further instructions. You'll probably get your back pay, if any, and be demobilized there. Have I missed anything?"

"Sir, there may come times when I will not want to be in uniform nor show my military identity card. Is it possible for me to get an American passport?"

He hesitated. "In a false name, sir?"

Nolan looked at him and then smiled. "Lieutenant, I think you have the makings of a first-rate intelligence officer. But I warn you, if you are out of uniform and using a false passport, there will be some who will think you are a spy. And you know what happens to spies. We would not intervene."

"I understand, sir. I'd still like that passport."

Nolan nodded and picked up a pad. "Okay what name do you want on the passport?"

Ashansky thought back to a day at Ellis Island when a clerk, probably Irish, told him he would have an easier time of it in the United States if his name was "Al Shannon."

He said, "I'd like it to be in the name of Al Shannon. I'll say I'm in the import-export business if I have to."

General Nolan smiled. "Albert, Alfred or Aloysius? That last one is common among the Irish, Al."

"Aloysius, it is, sir."

"How will you explain that accent which definitely is not a brogue?" asked Nolan.

"No problem, sir. I'll tell the truth. My mother was born in the Ukraine."

Nolan laughed. "That'll do it, Lieutenant. He handed Ashansky a letter in a waterproof pouch.

"Here is a letter describing you and your duties as an observer. It asks for the cooperation of anyone who reads it. It is signed by General Pershing and that should do you in good stead in most places."

Except in the Ukraine, thought Abie.

"Here is a chit. Take it to the paymaster and draw two months' pay."

"How much is that, sir?"

"About $280, I think," said the general.

Wow! I made thirty-eight bucks a month as a sergeant. Not bad.

"You shouldn't have any trouble converting dollars into French francs. They might be more useful where you are going."

"They will, sir." *And I'll get a much better exchange rate at a place I know in town than at a bank.*

Nolan reached into his desk and came up with two rolls of coins. "Here are a hundred British gold sovereigns. You'll find these valuable when paper money isn't." Each coin was worth a

British pound, or even more on the black market.

Hot damn, I'm rich.

"Okay, Lieutenant. You have your orders. You have your equipment. You'll be detached for service with Commandant Roche next Wednesday. Meanwhile, you'll be billeted with the junior officers. Hang around the mess and the officers' club. Get the feel for being an officer. You should be a good one."

"Thank you, sir."

Ashansky approached the mess warily. He had the experience in Kiev with mingling with the Russian upper class and it had not been a very positive one.

He needn't have worried. Captain Lynch introduced him to several junior officers. "This is Lieutenant Ashansky." Abie would say, "Pleased to meet you. Call me 'Al.'" These American officers, almost all of them college graduates, were open and friendly. If there were any who were offended by the presence of a jumped up enlisted man, they didn't show it. The snobs simply ignored him which was easy to do. There were a lot of junior officers at AEF headquarters.

His new peers liked to drink a lot more than Ashansky did. He would nurse a glass of wine all night. Ashansky had to pay for his food and drink now. His uniforms too. Ashansky was a frugal man.

The more they drank, the more they admired his Croix de Guerre ribbon. He retold the story of the fight at Apremont several times a night concentrating on General Nolan's heroics and downplaying his own.

One officer commented, "You don't want an American medal. It's either the Medal of Honor or the DSC. Either way, you'll most likely be dead when they give it to you. I wish we had something like the Croix de Guerre."

America would create the Silver Star in 1932 and gave it retroactively to all those men who had been cited for bravery in

World War I. The wounded would be given the newly established Purple Heart. Ashansky would get both.

Small talk at the officer's mess revolved around women, Paris, sports and "When the hell are we going home?" Ashansky participated but tried not to stand out.

But the mess men noticed him anyway. They knew everything about everybody.

One said to his partner, "I didn't know Jews could become officers?"

"What's the matter with you?" was the retort. "There are lots of Jewish officers."

"Yeah. But they're all doctors."

Commandant Roche was inside the general's office saying goodbye, while Ashansky was outside with Captain Lynch.

"You know, Abe, we're both from Jersey City," said Lynch, "You should look me up when you get back from the Ukraine. We might be able to do each other some good."

"I'll do that," said Ashansky. "I imagine I will find you in city hall, outside Mayor Hague's office?"

Lynch laughed. "Maybe, but I doubt it. Your buddy, Tony Aiello, will know where I am. I'll look forward to seeing you. You're tough and you're smart, Abe. Those are qualities much appreciated in our hometown."

"Thank you, Captain. It has been a pleasure serving with you. And I'll never forget that these good things wouldn't have happened to me, if you hadn't picked me out of a crowd at Camp Dix."

"True," said Lynch, "but your hard work helped get me promoted to captain. So we're even.

"'Captain Lynch.' Won't that look good on an election poster?"

Ashansky said, "You've got my vote, Captain."

"That makes two of us... I'm on my way," said Terry Lynch,

politician.

With that, the office door opened and Commandant Roche emerged with General Nolan behind him. "Goodbye to you too, Ashansky. Good luck on your mission."

"Thank you, sir," said Ashansky as the general went back to his desk.

"Here are your orders and travel vouchers," said Commandant Roche. "You are to report to the French Army liaison officer at the Naval Base at Toulon. He will give you further instructions. You have two weeks before we sail for Odessa.

"As for me, I am going to the Vendee to spend some time with my family before I report. Does this cause you any concern, Lieutenant?"

"Not at all, sir," said Ashansky who thought he might visit Paris before he headed south. There were bound to be some refugees from the Ukraine there and he might pick up some useful information and make some contacts.

Paris was already the refuge for aristocrats and other monarchists who were fleeing the Bolsheviks.

Talbot drove him to the train station and insisted he ride in the back. "Your gear rides up front with me, Lieutenant, not you."

Their goodbye was as emotional as the old Regular Talbot would allow. Then Ashansky was on the train in a first-class carriage.

From that instant until the train pulled into Gare D'Est, Ashansky was bathed in gratitude from the French passengers who sought him out.

He was eating a late supper is a brasserie when a highly attractive woman walked up to his table and said, in English, "Do you mind if I join you, Lieutenant. I have never met an American officer before."

She was a brunette with soft brown eyes. Tiny wrinkles at her eyes and mouth hinted that she might be a few years older than Abie. Not many, just a few.

Ashansky stood and answered, "It would be my pleasure, to converse with one as lovely as you, mademoiselle."

"Madame," she corrected.

"Madame," he said as he moved to seat her.

A waiter immediately approached. Ashansky said, "I am having a late supper, will you join me?"

"No," she said," I have already eaten but I would take a glass of that wine you are drinking."

"Garcon, another half-bottle, if you will," said Ashansky.

"Oui, monsieur," said the waiter who was unsure of Ashansky's rank but who cherished Americans since they tipped much better than the cheapskate French.

"My name is Loretta," said the Frenchwoman.

"A beautiful name for a beautiful woman," said Ashansky, "And mine is Al, madame."

"Ell?" she asked.

"What a charming accent you have, madame."

"I had no idea you Americans were so gallant. Some of my friends say you behave like cowboys. Wonderful cowboys, mind you. But cowboys."

"I assure you, Loretta, I am not a cowboy," said Ashansky who had made his living in America tossing scrap metal into a gondola car.

"Of course not. I see you are wearing the ribbon of the Croix de Guerre, Ell. You must be very brave."

"No more than the next man and less than many," he said.

"You know French officers wear the medal on their tunics and not just the ribbon," she said.

"I didn't know that," said Ashansky.

"Yes. It is very dashing."

The waiter returned and made a little ceremony of opening the new bottle and offering Ashansky a taste before filling her glass upon his nod.

"Where are you staying?"

"Nowhere, at the moment," he said. "I left my equipage at the train station and thought I would find a hotel room after I ate."

"Don't waste your money. My flat is within walking distance. You can stay with me. It is the least I can do for an American hero."

Ashansky thought he would test the waters. "And your husband, madame? He won't object to a late-night guest?"

Loretta looked straight at him and said, not unkindly, "My husband was killed at the front two years ago, Lieutenant."

He took her hands in his. "You've my most abject apology and my deepest condolences, Loretta."

"Thank you," she said. "Shall we go?"

Ashansky paid the bill and left both a big tip and the barely touched wine.

When they were both sweaty and satisfied, Ashansky lay on his back, uncovered, and Loretta was propped up one elbow. She reached over and caressed him with her left hand.

"You're circumcised, "she said. "Are you a Jew?"

"Yes," said Ashansky. "Does that bother you, Loretta?"

"Not at all. But I would have been very upset if you were a Muslim," she said, moving her hand slowly back and forth.

Three days later, Ashansky left and inquired at the Orthodox Cathedral. He made several contacts and gleaned much information on the current situation in the Ukraine. He got names and addresses that would prove very useful.

Then he headed south by rail to Toulon.

Ron Semple

The Black Sea

Lieutenant Ashansky emerged from his taxi about two hundred yards from the gate to the Catigneu section of the great French naval base, arsenal and shipyard at Toulon on the Mediterranean Sea.

Here was the protected anchorage that held the French fleet. It was vast and was shielded from the open sea by the two jutting peninsulas flanking it. The French had been improving it since Louis XII established a naval base here early in the 16th century.

Ashansky stood there with his duffle bag and a large suitcase. It would be unseemly for an officer to pick them up and haul them himself to the guarded gate.

An elderly porter, who didn't look like he weighed more than the bags, hurried over, put two fingers to his cap in salute and picked up the bags. Easily.

Ashansky tipped the porter with a few coins and handed his orders to the sentry who took them to a naval officer inside the guard shack.

Ashansky looked through the window and saw the officer pick up a telephone and crank it. A couple of feet away another armed sailor stared at the first American Army officer he had ever seen.

The officer came out and in halting English said, "Come you with me, if please it you."

Ashansky answered in French, "Of course. My pleasure, sir."

A relieved Frenchman ushered him in and sat him down on an uncomfortable chair.

"An automobile will be coming for you from the Army liaison office, Sous-Lieutenant. It is a great pleasure to meet one of our American allies. We gave the Boche a good beating, no?"

"Yes, we most certainly did, sir."

It began to drizzle and Ashansky's baggage was still outside.

He made eye contact and glanced out the window. The French officer's eyes followed his and he muttered, "My God."

He gave a crisp order and the bags were inside.

"Many thanks, sir."

"It was nothing. Ah, your car has arrived."

An Army officer briefed him at the Liaison Office. "You will be billeted with the junior officers until you embark and, of course, you will draw the pay and allowances of a sous-lieutenant."

The French are going to pay me too? Should I say something? I better.

"You know, Captain, that I also will be reporting as an observer for the American Expeditionary Force in Chaumont?"

The captain gave him a wry look. "We are not paying you to observe for the American Army. That's their problem. We are paying you, sous-lieutenant, to translate Russian and Ukrainian for Commandant Roche. You can observe on your own time."

"Yes, sir."

"Now if you don't have any more questions"—the word "silly" was unsaid—"I will have you taken to your quarters. I believe Commandant Roche will join you in two days. Here is a pass that will permit you to come and go or to walk around the base."

The captain smiled. "Observe, if you like."

Ashansky was in time for dinner at the junior officers' mess. He was wearing the Croix de Guerre medal on his tunic.

He sat down at a table with five other junior officers. "May I join you, gentlemen?" Ashansky asked. A chorus of "D'accord" greeted him.

None was wearing a decoration. They were all junior staff officers whose distance from the front was measured in miles, not yards. He noticed them taking surreptitious peeks at his chest during the meal.

The food was superb, the wines excellent. And, best of all, it was free to their "gallant ally from America."

"Do you always eat like this?" he asked a French sous-lieutenant.

"Not in the field, of course," he said, "But at a base like this, the food is always more than acceptable."

"How is that possible?" asked Ashansky.

The Frenchmen laughed. "Many of our great chefs and most of their sous-chefs were called up. Who do you think they cook for, the men in the trenches?"

"Oh. Who cooks for those poor devils?"

The Frenchman answered with a shrug, "Who knows?" he said. The "and who cares" was implicit.

Commandant Roche approached him two days later.

"Did you have a good Christmas with your family?" Ashansky asked.

"I did indeed," said Roche. "But they stuffed me like a Christmas goose." He touched the top of his fist to his chest as if dealing with indigestion.

"I could do with some plain food," he said.

"Well, you came to the wrong place," said Ashansky.

The briefings began the next morning and Ashansky was able to send out a report to Brigadier General Nolan in Chaumont every day before they sailed. The keyboard of the French typewriter he used was slightly different than an American one but easy enough to master.

General Nolan and his second-in-command, Colonel Conger, were seated side by side at a big desk discussing Ashansky's reports.

"So the French have a dual mission in the Ukraine," said Nolan.

"Look at this: 'Since by mutual agreement, the Ukraine is in the French sphere of influence, the expedition is to explore the political and economic gains to be had there.'"

"What does he mean by 'mutual agreement'? Who agreed to that?" asked Conger.

Nolan said, "The British." He explained that as soon as America entered into the war and it looked like the Allies were going to win it, the British and the French began to divide the spoils. The British would be dominant in Greece, while the French got the Ukraine and Romania. Now they both were busy carving up the Near East. France claiming Lebanon and Syria as Britain takes Mesopotamia, Trans-Jordan and Palestine.

"Didn't the British Foreign secretary say Palestine was going to become a national homeland for the Jews?" asked Conger.

"He did. But I don't think he got the okay from the Arabs who are already there. They'll probably have plenty to say later on. It won't be pretty."

"So what is the expedition's secondary mission?"

"To help the Whites put down the Bolsheviks, if they can." The French general in charge offered the Whites twelve divisions. The commander of the Whites, General Denikin, asked for eighteen. But, in truth, only three French divisions in the Balkans were available for deployment.

Ashansky reported that the deployment of those three divisions would be delayed because of the ravages of the Spanish Flu and the decision to wait for replacements for those men due to be sent back to France and demobilized. The surviving soldiers are discontented, sick of war, and eager to go home and get out of uniform.

Nolan digested this appraisal and turned to Ashansky's latest report. "Our man says the first French troops landed in Odessa on December 17, but it took a barrage of naval gunfire to end the fighting in the city."

"Fighting? Are the Bolsheviks there already?" Conger asked.

"No. Apparently there is continuous skirmishing between the Whites and a group of Ukrainian nationalists. The French are managing to enforce an uneasy truce."

"Dear God," said Conger. "I can't tell these people apart."

"Thank God, Ashansky can," said Nolan.

"So what is your conclusion, sir?" asked Conger.

"I'd say the French won't have enough reliable troops to do the job. I'll be very interested to in what Ashansky has to say when he gets there."

Roche and Ashansky were now as well briefed as any in General d'Anselme's entourage. That general was in charge of operations and was a tactician not a strategist. This would cause further trouble.

The small fleet that sailed from Toulon for Odessa on the Black Sea consisted of a command vessel with General d'Anselme's staff and its supporting troops and equipment, a warship as an escort and a couple decrepit freighters that looked like they had been in service since the Franco-Prussian War of 1875. It was not an impressive flotilla.

Presumably, more French transports were heading for the Ukraine carrying troops from the Balkans.

The command ship and its escort moved past the slower freighters. The war was over. Ships displayed their running lights at night, none zigzagged. German, Austrian and Turkish submarines had been cleared from the seven seas.

The perennial "Sick Man of Europe," the Ottoman Empire, had expired on October 30 when a Turkish functionary had signed the Armistice of Mudros. All that was left was the dissection of the corpse and that was well under way.

The Turks surrendered all their garrisons outside their heartland of Anatolia. The Allies manned the forts that guarded the Dardanelles and British, French and Italian soldiers occupied Constantinople.

Soon the French ships were in the Aegean, Homer's "wine dark sea," approaching the entrance to the Dardanelles.

Everyone came topside to look at the fabled straits. The Sea of Marmara was 112 miles to the north.

"Say, didn't Allied submarines have a field day here during the Gallipoli campaign?" asked Ashansky.

"They did indeed," said Roche puffing on his pipe. "As you can imagine, the straits were very well guarded. Forts, minefields, warships, even field artillery. And then there were the Narrows, the shallow depths and the unpredictable cross-currents. Even the Germans thought the Dardanelles were impregnable.

"But you know the British. The first one in was an English boat that went upstream a dozen or so miles. It sank an old Turkish battleship and its skipper received the Victoria Cross at the hands of his King."

"I'll bet every submarine captain in the fleet headed for the Dardanelles after that," said Ashansky.

"Not quite but they were very busy. British and French boats. Even an Australian submarine. One of them even made it into the harbor at Constantinople and sank a big transport at its mooring right by the Golden Horn."

"I'm sure the Turks loved that."

"They were very upset. The townspeople were very frightened and actually rioted in the streets," said Roche. "Yes, our submarines sank a lot of shipping in the Dardanelles and the Sea of Marmara. But most of the submarines were sunk too. Still, the Turks had to send supplies to Gallipoli by rail on a six hundred mile detour. So I guess it was worth it."

"But the Turks won, anyway," said Ashansky.

"Then, not now," said Roche contentedly puffing on his pipe.

As they passed through the Narrows, less than a mile shore-to-shore, British soldiers from the forts on both sides waved to them.

The Sea of Marmara was a bit of a letdown after the Dardanelles. Just another big body of water with not a lot of shipping on it.

Then, on the horizon, shimmering in the early morning sunlight was Constantinople. Lost to the Ottomans almost five centuries earlier, it was the door to the Mediterranean and the West. Constantinople, capital of Byzantium, the center of Eastern Christianity. Lost.

What Russia would have sacrificed to possess it—and it was almost hers. The British, desperate to keep the Czar's armies fighting against the Germans, had offered it to him. That unobtainable jewel of the East was within his grasp. And then—the revolution—the Bolsheviks.

The vision of that Byzantine jewel melted like a paste imitation in a furnace.

The convoy did not stop. Again, men lined the sides of the ships and looked first at Europe and then, turning, gazed at Asia as their propellers churned the waters of the Bosporus.

It was in the dark of night when they debouched into the Black Sea. In the morning a thick winter fog absorbed the light and the water of the sea indeed did look black.

The ships' foghorns were sounding and speed had been reduced.

Ashansky was at the port bow chatting with a seaman who stared alertly into the fog and turned his head back and forth in a slow arc.

Pointing at the dark water, Ashansky said, "So that is why they call it the Black Sea."

The man never looked down. "Maybe," he said, "but there is another reason, sir. The dead are safe in the Black Sea."

"What do you mean?"

"Shipwrecks, bodies, even rope from the old rigging, lie on the bottom of this sea uncorrupted. Even after hundreds of years, the bodies of dead seamen lie there as if they drifted to the bottom just minutes before."

"How can that be?" asked Ashansky.

"I don't understand these things, sir, but an officer once told me there is very little oxygen in the Black Sea especially in deep water. He said it is oxygen that condemns a body to rot. No oxygen, no rot. I really don't understand these things, sir."

"Neither do I," said Ashansky.

The ships passed Bulgaria and the mouth of the Danube in Romania without seeing either.

But it was obvious when they approached the port of Odessa in western Ukraine. There were ships anchored everywhere. Troopships from the Balkans and supply ships from France vied for moorings with ships that were beginning to ply the coast of the Black Sea.

It was still winter but it was said that timber being cut in the forests hundreds of miles away would come down the Dnieper River this spring to small ports where lumber trains would be waiting. The world war was over and trade was beginning to revive.

But war was not over—not in Odessa and not in the Ukraine.

General d'Anselme immediately grasped the situation when he was briefed ashore by his subordinate commanders. The littoral east from Odessa to Kherson was controlled by the Ukrainian nationalists. He would have to make an accommodation with them despite his orders to deal only with General Denikin's White Army.

He did. It was a military necessity. D'Anselme's forces were completely vulnerable to attack from the east.

The Whites were outraged and demanded to meet with him "at once."

Commandant Roche and Ashansky were to accompany General d'Anselme to the meeting.

Roche approached Ashansky and said, "My general has a favor to ask of you. He wants you to pretend not to know Russian. He wants you to listen closely and see if what Denikin tells his interpreter in Russian is what is passed on to our general in French."

"Of course I will. After all I am being paid to interpret for you. But now I want a favor in return."

"Oh? What is that?"

"I don't want either the Whites or the Ukrainians or anybody else to know I am a Jew. It will cause unnecessary trouble. Introduce me as Lieutenant Al Shannon, the American observer."

"Shannon? Like the river in Ireland?"

"Exactly."

"Certainly," said Roche, "but you know our paymaster and adjutant will know your true name and may get curious."

"In that case, sir, will you inform the general that Shannon is my 'nom de guerre'?"

Roche laughed. "An understandable ruse, even if seldom used these days, my boy. Lieutenant Al Shannon it is."

The respective staffs lined up behind their generals seated opposite each other. A Russian interpreter sat next to General Denikin.

The Russian leader looked pointedly at Ashansky and murmured to the interpreter who addressed d'Anselme.

"Before we start, your Excellency, my general would like to know the name and duty of that young American officer." He rudely pointed at Ashansky.

General d'Anselme did not look back. "Most certainly, sir. That is Sous-Lieutenant Al Shannon who has been attached to us as an observer."

Denikin said to his interpreter, "Good. Then he can tell the Americans what an idiot that Frenchman is."

The interpreter said, "General Denikin says, 'Good. Then he can tell the Americans what a good friend General d'Anselme is.'"

The French general nodded.

"General Denikin says he is dismayed. He wants to know

if the French government has changed its policy of supporting the Volunteer Army?" He left out the personal insults which Ashansky noted.

"Not at all. France supports the Volunteer Army and no other group in the Ukraine."

"Then why did the general conspire with the nationalist traitors?"

D'Anselme checked his temper. "A commanding officer must always consider his tactical position. It is a military necessity that my flank facing the nationalists be secure. I negotiated a truce as one might do with any hostile force."

For two hours, the charge "conspiring with traitors" and the answer "military necessity" went back and forth like the shuttlecock in an interminable badminton game.

Finally, the interpreter said, "The general says 'very well' and he accepts your apology."

D'Anselme actually gritted his teeth. "May I suggest to the general that he enter into serious unity discussions with the nationalists so that a united front can be made against the Bolsheviks who are the enemy of all?"

"Ha!" exclaimed General Denikin who spoke French fluently but who refused to use it with d'Anselme.

Ashansky's report intrigued General Nolan. He knew that the French were frustrated and puzzled by the refusal of the anti-Bolshevik forces to work together but he said, "This is a new wrinkle."

"What's that?" asked Conger.

"Ashansky writes: 'One outstanding element among the French forces is the shipboard Marine contingent. New to onshore duty, they are fit, well equipped, highly disciplined and very attentive to orders.'"

"So? They sound like our own Marines."

"I told Ashansky we would read between the lines. He's

telling us the rest of the French troops are exhausted, under supplied, war weary and, just maybe, ready to mutiny. I think he is telling us the French are finished. Maybe they will pull out of the Ukraine and leave the Whites, Reds and Nationalists to fight it out."

Just so. D'Anselme reached that decision after March 9 when two companies of his infantry simply refused to obey their officers' orders and demanded to be shipped home and demobilized. The general was convinced that Bolshevik propaganda was getting to his men.

It was time to get out.

Roche asked, "So I cannot convince you to come back with us to France, my friend?"

Ashansky shook his head. "No, sir. I hope I have discharged my obligations to you. Now I must find Rachel. Then we will go to America."

What optimism! The poor girl is probably dead by now, thought Roche.

"I wish you the best of luck. You will always be my dear friend. You saved my life and I will forever be in your debt, Abe."

The two men embraced.

Ashansky had no clothing but his Army uniforms. He went to a tailor in Odessa and said in Ukrainian, "I need a suit, two shirts, a tie, a warm wool sweater and a hat. Can you help me?"

The tailor rubbed his thumb and index finger together and said, "I can, if you can help me."

"I have money," said Ashansky.

"What kind?" asked the tailor.

"Francs."

"It is a pleasure doing business with you, sir."

He stood, a tape measure around his neck. "Now, let's get some measurements, Captain. When do you want these clothes?"

"As soon as possible."

The tailor eyed Ashansky. "If you pay for the suit now and give me a fair day's wages, I'll have it ready by nightfall."

"It's a pleasure doing business with you, sir," said Ashansky.

The suit, good wool and a good fit, was ready on time. Ashansky changed into his civilian clothes and put his uniform into his duffle bag. It was still chilly at night so he wore his army greatcoat. Many men his age were wearing the greatcoats of a dozen different armies. It attracted no undue attention.

Meanwhile, the Bolsheviks were on the move again and were menacing Kiev.

Shemuel said to his squad guarding the city's power station coal, "I hope you still have your red armbands, boys, the Communists are coming back." They did.

Heading North

Ashansky had dumped his suitcase in favor of a haversack. In it were a small sack with his Croix de Guerre and all the brass taken off his uniforms, a sweater, a change of underwear, an extra shirt, a pair of socks, a mess kit with a fork, knife and spoon. There was a cloth bag with a roll of toilet paper, a Gillette safety razor, a pack of blades, a bar of soap, a toothbrush and a tube of toothpaste. A khaki-colored towel filled the rest of the space.

On top of all this was a copybook in which he jotted down cryptic notes for his reports to General Nolan.

A canteen complete with cup and cover hung from a flap on the left side where a bayonet should have been.

His great coat was rolled like blanket and strapped to the top and sides of the haversack. A pouch on the cover held twenty five-ruble gold pieces and ten ten-ruble gold pieces wrapped in a handkerchief.

A smaller pack was attached by a strap to the bottom of the haversack. It contained his loaded .45 pistol in its holster, two loaded magazines, a box with twenty-five rounds, and a box containing small tins of gun solvent and oil, a wire brush, an old toothbrush, some cotton patches and a rag—all to clean his pistol.

Ashansky kept on his person the pouch with the letters from the generals, two pencils, his military identification, his false passport, his wallet with a few franc notes in it, a sharp clasp knife and a money belt with the two rolls of gold sovereigns and a wad of francs. A handful of Russian copper and silver coins were in his pants pocket.

The haversack never left his side. The bulky duffle bag could be abandoned if necessary. Ashansky was ready to begin his quest.

He was on a tram headed for an area away from the waterfront. Looking out the window, he saw few motor vehicles. Horses slowly plodded along the cobblestone streets pulling carriages or carts topped with immense loads.

The Ukraine was totally dependent on horses and its railroads for transportation as America had been a generation earlier. The once heavy boat traffic on its navigable rivers had virtually vanished with the advent of war. Many in the countryside had never seen a motor vehicle.

Once you left the cities, roads in the Ukraine were nothing but dirt, with thick, choking clouds of dust when dry, and almost impassable sloughs of mud when wet.

Kiev, where he would start his search, was more than four hundred miles away—too far to walk or ride a horse and no boats were going upstream on the great Dnieper River. Ashansky would have to use the railroads.

The railroads had not been destroyed during the war. All sides implicitly knew that the only way to move masses of men and equipment was by railroad and to deny it to your enemy was to deny it to yourself. So damage to the railroads, their equipment and their tracks was incidental, minimal and easily repaired.

This unspoken agreement even gave rise to a relatively new weapon of war, the armored train that roared through the land conveying much prestige and doing little damage. It was a beloved military toy favored by Soviet leaders.

Ashansky got off the tram in the center of the city at the railway terminal. He checked his duffle at the left luggage counter and looked at his map of Odessa. The address he wanted was about a half-mile from the terminal, an easy walk even with the haversack on his back.

The hand-painted sign on the door read in Yiddish: "Ferenikte Yidishe Sotsialistshe Arbeter Partey"—the Jewish Socialist Workers Party.

Ashansky had flirted with this group when he was at the

university, attended some of their meetings and could speak their language. He could use their help if he was to find Rachel.

He opened the door and walked into a large square room. Three young men, all thin, bushy haired and wearing glasses, were at desks typing away as fast as two fingers would let them. A sense of urgency hung in the air.

One of them stopped typing and looked speculatively at Ashansky who moved forward and stood in front of his desk.

"Good morning, Comrade. I am Abram Ashansky and I'd like to talk to someone who can tell me what is going on in Kiev."

"This isn't a newspaper," said the young man. "Why should we tell you anything? I've never seen you before."

The young man did not offer Ashansky a seat and a large man came to stand facing Abe. *An obvious and probably competent thug,* thought Ashansky.

"I was a supporter of the Ferenikte when I was at the university in Kiev, before the war," said Ashansky.

The young man paused to light an aromatic cigarette and said, "It is amazing how many supporters we seemed to have had and how few members. What university were you at?"

"The National University."

"St. Vladimir's?"

"Yes," said Ashansky.

The young man put his cigarette down, waved Ashansky into a chair and nodded a dismissal to the thug who walked away, disappointed.

"How did a Jew get into St. Vladimir's?" he asked.

"I don't know," said Ashansky. "My father had a Russian patron who arranged it but he wouldn't tell me his name."

"It must have been Czar Nicholas," said the young man. "Would you like some tea?"

"Yes, please." The young man caught the thug's eye and held up two fingers.

"My name is Moishe, Comrade," he said as the steaming tea

arrived in glasses set in cheap metal holders.

Ashansky sipped the hot tea and said, "Ah! I had almost forgotten what real tea made in a samovar tastes like. Thank you."

"You're welcome. Where were you that there was no tea?"

"In America. The tea comes in a little bag which you dunk in a cup of hot water."

Moishe stared at him, not really comprehending.

"I got out of the Ukraine just before the Czar conscripted me and I ended up in America."

"Smart man. I got nailed and spent two years trying to decide whether it was better to die at the hands of a German soldier or a Russian sergeant." Both men laughed.

"So tell me, Comrade. Why the interest in Kiev? Homesick for the old town?"

"Hardly. I'm an American now. But I have to go back there and I would like some idea of what I'll face—and whether I will have any problems along the way."

Moishe pointed his index finger straight up. "If I could stack the problems you are going to face, they would reach the ceiling.

"First off, the Bolsheviks have occupied Kiev again. But that doesn't mean the fighting has stopped. The Whites are around sniping at them. And worse, squads of the Black Hundreds on horseback are terrorizing the countryside. It's a mess."

"The Black Hundreds? I thought those miserable bastards were better at pogroms than at fighting."

"That too. You know they will turn on the Jews whenever they want."

Ashansky thought for a moment and asked, "Does the Ferenikte support the Bolshevik revolution?"

"No, not really," said Moishe puffing on his cigarette. "We favor a peaceful solution in Russia and an independent Ukraine. If the Ukraine is its own state then we Jews could have an extra-territorial autonomous nation within it."

Ashansky was puzzled. "An extra-territorial autonomous nation?"

"Yes, an extra-territorial nation. The two million Jews in the Ukraine are scattered from one end to the other. We already have local government in the shtetls and as an extra-territorial nation, we could make laws governing ourselves on a national level. We want to build a secular Jewish nation."

"I used to be secular myself," said Ashansky.

"Not anymore?"

"No. I'm still a young man but I've seen enough—and done enough—to know that man is not perfectible. If we are fallen creatures, and we are, then there must be a creator."

"So you are an observant Jew?"

"No. I'm not that either." *But I'm not a starry-eyed idiot like you people. Dreamers. You'll all end up dead,* thought Ashansky.

"Let's say, you are actually stupid enough to attempt the trip to Kiev, how do you intend to get there?" asked Moishe.

"I don't see any alternative to the railroad," said Ashansky.

"There isn't any," said Moishe. "The railroad is still running. It's in no one's interest to destroy it. There's a lot of useful smuggling going on. It will take forever to get there and you'll have to pass through territory controlled by the nationalists, then by the Whites and then by the Reds, none of whom will be happy to see a casual traveler, let alone a Jew."

"I see," said Ashansky. "Do you have anyone in Kiev that could help me when I get there?"

"Comrade Ashansky. If you don't tell me why you are so determined to get to Kiev right now, this conversation will end. And I most certainly will not give you the name of anyone we know in Kiev."

Abie decided to tell the truth. "I have to find my fiancée and then I'm going to take her to America."

"You're serious, aren't you? No sane man would make that up."

"Yes. I'm serious. This is the vision that has sustained me for more than four years."

Aaron shook his head and asked, "What is your fiancée's name?"

"Rachel Zeidman. Her father is Nickolay Zeidman. He used to be a goldsmith but now he's an agent for the Tereshchenko Sugar Refinery."

"A capitalist lackey, eh?"

"Just a Jew trying to make his way in life."

"Fair enough. So what will you do if you get to Kiev?"

"I'll try to find my people first. If they are alive, they'll know where Rachel is. I haven't heard from them since I went to America. If I can't find them, I'll search for her on my own."

Moishe snuffed out his cigarette butt. "Heaven knows why, but I am going to help you, Abram. I am going to give you the name of one of our people in Kiev. He's a bit too cozy with the Reds to suit us, but if he is still alive, he might be able to help you. He is pretty prominent in the Jewish community there. His name is Oleksandr Horwits."

"I know that name," said Ashansky. "But I never met him. Where can I find him?"

"Frankly, we don't know. We haven't heard from him in months. I'll write down his old address. You'll have to track him down yourself. If you find him, tell him to get in touch with us."

"I will. Thank you very much, Comrade," said Ashansky.

"Don't mention it."

Moishe walked him to the door, a smile on his face. "Tell me, Comrade. Are the streets in America really paved with gold?"

"Yes," said Abie the Jew. Moishe laughed, Ashansky didn't.

Ashansky picked up his duffle bag in the terminal and bought a second-class ticket to Kiev. The ticket seller was willing to take any currency or combination thereof. The exchange rates weren't very favorable.

There were no express trains nowadays. His would stop at every station along the hundreds of miles of its route north. This train would ultimately fetch up at Cherkassy on the Dnieper River, the route of the old lumber trains. Ashansky would have to transfer at a junction east of Kiev and catch another train which would arrive God knows when.

The trip, obviously, would take days.

He settled into a hard, straight-backed wooden seat, his haversack between his legs, and his duffle beside him. He thought if he stowed it in the baggage car, he would never see it again. Besides, he thought it might prove useful along the way. He was right.

No one sat beside him.

The locomotive huffed and puffed its way out of the terminal, cleared the city and made its way through the countryside that didn't seem like it was controlled by any political faction.

Hours later it stopped at a small station with a water tank. Two men entered from the connecting car. One was a heavy, older man wearing the impeccable uniform of a Czarist officer. The other was still a boy, wearing an ill-fitting uniform and carrying a rifle with a fixed bayonet. Whites.

The officer, clean shaven and sporting a monocle, walked slowly up the aisle carefully looking at each passenger. He stopped and talked briefly to two of them and moved on. His carriage and arrogant attitude seemed typical of a White officer, all of whom were drawn from the ranks of the aristocracy, the landowners or wealthy city dwellers. The boy soldier was typical too, a bored peasant.

Ashansky did not avoid the officer's scrutiny. The officer glanced at the duffle bag, the haversack and the man.

"And who are you?" he demanded in Russian.

Ashansky jumped to his feet and stuck out his hand. "Al Shannon, Eagle Uniform Company, Akron, Ohio. Glad to meet you, Colonel."

The captain stepped back. "What?"

Ashansky's hand remained in mid-air, unshaken.

Ashansky reached for his passport. "I'm an American businessman here to help you defeat the Reds." He offered it to the captain who examined it though he could not read a word of any language that was not written in Cyrillic.

"Your Russian is very good, American businessman," he said. *Too good,* he thought. "Where did you learn it?"

"From my mother," Ashansky said, a salesman's smile on his face, "She was born in Russia."

Reassured, the captain asked, "And how will you help us destroy the Reds, Meester Sha-known?"

Ashansky pointed to his duffle bag, "My company has acquired thousands of fabulous uniforms that the American army no longer needs. I have a sample right here in this bag.

"You won't believe the quality or the low price. Perhaps your own unit might be interested, Colonel. " He looked pointedly at the rumpled peasant boy. "Your men will be proud to wear our fine uniforms and, as you know, a proud soldier is a good soldier."

The captain had never heard of such a ridiculous concept. Soldiers fought because their officers would shoot them if they didn't. Who cared if they were "good" or not?

"I have my order book too. We'd be happy to extend credit on the signature of an officer and gentleman such as you."

The captain was eager to get away from this American imbecile.

"No. No. No. Thank you, no, Meester Sha-known. You need to see our Quartermaster General."

"Wonderful," said Ashansky. "And where can I find him?"

Anywhere you're not. "Our Divisional Headquarters is located three stops from here. You can get directions there."

"Oh. Thank you, Colonel," said Ashansky who again stuck out his hand. He was rewarded with a limp handshake. The captain left and did not return.

That was easy, thought Ashansky as he settled in again. *But somehow I don't think the Reds will fall for that little soft shoe.*

Near dusk, the train stopped for water again and the conductor suggested the passengers get off and get something to eat. The conductor was the son-in-law of the old woman selling grated turnip pancakes and hot tea.

Ashansky filled his canteen with hot tea and ate his meal out of his canteen cup. The food was all but tasteless. *I should have brought some salt and pepper with me.*

Night had fallen when the train pulled out again. Using his great coat as a blanket, his feet propped up on his haversack, Ashansky tried to sleep.

He didn't think he succeeded but the hours passed anyway. He was aware of the train starting and stopping several times and once he sensed men walking through the darkened coach with a flashlight but they didn't wake him.

The second day was much like the first with just one inspection. Ashansky said to the grizzled corporal who asked, "I'm a salesman on my way to see your Quartermaster General."

The corporal understood that he never wanted to the draw attention of any general. He said, "Good luck" and moved away quickly.

The private with him said, "Shouldn't we have questioned him further, Corporal. He seemed out of place."

"You're going to find that my boot is not out of place up your ass if you don't keep your mouth shut and do what you are told." The private believed him.

Later Ashansky got off to eat again, this time grated potato pancakes. And then the train rolled through the night as he slept soundly.

The sun was up when the train jolted to a stop in the middle of an open, plowed field. The signal alongside the tracks was red.

"What's going on?" Ashansky asked the conductor.

"Probably some shooting up ahead. It happens all the time. We'll stay here until it's over."

"How will you know that?"

"The stationmaster will turn the signal green."

Ashansky could envision the stationmaster, a pistol to his head, doing just that. He had a bad feeling about this and he had learned to trust his instincts.

A narrow road ran alongside the tracks. "How far is it to the station?"

"Not far. About ten or fifteen versts. "

Probably less than two miles. "Thanks. I think I'll walk a bit."

"Suit yourself," said the conductor. "But we may have left by the time you get there."

"No matter. I'll catch the train tomorrow. I'm in no hurry."

"Must be nice," said the conductor.

The haversack rode comfortably on Ashansky's shoulders but the duffle bag was awkward to carry and he wondered why he was hanging on to his army uniform. *Maybe I can barter it for something useful in the next village.*

Sure enough, in a few minutes the train passed him, the engineer pulling on the whistle. Ashansky was nonplussed by this. He still had that bad feeling.

He was less than a half mile from the station when he met villagers hurrying away on foot. One old man shouted, "Go back! Go back! They're robbing the train. They're stealing everything. Go back!"

Ashansky stopped him. "Who's robbing the train, my friend?"

"Them. The Reds. The Whites. The Greens. The Yellows. Who the hell knows? Them. Let me go, boy."

Ashansky did and moved off the road about a half mile and squatted down in a newly plowed field.

His instincts had been good. The old man was right. It didn't matter who was robbing the passengers and pillaging the village. The concept of "living off the land" was elastic in most armies.

Ashansky felt elated. His luck was holding. If he had been on that train, he would have been robbed of everything. No, he would have put up a fight and God knows how that would have ended.

Where there is a plowed field, there is a farmer, Ashansky thought as looked around carefully. In the distance, perhaps another half mile away, was a plume of white smoke emitting from a small copse of trees. *A strong farmer. A kulak. Someone with something to barter. Someplace to spend the night.*

Ashansky transferred his loaded .45 from his lower pack to the right-hand pocket of his jacket. The budge made by the big gun almost disqualified it as a concealed weapon.

Can't be helped, thought Ashansky who, like anyone really familiar with the Colt .45, would never put a loaded one in his waistband except in extremis. Never.

The kulak greeted him at the door with a leveled shotgun.

"What do you want?" he asked in Ukrainian.

Ashansky dropped his duffle and raised his hands in front of him and answered in Ukrainian.

"My name is Kristopher Boiko and I am traveling to Kiev. Our train was held up by brigands but I got away. I need something to eat and food to take with me. And a place in your barn to spend the night. And a horse and saddle to ride off on in the morning."

The farmer laughed. "And I suppose you want the moon too, eh? Even if I had these things, how would you pay for them? Don't tell me with paper money. That's good for starting a fire. Little else. Well?"

"I was thinking of gold coins and I have things to barter too," said Ashansky to the farmer who was almost broke after paying for the seeds he had just planted and was wondering how he and his wife would get by until the harvest.

The kulak gestured with the shotgun. "What do you have in your pocket?"

"A loaded pistol," said Ashansky.

"Take it out with your left hand and put it on the ground. We'll take it to the barn with the rest of your things. We can talk there. My wife is afraid of guns."

"Me too," said Ashansky, following orders.

Inside, they sat on bales of straw. The farmer said, "All right, Kristopher, what do you have to barter?"

Ashansky emptied the contents of his duffle bag onto the earthen floor. The kulak immediately picked up one of the shiny cavalry boots.

"Yes. These are enough to get you dinner, food for your trip and a pallet in the barn with a warm blanket. But it is nowhere near enough for a horse and saddle. You know that?"

"I do. We can bargain all night but I suggest you make me your best offer. If I think it is fair, I'll give it to you now. If not, well, I do know how to walk."

The farmer thought of his three horses. The oldest, a gelding, was still strong, docile, and would not balk at a saddle although it was much more familiar with a plow.

Somehow, he knew this man would walk if he set the price too high. He needed the money.

"I can let you have a good horse. A strong horse. For 100 gold rubles."

"Done," said Ashansky.

Searching for Rachel

The kulak was right. The horse was strong and easygoing. That was just as well since Ashansky was an indifferent horseman at best.

They would plod along steadily until the sun neared its apex at noon. Then Ashansky would find one of many small streams and rest while he and the horse ate. There was always greenery for the horse on the banks of a stream.

At first, Ashansky had tethered the gelding to a tree with a long, thin rope he had gotten as part of the barter but the horse showed no inclination to roam so the rope remained stowed on the saddle after the second day.

Ashansky did not know what the farmer had called the horse so he named him "Sergeant." That was whimsy. Ashansky hoped it would impel the horse to gallantry should that equine quality be demanded. Thus far, Ashansky had not attempted a canter, let alone a gallop, with Sergeant.

After lunch, when they had rested and the horse had drunk his fill from the stream and Ashansky had his tea, he would walk alongside Sergeant for a half hour or so holding a pleasant, if one-sided, conversation with his new companion.

Walking through ploughed fields was harder on Abie than on Sergeant who worked them all his life. It was worse when it rained and the mud was thick and Ashansky's great coat was heavy with rainwater. But he pressed on.

Ashansky avoided the road, keeping it in sight, but returning to it only when there was a fence or a bridge to cross. And then only after stopping and making a careful reconnaissance of the area. If he ran into real trouble, it would be on the road.

When dusk approached, Ashansky would look for a farmhouse. There he would offer to pay for food and a place in the barn for him and his horse. The offer was always accepted.

The peasants of the Ukraine were in a bad way and every kopeck helped. The food was plain but plentiful and palatable now that Ashansky had acquired some salt and pepper from the kulak's wife.

In the morning, with a canteen full of fresh tea and enough food for the day, Ashansky and Sergeant would be on their way, north and then west to Kiev.

As they ambled along, Ashansky's thoughts sometimes would wander. For example, Ashansky liked to think that not all of his ancestors came from the Twelve Tribes of Israel. There were the Khazars.

A semi-nomadic Turkic people, who intermarried with the local populations they conquered, once had an empire that stretched from the Ukrainian steppes to the Ural Mountains.

Their empire was a buffer state between Islam and Orthodox Christianity. The Khazars converted to Judaism en masse following the lead of their royal families sometime before the end of the first millennium.

The Mongols put an end to their independence in the 13th century and many Khazars fled west reportedly to mix with the Jews in Germany.

Ashansky liked to think of himself as at least part Khazar—a conqueror, not one of the eternally vanquished. Scholars would agree he looked like one: blue eyes, fair skin and even reddish tints in his brown hair when the sun hit it.

It was a harmless conceit which Ashansky confided to no one after he discovered the Khazars in history books at the university.

When Ashansky identified himself with a Ukrainian name at a Ukrainian farmstead, no one looked at him and questioned it.

Now, days later as they got closer to Kiev, the fields looked different than when they had been sowed with the potatoes and turnips that kept the peasants alive during the lean war years just past.

His suspicions were confirmed when he stopped at a farmhouse and the tenant was Jewish.

"You're right," he said, "the bastard that owns the land made me plant beets this year. I hope he is right or else my family is going to eat a lot of borsht this winter."

The countryside around Kiev was prime sugar country. In fact, it produced most of the beet sugar consumed by Russia. The great open black dirt fields of Russia were reserved for grain which was exported. Beets could be grown profitably on much smaller plots.

"The Russians love sugar in their tea and they've had to do without it for a long time. If my boss is right, he'll make a killing—he owns a lot of land, you know. If not, the skin will be off my ass, not his," said the tenant in Yiddish.

"Do you live in Kiev, Abram?"

"Not anymore. I am an American."

The old Jew was incredulous. "You left America—the promised land—to come back to this shithole? Forgive me, young man, but you must be crazy."

Ashansky laughed. "No, Uncle, I don't think I'm more crazy than most. I'm going to find my fiancée and then we're both going back to stay in America."

"That makes sense. My son is in America. You won't believe what we had to do to raise his fare. But now he is sending money back to us—although we haven't seen any since the war started. Like you, he calls himself an American, not a Jew. I don't understand that."

"In the United States, you can be both a Jew and an American," Ashansky explained.

"I still don't understand," said the old man.

"You will when you move there."

"Nah. My wife and I are too old to go. But I hope all my children join their brother in America."

"You won't mind being left alone back here?" asked Ashansky.

The old man laughed. "Hell no. My children will send us money. My wife and I will move to Kiev and live like royalty."

Then his face fell. "But I will never see my grandchildren when they come. My American grandchildren."

Ashansky enjoyed both the food and the company at the old Jew's cabin but, as usual, he left in the morning.

He always avoided villages, circling around them. Now, much closer to Kiev, there was one he could not bypass. It was built around a bridge and while the stream was narrow and not deep, its banks were steep. Too steep for Sergeant. Ashansky would have to go through the village.

He slowly walked alongside Sergeant, ready to spring into the saddle and gallop back the way he came. If Sergeant could gallop.

There was a crowd at a communal well on a patch of green down the road.

Uh-oh! Reds.

A man sat at a rough table with a semicircle of people facing him. He was in uniform with a red armband. Several other soldiers were lounging nearby, looking relaxed. Another serious-looking Red was standing behind them smoking a cigarette, holding it between his thumb and forefinger, Russian-style.

Ashansky stopped at the far edge of the crowd and asked the man next to him, "What is going on, friend?"

The man glanced at Ashansky and Sergeant and said, "Nothing that concerns you, stranger. The Bolsheviks are setting up some sort of new group that will run our village."

"What kind of new group?"

The man shrugged. "I don't know. " He pointed to a tall man standing in the front rank with his arms folded. "Boyar Pavlov has always told us what to do. His family owns all the land around here and always has. We just work it. He's a Russian too, so maybe he understands what they are talking about. I don't."

Ashansky nodded.

The speaker was droning on with one Marxist cliché tumbling out after another. Yet no one in the crowd drifted away.

Finally, he said, "Comrade Commissar."

The serious man, no longer smoking, walked up to the table. He gestured at the soldiers. Two of them brought their rifles to high port and walked up to the tall man who did not move. The crowd around him fell back a couple of feet.

"Comrade Pavlov, you are accused of being an enemy of the people," said the commissar. "You are accused of stealing the labor of the people of this village who work its land. You are accused of being a tyrant and a murderer."

The landowner cried out, "A murderer! What are you fools talking about? I've killed no one." The crowd murmured at his outburst.

The commissar pointed at him. "You drove Comrade Hordiyenko off the land. He could not find work and his child starved to death. You murdered that little girl."

"What rot," said the landowner. " I evicted him because he was a terrible tenant. His crops always failed. His fences were falling apart. And he couldn't find work because he was the laziest man in the oblast. That child died because he was her father. No other reason. This is my land—not the village's— and I'll farm it as I see fit." He waved his arm taking in the semicircle of people. "If it wasn't for me, these people would all starve."

The commissar moved towards the landlord. "Comrade Pavlov, your own words convict you."

"Don't call me comrade. I'm not your comrade. I've had enough of this nonsense," said the landowner as he turned to walk away.

"Just so," said the commissar who drew his pistol, elevated it slightly, and shot the landowner in the back of the head. The man dropped and hit the ground facedown.

The crowd was aghast, falling back from the body, a torrent

of sound gushing from them.

The commissar put his pistol back in its holster. The Red soldiers were alert and at port arms, their bayonets reflecting the sunlight. Ashansky got ready to flee.

The crowd quieted.

"This is how the Soviets deal with the enemies of the people. You will not have to live in fear anymore. We will protect you," said the commissar.

The people were very afraid. There was absolutely no sound now.

The man at the table said, "All right. comrades. Saddle up. We're moving out." The soldiers formed ranks.

The crowd did not linger either. Soon the untouched body, with its attentive flies, was the only thing Ashansky could see besides the bridge in the distance. He walked toward it.

There were two Reds guarding the bridge. "Where are you heading, Comrade?" asked one.

"To Kiev. To find my family."

"Where have you been?" asked the other.

"All over the world, Comrade. I'm a seaman. I used to work the lumber boats on the Dnieper. Then I signed on as a stoker on a French tramp steamer in Odessa and I was on her in the Mediterranean when war broke out. Then it was one French ship after another. I even got to America. But I couldn't get back to the Ukraine."

"You were lucky," said the guard," Show me your hands, Comrade. Palms up."

Ashansky did. The guard rubbed his fingers over them. Ashansky's hands were still heavily callused from his time in the scrap yard.

"You're a worker alright," said the guard." Why don't you join us? We're going to make Russia a worker's paradise."

"That sounds good. But I want to find my family first. Can I join up in Kiev?"

"Sure," said the guard. "Good luck on your journey, Comrade. Watch yourself. There are still some Whites and even some of those fucking Black Hundreds roaming around."

"Black Hundreds? Those bastards?"

"Those bastards," said the guard.

The rest of Ashansky's trip was uneventful.

He drew no notice in Kiev as he sought out his old home. He tied Sergeant to a hitching post outside and shouldered his haversack. He was anxious. What would he find?

He twisted the bell. In a few moments, the door opened and a face he had never seen before appeared.

"Yes?"

Ashansky stuttered a bit and then said, "I am Abram Ashansky."

"Yes?"

"Isn't this the Ashansky residence?"

The woman glared at him. "It is not. I live here. And I am certainly not a Jew." She slammed the door in his face. He heard the bolt slam home.

Ashansky didn't know what to do. He needed more information but he was sure that bitch wouldn't open the door again.

No one answered his knock at Rachel's home either. He couldn't go door to door in Kiev looking for her. He'd have to find Horwits.

Ashansky knew that it would be easier to move about Kiev on foot or on a tram rather than on horseback. He'd risk having his horse stolen the instant he entered a building.

So he took Sergeant to a livery stable. He paid for a week's board and gave the stable hand a nice tip.

"Don't worry, your honor. I'll treat your horse better than I treat my own wife."

I'll bet.

Ashansky looked at the disheveled man and said, "By the way, if my horse isn't here when I get back, I'll kill you." The stable hand blanched.

He took a tram to the center of the city, with his haversack between his legs. There seemed to be a sense of excitement in the air with some men laughing and joking. Others looked grim and seemed to withdraw into their jackets.

I'll try the Palace of Justice first.

The receptionist said, "Horwits? First door on your left."

Oleksandr Horwits was bent over a map, a red armband on the sleeve of his uniform jacket.

"Comrade Horwits?"

He looked up, showing very little interest in his guest. He was preoccupied.

"What now?" he asked.

"I am Abram Ashansky and I need your help?"

Horwits relaxed. *A fellow Jew.* "Everybody from Vladimir Lenin on down wants something from me. Why not you?"

"I am looking for my parents and for my fiancée. I haven't seen them since the war started."

"I'm sorry, young man. I don't know anybody named Ashansky. What is your girl's name?"

"Zeidman. Rachel Zeidman. Her father is Nickolay Zeidman. He's an agent for the sugar refinery."

"Him, I know," said Horwits. "Doesn't he have a son named Shemuel?"

"He does, Comrade."

"Well, I don't know where the father or daughter might be, but Shemuel is down at the power station by the river. He's been there for well over a year now."

"Doing what?" asked Ashansky.

"He leads a squad guarding the municipal coal supply for us," said Horwits.

Ashansky, loosening up now that he had a solid lead, asked, "But how is that possible? Kiev has changed hands several times since then, hasn't it?"

Horwits laughed. "Shemuel is a very resourceful young man. You'll find him there. Watch yourself. You know what's going on?"

"I'm not sure," said Ashansky.

"The world is in turmoil. When that happens, everybody turns on the Jews."

"A pogrom?"

"Yes, another one. Kiev is safe enough during the daytime but no place is safe at night," said Horwits. "But you shouldn't have any trouble. You look like a gentile."

"I'm not a gentile."

"Don't tell them that," said Horwits.

A tram took Ashansky within blocks of the big power station. As he walked toward it, he could see a huge mound of coal behind a barbed wire fence. He walked up to the locked gate and he could see a guard moving toward him.

"I'm sorry, Comrade," said the guard. "There is no coal for sale. It all goes to make electricity."

Ashansky said, "I don't want to buy coal. I'm looking for Shemuel Zeidman."

"Really? What's your name? I'll see if he wants to see you."

"Abram Ashansky. From America."

Another Jew, although this one doesn't look it. "Wait here. I'll tell Zeidman you're here."

Less than a minute later Rachel's brother came running towards the gate, a key to the padlock in his hand. "Abram! Abram! You're alive! You're here!"

The gate opened, the men embraced laughing and slapping each other's back. Shemuel paused to re-lock the gate. Then, arm in arm with Abie, they walked to the guard shack.

Shemuel stopped and said, "Let's sit down on those crates and talk. That'll give us some privacy. We'll go into the shack later and have tea."

Abie grabbed his arm, "Shemuel. Forget tea. Where is my Rachel?"

"Who?" Shemuel asked and, seeing the flabbergasted look on Abie's face, laughed and hugged him again. "Your Rachel is safe and as sassy as ever."

Sassy? Abe remembered Rachel as beautiful, sweet and very demure. "Thank God," he said.

"Boy, is she going to be happy to see you," said Shemuel. "We all told her you were probably dead but she would have none of that." He mimicked his sister's voice, "'My Abram will come back and take me to America.' That's what she would always say. Sickening." He laughed again.

"She is right. Here I am. And I'm going to take her to America. Where is she? No one answered the door at your house this morning."

"No one is there. There's been some trouble, you know. The whole family is at a house my father owns northwest of Kiev. He insists they'll be safe there until everything cools down."

"Wonderful news!" Ashansky stood up. "Let's go."

"Whoa!" said Shemuel," I can't just walk out the gate. I'm in charge here. I've got to make arrangements."

"So, make arrangements," said Abie.

Within two hours the men were at the livery stable collecting Sergeant and trying to rent a horse for Shemuel.

The stable owner said, "That's not the way it works anymore. Horses are too valuable. A lot of them were killed in the war. You can buy a horse from me. Then, when you are done, bring it back and I'll buy it back from you."

"At a lot less than I paid for it, I'll wager," said Shemuel.

The owner shrugged, "Not a lot less. But I have to make a living."

The price was set and the owner was willing to take francs. As they left, he said to Ashansky, "And next time, don't threaten my stable hand. This is a respectable business."

Shemuel was a competent but not an expert rider. "I don't like horses," he said. "They are big and stupid. Not a combination I've had much luck with in the past."

Abie was sure Sergeant gave Shemuel a dirty look.

It only took the men three hours to reach the modest farm which was not in sight of the main road connecting Kiev and Chernobyl.

"Who's there?" demanded the voice from behind the solid, locked door.

"It's me, father. And I've got a friend with me," said Shemuel.

His brother, Saul, rifle in hand opened the door. But before he could call out Abie's name, his brother put a hand over his mouth.

"Hello, Saul," Shemuel said. "Hey, Mama! Do you have anything to eat? I'm starving."

His mother turning around said, "What are you..." She saw Abram and clamped both hands to her mouth.

Now Rachel, curious, turned from the sink.

There she was. Even more beautiful than Abie remembered. Memory had blurred her image a bit. More mature. Even more ripe.

One has but few moment of total joy in this life. This was one of Abie's.

She stared at Abie for second or two. Then dropping her dish towel, she ran to him arms outstretched, "Abram! Abram!"

She kissed his lips, nose, eyes and cheeks. Then, putting her arms around his neck, she locked him in a passionate embrace. He felt her tongue against his teeth. He opened them and tasted her sweetness.

"Rachel!" her mother cried. "You're not married yet! Behave

yourself!"

"Leave them alone, Mama," said her husband. "They haven't seen each other for years." Nor had they ever kissed before.

I think I'm going to like being married, thought Abe who felt himself getting aroused and hoped his jacket would cover any embarrassment.

"Enough! Enough!" said Shemuel. "I'd rather my sister get married before I become an uncle." Everyone laughed and they moved towards the table, Rachel and Abram hand in hand.

For hours, they talked, ate, and talked some more.

"Do you know where my family is?" asked Abram. The table fell silent.

Nicolay spoke, "I am sorry to have to tell you this, Abram. Your father died three years ago. A bad heart. We sat Kaddish for him seeing as we are almost related. Your mother sold everything and moved to Galicia where she has family. Your sisters went with her and she told me your two brothers knew where she was going. They were in the army. God knows where they are now."

Abie felt a pang of sadness. Not only his father, but his whole family was lost to him.

"Do you have an address?"

"Lviv. That's all I know. I'm sorry."

"Thank you." Rachel squeezed his hand. Slowly the cheerfulness returned to the conversations at the table. Sometimes two or more were going on at the same time.

"So Saul, you were in the army too?" asked Abie.

"I was. I hated it," said the younger brother. "I was captured but the Germans didn't treat us much worse than the Russians did. They let us go after Brest-Litovsk. We had to walk home."

"How did you live?" asked Abie.

"Don't ask," said Saul.

Shemuel had learned about Abram's experiences during that three-hour ride from Kiev. "Tell them about the American army, Abram."

"What's to tell? An army is an army."

"Oh, no, it's not. " Shemuel turned to Saul. "He was an officer, a lieutenant on a general's staff."

"An officer? A Jew? Who ever heard of such a thing?" asked Saul.

"I didn't start out that way. I was a private when I enlisted…"

"You enlisted?"

"Yes. I enlisted. Nobody in America is conscripted except during a war."

"Such a place, America," said Saul.

"Yes, and we are going to live there," said Rachel proudly.

The elder Zeidman asked, "Are you sure you want to do that? This war here is bound to end and the demand for sugar will be incredible. I have room in my business for both my boys and you too, Abram. Things are bound to get better. It could be a good life."

"With respect, sir, I don't believe that," said Abie. "I think you will be at war in the Ukraine for decades. Things will get worse. Think about coming to America with us. If not now, later when we are settled."

"You're going to get married, before you go aren't you?" asked Rachel's mother.

"Of course, we are," said Abie. Rachel beamed.

In the Dead of Night

Pitr wasn't the ataman anymore. The commissar had told him, "We don't have an ataman. We are all equal here, Comrade." Then he put a Russian, half Pitr's age, in charge of this mounted band of irregulars.

So it was that Pitr was trudging along in the rear guard as they moved up the road towards Chernobyl on the lookout for any Black Hundreds that might be roaming about looking for easy prey this night.

The night was chilly and Pitr had drunk the last of his half-pint of vodka some time ago. Pitr had no interest in stumbling into a firefight with those hardcore Whites. In fact, Pitr, who didn't mind visiting violence on the helpless, was a bit of a coward.

He rode past an intersecting road that he remembered. Fondly. Pitr rode along for another half-mile or so then he reached over his saddle and said to his closest fellow.

"Hey, Pavlo. I'm not feeling so good. I think I have a fever. I'm going to go home and get into bed. Be a friend, don't tell our new boss I'm gone unless he asks."

Pavlo had an understandable fear of the Spanish Flu. The sooner he got away from Pitr, the better.

"Sure. Pitr. Go home. I hope it's just a cold. Get better soon, old timer."

Cold? I'm about to get nice and warm, boy, thought Pitr.

He turned his horse around and minutes later turned right on to what was little more than a cart track. It was dark but about a mile in, he saw a light through the trees.

Good, she's still here. Hot damn.

The family was still up chatting when Abie, who was closest to the door, heard a horse whinny.

Abie put his index finger to his lips. All fell silent. A horse whinnied again. Their horses were in the barn out back.

The men quietly moved to either side of the door, Saul taking his rifle, Abie holding his pistol. Abie and Saul to one side. Shemuel to the other side with Nickolay next to him.

Abie whispered, "Don't shoot unless I do. There may be others." Saul nodded.

A single kerosene lamp illuminated the room. But not evenly. There were shadows.

The women instinctively moved to the far wall and hugged each other.

Making no attempt to be quiet, Pitr dismounted and hitched his horse to a railing. He patted his pistol. If the Jew's husband was there this time, Pitr would tie him up and make him watch. *That would be fun. At least, for me.*

He tried the door. It was bolted shut. He banged on it, hard.

"Open the door, it's me, Pitr. I'm back."

"Oh, my God! It's him, Mama. It's him," cried Rachel. Her father was puzzled, her brother was not. Shemuel reached down into his boot.

"You remember me, you Jewish bitch. Open this door or I swear I'll burn the house down with you in it. You know I will. Move."

Abie knew what to do. He would knock this pig senseless with the butt of his .45. He nodded to the other men and quietly slid the bolt back.

Outside Pitr bellowed. "This is your last chance. I've got paraffin and matches. Open up. Now."

He waited a few seconds and then tried the door. He slowly opened it.

Pitr saw the two women cowering against the far wall. "Aha! I knew there were two of you. All the better."

Lust trumped prudence and he moved forward, his pistol still holstered. He sensed something to his left and turned toward it.

Before Abie could brain him, Shemuel pulled the Ukrainian's

head back by his hair and in one powerful slash cut the man's throat with a straight razor.

Pitr clutched his throat with both hands and dropped to his knees. Then onto his face. It was over in seconds. Shemuel shut the door with his left hand.

The women were sobbing. They had never seen a man killed before. Three of their men had.

Abie said to Saul, "Go out the back. Scout out the perimeter. See if there are others. Don't shoot unless you have to."

"Right," he said and was gone.

Nickolay went to his wife and daughter. "It's all over now, dear," he said caressing his wife's hair.

"It will never be over," said his wife.

Shemuel turned the body on its back and removed the man's pistol and ammunition pouch. "This might come in handy," he said.

"I hope not," said Abie, his mind racing with thoughts of what they should do next.

Saul came back through the front door. "He was alone. There's nobody else out there. I put his horse in the barn."

"How far did you go?" asked Abie.

"Far enough," answered the seasoned infantryman. Abie nodded. Everyone was relieved. They had some time. Time to think and act.

"But that doesn't mean they won't be back looking for him. We've got to hurry."

Shemuel was going through the man's pockets. Then he took the red armband off the man's arm and put it in his own pocket.

Abie knelt next to him. "Why did you kill him?" he asked softly.

Shemuel gave a reasonable, if inexact, reason, "What else could we do with a prisoner who had seen all our faces?"

Abie's own face was blank. "I never thought of that," he said. "I'm glad you did."

Not as glad as I am, thought Rachel's mother who had overhead the exchange. Rachel was facing away from the body.

Saul put a rag over the man's face. No one moved to clean up the blood he was lying in.

Abie spoke, "Saul, will you go stand watch down the road? If there's trouble, double back. One of us will relieve you in two hours."

"Yes. Good idea," said Saul. His father looked at his pocket watch. "At midnight, son."

"Whenever," said Saul and left.

The five of them sat at the table. "What will we do with him?" Abie asked.

"Bury him. Bury him someplace he can't be found if they come looking for him," said Shemuel.

"Here's a thought," said his father. "There is a woodshed out back. We take out the wood. We bury him there and then stack the wood back on top of the grave."

"That would take hours," said Abie.

"Do you have a better idea?" asked Shemuel.

"No," Abie said.

Rachel said, "I can go and take Saul's place. I can run back as fast as he can. Then there will be four men to dig the grave and stack wood."

Well, what do you know? My fiancée is a gutsy little thing. A nice surprise, thought Abie.

"I don't like it," said Rachel's mother. "I'm afraid you'll get hurt, Rachel."

"Mama. If we get caught, they will kill us all," said Rachel.

"There is that," said her father.

The burial took two hours from the time the first piece of firewood was put to the side of the shed.

While the men were digging, Rachel's mother had scrubbed the bloody wooden floor clean. She threw the blood-stained rags she used into the flames of the fire.

The men were dirty and sweaty. They washed up at the pump by the sink. They dried themselves with a rough red towel and then sat at the table again.

"What do we do next?" asked Nickolay.

"Get the hell out of here," said Abie.

"Look, the six of us traveling together are going to attract attention. Should we split up?" asked Saul.

"I don't think we have to," Shemuel said reaching into his pocket and pulling out a red armband. "I have two of these and we'll make two more from that towel. Papa, you'll drive the carriage with the ladies. Saul, Abie and I will be a mounted escort taking you to Bolshevik headquarters in Kiev."

"So, will I be under arrest?"

"Of course not, Papa. Who would arrest the agent who is going to make sure this year's beet crop gets into the hands of the Red Army?"

All six laughed. Abie said, "I was hoping you people had money. But I'm glad to know I am marrying into the smartest pack of Jews in the Ukraine."

He looked at Rachel, "Our children are going to be brilliant, my love." Rachel blushed.

They only got a few hours of sleep with one of them always posted a few hundred yards down the road.

When dawn broke, they had a breakfast of hot tea and stale bread. They were packed and ready to go in an hour.

Abie said, "I'm going ahead to see that all's well at the crossroads. It probably will be but why take a chance? Give me a good head start, and then come yourselves."

He mounted Sergeant and began the slow walk down the road.

Why not? He gently pushed the horse's flanks with the heels of his hob-nailed trench boot. To his surprise, the old farm horse started to canter. Abie went fifty yards or so and then dug his heels into Sergeant.

The horse broke into a full gallop, which Abie really wasn't expecting. It got out of hand quickly.

Instead of leaning forward, standing in the stirrups, thighs firmly clamped to the horse, Abie bounced up and down fighting to keep his balance and stay on the horse.

He pulled back on the reins. "Whoa! Whoa! Stop you stupid son-of-a-bitch!"

Sergeant skidded to a stop, reared up on his hind legs, front legs pawing at the air and snorting like the stallion he never was. Who knows what dreams horses have? Abie patted Sergeant's neck. "Good boy. Who would have thought? Well, I don't think we'll do that again unless we really, really, have to, eh?"

The road was still clear when the carriage and the two outriders came up.

"Saul, you take the point, no one knows you. I'll ride on the left side. No one knows me either. Shemuel take the right side. We don't want any of your buddies recognizing you. The carriage will screen you."

Saul rode slowly, his rifle fastened across his saddle.

They had but one moment of anxiety on the way back to Kiev.

A small patrol of mounted Reds passed, going in the other direction. Its leader nodded to Abe and looking at the carriage, said in Russian, "Sweet duty, Comrade."

"It happens," said Abie.

"Not to me," said the Red shaking his head.

Once in Kiev, they split up. The carriage headed directly to the Zeidman home. The mounted men took different streets. All kept their armbands on and tried to look like they were on important errands.

Safe inside the house, the four men were looking at a map of the Ukraine which showed all its rivers and railroad lines. It covered most of the dining room table. The women were in the kitchen.

"This is a great map. Where did you get it?" Abie asked Shemuel.

"It used to hang in the stationmaster's office. But it got lost, somehow." The men laughed.

"Good. Now let's see if we can figure out what's going on right now," said Abie. "You are probably better informed than any of us, Shemuel. You start; we'll fill in what we can."

"Very well. The big problem is General Denikin. His Volunteer Army and the Army of the Don are making a big push from the South. My people tell me the Reds are falling back. The Whites may be in force no more than thirty miles from Kiev." He drew his finger across the map.

"Shit," said Abie. "I sure as hell am not going to take Rachel and fight my way through the front lines to get to Odessa. So the railroad south from Kiev is out. What's going on to the West?"

Saul answered, "I came home from there. The Poles have taken most of Galicia and they are still pushing east." No going west.

Abe said, "When I left the Ukraine in 1914, I made my way to Petrograd and signed on a ship going to Denmark." He ran his finger to the top of the map and off it. "But as the British say, 'It's a Long Way to Tipperary.'"

"Where's Tipperary?" asked Saul.

"In America, I think," said Shemuel. Abie chuckled.

"Anyway," Abie said. "The only way we are going to get to America is by water. So we should head for water." He ran his finger back down to the Black Sea.

Shemuel said, "Abram, the nearest water is the Dnieper River."

Abie looked at him and then back at the map. "It looks like it would be twice as far to go by river and we'd end up in Kherson."

His finger traced the route of the river southeast and stopped.

"And there are the goddamn rapids. We'd have walk a million miles around them and take another boat. Too convoluted. We'd never make it."

"What's the alternative?" asked Nickolay.

Abie stared at the map. "The lumber boats used to pull in at Cherkasy and trains would take the wood south from there, didn't they?"

"They did," said Nickolay. "But the lumber boats stopped when the war started. If fact, there is virtually no shipping on the river even now."

"True," said Shemuel. "But one of my men, Sasha, used to have a boat on the river and he may know more than we do. What do you have in mind, Abram?"

"Do you have a ruler?" Abram asked Nickolay who fetched one. Abram made a couple of rapid calculations and seemed pleased.

"I make it to be a bit more than 100 English miles from Kiev to Cherkasy on the river," said Abram. "That's deep into territory the Whites already have. Right, Shemuel?"

"Yes."

"The train I was on from Odessa was bound for Cherkasy."

"Did it get there?" asked Shemuel.

"I don't think so. Some band of mounted men stopped and robbed it. I was already off it and moving north on foot."

"What makes you think, you'd make it south to Odessa this time?"

"If the Whites are controlling the whole route, I doubt that there will be any trouble. They will be using the railroad to move men and supplies," Abie said.

"Pity there aren't any boats," said Nickolay. "Perhaps, you and Rachel would be better off staying here in Kiev until the situation stabilizes. Nobody is going to burn down the city."

"I can't do that, sir," said Abie. "I'm still an officer in the American Army. I have reports to make to my superiors. If I stay here, I'll be a deserter and will never be able to return to America."

"So?" asked Shemuel who had no sense of nationality.

"I can't do that. I am an American. I have to get back to my people," said Abie. The other three men were astonished but remained silent.

Then Shemuel said, "I'm coming with you, Abram. I've had it with this godforsaken country. I want a life."

"You're welcome, my brother," said Abie. With that the two women walked into the room.

"Lunch is ready," said Rachel. "What is Shemuel 'welcome' to, Abram?"

"To come with us to America, my darling." Rachel's mother dropped a plate scattering food all over the floor.

"Oh, my God," she said, running into the kitchen for a towel to clean up the mess.

"Why don't we all go," asked Abie.

"I can't," said the elder Zeidman. "Like you, I have obligations."

"Neither can I," said Saul. "I'm courting a girl and she'd never leave her family." Rachel looked embarrassed and quickly joined her mother.

Lunch was finally served. Rachel's mother, red-eyed, said, "We have to plan your wedding, Rachel."

Abie said, "I'm afraid we can't wait for that, Mrs. Zeidman. We have to get out while we still can." Taking Rachel's hand, he said, "We'll get married in America, my love."

Rachel's mother opened her mouth to speak but Shemuel interrupted her, "Don't worry. Mama. I'm going with them. I'll be the world's best chaperone."

"Rachel?" her mother appealed.

Looking into Abram's eyes, Rachel said, "Whither thou goest, I go. Whither thou liveth, I will live. Thy people shall be my people." The eyes of all at the table filled.

Rachel's mother leaned over and kissed her, "And so it shall be, my child."

Lunch was unaccountably festive as though a bride and groom were being feted. Rachel's mother asked, "Are you sure there are rabbis in America, Abram?"

"On every street corner," he answered.

After they had eaten, Shemuel said, "Let's go down to the power plant and find my friend, Sasha, and find out what's up on the river."

"Let's. Meanwhile, Rachel, start picking out the few things you can take with you. I'm sorry but we have to travel light. We'll get what you need in America, my love."

He went and got his empty duffel bag which he had rolled on top of his great coat. Abie handed it to her. "Pick out some practical clothes to wear along with a pair of good boots and a warm jacket. Wool hat and gloves too."

"Boots? The only boots I have are good enough to get me to the carriage and back. I'm not sure I have anything that you say I'll need."

"Cousin Sarah does," said Shemuel.

Sarah Klinger was the most liberated woman in the Ukraine. She smoked cigarettes (or cigars), drank vodka, swore, wore her hair short, rode her horse as well as any man and did her riding with the Red Army. Her father was dead and her mother was exasperated.

Shemuel continued, "She's back in town with the Reds. She came and said hello to me at the coal pile. She might even be at her mother's house."

"I'll take you over to her house, Rachel," said her father, "I know she'll help if she can." The two girls had been close before the October Revolution. They were about the same size too.

His friend, Sasha, was pleased to see Shemuel. "You're back a couple of days early."

"I am. This is my brother-in-law to be, Abram Ashansky. From America. And we have a problem, Sasha."

The men sat down far from the guard shack to talk. Shemuel told Sasha of their plans and their need for a boat to get them to Cherkasy.

Sasha said, "You're both crazy. You know that. That's a two-day trip, at least. There are no boats working the river nowadays."

"No fishermen?" asked Shemuel.

"Sure. But the fishermen use oars or a small sail. No one is going try to make it back from Cherkasy against the current. You need a steam launch."

Shemuel thought for a moment. "Didn't you tell me you once had a boat on the river?"

"Still do. It's tied up across the river. I've got a wife and children to take care of so I do a little bit of smuggling on my day off," said Sasha.

"You old dog," said Shemuel.

"Will you take us to Cherkasy?" asked Abie.

Sasha looked thoughtful. "I suspect that would be the most dangerous trip I'll ever make. I can't do it just because we are friends, Shemuel. I can't leave my family destitute if something goes wrong. Can you afford to pay for the chances I must take?"

"Yes," said Abie. "We will give you twenty-five English gold sovereigns in advance and thank you every day of our lives."

"Gold sovereigns? How much are they worth?" asked Sasha.

Abie did some quick calculations. "More than 250 gold rubles at any bank you walk into and a lot more if you have clever friends." It was a princely sum in the Ukraine of 1919.

"I have lots of friends," said Sasha. "I'll do it. Just the two of you?"

"No. My sister will be coming with us. She's his fiancée. They're getting married in America," said Shemuel.

"Who will take your place at the coal pile?" asked Sasha.

"How about my brother, Saul?"

"Who will be boss?" asked Sasha.

"How about you, Sasha?"

Sarah was at her mother's house. The girls were delighted to see one another and when the hugging was over Sarah said to her cousin, "Why do you need traveling clothes, Rachel?"

"I'm going to America to get married to Abram Ashansky," gushed Rachel.

Sarah had heard of him, of course, but had never met him. "Mazel tov. But nobody can get from the Ukraine to America now."

"My Abram can. He's an American," said Rachel.

"Is he? Well, let's pick out what you need. But I'm not going to let you take them with you. I want to talk to this American of yours. Bring him with you when you come back tonight to get them," said her cousin who lit up a cigarette. Smoking, right in her mother's house. Shocking.

Abram knew he had to be careful how he spoke to Sarah. She was a fanatic and they were always dangerous.

"So what did you do in America, Comrade Cousin?"

"I worked in a junk yard, throwing scrap metal into gondola cars," said Abie.

"Let me see your hands," said Sarah.

Satisfied that he was a worker, she asked, "Were you in the 'movement'?"

Movement? All they did was sit around and talk, thought Abie.

"Yes, I was a 'Wobbly.' Industrial Workers of the World." That wasn't true.

"Good men. Bomb throwers," said Sarah. "You are marrying well, Rachel."

Two days later all was ready. They would leave at dawn. The goodbyes were long and tearful. Each aware that they might never see these loved ones again in this world.

Saul drove them and their gear to the coal pile in the carriage and helped put their baggage on board. Sasha had moored his boat at the coal pile pier and had stacked bags of coal on its foredeck. His wife, who cooked for the guards, was with him.

Saul hugged each in turn and said, "Who knows? Maybe I— we—will turn up in America someday."

"Please God," said Rachel.

Abie handed a sack with the gold sovereigns to Sasha who passed it on to his wife. She gave him a bag of food.

"Stay safe, old man," she said," I'm too fat to get a new husband." They kissed.

Sasha asked, "Who is going to tend the engine while I steer?"

"I will," said Abie," I was a stoker on a steamship."

"Of course you were," said Sasha, shaking his head. "Shemuel, you stay amidships with me. You're the lookout."

"What should I look out for?"

"Icebergs," said Sasha.

Ron Semple

Sailing to Byzantium

Sasha maneuvered the boat into midstream and headed down river.

It was a beautiful day, warm, with clear skies and no wind. To all on board, it was as if they were off on a carefree excursion. The fighting seemed quite distant although they occasionally could hear the far-off rumble of artillery.

The boat, which Sasha called "Iryna" after his younger daughter, comfortably held the four of them and all their gear. It was twenty-five feet long, its beam was a bit more than seven feet amidships and it drew but two feet of water.

Its steering station, steam engine and smokestack were amidships. Horseshoe-shaped seats curved around both forward and aft. Comfortable enough unless one intended to sleep on them. Neither had a surface long enough to accommodate an outstretched body.

Mooring lines were in the starboard lazarette aft and an anchor with its manila cable was under the forward seat.

The boat was exposed to the elements except for a canopy which would protect them from sun but not rain.

On the steep right river bank rose the Dnieper Mountains. Very picturesque foothills actually, rising to three hundred feet or so and broken by forested valleys and gullies. The river bank to port was virtually flat. Nothing but black earth and pine woods out to the horizon.

The Dnieper is a great river rising in a peat bog northwest of Moscow and flowing almost 1,400 miles to the Black Sea. It is a placid, slow-moving stream until reaches a ninety-mile stretch of very dangerous rapids which, fortunately, was many miles downstream from Cherkasy. Sasha had never attempted to take his boat through those rapids.

Once the fires were stoked, Abie came aft to join the others. They sat companionably and chatted watching the Ukraine slide by. Sasha could see over the coal sacks forward so he told Shemuel to keep an eye out aft lest any vessel gain on them. There were no vessels in sight all day.

The first crisis came when Rachel leaned over and whispered in her brother's ear.

Shemuel said, "Sasha, what does one do if nature calls?"

Sasha laughed and said, "Easy enough. Rachel closes her eyes. You stand on deck and grab that stanchion holding up the roof. Then over the side it goes."

"Suppose nature calls a lady?"

Rachel turned bright red.

Sasha didn't look back. "There's a bucket in the port lazarette. She can go forward and I will close my eyes."

Rachel stayed forward. Shemuel retrieved the bucket and remained aft while Abie came up to stoke the firebox.

"I am so embarrassed," said Rachel.

"Don't be, my love. I'm afraid before we're done you might think that bucket a luxury. We're not going to be traveling first class."

"Now you tell me," she said in Yiddish, They both laughed and spent the rest of the morning seated forward and talking. Getting to know one another which is harder to do than falling in love.

All four had lunch aft sharing hardboiled eggs, cheese and bread along with tea brewed with water heated atop the firebox.

All afternoon, they cruised down the Dnieper at a steady five knots. As the sun neared the horizon in the west, Sasha said. "There's a finger pier not far from here. If no one is there, we'll tie up for the night. Otherwise, we'll anchor on the shallow left side of the river."

The pier was empty. It was narrow, not two feet wide, and

not as long as the Iryna. There were three cleats attached to its planks.

Mooring lines were attached to the boat fore, aft and amidships.

Sasha gave instructions. "Abie, you go on deck forward with your mooring line. As I nose in, jump onto the pier and attach the line to the farthest cleat. Pull us up to you. Then just use a couple of figure eight turns. Don't lock it." Abie didn't know how to lock a line anyway.

"Shemuel, attach the aft mooring line to the closest cleat and pull us as close as you can. I'll make the spring line fast."

"What should I do," asked Rachel.

"Just stay out of the way," said Sasha, firmly.

It went smoother than anyone, especially Sasha, expected. He cut the speed to bare steerage. Abie jumped and moved forward to make fast his line. Sasha took the boat out of gear. Shemuel hopped onto the pier and pulled the boat close before he attached the rear mooring line.

Then Sasha stepped on the pier and adjusted the lines so that the boat was about a foot from the pier, held there by the current. Then he flemished the lines on the pier, turning them into tight concentric coils.

"I think you've been a seaman," said Abie.

"Maybe," said Sasha.

They dined on the crescent-shaped Ukrainian dumplings called "varenik," provided by Sasha's wife. "These dumplings are delicious, "said Rachel. "I can taste the cheeses, potatoes, and onions. Does your wife make them with meat too?"

"Sometimes, she adds bacon," Sasha said.

That's pork, thought Rachel.

Abie said, in Yiddish, "Bacon is the gift a compassionate God gave to the gentiles. It consoles them for not being the chosen people. You'd like it."

"No, I wouldn't," said Rachel.

Sasha looked at them quizzically. "Just discussing bacon," said Abie.

"Ah," said Sasha.

The men smoked cigars and drank tea as darkness surrounded them. A full moon shone overhead and the heavens put on a majestic display. It grew cool.

Rachel turned in first, forward, on the downstream side. She wore her coat, a blanket covered her and she propped up her feet on her duffle bag at the end of the horseshoe seat. Shemuel would bunk next to his sister. Sasha and Abie shared the aft seat.

Each man would stand a two-hour watch while the others slept. Shemuel stood the first watch. Abie, the second.

He was seated aft wrapped in his great coat, enjoying the quiet but fully alert. He heard them before he saw them. A murmur of voices moving toward the river. Abie cocked the .45 pistol in his right pocket, a round already in the chamber.

A light flashed in his eyes and blinded him. "Keep your hands in your pockets, man," the intruder said in Russian. "I have a gun. I don't want to hurt you but I will."

No one else in the boat stirred although they all heard what was being said.

The first Russian said to his mate, "Go get the others. I think we've found what we want."

"A way home, huh? Give me the flashlight. Otherwise, I'll kill myself."

"Here."

The second man left.

"So, where are you going?" asked the Russian.

"To Cherkasy," said Abie, hoping all they wanted was a ride.

"No, you're not. You're going to turn around and go upstream to Russia. We're getting the hell out of this lousy war."

Oh no we're not. We're going to America, Abie thought. He was close to panic. It was agonizing but he made his decision, *God forgive me.*

He pulled the trigger and the big slug tore through his great coat pocket.

Ashansky missed. The Russian unhurt but startled, stepped back and fell into the river, his arms waving, his pistol flying into the water.

"Don't shoot! Don't shoot!" he screamed in terror as he splashed ashore and scrambled up the bank. Rachel's screams mixed with his.

Sasha barked orders. "Shemuel take in the bow line and the spring line now. Abie take in the stern line when I tell you to."

Sasha lurched forward and took the helm.

The bow of the boat began to slowly move downstream pushed by the current. When it was perpendicular to the pier, Sasha yelled, "Now, Abie.

The boat headed downstream.

"Make steam, Abie," said Sasha. Abie shoveled fresh coal in and cleaned out the pan below the grate. They would have steam in about fifteen minutes.

"What the hell was that all about?" asked Shemuel.

"Probably deserters," said Sasha. "Looking to get out of the Whites' volunteer army. I don't blame them. Their officers treat them like shit."

"Don't I know it," said Shemuel as he moved forward with a boathook to fend off any nasty debris in their watery path.

They steamed downstream for an hour then Sasha carefully worked his way close to the left bank. "We'll anchor here and try to get a couple of hours sleep."

The anchor held and the bow was pointed straight upstream.

"We'll take one-hour watches," Sasha said. "If that anchor doesn't hold, there will be hell to pay. I'll take the first watch." The anchor held.

Rachel was thoroughly frightened. She was trembling despite her coat and the blanket wrapped around her. Abie had tried to soothe her and she pretended he did.

But soon all of them, save the watch, slipped into sleep.

They got underway again shortly after dawn. They were all more subdued. This trip was no excursion.

Abie, in particular, was brooding. *Thank God, I missed. Killing the Germans was war. But this would have been murder.*

Not really, he reasoned. *The son-of-a-bitch was armed and he might have killed us all. Maybe, maybe not. I'm just glad I missed and we got away.*

Rachel inspected the hole in his great coat. "I'm sorry, but I don't think I can mend the hole. The best I can do is put a patch over it."

"Don't worry, sweetness. I'll never wear it again once we get to America," said Abie.

The morning and afternoon passed without incident. Meals were eaten; the demands of nature answered discreetly.

Dusk was fast approaching when Sasha spotted the breakwater that formed Cherkasy's small harbor.

"We're almost there," he said. "Get ready to tie up the boat, boys."

Their haversacks and duffle bag packed, Abie said to Sasha, "The train for Odessa won't leave until tomorrow. We're going to find someplace to sleep and something to eat. Are you sure you won't come with us, Sasha?"

"No. Thank you. I'll sleep on the boat. Otherwise it might not be here in the morning. I've got plenty to eat and I'll bet that before eight o'clock tomorrow somebody will be asking if they can come north with me. It's happened before."

"Well, we owe you a great debt, Sasha. Thank you."

"You don't owe me anything, Abram. The money you gave me will change my family's life. Thank you," said Sasha.

None of the three had been in Cherkasy before. Abie asked, "What's the best hotel in town, Sasha, and how do we get to it?"

"The Slavyanskayk, hands down. It's on Khreshchat Street. You can't miss it. It's a very big, blue building with all kinds of spires. I've never been in it myself but I know people who have."

"Good enough for me," said Abie.

Shemuel asked, "Are you sure you want to do this, Abram? Go to a fancy hotel and call attention to ourselves?"

"Sometimes, that is the best way to hide," said Abie.

They were in the ornate lobby approaching the front desk. The desk clerk saw them, appraised them as riffraff, and offered no greeting.

Abie stuck out his hand and said, in English, "Howdy, partner. Al Shannon. Eagle Uniform Company, Akron, Ohio."

The desk clerk looked at him uncomprehendingly, wondering if he should pound his bell and get help.

"Oh, I forgot," said Abie in Russian, "none of you folks speak English. I'm Al Shannon of the Eagle Uniform Company, Akron, Ohio. I'm going to need two rooms for the night.

"Make them nice rooms. I just signed a big contract with your quartermaster general and I smell a big bonus coming my way."

"Yes, sir," said the desk clerk regaining his composure and putting on his professional smile.

"One room for me and my tailor and another for the little seamstress here."

"Of course, sir."

"Say, is there a bank nearby? I want to change some French money into rubles."

Sensing an opportunity, the desk clerk said, "The hotel can handle that exchange, if you prefer, sir. We offer the same exchange rate as the bank."

"Well, that's mighty decent of you, young man," said Abie reaching for his wallet. The desk clerk, on his lunch break, would seek out a man he knew who would give him much more for those francs. The hotel would never know. He would never mention that brash American from "Akronohio."

They ate in the hotel dining room, left their dirty clothes with the bell captain to be washed and dried overnight and made arrangements with the concierge to have a hack take them to the train station in the morning.

Rachel said to Abie, "We not even married yet and you have told me your first lie."

"What?"

"You said we weren't going to travel first class."

"Wait," said Abie.

They settled comfortably in a first-class railroad compartment. As Abie explained to Shemuel, "We're going to be traveling through White country now and they are not going to look too carefully at anyone who has money. The rich may be revolting, but they rarely revolt."

Just once during the long journey were they interrupted. A young White lieutenant popped his head in and saluted.

"Is everything going well, sir," he asked.

Abie jumped up. "Al Shannon. Eagle Uniform Company, Akron, Ohio."

"Yes, sir. I've heard of you," said the young lieutenant. His captain had entertained the officer's mess with the story of the insufferable American salesman.

"Everything is great. Tell that colonel of yours, I said 'thanks.' I got that big contract with your quartermaster general. Your colonel told me where to find him."

The lieutenant looked at Rachel and Shemuel.

Abie said, "I'm taking these two to America with me. We're always on the lookout for good tailors."

"I see," said the lieutenant. *Good riddance. We have too many Jews in Russia. Take them all.*

Their stay in Odessa, which Abie knew well, was brief. A night in a decent waterfront hotel and then berths on a Greek tramp steamer heading for Constantinople. The ship did not have to wait for the tide since there aren't any in the Black Sea.

"You know I am going to stop in Constanta and Constantinople but I am headed back to Piraeus," said the Captain, in French. "I can take you there if you like."

Abie was tempted. Greece was a step closer to America but he said, "Thank you, Captain, but no. I have business in Constantinople and I don't know how long it will take. We'll get off there."

"Too bad," said the captain who put unexpected passenger fares directly into his pocket.

The accommodations were better than on the steam launch. Just barely. The food was fair if you enjoyed lamb at every meal but breakfast and didn't mind watching the engineer scoff down his food making sounds seldom heard outside of a zoo.

The freighter tied up at Constanta, Romania, for a day unloading and loading small amounts of cargo. That was halfway to Constantinople. The trio never left the ship.

Abie and Rachel spent all of their waking hours together. Talking, laughing and, when no one was about, kissing.

Abie was getting desperate. "You know, Rachel, we can find a rabbi in Constantinople to marry us and then we can go to America as husband and wife."

She pushed him away. "No. I don't want that. I want a proper wedding. I am giving up all the people I love to marry you, except Shemuel, and I want it done right. I'm going to be an American. I want an American rabbi to marry us, dear."

Abie sighed and surrendered.

Soon they were passing through the Bosporus. Abie and Rachel were on the bow of the ship.

Abie pointed to his right and said, "That's Europe." Then he pointed to his left and said, "That's Asia."

A very excited Rachel said, "They're not very far apart, are they?"

"I'm afraid they are," said Abie.

They took a horse-drawn hack to a hotel the driver recommended. True, the desk clerk was his cousin but the rooms were comfortable and the price reasonable. Abie had his suit sponged and pressed and his boots shined.

In the morning, he handed Shemuel a sheath of francs and said, "Get these changed and take your sister to the Grand Bazaar. Let her buy what she needs, within reason, and get some clothes for yourself too."

Shemuel took the money but said, "Abram, I can't keep taking money from you. It's not right."

Abie said, "What are you talking about? You heard what I told that idiot officer. I hired you as a tailor. This is your pay."

Shemuel laughed. "Abram, you know I can't sew."

"So, you think you are the first incompetent I've had to deal with?"

He gave Shemuel a business card with the name and address of the hotel in Turkish. "Just in case you get lost."

"Just how incompetent do you think I am, boss?" Shemuel asked.

Abie had little difficulty finding the American military mission. He presented his military identification and his letter from General Pershing to the adjutant, a captain.

"Well, lieutenant, I see you have well-placed friends," said the captain handing the papers back to him. "What can I do for you?"

"Well, sir, I need a place to type up my reports to send back to the general at G-2. I presume you have contact with headquarters in Chaumont."

"We do," said the captain." A courier comes from France every two weeks but we can use the cable if it is more important."

"No, not urgent. But maybe interesting, sir."

Abie looked at the captain. "If fact, the captain might want to read my reports before they are sealed and sent. What I'm writing about is happening a lot closer to Constantinople than to Chaumont."

"Thank you, lieutenant. I'll do just that."

Abe was wary. "I take it your commanding officer will be discreet about this?"

The captain said, "It's unlikely the colonel will read those reports. He's not much interested in what's happening here. He didn't have a good war. He'll retire when he gets home."

"I understand," said Abie who glanced at the captain. The adjutant caught the questioning look.

"As for why I'm here, I've learned that one ought not tell a major to go fuck himself."

"Indeed, sir," said Abie.

Rachel was very excited about the clothes she had bought. Abie feigned interest as all aspirants to marriage do.

Shemuel was more practical. "I picked up a couple of big suitcases and I found a place where you can get some clothes. You're going to wear out that suit."

Reports finished, clothes purchased, Abie sought out the adjutant who said, "Let me see that Pershing letter again. He looked at the date.

"When were you last paid, lieutenant?"

"I got two months' pay in November, sir."

"Well, the Army owes you a batch of money. I can pay you now if you'll sign the pay book, lieutenant."

"With pleasure, sir," said Abie who had been worried about whether they had enough to make it to make it to America without traveling in steerage.

"Do you have any idea of when we can catch a ship to America or even to France?" asked Abie.

"America is out. No ships. Not sure about France."

The adjutant thought for a moment. "I think I can do better

than that. There's a Turkish ship leaving this week for Dover with 1,500 German soldiers who are being repatriated. If you don't mind the company, it would be a breeze catching a ship to America from Southampton."

"I don't mind at all. At least they won't be shooting at me," said Abie.

"Don't worry. Their NCOs will keep them in check. There will be some British officers aboard and some English and French civilians too. There might even be a couple of ladies to socialize with your fiancée.

"By the way, you get to ride free as an American officer but you will have to pay the Turks for your friends. But now, you're flush, right?"

The captain thought for a second, "You know, I've never seen you in uniform. Do you have one?"

"No. I had to get rid of it. The Reds would have taken too much of an interest in it and me," said Abie.

"Too bad. If you had the brass, I could have had my supply sergeant fit you out.

"I kept the brass, sir."

"Excellent. One more thing, I think it might be useful if my colonel provided a letter saying how useful your fiancée and her brother were in helping you in the Ukraine."

"Would he do that, sir?"

"He'll sign anything I put in front of him," said the captain.

Homeward Bound

The S.S. *Gul Djemal* had an amazing history. She was launched in 1874 as the S.S. *Germanic* of the English White Star Line. She was a champion in her day once holding the Blue Ribbon for the fastest trans-Atlantic crossing.

Thirty-six years later, the Turks bought her and she ended up as a troopship ferrying soldiers to the Gallipoli Peninsula. That's when a British submarine torpedoed her.

But the *Gul Djemal* settled in shallow water. She was raised and repaired and sent back to war.

She was 455 feet long and 42 feet wide and her engines were capable of pushing her through the water at 16 knots. She had room for 225 first-class passengers and the 1,500 disarmed German soldiers who would be crammed below deck.

The ship's first-class dining room was about two-thirds full. There were more than a hundred German officers, about two dozen British officers and the same number of civilians, mostly French.

Abie walked in alone. Rachel and Shemuel were already seated at a small civilian table.

The officers dressed for dinner and Abie was in his uniform with the Croix de Guerre on his chest and the wound stripe on his sleeve. As he walked to a junior officer's table, the civilians admired him, the British officers acknowledged him and the Germans nodded their acceptance of him as a fellow warrior. Few of them had ever seen an American Army officer.

Rachel had never seen him in uniform before and she thought him devastatingly dashing. She could hardly wait to get him alone. Frustration for both awaited.

That first night almost all sat at tables with people from their own country. But senior British and German officers dined with the ship's captain. Rachel and Shemuel were seated at a small table with two spinsters from England who were on holiday when they were marooned in Constantinople by the outbreak of war. That was almost five years earlier.

The four of them each knew a bit of French but not enough to carry on a conversation. The older women tried speaking English very loudly but even that perennial British ploy didn't work.

Shemuel, shaking his head said, "Je suis desole. Nous ne parlons pas l'anglais."

"Honestly, Mildred, you'd think these foreigners would learn a bit of English before they travel."

"Well, they don't, Emma. You know what they say. The wogs begin at Calais." They politely tittered. Then they all smiled at each other and fell into two-person conversations.

"Doesn't Abram look handsome, Shemuel?" asked Rachel.

"I guess so," said Shemuel who long since had stopped being impressed by officers. "I like him better in civilian clothes."

All the women got up and left for the ship's lounge when most of the men lighted cigars after the meal. Abie waited a few minutes and then excused himself and joined Rachel.

She said, "I'm so proud of you, Abram. But you behave yourself, I saw some of those ladies giving you the eye."

Abie laughed. "They wouldn't have looked at me a couple of months ago. I was just a corporal then."

"I loved you then too," said Rachel.

Abie kissed her hand. "Thank you, my love. Speaking of drawing attention. Not one of the officers, British or German, could take his eyes off you. You're that lovely."

That was true. Rachel did not have a formal dress but she still was a dark, riveting beauty.

The next day was very warm and Rachel stepped out onto the promenade with Abie. Hundreds of German soldiers sunning themselves on the bow sent up a raucous cacophony of appreciation. She laughed and waved to them before she disappeared back inside.

On the stern end of the promenade, the old maids emerged. The soldiers there made similar if lesser sounds. They hadn't seen any unveiled women for a long time.

Helen harrumphed. "Outrageous. The nerve of those German hoodlums."

"Oh, I don't know," said Mildred, waving to the half-clad troopers. "I'm enjoying myself. No man has paid attention to me since the turn of the century."

The second night out was different. The officers mixed and ate together although still segregating themselves by rank.

A German lieutenant said to Abie, "You know, we would have beaten them if you Americans hadn't joined in." "Oh, I don't know about that," said a British subaltern. "There was still plenty of fight left in us."

"We would have made peace with Britain after we defeated the French," said the German. "We didn't want to fight you in the first place."

"So, why did you surrender?" asked Abie.

"We didn't surrender. The revolutionaries and those cowardly socialists stabbed us in the back," said the German.

"What about your men," Abie asked. "Where do they stand?"

The German sneered. "That rabble? Most of them are infected with Bolshevism. We should have left them in Turkey."

The phrase "stabbed in the back" was heard virtually every time Abie was in the company of German officers. Obviously Germany's troubles were not over although the fires of revolution might seem to be banked.

Abie decided he'd have to send off another report when he reached Dover.

Rachel and Abie were on the promenade when Gibraltar was abeam. Abie pointed to it. "That's Europe." And then to his left, "That's Africa."

"What a world traveler I've become," said Rachel.

"You've just started. We're about to sail into the Atlantic Ocean. We're still a long ways from home," said Abie.

Other than at mealtimes, Abie and Rachel were always together, the darlings of the first-class passengers who alternately coddled and teased them. Shemuel was ignored.

He contented himself with studying English from a Yiddish textbook he picked up in Constantinople.

After just one reading, he asked the spinsters, "Und how ist der womens today?"

Mildred answered, "Just fine, thank you. And how are the mens today?"

He did make swift progress and by the time the ship approached the English Channel he was speaking broken English with Yiddish filling in the vocabulary gaps.

Once, when they were alone, Helen asked, "What language, besides ours, is that young man mangling? German?"

"Worse. I think it is Yiddish."

"Oh, my," said Helen.

The last night before the ship reached Dover was akin to the last night on a peacetime cruise, at least in first class. Wine and liquor flowed freely, toasts were offered, and songs were sung. Old enemies made slurred promises to meet their new friends sometime soon.

These promises were never kept, of course, except for a few who might face each other on a new battlefield some twenty years hence.

The check-in station at Dover was as hectic as expected but Abie found the American liaison officer and filed his report on the attitudes of returning German officers. Dover had daily courier service with Chaumont.

General Nolan was talking to General Pershing about Ashansky.

"I wish we would offer him a regular commission, sir. He has the makings of a first-rate intelligence officer and God knows we need them."

"Needed, Dennis. Past tense. We are about to be reduced in size to about what we were before the war," said Pershing.

"Besides, even if he accepted, we wouldn't be doing him any favor. He'd probably retire as a captain twenty years from now. Dennis, you're notoriously broadminded; promotion boards are not.

"Ashansky has three strikes against him. First, he's not a West Pointer. Second, he's a naturalized citizen and third, he's of the Hebrew persuasion. He wouldn't stand a chance."

Nolan asked, "How about a reserve commission, sir?"

Pershing laughed. "You really are determined, aren't you, Dennis? All right, we'll offer him one. But if he's as smart as we both think he is, he'll turn it down."

Back at Dover, the liaison officer who had examined Pershing's letter, asked, "Where do you go from here, Lieutenant? Chaumont or the States?"

"I think my work is done for G-2. I'm heading for New York and taking my fiancée and her brother with me."

"We'll give you a voucher for your passage to America but your fiancée and her brother will have to pay their own fares."

"Of course," said Abie, pleased that the cost had just been reduced by one-third.

"Okay," said the captain, "we'll inform G-2 in Chaumont and they can send your records to that unit on Whitehall Street in Manhattan. Do you know where that is?"

"Yes, I was inducted there."

So, you were an enlisted man. Interesting.

"You can resign your commission there. What'll you do if they offer you a reserve commission?"

Abie laughed. "I honestly don't know, sir."

The trio went by train to Southampton, a traditional port of embarkation for trans-Atlantic liners, checking into one of the better emigrant hotels there.

Ashansky's luck was holding. The RMS *Aquitania* was returning from a trip to New York and would be ready to turn around in little more than a week.

This gave Rachel and Shemuel plenty of time to get the pre-embarkation physicals and fill out the thirty-one-question form that the American immigration authorities required before they boarded the Cunard liner. Abie filled the forms out in English and they signed them.

Both were also vaccinated against smallpox.

Although the RMS *Aquitania* had been returned to civilian service, she still looked like she was at war.

Her spectacular dazzle paint job was designed to confuse any U-boat captain peering at her through his periscope. All the lavish fittings, portraits and decorations that had graced her when she was launched in 1913 were stripped from "The Ship Beautiful" when she became a trooper. They would be restored, including the Louis XVI dining room, when she was refitted later in the year.

Meanwhile, Cunard billed it as "austerity service" to New York and very welcome it was.

She was 901 feet long, 91 feet wide and drew 36 feet of water. Of primary interest to Abie was how fast she was. She could do 23 knots and would take them to New York in less than a week.

The Aquitania could hold 618 in first class, 614 in second class and 2004 in third class. Abie and the Zeidmans would sail in two second-class cabins.

This was not cheap. More than twice as expensive as third class where a berth could be booked for twenty-five dollars or so. But it was worth it for a number of reasons, the most important of which wouldn't be apparent until they reached New York.

Still second class on the Aquitania's "austerity service" was far more luxurious than any vessel the three of them had ever been on.

The food was plentiful, if British bland. The company was excellent and there would be a very tipsy last night gala. Prohibition was coming to America soon and even British ocean liners would have to obey the law. But not yet.

Many of the passengers made the most of it and every night was party night with Rachel quietly leaving the lounge early. Though Abie and Shemuel stayed on, they were light imbibers.

They were seated at a dining table for six. The other three were businessmen returning from England with fat contracts for practically anything they had to sell.

One of them was Jewish.

On the first night, the Jewish salesman was introduced to Shemuel and told he was immigrating to America.

He said, "Shemuel? Nobody in America is called Shemuel. From now on you are 'Sam,' pal."

"Gut," said Shemuel, "Now I, Sampal."

"No," said the salesman," Just Sam."

"Sam, it is," said Abie.

Sam and the salesman conversed constantly, the later having no trouble with Sam's combination of bad English and good Yiddish.

Rachel was becoming very frustrated. She said to Abie, "I can't understand anything anyone says. I've got to learn English."

"That's a good idea," said Abie. "But you are going to run into a lot of people in Jersey City who speak Yiddish or Russian or even Ukrainian."

"I don't want to speak Russian or Ukrainian. I want to speak English. Teach me. Now."

"Okay," he said in English. "Pass the salt, please."

She looked at him dumbly.

He pointed at the salt shaker and said, "Salt."

"Salt," she said.

Abie cabled Tony Aiello from the ship: "AQUITANIA RACHEL & BRO ABIE." He didn't think the detective would have any trouble deciphering the message.

Last night festivities over, the ship glided to a halt in the quarantine area off Swinburne Island, a few miles south of Staten Island in the Lower Bay.

Health and immigration officials climbed aboard using a Jacob's ladder. They were there to examine and quiz the first- and second-class passengers. The third-class people would have to go through that angst-ridden ordeal at Ellis Island.

Southampton was not an "infected port" so the doctors did not expect to run into cholera, smallpox or any other infectious disease. The doctors' examinations were perfunctory. All three were healthy.

Abie was in uniform and standing with them when the immigration agent and his Yiddish interpreter got around to the Zeidmans.

"Lieutenant, we're certainly not here to examine you," said the agent.

"I hope you will allow me to stay. The lady is my fiancée and the gentleman is her brother. Perhaps, I can interpret?" The agent's interpreter rolled his eyes. He could speak five languages fluently. One of his colleagues had mastered fifteen.

"Well, it's a bit unusual. But, why not? Anything for the Army," said the agent who had managed to avoid the draft.

The agent was a tad nervous about these two. They were from Russia which was in bloody turmoil. America had not avoided the violence roiling Europe. Anarchists, foreign born and home grown, had seen to that.

His boss, the commissioner of immigration for the Port of New York, got one of their bombs in the mail but fortunately it did not explode. Unhappily, some of the other thirty-five did, killing and maiming people who opened the packages.

A choleric commissioner had told his agents, "If you let one fucking anarchist or Red into this country, you're going back to Europe yourself."

Using the thirty-one questions on the form, the agent quizzed Rachel first, Abie serving as translator. The agent was satisfied. He really wanted to make sure of Shemuel.

"So, you say you were never an anarchist, Mr. Zeidman?"

"No. Never."

"And you never belonged to any Bolshevik organizations or served in their military?"

"No. Never," lied Sam Zeidman.

The agent put the same questions to him several different ways. The answer was always the same, "No. Never."

"Very well, let me see your passports, please," said the agents. All three blanched.

"I didn't know they needed passports," Abie said.

"Of course they do. Otherwise, how can we tell they are who they say they are?" asked the agent who sensed trouble ahead.

"I soldier in Czar's army," said Sam.

"Can you prove that?" asked the agent.

"Yes," said Sam, surprising Abie.

Sam reached into his jacket pocket and pulled out a small wooden phial. Inside was a piece of rolled paper containing details of his Imperial service.

The immigration interpreter said, "Yes. This is Shemuel Zeidman. He's legit."

"Okay. Now how about the lady?" asked the agent.

Rachel had no papers. Abie felt helpless and then he remembered. He pulled out the letter he had received in Constantinople from the adjutant.

"This letter identifies Miss Zeidman who assisted me in my official duties in the Ukraine. And here is a letter from General Pershing explaining what I was doing there."

The agent was more than satisfied. He was impressed and

he intended to move on to less well connected immigrants as quickly as he could.

He signed two forms and said, "Okay. You're both cleared to land in New York. Good luck in America."

"They don't have to go through Ellis Island?" asked Abie.

"No, that's for the poor people," said the agent moving on to the next immigrants in the second-class lounge.

The RMS *Aquitania*, guided by tugboats, moved upriver. Everyone who could was on deck as the skyline of New York came into full view.

And then, there she was, to their left. Lady Liberty. The Statue of Liberty. The symbol of their welcome to their new country.

Rachel was crying. Tears rolled down Abie cheeks too. Shemuel was dry-eyed but smiling.

Abie put his arm around Rachel and pointed. "That's where we are going to live, my love. Right behind Miss Liberty. In Jersey City."

"I want to kiss her feet," said Rachel.

Tony Aiello had pulled up the big Ford touring car next to a cop on the Cunard pier and flashed his badge. The policeman waved him into a "no parking" spot as a professional courtesy.

The ship had already docked and the gangway was positioned. He walked up to it and again flashed his gold badge to the officials at its foot.

The first-class passengers disembarked first, hundreds of them. They quickly got into limousines, taxi cabs and a few horse-drawn carriages. Their luggage would follow them forthwith.

Then came the second-class passengers. Abie in his officer's uniform was hard to miss. He had Rachel by the arm.

"Abie! Abie! Over here," cried Tony. He pulled the three of them to the side of the gangway, laughing, talking, and hugging Abie.

"You did it, you son-of-a-gun," he said. Then he turned to

Rachel, who curtsied.

"None of that now, sis," said Tony who yanked her towards him and kissed her on both cheeks.

He stepped back a pace, still holding her arms. "What a beauty!" he said. Rachel didn't understand what he said but she knew she liked it. She laughed and smiled.

Now for Sam. They shook hands and Tony said, "Welcome home, Sam."

Beaming, Sam said, "To meet you a pleasure is."

"Wow! He's here two minutes and already he's speaking English," said Tony.

"It may need a bit of polishing," said Abie.

Less than an hour later they had their luggage which the men piled into the touring car. Abie sat up front with his old friend. They tried to catch up on their lives.

Brother and sister spent the drive to the ferry pointing and yelling, "Look! Look!"

They enjoyed the ferry ride across the wide Hudson River to the Jersey Central Railroad terminal which was near an empty, scarred place called Black Tom which linked them all.

It wasn't very far to the Aiello house. The newcomers were fascinated with the bustle of the gritty, industrial city. "Many, many automobiles and trucks. Not many horse, eh, Rachel? Not like the Ukraine."

"No, not a bit like the Ukraine," said his sister who was looking for Jews on the street but if there were any she couldn't identify them.

"The trams look much bigger too," said Sam.

Abie turned in his seat and said, "We call them streetcars or trolleys, Sam." His brother-in-law to be concentrated on memorizing two more English words.

They were on York Street when Rachel saw it. *Please! Please!*

She pointed and asked in Yiddish, more calmly than she felt,

"Abram, is that a synagogue?"

Abie looked and said, "Yes. Temple Beth-el. Why?"

"That's where I am going to get married, that's why," said Rachel.

They pulled up in front of the four-flat Aiello home. Tony jumped out and ran up the stairs ahead of them.

"Mama! Mama, guess who's here?"

Carmella Aiello, that squat, unflinching, Catholic, Sicilian peasant, opened the door and with a beautiful, if rare, smile, said, "My family."

The Family Circles

Carmella wiped her hands on her apron and hurried out into the hallway with her arms open.

Rachel reached the top of the stairs and walked towards her smiling but unsure.

Carmella said to Abie, "You tell her what I say." He nodded.

"Rachel, dear Rachel, I am not your momma—God bless her wherever she is—but I swear to her that I will love you like I love my own daughters. I am your Aunt Carmella."

Those strong Sicilian arms enfolded the taller, slender girl and she kissed Rachel on the cheeks repeatedly.

Rachel, through tears, said. "Tank you. I love too, Mume."

Carmella looked at Abie. "Mume?"

"It means 'aunt.'"

"Mume Carmella. I like," said Carmella. "Come. Meet your new American family, *cara mia*."

Carmella kissed Sam and said, "You too."

The Sicilians awaited inside Carmella's flat. First came her husband, daughters, son and daughter-in-law who all laughed, kissed, squeezed, and hugged Rachel and Abie.

Waiting their turn, grinning, laughing and commenting on Rachel's beauty, was the extended family, the Aiello children's godparents and their children, Carmella and Antonio's godchildren and their parents, some cousins and some close friends.

Hard people. People who suspected everybody and trusted nobody—but their own. They understood, and accepted, that these three—these Jews—were now their own. To be protected and to be trusted. To be loved. Or they would have to deal with Carmella.

One, summoned by Carmella, had asked, "Didn't the Jews kill Jesus?"

Carmella said, "Of course not. The Romans killed Jesus. You know they are capable of anything."

"I do," said the Sicilian woman, ending the theological discussion.

Rachel was all but overwhelmed. Abie translated as fast as he could, giving names and relationships which rarely registered with Rachel. But she felt the welcome, the acceptance, the love. She repeated "Tank you" endlessly.

The crowd was so big that it spilled over into the parlor that had been unused in the years since Carmella's father-in-law had been laid out there before his funeral.

It was a well-dusted museum of the good life in America and Carmella's people were careful not to disturb anything. They sat on the edge of their seats and admired her taste. The framed picture of the Sacred Heart drew several envious glances.

Rachel was steered there too and was greeted the same.

Then Carmella's daughter-in-law, Peggy McCann Aiello, took Abie and Rachel by the arms and wheeled them out of the room. "You're not done, kids," she said. Sam trailed them.

In her flat across the hall was Peggy's tribe: Poppa Jim and Momma Agnes McCann; Amelia McGurk, Mickey's mother; Hannah McGurk and her parents, Otto and Sophia Ganz; Heidi Mannstein; Father McBride and Fat Jack Lynch, his wife, Maureen, and his brother, Captain Terry Lynch.

Abie was moved. He knew them all, some better than others, but he never expected them to be here to welcome him—and Rachel—home. The only one missing was Mickey McGurk, the police lieutenant, now a Marine and on his way home from France.

The same scene unfolded—this time with more sedate Celtic and Germanic overtones— but no less sincerity.

Abie even got to speak a few words with Terry Lynch. "When did you get back, sir?"

"No more 'sirs,' bucko. We're civilians now. Friends." They

shook hands.

"Just a couple of days ago. I'm staying with Jack until I get settled. You didn't tell me you were involved with him in all that skullduggery before the war."

"I didn't tell anyone...Terry?"

"Yep. That's my first name. Terry. Let's get together soon, friend."

People were moving freely between the two flats. Eating, trying to find a place at a table, or failing that sitting with a plate on a knee praying not to make a mess. Both kitchen tables and stoves were stacked with food. It was Friday so there was no meat eaten in these Catholic households and Father McBride had said grace in both kitchens.

There were ravioli, pasta and manicotti, all with marinara gravy, baccala, clams, mussels and shrimp, salads with anchovies, olives, dates, figs and loaves of Italian bread to mop up the gravy.

Despite the oncoming Prohibition, there was no shortage of wine and beer. In Peggy's kitchen was also a treasured bottle of Irish whiskey for those who preferred something stronger. Sicilians usually did not drink whiskey.

It was hours before the well-wishers made their goodbyes and the intimate family, now numbering nine, gathered to discuss the future.

Abie translated. Rachel's and Sam's English was improving by the hour but nowhere near ready for a serious conversation.

Carmella said, "Rachel stay with me and the girls."

"You can have my room, Rachel, I'll share a bedroom with my sister," said Doreen who hated the idea of sleeping with her sister.

"Tank you," said Rachel.

Peggy said, "Abie, you and Sam can stay with us. We have room." The spare room was to be a nursery for their daughter.

The girl was stillborn and the Aiellos were still grieving. Peggy was unaware that she was pregnant again.

"You are very kind," said Abie. "I hate to inconvenience you. Sam and I could stay at a boardinghouse. I'll bet there's one nearby."

"Nonsense," said Peggy. "Stop talking nonsense, Abie."

"Okay, Peggy. Thank you."

Sleeping arrangements out of the way, Tony asked, "Do you have any idea what you are going to do next, Abie?"

"Yes, I do," said Abie. "I have four things to do as soon as possible. One, I have to get out of the Army. Two, I have to get married. Three, I have to find us a place to live. And four, I have to find work. I have enough money to tide us over but it won't last forever."

He then translated for Rachel who smiled and kissed him on the cheek.

Doreen said, "Mama. Isn't there a flat for rent next door to my godmother's store?"

"That too far," said Carmella.

"Mama, it's only four blocks away."

"See! Find something closer. That poor girl can't stay alone all day."

She turned to her husband, "What about our tenant on the first floor? You know, Giatano. Maybe, he want smaller place. Maybe, he lonely."

Giatano was recently widowed and had daughters not far away. "I'll talk to him," said Antonio Aiello.

"How about you, Sam?" asked Tony.

Abie translated, "He says he has no idea. He can stay with us until he gets on his feet. It will all work out."

Later, Abie kissed Rachel, Carmella, Doreen, Theresa and Peggy goodnight and headed for a makeshift bed shared with Sam.

The next morning, Sam approached Peggy and said, "Okay I

sleep on couch? He snore."

Peggy laughed and said, "Of course, Sam."

At breakfast Abie said to Rachel, "I am going to see the rabbi this morning, love."

"Should I come?" asked Rachel.

"I don't think so. I'm not sure how these things work. You'll get to meet him when we go to shul."

Rachel was thrilled. "You'll come with me?" she asked. "My father never went except on the high holy days."

"I'm not your father, thank God," said Abie.

Abie found the rabbi in his study in Temple Beth-el.

"I'm Abram Ashansky, rabbi, and I want to get married,"

Doctor Maurice Thorner removed his reading glasses, looked up and said, "How is it that I have never seen you before, Mister Abram-Ashansky-I-want-to-get-married?"

"I was in the Army, serving in France, and I just moved into the neighborhood," said Abie.

"I don't suppose I know the bride-to-be either?"

"No, Rabbi. I just brought her and her brother here from the Ukraine," said Abe.

"The Ukraine? Now? How the devil did you pull that off?"

"It's a long story, Rabbi. Are you sure you want to hear it?"

"Yes."

So Abie told him. It took a half hour.

"Remarkable," said the rabbi. "You should write a book. Okay, Mr. Ashansky. Now I know all about you. But what do you know about us?"

"What do you mean, Rabbi?"

"We are a Reform congregation, Mr. Ashansky. Orthodox Jews might be more comfortable at another synagogue."

Abie had heard of the Reform movement which started in the 19th century in Germany and had spread to the United States but not being very religious himself, he knew very little about it.

Rabbi Thorner had been at Temple Beth-el for five years and led the congregation into the Union of Hebrew Congregations. That was the central body of Reform Judaism in America.

Abie asked, "How are you different from the Orthodox Jews, Rabbi?"

"Well, we're much less rigid than our Orthodox brethren, that's for sure. We believe Judaism is always evolving and adapting itself to modern life. We are much more concerned with what people do than in any rituals or Talmudic law."

Abie was suspicious. "But you believe in our God?"

"Of course?"

"And an afterlife?" asked Abie.

"Maybe," said the rabbi.

"Good answer. So, maybe we don't get punished for our sins."

"Maybe everyone gets punished enough on earth," said the rabbi.

"No 'maybe' there. What about the dietary laws?" asked Abie who had been violating them daily for years.

"If you feel you must obey them to get closer to God, obey them. If not, don't. We feel all such Jewish law is not binding on the individual. You decide for yourself. We're more rational, less biblical."

"But you're still Jews?" asked Abie.

"You bet," said the rabbi, "Ask any gentile." Both men laughed.

"I think I'm going to be very comfortable in this congregation," said Abie.

"How about, what's her name? Rachel? Will she be, as well? We don't have ritual baths or anything like that. People worship here as families. The women don't sit in the balcony," said the rabbi.

"I think so. As I told you, it was a rough journey and she ate everything but the pig's whistle and never complained. She's a good girl but not a particularly pious one. She'll always be a Jew but she wants to be an American Jew."

"Well, we're certainly that," said the rabbi. "Okay. Now what about the wedding?"

"I think that's a different story," said Abe. "She going to want a traditional one. Canopy, crushed glass, Hebrew. All of it."

"The Hebrew and glass we've got," said the rabbi. "And we use the chuppah a lot. I think we can do it. First thing, we'll need two witnesses."

"Well, there's her brother, Sam," said Abe who then fell silent with a slight shrug of his shoulders.

"Don't you know any Jews?" asked the rabbi.

"No. I was hoping you would introduce me to some. "

"I will. In fact, there's a man I want you to meet anyway. I'll ask him to be a witness."

The rabbi started counting on his fingers. "So far, I count six people coming to your wedding including me. Anybody else?"

Abie said, "But don't worry about wedding guests, Rabbi. I'm going to pack more goyim into your temple than you have ever seen."

"That'll be different," said the rabbi.

"How quickly could we hold the wedding," asked a very anxious Abe.

"Well, you have to get a marriage license at City Hall and arrange for flowers, caterers, things like that. But I suppose we could do it in two weeks or so if we had to."

"Good. We won't need caterers. My goy family will provide the food, believe me."

Abie broke the good news about the wedding date at lunch with Rachel and Peggy.

"Are you insane?" Peggy demanded. "There is no woman alive who could plan to get married in two weeks unless she's eight months pregnant.

"Two weeks! It'll take longer than that just to find a decent wedding dress.

"Men! Even when you think they're smart, they turn out to be morons. We're going to need two months at the very least, dodo."

Rachel could understand a few of the English words but she knew what the subject was. Her wedding day.

She put her hand on top of Peggy's. "I wait years," she said and then raised her index finger. "I wait month."

Peggy sighed. "Okay, Rachel, but we're going to have to work night and day." She glared at Abie once more.

Then Peggy smiled sweetly at Abie and said, "Go to the rabbi, see if you can find a girl who speaks Yiddish to go shopping with us. I want Rachel to get the perfect dress and my Yiddish is confined to a term that describes you perfectly—schmuck."

Abie winced and Rachel giggled.

The rabbi was relieved. His wife had given him a similar blistering when she heard of the two-week deadline. His unmarried niece, Esther Katz, agreed to go shopping and translate for Rachel.

The quest for the wedding gown would begin in the morning in Manhattan since, as the rabbi's niece said, "There's nothing in Jersey City but rags. Believe me, I know."

Tony said to Abie, "The girls are going to be gone tomorrow. Why don't you come with me to the parade?"

"What parade?" asked Abie.

"Mickey McGurk's Marines are going to march down Fifth Avenue. I'm taking Hannah, Francis and Mickey's mother to see them. I doubt that we'll be able to pick him out but at least we'll know he's there."

"Count me in. Is Mickey coming back here after the parade?"

"No," said Tony. "I understand they'll be taking a train down to Quantico. They've got another parade in Washington. Then they'll be demobilized."

"So he'll be home in time for the wedding?"

"Yep," said Tony.

A Navy band playing rousing marches set the pace for the thousands of men of the 4th Marine Brigade as they marched down Fifth Avenue from 102nd Street to Washington Square.

Major General John A. Lejeune, commanding general of the 2nd Division, led his marching Marines just as he had led them in combat at Belleau Wood, Blanc Mont Ridge and the Meuse.

They were in perfect cadence but their backs seemed just a tad stiffer when the band boomed out Sousa's "Semper Fidelis."

John Phillip Sousa had served in the Marine band for eight years and later led it for twelve. He was commissioned a Navy lieutenant in 1917 at the age of sixty-two but was no longer on active service.

The crowds were four deep in places and cheered, whistled and shouted for the Marines during the six-mile route. The Marines did not respond. Each man's eyes were fixed on the back of the head of the man in front of him. They were nothing if not disciplined.

Their uniforms were indistinguishable from those of soldiers but they sported the Marine Corps emblem—Eagle, Globe and Anchor—on both sides of their high collars. Their courage at Belleau Wood prompted the assistant secretary of the Navy, Franklin Delano Roosevelt, to authorize that.

Tony had flashed his badge and found his group of five a prime spot directly opposite St. Patrick's Cathedral. This proved to be a mistake.

They could see Archbishop Patrick Joseph Hayes and a covey of monsignori standing on the stairs of the towering Gothic structure, perhaps the most famous Catholic Church in America.

Six-year-old Francis McGurk, was excited. "I hear them, Mommy. They're coming. Daddy's coming, Mommy. I hear them."

It took the Marines a few minutes to get there and when they did Major General Lejeune gave the command "Eyes Left" and saluted. The archbishop acknowledged the salute with a blessing.

As each unit—regiment, battalion, company and platoon—came abreast of the archbishop, the command was given and heads snapped to the left.

Most of the Marines were Protestant, of course, but they didn't mind being blessed by a man who would receive the red hat of a cardinal in a few years. They were grateful to be home and able to march.

Tony, Abie and the McGurks were a bit disappointed. They couldn't see any Marine's face let alone pick out Mickey's.

That didn't faze Francis. "There he is!" he shouted and pointed." There's Daddy! Hello, Daddy!" The people around him cheered and applauded.

The adults went along. "You're right, Francis. There he is. What a good boy! You found your Daddy!"

"Well, he's in there someplace," murmured Amelia McGurk to her daughter-in-law.

Then the Marines were gone and the crowd was breaking up.

"Weren't they splendid looking?" Hannah asked Abie.

"They certainly were. You know the 2nd Division was one of the best we had in France. Those Marines and the Army regulars in the other brigade never failed. General Pershing knew he could always rely on them."

Francis was telling anyone who would listen, "I saw my Daddy. He's coming home soon."

With her house empty, Carmella Aiello decided to wait on the stoop and intercept Lillian Giatano Moretti on her way out from visiting her father.

They spoke in English. Lillian was born here. "How's your

father, Lillian?"

"Not so good, Mrs. Aiello. Ever since my mother died, he mopes around. My sister and I bring him food and do his laundry but he puts the dirty clothes back on anyway."

She paused. "I think he's drinking more wine than he should too."

"I'm so sorry." said Carmella, "What you going to do?"

"My sisters and I have talked it over. We think he should come and live with me before he burns the house down."

Carmella laughed. "Me, I no like burning the house down either. When do you think it's gonna happen?"

"I don't know. Soon, I guess."

Carmella said, "Lillian, I got a problem too. Maybe you can help me. I got relatives. They're getting married. They need a place to live."

"Oh, I see," said Lillian. "When are they getting married?"

Carmella gestured palms up, head tilted, "In a month."

"Oh boy!' said Lillian "So you'd like to see my father gone in a week or two so you could get the place ready?"

"It would be a great favor to me if that could happen."

Lillian liked the idea of having the Aiellos beholden to her. Tony was a cop and you never knew when that would come in handy.

"For you, Mrs. Aiello, we'll do it. My father will be happier and better off with me anyway."

Carmella pressed on. "What about his furniture? You gonna take it with him?"

Lillian hadn't thought of that. She did a quick inventory of his flat.

"I don't think we can. Maybe his bed and some pictures and that old trunk, but not much more. We don't have room. I'll have to sell it."

Carmella said, "My relatives don't got no furniture. If you want, I'll buy it from you. I give you fifty dollars."

Lillian calculated. "That's a lot more than I could get from the junk man. I don't want to cheat you, Mrs. Aiello."

"You no cheat me. You do me a favor."

"We're doing each other a favor, Mrs. Aiello," said Lillian, serenely considering the prospect of a fifty-dollar windfall.

Tony and Abie came home. So did her husband. Carmella began to prepare dinner.

"Say, Abie, I've got something of yours you are going to want," said Tony handing him the key to a safe deposit box. That box contained Rachel's dowry smuggled out of the Ukraine by Abie when war broke out in Europe in 1914.

Abie fingered the key. "Thank you, my friend. I truly appreciate it. What do I owe you for paying the rent on the box while I was gone?"

"Forget it," said Tony. "I'll just buy you a cheaper wedding present."

"Tony. Tony. How can I ever repay you—for everything?"

"How about we split that dowry?"

Abie was taken back. Then Tony laughed and said, "Gotcha, pal."

The women came barreling in. Rachel, Peggy, Theresa, Doreen and Esther Katz still chattering but suddenly as weary as soldiers returning from the front.

Theresa said, "Esther is staying for dinner, Mama."

"Of course, she is."

"So, did you find a wedding dress," Abie asked Rachel.

Esther answered in English. "We're going to have trouble with that one. She wanted to buy the first one we saw. And the second, and the third. We explained to her that she would have to try on at least a dozen of them before she makes up her mind. That's the American way."

Rachel said, in Yiddish, "They are all so beautiful. I can't make up my mind. I said I want you to come help me but they said you can't see me in my dress before the wedding. It's bad luck." Abie translated and everyone laughed.

When talk about the wedding dress didn't peter out at dinner, Carmella interrupted. "I found you a place to live, Abie."

"You did? Where?"

"Downstairs. Mr. Giatano is moving in with his daughter."

"When?" everyone asked.

"Next week, maybe."

The table erupted with excited chatter. Carmella waited a minute or so and then said, "He's leaving the furniture too. You no like, you buy different stuff later."

"Mume, I love you," said Rachel.

Tony said, "We're gone for a couple of hours and you manage all this, Mama. You're a wonder."

"I was going to talk to him," said Antonio, somewhat defensively.

"When? Next year?" asked his wife.

Back in Harness

"This place stinks," said Carmella Aiello, inspecting the flat just vacated by Frankie Giatano who was carted off to live with his daughter.

"It's them 'guinea ropes,'" she added.

"Guinea ropes?" Abie was lost.

"De Nobili cigars," said her husband, Antonio. "Small, hand twisted and soaked in wine. I smoke them myself."

"Not in my house, you don't," she said.

Carmella went room to room criticizing Giatano's habits and cleanliness.

"Look at the walls. They're yellow from that stupid tobacco. Get them painted, Antonio."

"Yes, *cara mia*."

Carmella was horrified. She pointed to a number of burns in the wooden floor where Giatano's bed had been.

"That bastardo!" she cried, "He was smoking in bed! Look at those burns. Lillian was right. He was gonna burn the house down. See what comes from renting to some *cafone* who's not Sicilian?"

Giatano was Neapolitan, one of that hardworking, fun-loving folk disparaged by the more austere Sicilians as "not serious people."

"Abie, you no smoke in bed. You hear me?"

"I do, Mume Carmella," said Abie. Then he teased her. "You know I'm not Sicilian either."

She looked at him sternly. "You're family. Of course, you're Sicilian."

"Sort of," said Antonio, very quietly.

"So who is going to paint the place, Uncle Antonio?"

"Not me," he said, "I have a rule. You don't lay brick, I don't paint. I'll get my cousin, Lutz, to do it. I owe him a favor anyway."

Within days the flat was painted a bright, shiny white.

"Nice," said Carmella.

"Beautiful," said Rachel.

Less than a week later, the letter summoning Abie to Whitehall Street came. It also instructed him to bring a "passport in the name of Aloysius Shannon" which he was to surrender to the officer-in-charge.

The officer-in-charge was a balding young, blond captain who had spent the entire war at Whitehall Street, first processing men into the Army and now processing them out.

He had Ashansky's records in front of him.

"I see you were paid in Dover, Lieutenant. So the Army owes you two months and eleven days pay as of today." He made some calculations on a scratch pad.

"That comes to $311.24" He offered Ashansky the pad. "Do you want to check my arithmetic?"

"No, sir," said Ashansky.

"Okay. Sign the payroll, Lieutenant, and I'll have my clerk get your money."

"Good," the captain said as he looked again at the records. "It says here you are to turn over a passport in the name of Aloysius Shannon."

Abie who was wearing civilian clothes reached into his inner jacket pocket. "Here it is, sir."

The captain inspected the passport and asked, "Where did you get this?"

"General Dennis Nolan gave it to me, sir." The captain waited for further explanation. He got none.

He handed Abie a form. "It's your resignation. When you sign this, you are no longer an officer on active duty with the United States Army."

Abie read it and signed.

The captain was carefully reading the next document which

had a note attached to it. "Now I'm supposed to offer you chance to apply for a commission as a second lieutenant in the Reserves."

Abie didn't get a chance to say, "Don't bother."

The captain continued, "Not many officers accept but those that do have to fill out another batch of application forms. But not you, Mr. Ashansky. I have your commission, already signed, in my hand. I've never had this happen before."

"Really? Tell me what I have to do as a lieutenant in the Reserves."

"Actually, nothing. Of course, they'll call you up immediately if another war breaks out," said the captain.

"I'd say that was a pretty remote possibility now that we've won 'the war to end all war,' wouldn't you?"

"That's not for me to say, Mr. Ashansky."

"Captain, does that chit you're holding say where I am to report if I am mobilized?"

The captain looked again. "It does. You would report to G-2 of the General Staff at the War Office in Washington."

General Nolan, Abie thought. "I'd be honored to accept that commission, sir."

"I will swear you in myself," said the captain.

Minutes later Abie left with his commission and a bundle of cash.

The Captain thought, *That's one hell of an interesting story walking out the door. It's a pity I'll never hear it.*

Mickey McGurk's homecoming was held in his mother's flat in the Horseshoe, her boarders shooed away for the evening. There were more Irish and German guests and fewer Sicilians. Policemen wandered in and out all night.

More whiskey was drunk and less wine and the food was, well, more to Irish tastes.

"What's that?" Carmella asked quietly as she poked it with her fork.

"That's potato salad, Mume," answered Abie.

She tasted it and made a face. *"Gesu dolce, questo e terribile."*

"I like it, Mume. Why don't you just put it on my plate?"

Carmella gratefully followed instructions and said, "Abie, you a good boy."

Then she bit into a ham sandwich made with a slice of rubbery ham between two slices of Dugan's bread. She looked at Abie.

"Sorry," he said.

Terry Lynch steered Abie to his brother, known as but never referred to as, Fat Jack Lynch.

"Abie," Fat Jack said, "we didn't get a chance to talk the other night. Are you registered to vote yet?"

Abie knew Fat Jack was a Democratic ward leader and thus a very important man in Jersey City. *I wonder if he could help me find a job?*

"Yes, sir." He pointed to Tony Aiello.

"Tony took me up to the courthouse. I voted for Mr. Hague before I joined the Army."

"Good man. My brother tells me you were a real hero in France. A medal. A battlefield commission. That's something to be proud of, Abie."

"Thank you...Jack. But I don't think I was a hero. I was scared to death most of the time." The Lynches laughed with him.

Fat Jack said, "Well, I want you on my side. I'd be honored if you would join the John J. Lynch Association. You know, your buddy here is thinking about getting into politics himself. But he'll have to do a couple of years in the trenches first."

That'll be the first trench he's been in. Still I owe him, thought Abie.

"The honor is mine, Jack," said Abie.

"Good. Now if you gentlemen will excuse me," said Fat Jack, seeing a precinct committeeman he wanted to talk to.

"So, Terry, what are you going to do before you become governor?" asked Abie.

"That's a long ways off," said Terry without the trace of a smile. "I'm going to work for Tom Flaherty. He's got an insurance agency in Greenville."

"Is he a ward leader too?"

"No. A precinct captain and a Democratic committeeman. My brother thinks he's the right guy to show me the ropes. Besides the insurance business is a great trade to fall back on."

"Sounds like a good deal."

Terry said, "It is. Now, you don't have to come to regular meetings of the association. I'll keep you informed. But we throw a racket every so often and I'd like you to come to those. Bring Rachel."

"Thanks, I will."

"When you come, wear that Croix de Guerre ribbon on the lapel of your jacket. The vets will know what it is."

"I don't want to pass myself off as a hero," said Abie.

"You are a hero, Abie. You don't have to say anything; people will draw their own conclusions."

They were all there in Mrs. McGurk's flat except Frank Hague who was in Trenton. Mickey McGurk and his detective sergeant colleague, Tony Aiello, and their confidantes, Fat Jack Lynch, Peggy McCann Aiello and Abie Ashansky. Sadly, the Bomb Squad's third policeman, Hans Mannstein, died from the Spanish Flu at Camp Upton the year before.

They tried to protect Jersey City from possible harm by radical or foreign groups during the two years before America entered the war. They failed.

German saboteurs literally blew the massive munitions terminal at Black Tom out of the water. The devastation was complete. Four people were dead, hundreds injured, millions panicked on both sides of the Hudson River and the damage ran into many millions of dollars.

But the Germans got away with it. Mickey suspected them but couldn't prove it.

Now back at the Ganz house, Mickey and Hannah were bleary-eyed. Hannah got ready for bed making her preparations in the bathroom. Mickey lay down the bed almost giddy with anticipation.

He had dreamed of this moment during those long, lonely months in France. The dream of long, languorous lovemaking with his lovely wife just like on their honeymoon.

Hannah slipped into bed and threw her arms around Mickey. "Oh, I've missed you so, darling," she said as she kissed him.

Mickey's resolve vanished and within seconds they were naked. Mickey and Hannah coupled and Mickey came close to setting the state record for premature ejaculation.

"Well, I see you're glad to see me too," Hannah said to a spent but dejected Mickey.

He made it up to her less than an hour later and from then on every night went on as he had dreamed. Hannah was content. Her husband was home and he loved her.

Mickey McGurk and Tony Aiello waited in Frank Hague's outer office. Neither of them knew the mayor's new secretary, Alice Patterson.

Miss Patterson was a longtime suffragette and there was a good chance that women were going to get the vote soon. A chance Frank Hague intended to exploit fully.

Women had been agitating for the vote for decades. Hundreds of them had been injured in a riotous demonstration in Washington, D.C., on the eve of President Wilson's inauguration in 1913.

The president changed his mind on suffrage years ago and endorsed it.

The 19th Amendment to the Constitution that would give them the vote cleared Congress in June. Six states, including New York, had already ratified it.

But getting two-thirds of the states to ratify it wasn't a sure thing. The Southern states were adamantly opposed.

A buzzer rang on Miss Patterson's desk. "You may go in now, gentlemen."

Frank Hague, fairly tall, balding, lean and always dapper, jumped up from behind his huge desk and took Mickey's hand in both of his, "Mickey! You're back! You look great, boy."

"Thanks, Uncle Frank... I mean Mr. Mayor."

"I'm still your Uncle Frank, Mickey, and I'll bet Sergeant Aiello already knows that."

"I do, sir," said Tony. McGurk and Hague were related by marriage and he was responsible for McGurk's meteoric rise on the force.

"Sit down, men. I'm glad to see you, Mickey, and, by the way, you're back on the force as a lieutenant. But I want to talk you both about something serious."

"The Zeppelins, sir?" asked Mickey referring to Hague's hard-nosed, elite squad.

"No. The Zepps did a great job. The police force is first class now and so is the fire department. They're back on regular duty now but I can call them out as a riot squad if I have to," said Hague.

"No. We have other problems now. You know how we were afraid of the anarchists blowing up places before the war? Well, you fellows barely stopped shooting in France before they started with the bombs again.

"This time they're sending them in the mail to people they hate. Senators, governors, prosecutors, people like that. One poor lady got her hands blown off when she opened the goddamn package. The damn things have been going off all over the country.

"It's been a hellava summer. General strikes, just like it began in Russia. Bolsheviks, socialists, all those assholes riling up the coloreds. There have been race riots all over the country. They even had a dustup across the river."

Hague looked at Aiello. "Are you up to speed on this stuff, Sergeant?"

"Only what I read in the papers, sir. I know that a bomb they mailed blew up the attorney general's house in Washington."

That particular twenty-five pound dynamite bomb was so powerful that debris flew across the street and landed on the front stairs of the assistant secretary of the Navy, Franklin D. Roosevelt. Incredibly no one was hurt in the explosion.

"Have any of those bombs shown up in Jersey City, Mr. Mayor?" Mickey asked.

"No. But monkey see, monkey do."

Mickey then asked, "Any anarchist activity here that you know of?"

"How the hell do I know? That's why you people are here," said Hague. "Your little Bomb Squad is back in business, Mickey."

Mickey and Tony looked at each other and smiled.

"Yes, sir. Thank you. What about a third man, Uncle Frank?" Mickey asked.

"Yeah. Poor Hans Mannstein. He was a good cop," Hague said. "Well, I have a man for you. Vince Crehan, he's some sort of cousin to Jack Lynch. From the other side."

"I think I know him to say hello to," said Mickey.

"I know him," said Tony. "He's a good cop. Works out of the 6th Precinct up in the Heights. But he's not a detective. He walks a beat."

"Jack tells me he's ambitious," said Hague," so he can work in plain clothes for the time being. You let me know if he is detective material."

"Okay," said Mickey.

"Another thing. Keep your eye out for radical labor union people too. You know, Wobblies. People like that. God knows I'm not against labor unions. Decent ones. The AF of L unions are okay. Their Central Labor Council endorsed me. You remember when I ran those strikebreakers out of town don't you, Mickey?"

"I do, Mr. Mayor."

"But the world has changed what with those Bolsheviks causing all that trouble in Europe. What are they called again?"

"Communists," said Mickey.

"Yeah, communists. Well, I don't want no communists, Bolsheviks, Reds, anarchists or any other assholes like that in my city. If there are any here now, I want you to root them out.

"But back to bombs. I can tell you this," said Hague, "some of those bombs are going to New York. They even sent one to the police commissioner. It didn't go off. A lot of them didn't even leave the post office. Not enough stamps. Stupid foreigners.

"I think a visit to your old friend, Captain Tunney, over in the city might be a good idea. He can give you a good picture of what's going on, I'll bet."

"Yes, sir," said Mickey.

Mickey had consulted with Tunney profitably several times when he was running Jersey City's little Bomb Squad.

His old badge in hand, Mickey and Tony went from City Hall to Police Headquarters.

His old office was being used as a storage space. His desk and chair were still there and the calendar on the wall still said 1917. The two straight-backed chairs and his filing cabinet were gone. So was his typewriter. Boxes were piled on one another.

"What is this stuff?" asked Mickey.

"I don't know," said Tony. "But it can't be every important if it's stored here in an unlocked office."

"Well, let's get rid of it. And let's get a couple of chairs," Mickey said.

"I'll talk to the desk sergeant."

"When do I get to meet this Crehan guy?" Mickey asked.

"I called his precinct before we left City Hall. He's on duty. They're going to relive him so he should be here pretty soon."

A couple of civilian janitors showed up each bearing a chair and they started to move out boxes. They hadn't finished when a young cop knocked on the open door.

"Lieutenant McGurk? I'm Vincent Crehan and I was ordered to report here to you, sir."

"Okay," said McGurk looking at the remaining clutter.

"Let's go get a cup of coffee. You know Sergeant Aiello?"

"I do, sir. How are you, Sergeant?"

They sat a table in a nearby greasy spoon much favored by policemen. McGurk wasn't worried about being overheard. The news of a resurrected Bomb Squad would be all over the department by roll call tonight.

"Okay, tell me about yourself, Vince."

"Not much to tell," said Crehan with the lilting tones of the west of Ireland. "I came over with my sister, Katie, when I was sixteen. My cousin, Jack Lynch, got me in with some of his longshoreman friends and I worked the docks in Hoboken until I was old enough to get on the force three years ago."

"I remember you now," said McGurk. "You replaced one of those lazy assholes Mayor Hague dumped."

"He wasn't mayor then," said Crehan. "But you're right. I've been working in the 6th ever since."

"Are you married?"

"No, sir."

"Still living with your sister?"

"No, sir. She's married and has three kids. She lives on Griffith Street. Once I was on the force, I got a furnished room over on Booraem Avenue."

Well, I'll be damned." said Mickey. "I used to live over there myself. How do you like the job?"

"Fine, sir. It's pretty quiet up in the Heights. Except on Friday and Saturday nights, we might have a bit of excitement."

"I know," said Mickey, "I worked there and I live there now."

"Where, sir?" asked Crehan.

"I'm not sure," said McGurk. "My wife and kid bunked in

with her parents when I was with the Marines. We have to get our own place. But it will be in the Heights.

"You know, I would have thought that a young, unmarried guy like you would have enlisted."

Crehan looked thoughtful and hesitated before he spoke. "No offense, sir, but England is no ally of mine."

Of course. Fat Jack Lynch, the head of the Clan na Gael in Jersey City. Young Vince here is another Irish nationalist, McGurk thought.

"No matter. The war's over," said McGurk. "Do you know why you are here, Officer Crehan?"

"No, sir," he said. *But I hope it is what I think it is.*

"With all the anarchist agitation going on, Mayor Hague has decided to revive the Bomb Squad," McGurk said. "Do you want to be on it? It's a plainclothes job."

Crehan's grin was answer enough, but he said, "Yes, sir. I do. When do I start?"

"As soon as you get out of that uniform," said McGurk. "Report here to Sergeant Aiello tomorrow morning."

"Yes, sir. Thank you, sir. Thank you, Sergeant." Crehan couldn't wait to get back to the Heights to tell his sister the good news. Then he'd go to his Cousin Jack's house to thank him. Life in America was good.

His sister Katie was ecstatic. "On the job just three years and already you've been promoted. Oh, I am so happy, Vincent. I'm that proud of you. Imagine, my little brother, a detective."

"Plainclothes, Katie. I'm not a detective yet."

"It's almost the same thing," said his sister, "And tell me how much more money will you be making?"

"My pay stays the same."

"What manner of promotion is it when the pay stays the same?" asked Katie.

"It's a real opportunity for me, Sissy."

"It is now, is it? Apparently when opportunity knocks for my brother, it knocks on his thick skull," she said. "Well, don't get yourself blown up."

"Don't worry, Sissy, we don't defuse bombs. We catch the guys who throw them."

Katie laughed. "Well, I'm your big sister and I remember when the only thing you could catch was a cold."

The Wedding

Abie Ashansky took seriously Peggy's admonition "to stay out of the way" as the women prepared for Rachel's wedding.

He had a few chores of his own. Two of them were accomplished at a jeweler's on Newark Avenue recommended by Rabbi Thorner.

They recognized each other. Abie had gone to shul with Rachel to meet the rabbi and he had seen the jeweler there.

First, he bought a solid, gold ring that he would give to her during the wedding ceremony.

Next, he placed a sack with the contents of his safe deposit box on a piece of velvet on the jeweler's glass case. "I'm going to need these things appraised and listed. For the ketubah."

That was the marriage contract the couple would sign before the ceremony.

"Yes, I know," said the jeweler, "I've done this before." He fixed his jeweler's eye over his glasses and ran his fingers over the small pile spreading it out.

After a minute or so, he said, "Gold is gold. Platinum is platinum and silver is silver. Easy. But there are some nice gems in settings here too. It will take a while to come up with an honest appraisal but I can tell you now, your beloved isn't going to have too many problems if you get hit by a streetcar." *And she's beautiful too; the line would go around the block,* thought the jeweler.

He picked up one ring. "Granted, these pieces are a bit old fashioned but if she wants to sell, I'll make her a good offer."

"I'm sure you would," said Abie. "But I'll try not to get hit by a streetcar."

Abie also bought a bed, pillows, bedding, linens and towels. The kind of things single women in America bought or received as gifts and were stored in a wooden, cedar-lined hope chest. Rachel came with little more than the clothes on her back. He bought only enough for the time being. Rachel could buy more of her choosing later.

She could also fit out her kitchen although Mr. Giatano's daughter left his dishes and pots and pans taking only his espresso coffee pot. There was an ice box.

The ice box would do fine. The iceman would stop by every week in his horse-drawn wagon with cakes of ice to help keep food fresh.

Still, Rachel would have to shop for groceries virtually every day. Food spoiled fast, especially in summer.

The quest for the perfect wedding dress ended successfully with Rachel and the girls rhapsodizing over it. Abie, of course, was forbidden to see it.

All Peggy would say to him was, "The big problem was finding a veil short enough that Rachel could pull over her face and then toss it back behind her head. God only knows why she insisted on that." Rachel, Esther, Sam and Abie knew why.

The wedding was set for 11 a.m., Sunday, September 7, 1919— that is the twelfth day of Elul, in the year 5679.

The Catholic guests, and there were many of them, would go to an early mass before they headed for the synagogue downtown. Almost none of them had been in a temple before and most were not sure they should be going there.

"I tell you, Mike, it's not like going to a Protestant church," said one. "That's a mortal sin. I'm pretty sure going to a synagogue is just a venial sin. Hardly worth mentioning in confession."

No one bothered to ask their parish priest less they get an answer they didn't want to deal with. They'd ask for forgiveness later, if that was necessary.

For a Jewish couple, their wedding day was also a day of repentance and forgiveness. Rachel and Abie had decided to fast although Rabbi Thorner did not require that.

The guests began to arrive at Temple Beth-el and were ushered to the bride's side on the right or the groom's side on the left. Rachel's side had the Aiellos in the first row backed up by many Sicilians and by Jews she and Abie had met at shul and had invited to the wedding.

On the left were more people, all of them gentiles, and most of them friends of Abie's or friends of his friends.

The gentile men had ditched their straw boaters on Labor Day and many of them were hatless. They were offered yarmulkes which they accepted.

"I know all about these hanukahs," said one man, "I saw the bishop wore one of these beanies when my kid was confirmed. You're supposed to wear a hat when you're in a Jewish church."

Tony Aiello saw two guests that he couldn't quite place at first. Then it registered. *That's Peter Capparelli and his Irish wife. I haven't seen him since the murder.*

Capparelli was an uncle-in-law to Billy Cunningham, the hapless young man who killed the arrogant son of a powerful politician. Billy had hid out with his relatives in Newark and worked for his uncle in a scrap yard in Kearny. So did Abie Ashansky. That's where Tony Aiello met him during the investigation.

The interaction between the two sides was silent but obvious. They looked at each other as though they were observant tourists in a far-off land.

Of course, as at all weddings, the women were very interested in what other women were wearing. They were surprised to discern no differences.

Rachel and Abie first saw each other when they joined to sign the ketuba, the marriage deed.

The sight of his beautiful Rachel caused Abie to actually hold his breath. Her ankle length, white dress was form fitting and quietly spectacular. Her veil attached to a Juliet cap perfectly framed her lovely face. She wore no makeup save a bit of lipstick but, then, she didn't need any.

Abie was handsome in the uniform Rachel had insisted he wear. His boots and Sam Browne belt were polished to a high gloss and his Croix de Guerre glistened on his chest. The wound stripe was a highlight on his sleeve and he wore an overseas cap.

All in all, they made a grand couple.

The ketuba was the bride's protection from widowhood or divorce.

Once written in Aramaic but now in English, it listed all the contents of Rachel's dowry.

Also listed were what she would get from Abie's estate should he die or divorce her. In the old days it was 200 denarii. Now it read "all my worldly goods" plus fifty British gold sovereigns the Army hadn't asked Abie to account for.

The ketuba is the property of Rachel as is the key to that safe deposit box at the Provident Savings Bank.

Abie signed first, then Rachel and finally, the two witnesses, her brother and Charles Schor, a man anxious to spend more time with Abie.

Then Rachel was taken to a small room by the rabbi and Antonio Aiello, followed a few minutes later by Abie, and most of the male Jews present. The gentile men stayed put in puzzled ignorance.

Rachel was veiled. Abie lifted the veil to reveal her sweet face. Her smile bewitched Abie whose hands shook.

This little custom went all the way back to Jacob who wanted to marry his Rachel. Her father secretly substituted her heavily veiled older sister, Leah. Since then Jewish men have insisted on seeing their brides face-to-face before they wed.

Now the marriage ceremony was ready to begin, and all the guests went back in their seats.

The wedding canopy, the chuppah, was held up by four stanchions. The rabbi and the cantor were waiting inside it.

Sam Zeidman, the best man, came down the aisle first and stood to the left outside the chuppah. Next came the fatherless Abie who stood to the left of Sam.

Then came the bridesmaids, Esther Katz, Theresa Aiello, and Doreen Aiello who stood to the right of the chuppah.

The matron of honor, Peggy McCann Aiello, followed and joined them.

Then came Rachel, escorted by her surrogate parents, Carmella and Antonio Aiello. Rachel walked slowly down the aisle, the oohs and aahs audible in her wake.

Antonio lifted her veil and he and his wife kissed Rachel and went to the first pew.

Rachel took three steps forward, indicating that this was her free choice, and Abie joined her. They went under the chuppah with Rachel to the right.

Rabbi Thorner read the ketuba aloud. Then he blessed a glass of wine the couple sipped.

Abie took Rachel's left hand and placed the gold ring on the fourth finger repeating a vow in Hebrew which he had memorized, "Behold, thou are consecrated to me with this ring, according to the laws of Moses and Israel."

Even the gentile women were tearing up now although they didn't understand a word.

"What's he saying?" one asked her husband. "How do I know? Probably what we say in Latin. I can't understand that either."

The rabbi asked Sam to put a wineglass in a special pouch the bridegroom had provided. Sam placed it under Abie's right foot.

Abie crushed it reminding the congregation of the destruction of the Temple in Jerusalem and the bride of the shortness of human life.

With that the congregation began to shout, "Mazel Tov!"

Some of the gentiles joined in although the sound emerging from a few Irish mouths sounded more like "Matzoh Toff."

The Jews began to clap hands, sing and embrace each other. The flummoxed gentiles just clapped.

The cantor began to chant the Seven Blessings and the rabbi repeated them in English.

Then he pronounced Abie and Rachel man and wife. They kissed to tremendous approval and loud applause.

The couple, holding hands, rushed up the aisle to a little room where they would be alone for a few minutes while their guests moved to a large meeting room where the reception would be held.

Abie and Rachel broke their fast, taking some soup, the bride careful not to spill any on her dress.

They were laughing. Abie was kissing her between spoonfuls.

"That idiot brother of yours," said Abie. "I expected him to put the wineglass under my heel. But that numbskull puts it under the front of my shoe. I thought I was going to have to jump up and down to break it."

"You did beautifully, my love," said Rachel. "You can get even with him at his wedding."

"Ha! Who would marry him?"

"Maybe Esther," said Rachel.

"What! She's just a kid."

"Men. You're all blind. Don't you see how she looks at him with—what do you call it in English—goo-goo eyes?"

"Who knows?" said Abie as he took Rachel by the hand. "Come on, let's go and enjoy our own wedding."

They sat down at a table in the middle of a big circle of guests' tables.

Rabbi Thorner and Antonio blessed the challah bread, big, soft, egg-rich loaves, which the couple broke and brought large pieces to each table of guests.

A klezmer band played fantazi tunes while the guests ate their chicken, fish and beef. No one seemed to notice the absence of dairy products. There was plenty of wine.

"Good lord, this stuff is terrible," said one Irishman who rarely tasted wine before. "No wonder those old biddies don't want them to make it."

"That's Manischewitz," said a more astute friend. "They make it in Upstate New York from those sweet Concord grapes."

"Well, it's enough to put you into a diabetic coma."

"But this stuff will be perfectly legal," continued his friend. "The Jews are getting an exemption. They can have all the sacramental wine they want."

"Hey, that's not fair," said the Irishman. "Whiskey is practically a sacrament with us, you know."

"Maybe. But the church is getting an exemption too. The priests can buy all the sacramental wine they want."

"I'll bet they won't buy this Manischewitz stuff." They didn't.

After eating, the guests started to form a circle around Rachel and Abie. McGurk was briefed on what was coming next. He cornered three burly policemen, "Come with me. We're going to lift Abie in that chair. And don't drop him." Four husky Jews headed for Rachel.

The band struck up a hora. The Jews began to dance in a circle around the elevated couple.

The gentiles, seeing there was little skill involved, joined in, after the Jews invited them.

The band played a new hora called "Hava Nagila" which means "Let's Rejoice" in Hebrew.

The song had been written but five years earlier in Palestine but it was already the informal anthem of the Jews there who were basking in the Balfour Declaration that proclaimed it their homeland. The song was spreading through Jewish communities throughout the world.

Few Jews and no gentiles knew the words yet but the cadence and melody were infectious and soon all were singing "Da—da—da-da-da" at the top of their lungs and having a great time.

When the dance ended, one older Jewish man called out, "Officer McGurk! Officer McGurk! It's me, Cheap Sam. Cheap Sam from Central Avenue."

Mickey turned around, spotted the man, moved forward to shake his hand, and said, "Mr. Schor! How are you, sir? I haven't seen you in years."

Sam Schor who had immigrated to America from Germany in 1885 had parlayed a pushcart on the Lower East Side of Manhattan into a toy store on Patrolman Michael McGurk's beat in The Heights.

"We miss you, Mickey. All us storekeepers liked it when you were on the beat." He turned to the small crowd that had gathered around them. "Back then, if any *momzer* tried to rob us or even say 'boo' to us, Mickey would break his head."

His wife, who frequently despaired to raising Sam to total respectability, sighed.

He heard her and said, "Well, he would've. I'm honored that my son was your witness. I'm proud of him too. He's a lawyer, you know."

"Really," said Mickey as they fell to talking about old times as men do at weddings.

The band played waltzes too which the gentiles were quick to dance to. A few lead-footed Irishmen did their best all but crippling their still smiling partners in the process.

Then there was the Krenzel Dance, the last dance. Carmella and Antonio, Rachel's surrogate parents for the day, were seated on chairs in the middle of the floor. A crown of flowers was placed on Carmella's head and the couples began to dance around them.

Each couple stopped to congratulate them, kissing them both. Most of the Irishmen kissed Carmella on the cheek and shook hands with Antonio. Men kissing men was not a widespread Irish custom.

"I like this," said Carmella to her husband. "We gonna do this at the girls' weddings."

The crowd quieted down and filled their wineglasses.

Once again, the cantor began to sing the Seven Blessings in Hebrew. Many of the Jews joined the cantor in singing parts of the blessings. The rabbi repeated each, in turn, in English.

"Blessed are You, Adonai our God, King of the universe, Creator of the fruit of the vine."

"Blessed are You, Adonai our God, Creator of all things for Your glory."

"Blessed are You, Adonai, our God, Who has created man and woman."

One cop whispered to his friend Jerry, "Who is this Adonai he keeps blessing?"

"I'm not sure but you can bet your sweet ass it's not Jesus," said Jerry.

Some decades later Jerry would be sternly reminded of this bit of blasphemy as his soul was dispatched to Purgatory for a well-deserved cleansing. Heaven would wait.

And finally: "Blessed are You, Adonai, our God, King of the universe, Who created joy and gladness, bride and groom, mirth, glad song, pleasure, delight, love, brotherhood, peace and companionship. Adonai, our God, let there soon be heard in the cities of Judah and in the streets of Jerusalem the sound of joy and the sound of gladness, the voice of the groom and the voice of the bride, the sound of the groom's jubilance from their canopies and the youths from their song-filled feasts. Blessed are You Who causes the groom to rejoice with his bride."

Then a cup of wine was presented to Rachel and another to Abie. These cups were then poured into a third which was offered to all present. The symbolism was obvious.

With that, the congregation began to shout out individual blessings on the couple. The gentiles joined, mostly with "God bless you."

One young woman yelled, "May the Blessed Virgin keep you both."

Her sister poked her in the ribs, "Deidre!"

"What? Sure wasn't Mary a Jew herself?"

The bride and groom vanished and the guests said their goodbyes and most of them headed for a second reception at the Aiellos.

Here the Sicilians got wine they relished, the Irish and Germans headed straight for the beer and not a few of them downed a shot of Irish whiskey in Peggy's kitchen.

"Ah! That was good," said one policeman. "Mind you, I really enjoyed myself at the wedding but you have to admit, those poor Jews aren't much for decent booze."

"Well, if those bluenoses have their way, none of us will be drinking anything what with their Prohibition arriving in January," said his friend.

"Do you really think that is going to happen in Jersey City?"

The second cop thought for a moment and then said, "Nah."

Tony Aiello found Peter Capparelli and his wife in his mother's parlor. "Mr. Capparelli, it is good to see you again. Tony Aiello."

Capparelli shook his hand and said, "I remember you, detective." His wife's memory was even more vivid. Billy Cunningham was her nephew and now he was in State Prison doing seven years for manslaughter.

The prosecutors had decided not to accuse him of second-degree murder for two reasons. They were afraid Billy would get a lawyer and all they had was an easily retracted confession. Second, they liked Billy a lot more than they liked his arrogant, bullyboy victim.

Tony did not ask about Billy. "How have things been going,

Mr. Capparelli?"

"Great. We got a lot more work when war broke out and they made me the superintendent." His wife looked at him proudly.

Tony did not know that Peter Capparelli had been a "Wobbly," a card-carrying member of the Industrial Workers of the World. He did know that Abie had traveled in radical circles and he had heard that the Capparellis had taken in two emaciated boys during the ill-fated Paterson Silk Strike in 1913.

Capparelli struck up a conversation with Sam, speaking simply and slowly since he knew the immigrant's English was limited. "I heard you are from Kiev, Sam."

"Yes."

"Are the Reds in Kiev now?"

"Yes."

"What do you think of the Reds, Sam?"

"More good than the Whites."

"Why do you say that?"

"I guard coal pile in Kiev. For electric. One day I am Red. Then I am White. Then I am Red again. Reds gonna win. People hate Whites."

Suddenly, there was a buzz in the front of the flat. In the doorway was a fairly tall, impeccably groomed middle-aged man. It was Frank Hague, mayor of Jersey City and the most powerful Democratic politician in the state.

He headed straight for Mickey McGurk who said, "Uncle Frank, what a pleasure to see you."

"I was on my way to a wake at McLaughlin's. Jack Lynch suggested we stop by and wish the newlyweds good luck. It seems Jack's kid brother and Ashansky served together in France."

"Yes, sir, and I'm sure you remember the work Ashansky did for us before Black Tom blew up."

"Of course, I do," said Hague who didn't.

Hague found the couple in the senior Aiellos' flat. The mob

pushing in behind him brought the kitchen to almost suffocating density.

He glanced at the medal on Abie's chest and said, "Lieutenant, I always knew you were a patriot. Now I see that you are a hero too. I want to welcome you and your bride back home to Jersey City."

Abie said, "Thank you, Mr. Mayor." He shook Hague's hand. Rachel, who understood some of what Hague had said, smiled and said, "Tank you, Mayor."

Hague shook her hand too. Hague did not kiss women other than his wife.

The mayor was introduced to Rabbi Thorner. "I've heard of you, Rabbi. I'm delighted to meet you."

"Likewise, Mr. Hague."

"I hear you folks are thinking about building a new synagogue up on the Boulevard."

The rabbi was taken aback. Only a handful of people were privy to that information.

"Why am I not surprised that you know that, Mr. Mayor?" he asked.

"Well, if there is any trouble with permits or inspections or any nonsense like that you just come and see me at City Hall."

"That's generous of you, Mr. Hague. I'll remember that."

Hague gave the rabbi his serious "I mean it" look.

It was a less politically correct era and the mayor said, "I like Jews. They don't cause any trouble. They vote. And they vote Democratic."

His ultimate seal of approval.

Making a New Life

Rachel and Abie had slipped away from the reception separately and went downstairs to their flat. It was easy to do since they were frequently moving back and forth between the two Aiello apartments. No one noticed.

It was still early, nine o'clock, but both of them were drained.

They had decided not to trek off on a honeymoon. It didn't make sense.

As Rachel had said, "Where are you going to take me? On an ocean voyage?"

Rachel had said she wanted the Sheva Brachot, an old Hebrew custom where the newlywed couple was honored at special family dinners every night for a week. The idea, thousands of years old, was to bind the couple to the community and vice versa.

Rachel understood this. "I want to meet the people I am going to live with. I want to learn English and I want to learn how to be an American. An American Jew," she said.

She was particularly frustrated by her inability to understand the conversations around her. "If they talk English, I understand a word here and a phrase there. By the time I've translated it in my head, they've moved on to something else.

"And the Yiddish! I understand the older people easily but when do I talk to them? Over a piece of cake at Oneg Shabbat?

"The young people speak Yiddish badly or not at all. Except my precious Esther. Most of them sprinkle their English with a few Yiddish phrases and that's it."

A sympathetic Abie said that he would speak English to her exclusively, translating into Yiddish only when she did not understand. That was working. Their conversations were in English— with Yiddish interjections and a word or two in Russian or Ukrainian when it seemed apt.

But a wedding night was not one for long conversations in any language but that of love.

When Abie arrived downstairs, Rachel had already removed her wedding gown and hung it up. She was in the bath, he could hear the water running. He walked into the parlor and into the connecting big bedroom.

The day had been warm, it was one of the last days of summer, and he thought, *I could use a bath too. I'm sweaty. But God knows how long she is going to be in there.*

He stripped to the waist and went into the kitchen. All rooms in the flat connected to the center of family life, the kitchen.

Abie sponged himself at the sink and dried with a rough towel. He looked at the bathroom door and could hear Rachel softly singing.

He had never seen his wife naked. He thought, *I wonder.*

Abie walked quietly to the bathroom door and, eager as a teenage boy, knelt down. The key inside the lock blocked his vision. He smiled, *Ah, well. That was sort of weird anyway.* He did not try the handle for fear it would open.

In their bedroom, he removed the rest of his uniform and hung it up in the wardrobe. He put on a pair of light pajamas — purchased for the occasion.

Abe lay down on top of their made bed, his hands behind his head, waiting for whatever would happen next. He knew his wife was a virgin; he knew he had to be gentle. No, more than that, he had to be considerate, patient. This wasn't a wild one-night stand, this was forever.

Without knocking, Rachel walked in, still drying her hair with a towel. "There you are," she said,

"Where did you think I'd be?" asked Abe. She laughed.

Rachel was wearing a silk dressing gown over what seemed to be a black negligee. She was barefoot. All Abie could see of her was her instep. But what a lovely instep it was.

She sat at a chair in front on her vanity to finish drying her hair. She could see Abie in the mirror, hands still behind his head. Rachel was more nervous than she looked. Her mother had told her all that would happen on her wedding night but listening was not doing.

Here we go, she thought as she placed the towel on the back of the chair and walked towards the bed, Abie's arms reaching out to enfold her.

They lay side by side. They kissed, their tongues exploring each other. Abie was getting aroused. *Control yourself,* he thought. *Slow down! Slow.*

As they kissed Abie, slowly, gently felt the contours of her body through the soft fabrics. Everything. Even the nipples on her breasts.

Rachel, stiff at first, began to relax. Abie made a quick adjustment freeing his erection. He whispered, "You can hold me there, if you like."

"Why?" asked Rachel.

"Because I like it," said Abie.

"Okay," she answered in English. Rachel had been dubious when her mother told her the male organ would expand in size simply because it was touched by a woman.

Mama was right.

When they awoke, light was peeping in through the sides of the front window curtains. They were lying on their bed, she on her side facing him, Abie on his back with his limp organ barely protruding out of the fly of his pajamas. They were clothed as they had been some hours earlier. They had fallen asleep while they were petting.

"Good morning, Mrs. Ashansky."

"Good morning, my love. What happened?"

"We fell asleep," said Abie.

"Well, we're awake now," said Rachel reaching for her husband. This time there was no hesitation. Her hand did its magic and Abie tore off a button from his pajama top freeing himself.

They were naked and could see each other as the morning light grew in the bedroom.

"I like this better," said Rachel determined to act as her mother had told her. "This is a gift from God," she had been told. As Abie fondled her, her belief in that grew.

It was time. Abie was very gentle as he entered her and felt that membrane of maidenhood. He pushed very slowly but insistently. Rachel's hands bit into his shoulders and she winced.

Abie stopped. "I'm sorry, sweetheart. I don't want to hurt you."

"It's nothing," Rachel said. "It's over." She wrapped her legs around his and started to move. Abie made no more apologies.

When, at last, the very happy couple left their flat to get something to eat, Carmella Aiello opened their door with her skeleton key and replaced the sheets on their bed with those she brought.

When Abie and Rachel returned they saw the bloody sheet hanging from Carmella's front windows.

"Oh, my God!" said a mortified Rachel.

"Don't fret about that, sweetheart. It's an old Sicilian custom. She's just showing the neighborhood that you were a virgin. That's important to them. Little does she know what a vixen you turned out to be."

"Oh, you!" said Rachel, contentedly holding her husband's arm.

Rabbi Thorner had set up the Sheva Brachot choosing families most likely to help the young couple or just make them more comfortable. First on his list was Charles Schor who had witnessed Rachel's marriage deed.

The Schor family lived on the Hudson Boulevard near Lincoln Park and it took a streetcar and a bus to get there.

Their home was large, well furnished and comfortable. A maid served the dinner. Charles and his wife; their three children, Stanford, Allan and Anita; his parents, Sam and Fanny; and his in-laws, Morris and Sarah Rubenstein formed the core of the guests.

The dinner conversation was lively. Sam Schor spoke fluent and colorful Yiddish to Rachel's delight and the two little boys simply would not leave Abie's side. He was the first war hero they had actually met.

"How many Germans did you kill to get that medal, Mr. Abie?" asked Sanford.

"I'm going to kill lots of Germans when I grow up," said his younger brother who, indeed, would.

Abie, like most combat veterans, was reluctant to get into the details of his derring-do. He preferred to tell funny stories about his time in basic training or in France, usually with himself as the butt of the joke. That diverted the boys and entertained the adults.

Charles Schor was unable to get more than a moment alone with Abie and he wanted a lot more.

As the evening was ending, he asked Abie, "Can you get away tomorrow morning?"

"Yes. After breakfast. Why?"

"I want to talk about the law with you. I don't have to be in court. So we would have plenty of time. Say around nine?" He handed Abie a business card.

"Sure," said Abie. "That would be fun."

Rachel arranged to go off with Peggy to buy some needed items for the apartment.

Abie walked straight up Newark Avenue. He saw the great Roman-style county courthouse on the corner and found Schor's office midway up the block, on the other side of the street. The sign on the door read, "Charles Schor, Esq." And on the line below, "Counselor-at-Law.

Abie sighed and thought of what could have been.

He walked in and was greeted by a woman in her early thirties typing at her desk. "Counselor Schor is expecting you, Mr. Ashansky. This way please."

Schor rose to greet him and waved him into a comfortable chair in front of a large desk. Schor pulled up a chair beside him. "What do you know about contracts?"

"Ha! Contracts!" said Abie, eyes sparking as he retrieved knowledge gained years earlier. Their conversation went on all morning. Wills. Torts. Corporate Law. Rules of Evidence. Property law. Civil procedures. Criminal law.

Abie was thoroughly enjoying himself, learning the differences between the Russian and American legal systems as they spoke. Periodically, the secretary brought them coffee and removed the old cups.

At noon, Schor said, "I don't know about you but I've got to use the men's room. Then let's go to lunch."

They were seated in a crowded lunchroom next to the bail bondsman's office. They were munching sandwiches. No one paid attention to them.

"Well, Abie, I don't think you could pass the bar exam today," said Schor. "But you'll sure be ready in three years."

"I'm sorry, Counselor. But I really don't know what you are talking about."

Schor smiled, "The rabbi told me. You told me. You studied law in the Ukraine. Don't you want to be a lawyer, Abie?"

Abie dropped his sandwich onto his plate. "Sure. But that's impossible, isn't it? I don't have my diploma from the university and it looks like I am never going to be able to get it. I can never be a lawyer here."

"Who says so?" asked Schor. "That's not the way it works here in America. Not in New Jersey. You want to be a lawyer here? You clerk with a lawyer for three years and then you pass the bar examination. That's it."

"You don't need a diploma?"

"No. But if you have one, the bar association might knock off some time you have put in as a clerk."

Abie was flabbergasted. He knew his future was changing as the words registered.

"Did you go to law school, counselor?"

"I did. My mother wanted me to go to college so I enrolled in the first class at the New Jersey Law School in Newark. Two years. Then I clerked with Harry Rosenberg—a great lawyer. He's dead now. But still it took me nearly another year to master what I had to know."

"Why is it that I never heard of this until now?" Abie asked. The question was more for himself than Schor.

"Probably because you never talked to an American lawyer before. Well, do you want to be a lawyer?"

"Yes, sir," said Abie.

"Can you type?"

"Yes'

"Can you take shorthand?"

"No."

"Too bad," said Schor. "Okay. My secretary has given me her notice. Her husband is coming home. He's in the National Guard. An officer.

"I'll pay you what she was getting, twenty-eight dollars a week. Once you begin to be useful, I'll raise your pay. I won't cheat you. With any luck, you'll be my partner in a few years."

That was less than Abie made as a lieutenant in the Army but just enough to live on. He and Rachel could get by on it and their future would be bright. *What a country!*

"So what do you say, Abie?"

"I say, 'yes, sir,' with great gratitude and I promise that I won't disappoint you.

"Yeah. Yeah. Okay. Let's get back to the office."

Schor sat down behind the big desk. Abie sat in front of him.

Okay. He's the boss now, thought Abie.

Schor spoke. "You speak English very well but how well do you read it? Do you truly understand what the words mean or do you do a lot of guessing?"

"I think I read English even better than I speak," said Abie. "Certainly, my reading vocabulary is larger than my spoken vocabulary. But there are words that I'm not sure how to pronounce since I have never heard them spoken."

"For instance?"

"Archipelago." Abie pronounced it archy-pell-ah-go.

"Archipelago," said the lawyer pronouncing it arc-a-pell-ago.

"Thank you," said Abie.

"But how do you know you really understand written English? It's a tough language."

Abie answered. "You know, all educated Russians can speak French. I am fluent in it. When I was learning English I realized that my French would be a great help in understanding the English the Normans created. I tended to use those Latin-rooted words while I learned the Anglo-Saxon words one at a time.

"When I read novels, I picked English translations of French and Russian novels that I had already read. I knew where the plots were headed and that helped my comprehension a lot."

"Clever little devil, aren't you?" said Schor. "Do you have a briefcase?"

"No, sir."

Schor got up and rummaged in a small closet emerging with a somewhat battered brown briefcase. "Here is one you can use. My wife got me a new one for my birthday. Said I looked like some waterfront shyster."

I'll settle for that. "Thank you, Counselor."

Schor turned to the bookcases that filled the wall behind his desk. He took down four volumes and stacked them on the desk.

He pointed to the books. "American law is based on English

common law," he said, "and the best authority on that is Blackstone. William Blackstone. He wrote these books more than 150 years ago but you will find our Supreme Court quoting them to this very day.

"Take them home and study them. Read them thoroughly and you will understand the roots of American law. Pay particular attention to his commentaries."

Abie looked at the titles as he put them into his briefcase: "The Rights of Persons"; "The Rights of Things"; "Public Wrongs" and "Private Wrongs." He would often read far into the night mastering Blackstone.

Schor handed him a box of business cards. Abie put it in his briefcase.

"You give these out to everybody you know. My business— our business— depends on contacts. When somebody suddenly needs a lawyer, I want them to think of us. I'll have new cards made up listing you as the law clerk.

"Now, do you belong to any organizations, Abie?"

"Yes. I just joined the John J. Lynch Association."

"Great. I saw Fat Jack at your reception and Mayor Hague too. And all those policemen. Those kinds of contacts are invaluable to a lawyer. I'm in the Elks, myself.

"I see that a veterans' organization was formed a few months ago—the American Legion or something like that. You should join as soon as they have something locally. I think it is going to be as important as the G.A.R. was."

"The G.A.R.?"

"Grand Army of the Republic. Union veterans of the Civil War. They dominated politics in America for more than a generation. They're dying out now, of course."

"I'll join the American Legion," said Abie.

"Okay. That's about it."

Abie asked, "When do you want me to start, Mr. Schor?"

"I don't want to push you, Abie, but if you could be in next

Monday, Monica could show you the filing system, the calendar. You know, things like that before she leaves for good on Friday."

"Monday, it is, sir."

"Good," said the lawyer rising to shake hands.

"Another thing. When we're in the office, it's 'Charlie.' Sir, Mister and Counselor are for when we have company or we're in court."

"Okay, Charlie. You have thanks, my wife's thanks and when I have them, my children's thanks."

Abie was absolutely buoyant as he walked out of the office, briefcase in hand. He felt like a lawyer already.

He instinctively jaywalked across the street and walked past the courthouse. Several men, obviously attorneys, nodded to Abie as if they knew him but not well enough to speak to. He nodded back. Professional courtesy.

Abie walked on, his feet barely touching the ground. He took the streetcar down Newark Avenue. He wanted to get home as quickly as he could.

Rachel was sitting at the kitchen table snapping peas into a bowl.

Without preamble, Abie blurted out. "I'm going to be a lawyer!"

Rachel turned to him, trying to take it in. Abie said, "I start work as a law clerk on Monday and I'll be a lawyer in three years. Maybe even sooner."

Rachel jumped up and hugged him. "Oh, my sweet! My love, how wonderful! How did this happen?"

"Mr. Schor," said Abie.

"You mean our Mr. Schor?" Rachel asked.

"Yes," said Abie who happily related everything that had occurred after the lawyer asked if he had anything to do on Monday.

"I can't believe it," said Rachel. "I am so happy."

Then she started crying. Abie was mystified.

"Oh, how I wish my parents and yours could be here to share our happiness. How proud of you they all would be. Your sisters and brothers and my other brother too. Everybody."

Abie understood. They sat down and he held his wife's hand.

"Yes. It is a happy day but you're right, it's a sad day too. I think of my mother often. Sometimes it's as if she was dead. I know that I probably won't ever see her again. How hard it is to leave everything and everyone behind."

"That's exactly how I feel," said Rachel. "I miss my family. I miss Kiev. Yes, we are going to live a good life here in America but we have to pay a terrible price."

"True," said Abie. "But everybody that came to America—for hundreds of years—has paid the same price. Maybe, it's what makes us strong. We know there is no going back."

Rachel dried her eyes with a handkerchief. She had a sad smile on her face, "There is no going back. But maybe someday, we can send letters back and forth. Maybe we can send for my brother."

"Of course," said Abie who didn't believe that either would ever happen.

Abie kissed his wife and stroked her hair. "Let's go upstairs and tell the good news to the Aiellos."

Carmella, Peggy and the girls were scurrying around the kitchen getting ready to put supper on the table.

Antonio, Tony and Sam sat at the kitchen table.

"You just in time. Sit down," said Carmella. There would be plenty for all. She believed that if you didn't have leftovers you didn't cook enough food.

"No, no, Mume, we have to eat out tonight," said Rachel. "We just wanted to share the good news."

All looked at her expectantly but it was Abie who spoke, "I got a job as a law clerk. I'm going to be a lawyer in three years."

Their joy burst like a bomb. The men leaped up shaking his hand, patting his back, hugging him. The women were kissing and hugging Rachel. Everyone was talking at once.

"I knew it," said Carmella. "I knew you would be successful. Everyone in my family is successful."

"Except me," said Theresa who now had seven years on the line at the Dixon Pencil Company.

"Someday, you get married. That's successful," said Carmella.

Tony said, "Congratulations, brother. I'll tell every criminal I arrest to hire you or else."

"Suppose I get them off?" asked Abie.

"No problem," said Tony. "I'll arrest them again. More work for you."

Abie Ashansky started work as a legal clerk for Charles Schor on September 15. Monica showed him her filing system which was easy to understand. Then they went over a number of standard forms which, again, were easy to master.

Finally, she said, "Now let me show you how we handle money."

She produced a large ledger. "You're familiar with double-entry bookkeeping, I take it."

"Of course," lied Abie who figured he had until Monday to figure out what it was and how to use it.

Schor looked in on them. "How's it going, Monica?"

"Fine, Counselor. Mr. Ashansky is a fast learner. I think he has picked up in just hours what it took me weeks to understand."

"Great," said Schor.

When the work day was done, Abie headed straight down to the Main Public Library on Jersey Avenue which was, thankfully, still open. He checked out a book on double-entry bookkeeping and it came up in conversation at the Sunday dinner at the Aiellos.

"I had a bookkeeping class in high school," said Peggy. "All you have to remember is that the debits go on the left and the credits go on the right."

Abie held his thumb and forefinger an inch apart. "How come the book is this thick?"

"Padding," said Peggy.

Sam Zeidman started work as a helper at Al Smith's Moving Company on Bowers Street in the Heights. Abie had used his clout.

Al, at the end of the day, asked his driver," How'd the new guy do?"

"Okay, I guess. He's strong enough. He's not afraid of work. His English ain't that great but he knows enough to take orders. He's polite with the customers.

"But I still don't see why you hired that sheeny, Boss. There's lots of micks who need work. Vets too."

"What could I do?" asked Al Smith, a practical businessman. "Fat Jack Lynch's kid brother comes and asks me for a favor. I couldn't say no. Besides Sam fought in the war too."

"Yeah? On whose side?"

Boxed In

Emory Jackson was a malcontent but he learned early in life not to show it.

He thought his mother loved him but he knew she didn't like him much. She complained that he was a "colicky" baby, far more trouble than his brothers and sisters.

Emory remembered that if he cried about anything other than a visible injury, she would say, "I'll give you something to cry about." A sharp smack would follow.

So Emory Jackson learned not to complain out loud. Bad things would happen to him but he would not say a word. Instead, he'd smile slightly and plan to get even.

Young Emory was caught up in the turmoil of the Paterson Silk Strike in 1913. He listened to all the great Wobblies — "Big Bill" Hayward, Elizabeth Gurley Flynn, Carlo Tesca and was unimpressed. The strike collapsed and the IWW left town.

All talk and no action. Emory was more impressed by Luigi Galleani, the Italian anarchist leader who had been shot in the face during an earlier silk workers strike.

Galleani preached the "propaganda of the deed." No talk, all action. That made sense to Emory. He considered himself a Galleanist even though he wasn't Italian.

After the strike was broken, he bounced around America finding work where he could. Picking crops, working in factories, unloading freight cars, working on a barge. Nothing satisfied him.

Inevitably, some boss, supervisor or foreman would offend him and Emory would move on without complaint. Sometimes, they didn't even know he was gone.

Certainly they never connected him with the fires that would break out just after he left. Emory had learned that kerosene and matches were the best tools for revenge.

Then came the war.

Emory didn't like the idea of serving his capitalist masters but he wasn't willing to go to jail as a draft-dodger. He hoped he was too short at five foot two inches to be inducted.

"You're fine," said the doctor. "You cleared the minimum height by a full inch and at 120 pounds, you're a solid featherweight."

"Lucky me," said Emory.

Emory did his basic training at Fort Dix and he expected to be sent overseas. But the Army ordered him to permanent duty in supply at Camp Merrill, less than twenty miles from his hometown in Clifton.

For months, he helped an amiable old supply sergeant hand out clothing and equipment to thousands of men headed for France.

That's how he got the Mark I trench knife.

This new model was produced too late to be issued to troops going to war. The Armistice had been signed. There were crates of them piled high in warehouses.

It is axiomatic in every army that the men in supply will be equipped with the best of everything long before anything ever reaches the front lines.

The supply sergeant took a trench knife for himself and gave one to Emory. "It's a beauty, isn't it?"

The blued, double-edged, steel blade was almost seven inches long but it was the handle that captured one's attention. A set of brass knuckles curved around it. A small spike stuck out from each knuckle.

A prudent man would flee just from the sight of that knife.

Emory gripped his and held in before his eyes for a closer look.

This is mine. I'll never be picked on again. He put the trench knife in its scabbard and said, "Thank you, Sergeant." Emory rarely thanked anyone for anything.

The Army cut him loose in September giving him sixty dollars' mustering out pay. He went home and packed a suitcase with civilian clothes and hung up his uniform for good.

"Where you going now?" asked his mother, not really interested.

"There's a strike going on down in Jersey City. I think I'll go down there and nose around."

In his room in a West Side Avenue boardinghouse, Emory donned on old set of his father's bib overalls. His father was a much bigger man so Emory rolled the cuffs up a full six inches.

He put the overalls on over his trousers. They were baggy on him but they concealed the trench knife on his pants belt.

Emory found he could draw the knife easier by placing it on his right side even though he was left-handed. The knife cut the air in a smooth arc. He repeated the motion many times.

The union at Ryerson was relatively weak but it walked out with the rest of the nation's steelworkers. Many of the skilled men crossed the picket line and the company hired black strikebreakers to do the less demanding work.

The Jersey City policemen at the scene were sympathetic to the strikers. They knew many and were related to some. But they were determined there would be no trouble.

The sergeant in charge of the detail talked to the picket captain. "Now, Ted, here are the ground rules. You can make all the noise you like. You can call those scabs all the names in the book but you can't touch them. You can picket and harass them but you can't stop them from going into the plant and you can't stop any trucks, wagons or trains making deliveries. You understand?"

"Jesus Christ, Bob, if we can't do anything to stop them, how the hell are we going to make the bosses give in?"

"Ted. You know I have my orders. You know where they come from. Don't make us break your heads. You know we will.

Let them win or lose the strike somewhere else. You and I know that Ryerson doesn't mean shit. Go through the motions."

The picket captain said, "You're right, Bob. I'll keep my people in line. That way we'll all go home to our families at night. But I'll tell you this; we're going to make a hell of a lot of noise."

The sergeant looked around at the empty meadowlands. "Go ahead. There isn't anyone around to annoy."

Early each morning, surplus Army trucks slowly cruised the black neighborhoods of Jersey City. Canvas signs on their sides asked, "Need Work? $5 a day. Paid daily."

Black men clutching lunch pails climbed aboard. They would nod to each other but there was little talk as they headed for Ryerson's. Jobs were hard to find now. Work was work.

They were greeted by a cacophony of curses when they slowed to enter the plant. Strikers on both sides of the road cried out, "Nigger bastards!" "Scabs!" "Cocksuckers!" "We'll get you for this, Sambo!" and other, more imaginative, epithets.

One striker tried to tear the sign from the truck as it inched by. A cop stopped him, "None of that. Keep your hands to yourself."

"Jesus, Bob, they're paying those black sons-of-bitches the same as us. We'll never get our jobs back!"

"Just behave yourself."

The strikebreakers inside the trucks could hear the curses but they couldn't see the men making them. The canvas sides blocked their vision. Only the men in the last couple of seats could see their tormentors. They said nothing. One of them was named George Williams.

Lieutenant McGurk reported to Mayor Hague. "There probably won't be much trouble at Ryerson's, Uncle Frank. The union guys are all local. Not a radical in the bunch." He was wrong.

The pickets stood around a steel barrel filled with burning scrap wood though the temperatures were still warm in late

September. They expected a long strike.

Emory joined them and enjoyed the hooting, hollering and cursing as the strikebreakers' trucks rolled through.

No one asked Emory if he worked at Ryerson Steel. Each assumed that he worked in a different department.

A week later, the picket captain said, "I'm tired of this 'behave yourselves' shit. We're not getting anywhere. We have to do something. Something that won't bring the cops down on us."

That's my specialty, thought Emory. *The propaganda of the deed.* He said nothing.

Emory didn't show up at the barrel the next morning. Unseen, he made his way through the spongy meadows on the far side of the plant where the railroad siding was. He easily scaled the chain-link fence with its three strands of barbed wire. The trick was to climb where sections of the fence met at a right angle. You could slip through the gap in the barbed wire.

He had a pint whiskey bottle filled with kerosene in his back pocket and a batch of kitchen matches in the chest pocket of his bib overalls.

Crouching behind a cable spool near the fence, Emory looked around for something to burn.

He eyed the freight cars at the loading dock. *I'll bet there is something there that'll burn.*

Minutes before, the foreman questioned George Williams.

"Hey, Rufus, where'd you work yesterday?"

"My name is George."

"Whatever. Where'd you work?"

"Right here in the warehouse, Mr. Foreman. I was here all day cleaning and sweeping."

"Well, there's no soft job like that for you today, boy. I got a boxcar that has to be emptied this morning. Mostly boxes, some carboys of chemicals."

He pointed to the far wall. "Stack the boxes over there with the others. Put the carboys next to them and don't you dare break one. It'd be your ass."

"I won't." said George Williams who added, "Sir."

"That's the boy," said the foreman, slapping him on the back. "There's a hand truck on the loading dock you can use. The door to the boxcar is open."

"Is anybody going to help me...sir?"

"You don't need no help. A big strapping buck like you. Half that car was emptied yesterday. Now get to it."

Williams was six feet three inches tall and weighed more than two hundred pounds.

He, his wife and his two small children had come north from the Mississippi Delta in search of a better life. He was the son of a sharecropper who had too many sons.

Williams found work that paid well and they lived in a house that by most standards was a slum but it was better than anything he or she had ever lived in. It had an indoor toilet and a deep sink in the kitchen that the kids used as a bathtub.

That good life ended when the war ended. Soldiers were demobilized almost at random and came home looking for their old jobs.

His foreman had said, "I'm sorry, George. I really am. You're a good worker but I have to let you go." The returning soldier was his wife's cousin.

Strikebreaking was all the work Williams could find. He didn't like it but he was determined to keep food on the table.

So he told the foreman at Ryerson's, "I'm on my way, boss."

Emory was already inside the boxcar, the uncorked whiskey bottle in his hand, when Williams walked in.

It took a second or two for Williams to assess what he was seeing. "Excuse me? I got to unload these boxes."

Heart racing, Emory turned towards him and calmly said, "So, unload."

Williams thought, *Something's wrong here. I seen that little ofay on the picket line. He's a striker.* He said, "What's that funny smell?"

"That's none of your business, boy."

Williams looked down on the little man in front of him and said, "Don't call me that."

Emory felt an onrush of familiar fear which produced a burst of adrenaline.

"Oh, no? Did I offend you?"

Williams stood there with his hands on his hips. *I've had enough of this shit.*

"Let me call you by your real name," Emory said softly. He dropped the bottle which shattered.

Then he yelled, *"Scab!"* and in a practiced motion pulled his trench knife from its scabbard underneath the bib overalls.

As it arced from right to left, the brass knuckles hit Williams on the left side of his chin, piercing his skin and breaking his jaw. As Williams staggered back, Emory plunged the blade upwards and in just below the sternum.

The man dropped and was dead in seconds but not before splattering blood on Emory's overalls.

Emory straddled the black man's body pumping his trench knife in triumph. "Now who's the big man? Tell me that, Mister Scab!" He laughed. Then exhilaration gave way to fear.

The little man had not survived this long by being stupid. He realized that he had to get out of that boxcar, out of Ryerson's and out of Jersey City. It wouldn't be long before someone came looking for the dead man.

He peered out of the boxcar. No one else was on the loading dock. He walked at the normal pace to the end, still holding the trench knife in his left hand, and jumped down. Emory walked just a bit faster towards the fence. It wouldn't do to run. That might draw attention.

Emory didn't know it but someone saw him, the foreman

who came out to open another boxcar door. Seeing Emory, he thought, *I wonder where that guy is going. Probably to take a piss.*

He didn't see Emory climb the fence and crouch down to look around. No one was in sight. Emory was very frightened. *I just killed a man. They'll hang me if they catch me. I've got to get out of here.*

He took off the bloody coveralls and dropped them in a pile. Emory removed the sheath from his belt and encased the knife. He put it inside his khaki shirt. Some blood had seeped through the overalls and stained the shirt. But it just looked like he had spilled something on it, maybe fruit juice.

Emory walked down the road away from Ryerson's, never looking back. It was less than a mile to his boardinghouse.

He quietly climbed the stairs, used his key to open the door to his room, changed his shirt and packed his suitcase with the trench knife inside. He shut the door to his room.

As he put the room key on a hall table downstairs, his landlady emerged from the kitchen. "Oh! Mr. Jackson," she said looking at his suitcase.

"Mrs. Kierce, I'm glad I caught you," said Emory. "I have to leave. There's been a death in the family."

"I'm sorry for your troubles, Mr. Jackson. I'm sorry. I know you have three days left on your rent but I don't give refunds."

"I understand. Now if you will excuse me, I have to go. Goodbye, Mrs. Kierce."

"Goodbye, Mr. Jackson."

It wouldn't be easy for Emory to get from Jersey City to Clifton. It was only about thirty miles away but it would take several hours.

No one took notice of him. Just an ordinary little man carrying a suitcase.

Emory was about an hour into his journey when the foreman at Ryerson's noticed that the pile of boxes on the far wall didn't seem to be getting any bigger.

He walked out onto the loading dock and saw the empty hand truck.

That lazy son-of-a-bitch. I'll bet he's sleeping in there. Ready to fire the black strikebreaker on the spot, the foreman stepped into the boxcar.

Oh, shit.

The sergeant in charge of monitoring the pickets was on the scene in less than a minute. He saw the body. He saw the broken whiskey bottle, its contents long since absorbed into the rough boxcar floor, and came to a quick conclusion.

He turned to the patrolman with him. "Okay, don't let anybody into this boxcar. I'll go to a call box and report this. They'll send somebody down to handle it. It's not our job."

"Right, Sarge."

Lieutenant McGurk and his two-man Bomb Squad were in his closet of an office when a desk sergeant stuck his head in.

"Hey, Lieutenant, you said to let you know if anything was going on at Ryerson's. Just got a report that some guy was killed down there this morning."

"On the picket line?"

"No. The sergeant that called it in said that it had nothing to do with the strike. Just a couple of black boys fighting over a bottle of whiskey."

"Thanks," said Mickey McGurk.

He looked at young Vince Crehan, the new third man of the Bomb Squad, who was as alert and eager as a puppy waiting for someone to throw him a ball.

"This looks pretty routine," said McGurk. "It's a nice chance for you to break in, Vince. Go on down there and play detective. Interview whoever found the body. Pick up and bag the weapon if it's on the scene and any other evidence you find. Follow your nose. Find out what happened. Make the arrest if you can. There's lots of uniforms there to help you if you need it.

"Don't worry. It's hard to screw up a killing like this. It's routine. The only difference I can see is that this one didn't happen on a Saturday night.

"Take the car," said Tony Aiello. "If we need transportation we can bum a ride from someone."

"Thanks, Sergeant."

Crehan was very happy when he pulled in next to the other police cars at Ryerson's. *It's like I'm a real detective*, he thought. He tried to look blasé as he walked up to the sergeant in charge.

"Crehan—Bomb Squad," he said.

"I don't know why they are bothering you people," said the sergeant. "Seems cut and dried to me. One shine shanked another shine."

Crehan examined the body while the sergeant looked on from the boxcar door.

"When I'm done here," said Crehan," we've got to call the coroner to pick up the body. This is obviously a homicide. There will have to be an autopsy."

"Even for a nigger?" asked the sergeant.

"Yep," said Crehan who then carefully put the shards of the whiskey bottle into a paper bag and marked the time and date on it. He didn't smell any whisky. He looked around the boxcar very closely and saw nothing else.

"Secure the scene, Sergeant, while I go talk to that foreman who found the body."

"Right, Detective," said the sergeant thrilling Crehan, who was merely a 'plainclothesman,' right down to his toes.

The foreman was anxious to help but he knew little.

"What was the dead man's name?" Crehan asked.

"George," said the foreman.

"George what?"

"I don't know," said the foreman. "But one of those darkies should know. They hang out together at lunchtime."

236

The foreman said he had neither seen nor heard anything unusual after the strikebreaker had left him.

"You didn't see anyone outside on the dock before you found the body?" Crehan asked.

"No. Not on the dock. Wait. Just before. I did see a guy walking towards the fence. I think he was going to take a leak."

"Who was it?"

"I don't know," said the foreman.

Crehan asked, "What did he look like?"

"I don't know, really. White. Short. Brown hair. Tan shirt. Carrying something in his hand. Wearing bib overalls, I think," said the foreman.

"Would you know him if you saw him again?"

"Nah. He was facing away from me and he was a good ways off. I didn't pay no mind to him. I was pissed at that nigger. Poor bastard."

Crehan walked towards that back fence and noticed something just outside where the sections met."

He scaled the fence, bent down and slowly unraveled a pair of bloody bib overalls.

The killer dumped these. A white guy, thought Crehan as he placed them in a large paper bag. *I'm in over my head. I've got to call the big boys.*

McGurk and Aiello arrived within minutes. McGurk split up the chores. "Vince, you talk to the people on the picket line. See if you can get a lead. Tony you go inside and talk to the strikebreakers. I'll talk to the foreman again and see if I can wring more out of him. Then I'll talk to the superintendent. I'm sure Ryerson's is making its own investigation. The company police might have something."

Tony learned George Williams' name and address and found a man who was working in another boxcar who thought he heard someone shout "Scab."

"Weren't you curious why someone would yell 'Scab' inside

the plant? Why didn't you go check it out?"

The black man sighed. "Mr. Detective, I'm a black man living in a white man's world. I've got enough trouble without looking for more."

None of the other black strikebreakers heard or saw anything. Many of them believed that story about a fight over a whiskey bottle.

Mickey interviewed the foreman at length and was convinced that he couldn't coax any more details out of him because there weren't any to be had.

Maybe I'll have better luck with his boss. He didn't.

Mickey received a cordial welcome from the superintendent. "We're very grateful the police are keeping that rabble in line. Now, what can I do for you, Lieutenant?"

"Well, I presume your company police are making an investigation into the killing and they may have come across something that we haven't. So as a courtesy, I thought I'd check with you before I talk to your security people."

The smile faded from the superintendent's face. "I'm glad you did, Lieutenant. I'll save you the trouble. There is no internal investigation, nor will there be any. George Williams was not an employee of ours."

"What? I don't understand. He was killed working in one of your boxcars."

"That's true and that's why you are here," said the superintendent. "But George Williams did not work for us. He was an independent contractor working for himself. We take no responsibility for him. He worked here at his own risk."

You bastards. He does your dirty work for you and you're not going to give his widow a fucking dime. Bastards.

"I see. Could I see that contract, sir?" asked McGurk.

"It was a verbal contract," said the superintendent, well coached by a company lawyer.

Vince Crehan was by the burn barrel talking to the men. "Say, has anybody seen a really short guy with brown hair? Wears bib overalls. I don't know his name but I owe him a quarter and I want to pay him back."

One man answered, "That sound like Em."

"M? What kind of name is M?" asked Crehan.

"Part of a first name he doesn't like. You know, a fancy name your mother hangs on you."

"Oh. Em— e-m."

"You got it, bud. I haven't seen him in a couple of days though."

"What department does he work in?" asked Crehan. No one knew. Neither did accounting when McGurk asked. No one on Ryerson's payroll had a first name that began with E-M.

"Okay," said McGurk." We're making progress. We know the guy we are looking for is nicknamed Em. His first name could be Emmet, or Emory or Emerson. Something like that. We know he's white, he's short, has brown hair, he wears bib overalls and he doesn't work for Ryerson's but he's been on the picket line. And he hasn't been seen there for two days. Not since the murder.

"We need to find out where he has been living. The odds are that he's walking to that picket line in the morning.

"Ryerson's is pretty isolated so he might be staying somewhere on West Side Avenue.

"Tony, you head north, Vince you go south. Check every rooming house within a half-mile or so."

"How will we know which houses are rooming houses?" asked Crehan.

"They'll usually have a sign in the window. Either 'Room for Rent' or 'No Vacancy.'"

Crehan felt stupid but merely said, "Thank you, sir."

Frank Hague was not pleased. Young Fred Martin and a black clergyman had showed up at his office without an appointment.

Intuitively, Hague knew he couldn't tell his secretary to inform them that he was unavailable. Martin was not part of the Hague organization but they had an understanding and the entrepreneur had delivered several hundred black votes to help elect Hague two years earlier.

It was an alliance to be nourished. *If I can do him a favor, I will.* "Show them in, Alice."

Hague rose to greet them, "Mr. Martin. It's always a pleasure to see one of our city's brightest businessmen." They shook hands.

"Good morning, Mr. Mayor. I apologize for barging in on you without an appointment. I know how valuable your time is but this is something that demands immediate action."

Hague was instantly on guard but said only, "Oh?"

"Yes, sir. Before I explain, may I introduce you to the Reverend Elijah Stiles? This concerns him too." Hague and the minister exchanged greeting and handshakes.

"Now, Fred, what is this about?" asked Hague.

"Murder. One of Pastor Elijah's congregation was murdered yesterday. At Ryerson's Steel."

Oh, shit. A fucking strikebreaker.

Hague was extraordinarily quick on his feet and was a nimble liar.

"I know," he said," I put my best detectives on the case."

Both black men looked relieved and Martin said, "We are very glad to hear that, Mr. Mayor. We were afraid this murder was going to be neglected. Just one Negro killing another over a bottle of whiskey. That's what people are saying."

"Well, they're wrong," said Hague. "My police department is here to protect all the people of Jersey City." That would be news to the numerous black people who were stopped, frisked, clubbed and arrested while the rest of their community was generally ignored by the cops.

Frank Hague never let a political opportunity go by. "What about Mr. Williams' widow. How is that poor woman doing?"

The pastor answered, "Not too well. You expect your husband to come home from work. Work he didn't want to do, I might add.

"Things up North were better for them. She has a few dollars put aside. But now she has to make a terrible choice. Either she pays for her husband's funeral or she and her children head back to Mississippi where she has people. She can't afford both.

"My congregation is as poor as she is, so we can't help much," said Pastor Stiles.

Hague smiled. "Maybe I can help. Of course, the city can't give her anything. That would be against the law. But my organization—the Democratic Party—can. Let me send a bright young man, Terry Lynch, over to meet with you and the widow."

"That would be most generous of you, Mr. Hague. My community, my congregation and I are most grateful."

Martin interjected, "You know most Negroes are Republicans, don't you Mr. Mayor?"

"So I've heard. But they are a hardhearted bunch, those Republicans. I don't think they would help Mrs. Williams much."

The pastor got the message as Martin knew he would. Hague just did you a favor but he'll be around on Election Day to collect.

After his guests had left, Hague told his secretary, "Alice, get me Mickey McGurk on the telephone now."

He was barely back at his desk and staring at the phone when his secretary looked in.

"Mr. Hague, the chief of police says Lieutenant McGurk is at Ryerson Steel. Apparently there's been a killing down there. Do you want the chief to get him?"

"No. I don't want to interfere with McGurk's investigation. Just have him call me when he is done for the day. Thanks, Alice."

Hague was well pleased. You knew your organization was running smoothly when your people knew what you needed before you did.

The Chase

"Yes?" asked the landlady.

"I'm Detective Sergeant Aiello. I'm looking for a man who calls himself 'Em.' I wonder if he could be a tenant of yours?"

"No, I don't have a tenant named M."

"No? Let me describe him. He's very short." Tony held his hand up to the level of his chin. "Brown hair and he likes to wear bib overalls to work. The legs are rolled up about six inches."

The landlady thought for a moment, "You know that sounds like Mr. Jackson. But he's gone. He left two days ago. Had a death in the family. Too bad though, his rent was paid through the end of the week."

"Do you know where Mr. Jackson went?"

"No."

"Do you know where he came from?" Tony asked.

"Could be on the register," said Mrs. Kierce. "Do you want to look at it?

"Absolutely."

He signed himself "E. Jackson" and gave "Tenafly, NJ," as his previous address.

Tony said, "There's no street address."

"Look, Sergeant, this ain't the Waldorf Astoria. All I ask for is a week's rent in advance."

The Bomb Squad was discussing how to take the investigation to Tenafly when the coroner brought his report to McGurk in person.

"Hello, Doc. It's a bit of surprise to see you here," said McGurk, who took the report from him.

"Read the report first, Mickey. Then I want to discuss a few details that might help you out."

Mickey read and then looked up from the report. "Seems pretty routine, Doc. Williams had a fight with somebody who stabbed him to death."

"Looks that way but there are several things that intrigue me. Sure, the victim's jaw was broken but I don't think there was a fight. There was no mark on his knuckles and there usually is in a fight. I think he was sucker punched—with brass knuckles."

"What?"

"The brass knuckles apparently had little spikes on them. Two of them made punctures on the left side of his chin."

"Yeah. I was going to ask about that. What else?"

"The knife he was killed with was double bladed and cut tissue on both sides before it split open his aorta. The angle of entry suggests that the victim was standing and his assailant may have been a foot shorter."

McGurk smiled. *Em Jackson.*

"There's more. But this is just conjecture. I think the brass knuckles were part of the knife. I think you have an unusual murder weapon. A trench knife."

Mickey was dubious. "Doesn't sound like a trench knife, Doc. The blade on a trench knife is triangular and is meant to puncture not to cut or slice."

"Oh, I see," said the pathologist.

Mickey thought for a moment and then said, "Wait a minute. I heard they designed a new trench knife. The old one wasn't much use. But the war ended before the new one could be issued to the troops."

The pathologist grinned, not humbly. "Very well. I am going to release the body now. To Terry Lynch, of all people."

When the coroner left, Mickey said, "I told you Mayor Hague was interested in this case. There's politics in there someplace."

"Where would our boy get a trench knife like that?" asked Aiello.

McGurk answered, "At an Army depot, obviously. But which one?"

"Say, isn't Camp Merritt, you know, that embarkation center, near Tenafly?" asked Tony.

"By God, Tony, I do believe you will be chief of detectives someday. Let's go."

The corporal on the main gate at Camp Merritt was helpful. "I have no idea where they keep the trench knives," he said. "But the regimental supply sergeant would know. He's in Building 231, second floor."

The regimental supply sergeant was a Southerner. "Y'all know this camp is closing down soon. Most of those boys playing soldier have been demobilized already. Their records are gone too."

"We know that, Sergeant," said Mickey. "We were hoping you could tell us who issued those new trench knifes."

"The Mark I? Nasty looking thing. Why do you want to know that, lieutenant? What kind of case are y'all working on?"

"A murder, sir."

"Don't call me 'sir,' I'm just a sergeant. Well, those knives were never issued. They are still in their packing cases. They'll be shipped somewhere else when we shut down."

McGurk was dejected. "So nobody got one of those knives."

"I didn't say that. I said they weren't issued." The regimental supply sergeant spent a few seconds scrutinizing McGurk.

"Were you in the military, Lieutenant?"

"I was. A sergeant, in the Marines."

"Did y'all ever know anybody in supply who lacked for anything? Let's see if I can find the paperwork on those knives." He took him about thirty seconds.

"Here we are. There were a hundred cases with fifty knives each sent to us. Aha! One case was lost in transit."

"What does that mean, Sergeant?"

"It means, Lieutenant, the supply boys helped themselves to fifty Mark I trench knifes."

McGurk quickly asked, "Is it possible that you would have

the names of the men who worked in supply, say from daily muster sheets going back to when you received those knives?"

The regimental supply sergeant smiled. "I do, Lieutenant. As y'all knew I would. What's the name of the fellow y'all are looking for?"

"E. Jackson, Sergeant." McGurk all but held his breath.

"Why here he is. Emory Jackson, working in the 2nd Battalion supply room."

"Has he been demobilized?"

"You betcha. Two weeks ago. There's nobody down there now but the supply sergeant. He's a regular waiting for orders reassigning him."

Sergeant Dobson, an older, overweight, cheerful man, was sitting in an easy chair, reading a newspaper, when McGurk and Aiello knocked on the doorframe of his small office. "Gentlemen. What can I do for you?"

"The regimental supply sergeant sent us down to see you. We're police officers from Jersey City. We're looking for a man you know."

"And who might that be?"

"Emory Jackson."

"Em? I'm afraid he's been demobilized. He ain't here. Besides, I can't imagine why the police would want to talk to that boy. Quiet as a mouse. Always a smile on his face."

"Did you give him a Mark I trench knife?"

Dobson popped up out of the easy chair and went to the door to look both ways in the corridor. "Did you talk to the regimental supply sergeant about this?"

"We did."

"Shoot. Ah, well. Yes, I gave him a knife and kept one for myself. I think everybody in the supply section got one," said Sergeant Dobson.

"Did he take it with him when he left?" said Aiello.

"Of course, he did. Great souvenir of the war. Why are you

looking for him anyway?"

McGurk said, "He's a suspect in a murder case. A man was killed with a Mark I trench knife."

"Oh my God! Em? Em did that?"

"We don't know. We've got to question him first. Do you know where he went?"

The sergeant said, "He was heading home. A town around here someplace. He went there every time he got a weekend pass. Cliff-something or other."

"Cliffside Park?" asked Aiello.

"No. Cliff-town. Something like that."

"Clifton?" asked McGurk.

"That's it!" said the sergeant. "But I don't have the address."

"Okay," said McGurk. "Describe him for us." Aiello took out his notebook and a pencil.

"Describe him? I can do better than that," said the sergeant pointing to a wall.

"That's his picture right there."

The photo showed Private Emory Jackson and his sergeant posing menacingly with Mark I trench knives.

Lieutenant Mickey McGurk made a telephone call to the chief of police in Clifton.

Emory Jackson slipped out the back door of his mother's house and made his way to the candy store where he would buy a newspaper searching for a story on the killing at Ryerson's. No story.

An old friend was there buying cigarettes. "Hey, Em! You're out of the Army."

"Yeah, Charlie. How are you doing?"

"Great," said his friend who then lowered his voice. "Say, Em, there was a copper at the pool hall last night asking about you. Wanted to know where you lived."

"Did you tell him?"

"Hell, no," said his friend. "I hate cops."

"Me too," said Em.

That's it. I've got to run. Now. That $35 I have isn't going to last long if I have to buy clothes too. I've got to go back for my suitcase. I've got to be careful. Real careful.

He made it back home unseen and went upstairs to grab his already packed suitcase.

His mother saw him on the way out. "Where you going?"

"I'm going to stay with a friend for a few days. He might be able to line me up with a job," said Emory.

"Good. I can't keep feeding you for free."

Emory slowly made his way to a streetcar stop where an interurban trolley would take him to Paterson and the Lackawanna Railroad Station. He stood in the hallway of a building where if he saw a policeman he could dash in and emerge out the back.

No cop appeared and Jackson disappeared from Clifton.

As Jackson headed for Paterson, the chief of police was talking to Lieutenant McGurk and Officer Crehan who had just arrived from Jersey City.

Pleased with himself, the chief said, "I've got an address for you. I'll take you there myself and if your boy is there I'll arrest him and you can haul him off to Jersey City."

"Good work, Chief," said McGurk. "Do you have the house staked out?"

The chief of police hadn't thought of that. "No. I didn't want to spook him."

"Good thinking, Chief," said McGurk. The chief was relieved. He was a bit intimidated by big city cops and he didn't want them to think him a rube.

They pulled up to the Jackson house in two automobiles. The chief told one of his men, "Go around back. He might run." He said it loud enough for McGurk to hear.

The chief knocked on the door and Emory's mother answered.

"Good morning, Mrs. Jackson. I'm the chief of police and I'd like to talk to your son, Emory."

Mrs. Jackson said, "Well, you just missed him. He's gone to stay with a friend."

"Where?" asked McGurk.

"I don't really know," said Mrs. Jackson. "Why do you want to talk to him anyway?"

"He may have seen something that happened in Jersey City," said McGurk.

"Could be. He was there last week. Anyway, he's gone. Sorry," said Mrs. Jackson as she moved to close the door. The chief stopped her.

"Do you mind if we have a look at his room?"

"I don't know why you'd want to do that. He's gone. But suit yourself. Upstairs, to the right," she said as she opened the door wider.

"Vince," said McGurk. Crehan went inside and up the stairs and was back in a few minutes.

"He's gone. Nothing there. Just a uniform hanging in the closet."

"I told you so," said Mrs. Jackson. "Emory's gone."

The policemen stood by their cars. "Where do we go from here?" asked the chief.

McGurk said, "Well, chief. Your people should keep looking for him here but I think he's on the run."

"Where?" asked Crehan.

"New York is my best guess," said McGurk. "I need to use a telephone, chief."

"There's one in my office."

McGurk left Aiello back at headquarters just in case. His instinct had been good.

"Tony? Our boy has flown the coop. I think he's headed for the city.

"Take a couple of uniforms and stake out the Lackawanna terminal in Hoboken. You'll need a Hoboken cop to make the arrest if he shows. I don't want any problems with jurisdiction.

"Tony, if he makes it to the city, I don't think we'll ever see him again."

Aiello said, "I'm on it, boss."

Emory Jackson saw no policemen outside the Paterson terminal so he went in but he didn't buy a ticket. He'd pay the conductor on the train. Harried commuters did this frequently.

Jackson concealed himself behind a steel post holding up the platform roof.

The train he wanted arrived less than a half hour later.

Emory Jackson paid the conductor and took a seat by the window where he could see the platforms of every station along the way to Hoboken.

McGurk showed a copy of Jackson's photo to the ticket agent in Paterson, "Did this guy buy a ticket this morning?"

"Weren't no soldiers buying tickets this morning," said the agent.

"He wouldn't have been in uniform," McGurk said.

"The answer is still 'no,' mister."

"That little son-of-a-bitch is always one step ahead of us," said McGurk showing a trace of temper.

"I still think he's headed for Hoboken. Nothing else makes sense."

The conductor called out, "Hoboken. Hoboken. Last stop. Hoboken." The train glided into the station.

Jackson spotted the policeman on the neighboring platform.

Shit. They're here, he thought.

There was a policeman on the other platform too. Jackson's options evaporated. *I've got to hide.* He made it to the tiny toilet at the end of the car, went in and latched the door.

Tony and a Hoboken cop flanked the gate through which all the passengers would pass. The commuters had to show a ticket stub to an agent there.

The line, as usual, backed up which gave the policemen time to look for a very short man. There were several but none looked like the photo of Jackson.

"We're going to search the train," said Aiello to the agent.

"Have at it, detective."

The first two cars were empty. In the third, Tony saw a suitcase on the overhead rack.

"He's here," he told the Hoboken policeman. "He's got a bad ass knife. Don't take any chances." Both men drew their pistols.

Seat by seat they slowly moved through the carriage. Tony pointed to the tiny toilet and tried the handle. It was locked.

"Jackson! We know you're in there. Come out with your hands up. Don't make us kill you." There was no answer.

"Emory, come out now. With your hands up. If you don't, I'm going to shoot through this door twice and then I'm going to break it down. I'll count to five. One...two..."

The latch slid back and the door opened. Jackson stood there with his hands held high.

"Come out slowly, Em. Keep those hands in the air or, by God, I'll shoot you between the eyes. Do it."

Jackson moved forward, saying nothing. Tony spun him around and handcuffed his hands behind his back. The Hoboken cop said, "Emory Jackson, you are under arrest for the murder of George Williams."

"I didn't murder nobody," said Jackson in a normal voice.

Tony searched him finding the trench knife on the inside of his right pants leg, the scabbard was inside his sock resting on the bottom of his shoe. It was tied to his leg by a shoelace.

"Looky, looky what have we here?" asked Tony. "A nasty pig sticker. Is this the knife you used to kill George Williams?"

"I didn't murder nobody," said Jackson.

Within a half hour, Jackson was being booked at headquarters.

Fingerprinted and photographed, he told the police his name and address but would say no more.

Tony had him in a little room awaiting the arrival of McGurk and Crehan.

"Make it easy on yourself, Em. Tell me what happened. Did that big, black guy come at you? What?"

Jackson said, "I told you. I didn't murder nobody. That's all I am going to say."

Tony tried several other approaches and failed. He got the same answer.

Finally he said, "I'll tell you one thing, Em. You are going to need a good lawyer. Here."

Jackson looked at the business card Tony had handed him: "Charles Schor, Counselor-at-Law" and beneath that "Abram Ashansky, Law Clerk," an address and a telephone number.

"Thank you, Detective." *They're Jews. They're always smart. I'm going to need a smart Jew lawyer.*

McGurk and Crehan arrived. "What did he say, Tony?"

"Absolutely nothing."

"Well, let me have a crack at him."

Jackson looked at McGurk with little interest.

"You might as well come clean, Emory. We've got witnesses. We've got your knife and we have your fingerprints. Do yourself a favor, tell us about it. Maybe they'll take the death penalty off the table."

Bullshit, thought Jackson. "I didn't murder nobody. That's all I have to say. I want to speak to my lawyer."

"Who's that?" asked McGurk.

"Charles Schor. Do you want his telephone number?"

McGurk looked at Aiello who looked away.

"Later."

Jackson was interrogated for twenty-four hours straight by shifts of detectives including one who was not very nice. Though he grew somewhat bruised, exhausted and hungry, the answer remained the same. "I didn't murder nobody."

The next day, McGurk said, "He's a tough bird. He's not going to talk. Feed him, let him sleep and then let him call his lawyer. Tony, a word please?"

"Sure, boss."

"Did you really give him Schor's card?"

Tony answered, "I did. Look, it's our job to identify him, gather evidence, track him down and arrest him. We did that. It's somebody else's job to try him and convict him. Jackson was going to get a lawyer anyway. Why not one we know? This way Abie gets to eat."

"Hmmm," said McGurk who knew when he was beaten. "Okay, but it our job to help convict him. Right?"

"Right, boss."

Getting Ready for Trial

Abie knew Tony had given Jackson the business card so the phone call came as no surprise. Schor said to him, "Come on. We're going down to police headquarters to meet a new client. He's charged with murder so this should give you a chance to prepare a case I can argue in court."

"So I'm the solicitor and you're the barrister like in England?" asked Abie.

"Might as well start now. Let's see if you can earn your keep."

McGurk greeted them. "Counselor. Abie."

"Lieutenant. What is my client charged with?" asked Schor.

"He was arrested on suspicion of murder. I understand the case is going before the Grand Jury but I don't know when. Do you want to see Jackson now?"

"I do. Thank you."

Emory Jackson was waiting for them in a small room with a table and four chairs. A policeman was watching him. Jackson was not handcuffed. The policeman left and shut the door.

"My name is Charles Schor. I'm an attorney. This is Abram Ashansky, my associate. I understand you wanted to talk to us?"

"Yes, sir," said Jackson. "I most certainly do. These people are accusing me of murder. I never murdered nobody and I want you to defend me."

It was self-defense. That big nigger could have killed me. But I'm not going to tell you that.

"Indeed. Well, let's all sit down and talk." Schor and Ashansky sat on one side of the table, Jackson on the other.

"First thing, Mr. Jackson, the law presumes you are innocent until you are proven guilty. We too will make that presumption."

"Damn straight," said Jackson.

Schor gestured with his hand and said, "Mr. Ashansky."

Ashansky looked at a sheet of paper. "Now let's see. You are accused of killing a George Williams in a boxcar at Ryerson's Steel. Did you know Mr. Williams?"

"I did not."

"Did you work at Ryerson's?"

"I did not."

"Were you at Ryerson's on the day of the murder?"

"When was that?" Jackson asked. Ashansky told him. "I wasn't there that day. I packed up and went home to Clifton."

"But you had been there before. What were you doing at Ryerson's?"

"I helped the strikers picket."

"Why."

"Because I'm sympathetic to them. I was on strike myself once when I was a kid. Worked in a silk mill. Lots of people who didn't work in a silk mill came to help us. I just got out of the Army, so I wanted to help the Ryerson people."

"Was that the Paterson Silk Strike?" asked Ashansky.

"Yes."

"Did you know Mr. Williams was a strikebreaker?"

"I didn't know him at all."

"Did you know the company hired Negroes as strikebreakers?"

"Yes."

"How did you feel about that?" asked Ashansky.

"I hate scabs. I don't care what color they are."

"So, tell me what you did the day Williams was killed."

"I got up. Ate. Went out for a newspaper. Came back. Said goodbye to my landlady and left for Clifton where I live."

"Why?"

"I had to find work. I was running out of money."

"Is there anyone who can confirm your story? Give you an alibi."

"Maybe Mrs. Kierce. The landlady. Or my mother. I didn't see or talk to anyone else," said Jackson.

"I see. No solid alibi. So, if you never were at Ryerson's that day, no one can come forward and say they saw you there?"

"No, sir," said Jackson, confidently.

"Okay. Tell me about the knife you had on you when the police arrested you in Hoboken."

"It's a Mark I trench knife. I got it when I was stationed at Camp Merritt."

"Why did you have it strapped to your leg?"

Jackson answered, "For protection. You may not have noticed it, Mr. Lawyer, but I'm not a very big guy. Lots of people like to pick on me. Nobody would pick on me when I had that knife."

"No. I don't think they would. Did you ever use that knife— to protect yourself, I mean?"

"No, sir," lied Jackson.

"So, the police are not going to find blood on that knife?"

"No, sir. I never cut myself with it and besides I clean it with gun solvent and oil it."

"Why would you do that if you never used it?"

Jackson seemed incredulous. "You've got to keep your equipment clean. If you don't, it'll rust." Jackson may not have seen combat, but he was a soldier.

A nice answer to a question I'll never let them ask you, thought Schor.

Ashansky continued, "Where were you going on the day the police arrested you?"

"I was going to New York. I was hoping to stay with some friends. Look for a job."

"Did those friends know you were coming?"

"No, sir. I was just going to look them up."

"Do you have any names for me?"

"No," said Jackson.

"Pity."

"Now, what have you told the police?"

"Nothing."

Schor interrupted, "You didn't tell them about your

movements on the day of the killing?"

"I did not. All I told them was my name and address. I did tell them I didn't murder nobody. But that's it. Nothing else. I swear."

Schor, who was taking notes, smiled for the first time. "Keep it that way, Mr. Jackson. I'll do the talking from now on. If you so choose, I will be your attorney of record."

"Yes, sir. I sure want you for my lawyer. Yes, sir." *Hot damn! I got me a smart Jew lawyer.*

Schor continued, "Very well. Here's what will happen next. The prosecutor will take the case to the Grand Jury. You will be indicted, arraigned and then face a trial. Do you have any assets, Mr. Jackson?"

"Assets?"

"Money, real estate, property of any kind."

"I don't have nothing but thirty-five dollars and that trench knife, Mr. Schor."

I was afraid of that.

"So you won't be able to post bond even if I could get it. Okay. You'll have to sit in jail until the trial is over.

"So that thirty-five dollars will have to do as our fee. I'll arrange for it to be released by the property clerk.

"Mr. Ashansky or I'll visit you from time to time. We may ask more questions and we'll inform you what progress we are making in our investigation?"

"Your investigation?"

"Yes. If you didn't kill George Williams then someone else did. We will make every effort to make sure the jury understands that.

"Meanwhile, you think of some respectable people we can call as character witnesses."

Respectable? Jesus, that ain't going to be easy. "I know some people from the Army."

"Wonderful," said Schor. "Soldiers in uniform make great

witnesses. We'll say goodbye now Mr. Jackson. Keep your spirits up. You're not alone. We're on your side now."

"Thank you, Mr. Schor."

When they were well clear of police headquarters, Abie asked, "Well, what do you think, Charlie?"

"He's lying," said Schor. "Did you notice how he kept saying he didn't 'murder' anyone? Not once did he say, 'I didn't kill him.'"

"So you think he's guilty?"

"That is of no interest to me," said Schor. "Knowing guilt might cloud my judgment. Emory Jackson is entitled to the best defense I can provide and that's what I'm going to give him."

"For thirty-five dollars? Just doing interviews and tracking down witnesses is going to cost more than that. You're going to lose money on this case, Charlie."

"No, I'm not," said Schor. "Lawyers aren't allowed to advertise anymore. It's unethical. This case is going to be in the newspapers every day from start to finish. You can't buy publicity like that. Cases are going to pour in. And if we win, they'll be coming in over the transom."

"Any chance of that, Charlie?"

"Yes, I think so. From what I can see, the state's case is going to be purely circumstantial. I like that."

That's what the Hudson County prosecutor was explaining to Mayor Hague.

"Mr. Mayor, we don't have a strong case. There're no witnesses and we can't put him within a hundred yards of the scene of the crime."

"You have that goddamn knife he used to kill that darkie. You go and get a goddamn indictment," said Hague.

"Well, certainly I can have him indicted but it won't be for first-degree murder. We'd never be able to prove 'premeditation.'"

"I don't care whether it's first-degree murder or thirty-second degree murder as long as the word 'murder' is in the indictment. You may recall we've got an election coming up in a few weeks. I promised those Negro leaders I'd deliver that boy's killer. I want those black votes."

Hague became less strident. "Besides, the election will be over before the trial begins. Right? I don't care whether or not you convict that asshole. I just want an indictment."

"You got it, Mr. Mayor." The indictment was for second-degree murder.

Emory Jackson was sitting out the weeks in the Hudson County Jail until his case showed up on the docket of the Superior Court. No one visited him except his lawyer and Ashansky who brought him a couple of cigars which he enjoyed. He didn't smoke cigarettes.

He was a quiet prisoner who made no friends. At first, two or three inmates tried to get close hoping he would spill something they could use to bargain with in their own cases. They failed. Jackson's conversation usually consisted of "Yes," "No," and "I don't know." He was soon left alone which suited Emory just fine.

He didn't even complain about the plain jail grub. Jackson relished the bologna sandwiches that showed up on the menu with depressing regularity.

The prosecution had concluded its investigation, such as it was, and now the defense attorney has access to the police reports, the coroner's report, the witness list and a list of exhibits.

Charlie Shaw and Abie Ashansky studied that material very closely looking at what was there and what wasn't.

"The case against our client is purely circumstantial," said Schor. "There nothing or no one that even puts Jackson at the scene of the crime.

"It's all built around that unique trench knife and the fact that it was found on Emory when he was captured. Their case is very thin. What they needed was a confession and that's what they didn't get. Thank God."

Ashansky said, "What's interesting is what isn't there."

Ashansky held up the list of exhibits. "The police report says a shattered whiskey bottle was found at the scene of the killing but it is not listed as an exhibit."

"Bingo! You found it," said Schor. "No fingerprints on the shards of the bottle and the state wants to avoid anything that would suggest a fight over a whiskey bottle. We'll enter that whiskey bottle into evidence."

Then picking up the coroner's report, Ashansky said, "The coroner didn't do a full autopsy. He just ascertained the cause of death. There's something else that bothers me."

"You mean those two puncture marks on his chin left by the brass knuckles?" asked Schor.

"Yes." Abie looked at the report again. A minute later, he said, "Of course, how stupid of me."

"You're hardly stupid, young man. I can't believe how quickly you've picked up on that."

Schor said. "The coroner could be our best witness." Both men laughed.

Schor said, "Okay. I think we've made a reasonable start in dismantling the state's case but I want to attack the uniqueness of that knife too. Get up to Camp Merritt and talk to those supply sergeants. I hope they haven't been transferred. "We're going to need some character witnesses too."

"You mean other than his mother? And I'm not too sure about her either," said Abie.

"That's right, you've been nosing around up in Clifton, haven't you?"

Ashansky said, "If we turn to the bums who know him, Jackson will be found guilty by association. Are you going to put him on the stand?"

"Not a chance," said Schor. "His silence is golden. I don't want the prosecutor cross-examining him. No, I'm going to convince the jury the other guy did it."

"You know I've never tried a murder case before, sir," said Jeremiah O'Flanagan.

"Yes, I do," said his superior, the Hudson County prosecutor. "But I think it will be good experience for you. Granted, the case isn't that strong and you might not thank me for assigning it to you. I just want you to do your best and learn as you go along."

"You can count on me to do my best, sir."

O'Flanagan was a newcomer to the prosecutor's office but in a few months he had shown great promise. He was a favorite in the courts. His flaming red hair distinguished him almost as much as his good humor.

O'Flanagan studied the police reports and the statements of witnesses. He examined the trench knife himself.

Shit! The whole case is built around this goddamn knife. Calling the case circumstantial overstates it. Too much "if this, then that" to suit me. I'd rather be the defense attorney.

Not one to give up, O'Flanagan found his hook. *If I can't convict him for murder, then I'll convict him of being a radical.*

It was a more cheerful O'Flanagan now that prepared for trial.

When Charles Schor learned who would be his adversary in the trial, he discussed it with his law clerk, "I believe that our beloved county prosecutor doesn't want anything to do with this case himself so he sent a boy to do a man's job. That's encouraging."

"Do you know anything about this O'Flanagan?" asked Abie.

"No. Not really. I've never seen him in court. I know he's a new hire. Probably someone's nephew."

"Isn't everyone in Jersey City?" asked Abie, well versed on the local reliance on nepotism.

Schor said, "There is that. Still, it is always a mistake to underestimate one's adversary." He was right.

Now the day had come to pick a jury. Jackson was on trial for the murder of George Williams, a black man, a strikebreaker.

Judge Redmond Barkley was on the bench. He had a reputation as a fair jurist who tolerated little "nonsense" from either side.

Jackson's defense counsel was well prepared to pick a jury. Charles Schor had told his law clerk, "We're going into 'voir dire' with an edge."

"How so?" asked Abie Ashansky.

"Well, most of the potential jurors will be reluctant to find any white man guilty of killing a Negro. That works in our favor. But it's not a sure thing.

"If the electric chair was a threat, I believe they would acquit. But second-degree murder only carries a ten- to twenty-year sentence. The jury might go for that if they don't like Emory Jackson."

"He's not a lovable man," said Abie. "Say, explain to me why the prosecution didn't ask for the death penalty?"

Schor said, "I don't think they could begin to prove premeditation. And most juries won't condemn a man to death on purely circumstantial evidence. They want a smoking gun.

"No. Our job is to get a jury that won't think Emory Jackson is a complete jackass.

"What we want is a couple of veterans and at least one or two men sympathetic to labor. What we don't want is a Negro juror. I want an acquittal. I'll use a preemptory challenge if I have to."

Schor was amiable with the potential jurors, but he did have to use that peremptory challenge when a dignified, middle-aged black man was called. He smiled his apology as the man left.

He noticed O'Flanagan was positively cordial in questioning jurors. He didn't challenge anyone.

I think that's deliberate. He wants to give the impression that it doesn't matter to him who's in the box, he's going to win. Is he stupid—or smart?

Schor was satisfied with the jury. It was all white with two veterans and a pro-union man on it.

Judge Barkley sat down on the bench—actually, a comfortable, high-backed leather chair—elevated about three feet higher than everyone else. When lawyers stood before him, they would have to look up at him. That was the idea. The judge could easily address either the jury or the witnesses. The jury box was to his right, the witness stand to his left. The acoustics in the room were excellent.

O'Flanagan was seated alone at a table to the right of the aisle that led to the witness stand. He was reading his notes.

Emory Jackson was sitting at the left side of the table next to Charles Schor with Ashansky on the right. Jackson was wearing a decent, well-pressed, brown suit, a white shirt, light-green tie and polished brown shoes. Jackson was well groomed, clean shaven with his brown hair neatly trimmed and parted on the right. He looked like a harmless, little clerk, much as he did in the Army.

The Opening Salvos

The judge banged his gavel and asked if the State was ready to proceed. The prosecutor rose to make his opening statement.

"Gentlemen of the jury. What a sad world we live in. Not much more than a year ago, an Armistice was signed that was to put an end to the Great War. But did it? It did not. In the short months that followed the world has been turned upside down. America, herself, has been subjected to bombs, race riots, radical agitation and hundreds of crippling strikes led by Bolshevik agitators. Our own community has not been spared.

"As I speak, men at Ryerson Steel on the West Side of Jersey City are engaging in such a strike. Some are on a picket line while others are enduring their threats and venom just because they want to go to work and feed their hungry children.

"George Williams was one of these men; a man doing the only work he could find. A pitiful man brutally murdered by a coward who butchered him like an animal.

"Who would do such a thing?" He paused and then wheeled, pointing a finger at the defendant.

"Emory Jackson, that's who. Emory Jackson is the vicious radical who cut down George Williams without mercy because that poor man—that man who had no other choice—crossed a picket line.

"The state will prove that Emory Jackson had the motive, means and the opportunity to murder George Williams. He did it. No doubt about that.

"Emory Jackson had no reason to kill his victim other than George Williams dared to cross a picket line. This was something that the radical Mr. Jackson could not abide.

"We will prove that Emory Jackson confronted and insulted George Williams in a boxcar at the loading dock at Ryerson's Steel. It never came to fisticuffs. There was no fair fight.

"The state will prove that Emory Jackson, without warning, took out his wicked trench knife—a knife designed only to kill— and plunged it into George Williams' chest. Emory Jackson murdered George Williams with no more concern than one would give to a fly.

"Oh, yes. He did it."

O'Flanagan turned to the jury, "Look at him, gentlemen."

"Looks like a pretty nice fellow, doesn't he? But you didn't see him on the picket line, screaming, yelling, cursing and, yes, threatening to kill the men who crossed that picket line.

"He didn't look like this either when he killed George Williams. He was wearing his trademark bib overalls and carrying a knife almost as long as your arm.

"Who is this man? Just who is Emory Jackson? He didn't work at Ryerson Steel yet he was on the picket line. Why was he there? Where did he come from? Who sent him there? What was he ordered to do?

"We don't know the answers to those questions yet, but we may find out during this trial if Emory Jackson is man enough to take the stand and let me ask him.

"We do know Emory Jackson thought he would get away with murdering George Williams. But he was wrong.

"He didn't reckon with Jersey City's elite Bomb Squad. Those stalwart and crackerjack policemen who protect us—yes, us— from radicals such as Emory Jackson. And if they cannot prevent an outrage like this murder, then they will relentlessly track down the killer and bring him to justice.

"It was the Bomb Squad that identified Emory Jackson as the murderer, placed him at the scene of the crime, found his blood-soaked overalls, identified the trench knife he used, traced him through flawless detective work and arrested him as he tried to flee to New York. When the Bomb Squad cornered Emory Jackson in the toilet of a railroad car at the Hoboken ferry, he still had that terrible trench knife strapped to his leg, ready to kill again.

"In short, gentlemen of the jury, the State will prove that Emory Jackson murdered George Williams.

"It is your duty to find the murderer Emory Jackson guilty. He should spend at least two decades in prison for this heinous crime. In prison, where—I might add—he can harm no other innocent. That only would be just. You would just be doing your duty.

"Thank you."

The prosecutor glared at Jackson who sat there, a slight smile on his face. Ashansky took notes.

The judge spoke. "Mr. Schor, your opening statement, if you will."

Schor faced the jury, smiling and said, "Good morning, gentlemen. You have heard the tall tale that my learned colleague has concocted for you and I must say he made a dramatic show of it.

"But be that as it may, the state cannot prove that Emory Jackson killed George Williams for one simple reason. He didn't do it.

"In fact, Emory Jackson told the police that he didn't murder Mr. Williams. He told anyone who would listen that he didn't murder anyone. Emory Jackson did not confess to any crime let alone murder. Emory Jackson is not guilty. It's that simple."

Here Schor improvised. "The prosecutor asked, 'Who is Emory Williams? Where did he come from? What was he doing at Ryerson's?'

"Emory Jackson is the decent young man you see before your eyes. What you see is what you get.

"Emory Jackson came to Jersey City straight from Camp Merritt in Tenafly where he was serving as a soldier in the United States Army.

"Emory Jackson is an honorably discharged veteran of the

Great War.

"Emory Jackson walked the picket line even though he didn't work at Ryerson Steel because he sympathized with the men that did, as many of us do.

"Emory Jackson was never seen in or near the boxcar where the murder was committed.

"Emory Jackson was never seen on Ryerson Steel property by anyone. Period.

"Emory Jackson was not on the picket line the day poor Mr. Williams was killed.

"Emory Jackson was not fleeing the state when he was surprised by the police and arrested. He was off to visit friends.

"Emory Jackson had no motive to kill George Williams who was a stranger to him.

"Emory Jackson had no opportunity to kill George Williams."

Schor paused.

"The prosecution will make much of the means used to kill George Williams—an awful trench knife. But the defense will have much, much more to say about that knife. And you will be satisfied when we finish. I promise.

"In the end, you must decide Emory Jackson's fate. Emory Jackson is presumed to be innocent. The state must prove otherwise. To convict, you must find the defendant 'guilty' beyond any reasonable doubt. I contend, gentlemen, that isn't possible.

"It wouldn't shock me if some of you were already harboring reasonable doubts to go along with the presumption of innocence.

"Someone did murder George Williams. That's very sadly true. But it wasn't Emory Jackson. The state cannot prove that he did because that, simply, is not true. Emory Jackson did not murder anyone. The real murderer of George Williams is still out there. And no one is looking for him. How sad. The man deserves better.

"Thank you."

The court took its lunch break after the opening statements. "How do you think we did, Charlie?" asked Abie.

"Not as well as I'd like. We've got to talk to our client now."

Jackson was in a holding pen in the courthouse's cellar eating a bologna sandwich and washing it down with a cold cup of coffee. He said nothing as Schor and Ashansky joined him.

"Emory, there are a couple of questions I have to ask you. Whether the answers are yes or no, I'll deal with them. But you must tell me the truth. It's important."

"Okay," said Jackson.

"Are you a member of the International Workers of the World? A Wobbly?"

"No."

"Are you affiliated with the Communists, Anarchists, Socialists or any other radical organization?"

"No."

"Have you ever been arrested before?"

"No."

"Okay, thank you, Emory," said Schor as he rose to leave. Jackson asked his counsel no questions. He finished his bologna sandwich.

At lunch, Abie asked, "What's up, Charlie?"

"Young Mr. Flanagan is going to paint our client a bright red. He trying to force me to put Jackson on the stand to defend himself and I won't do that."

"Hey, being a radical isn't against the law," said Abie.

"In Hudson County it might as well be. We've got problems," said Charlie Schor, counselor-at-law.

Back in the courtroom, Abie asked, "Do you expect any surprises from the state's witnesses this afternoon?"

"Not really. He has to start off with the cops and they'll walk a pretty straight line. I don't expect anything that isn't in their reports. That goes for the coroner too. Thank God.

"I'll have to be careful on cross-examination. Barkley can be strict. If I try to weasel in anything that wasn't mentioned in direct testimony he'll shut me down. I don't want that."

"What will you do?"

"I'll ask the judge's to instruct the witnesses to keep themselves available. He's done that before. Then I'll question them when it's our turn and that'll drive the prosecutor crazy wondering what we have."

Officer Vince Crehan was sworn in as the first state witness.

The prosecutor said, "Officer Crehan, in your own words, tell us what you first found when you were sent to investigate a murder at Ryerson Steel on the morning of September 28, this year."

"Yes, sir. When I arrived, a police sergeant had already secured the boxcar and a uniformed policeman was guarding it against intruders. I examined the victim's body and saw the injuries to his chin and the chest wound. It was obviously a homicide. No weapon was near the body and none was found later when we emptied and searched the boxcar. Then I questioned the man who had found the body."

"Who was that and what did he tell you?"

"He's the foreman, a Mr. Bramhall. He had put the victim to work unloading the boxcar and when he went to check on him later, he found him dead. When I asked him whether he had seen anyone else on the loading dock, he said he hadn't. But then he remembered he had seen a short man, a white man with brown hair, wearing bib overalls, walking away from the railroad siding towards the perimeter fence."

"Did you check out the area near that fence?" asked the prosecutor.

"Yes, sir. Leaving the scene guarded, I went to search the area around the fence. I found a pair of bloody bib overalls with the cuffs rolled up about six inches."

"What did you surmise, Officer Crehan?"

"I surmised that this was the outer garment worn by the short man the foreman saw. I also suspected he was the killer since the overalls were still wet with blood."

The prosecutor offered the overalls and they were marked Exhibit A.

"What happened next, Officer?"

"I telephoned my superiors and told them what I had learned."

"Is this when the Bomb Squad took over the investigation?"

"Yes, sir."

"I have no more questions for this witness, your honor."

"You may cross-examine, Mr. Schor."

"Officer Crehan—it is 'Officer' is it not?"

"Yes, sir."

"You're not a detective?"

"No, sir. I'm a patrolman but I work in plainclothes."

"I see. I noticed you mentioned uniformed policemen assisting you. Were there any detectives down there while you were investigating?"

"No, sir. They came later."

"But your superior sent you to investigate initially? Why was that?"

Crehan hesitated and then said, "At first, it was thought to be a couple of hotheads fighting over a bottle of whiskey. My lieutenant thought I could handle the investigation alone."

Schor said, "You said you did not find a murder weapon. Did you find anything else unusual in the boxcar?"

Crehan said, "Yes, sir. A broken whiskey bottle."

Schor looked at the jury. "A broken whiskey bottle. Hmmm."

Son of a bitch. He got it in. Using my witness. Damn it to hell, thought O'Flanagan.

Schor turned and addressed the judge, "No more questions

for this witness, your honor."

I don't dare re-direct. He'll drive a truck through it.

The judge asked, "Mr. Flanagan?"

"No more questions, your honor."

Schor spoke up, "Would your honor instruct this witness to make himself available for direct questioning should the defense present a case?"

"I object!" shouted O'Flanagan.

"To what, Mr. Prosecutor," asked the judge?

"The defense counsel should ask whatever questions he has now during cross-examination." *I don't want any fucking surprises later.*

"Overruled. Apparently the prosecutor didn't hear the defense counsel say he might want to question the witness later and elicit more direct testimony."

Oh, shit. I forgot that you could do that.

"You may step down officer, but make yourself available for additional questioning by the defense."

"Yes, sir."

Lieutenant Michael "Mickey" McGurk was the next state's witness.

"Lieutenant McGurk, you're the head of the city's Bomb Squad, are you not?"

"I am, sir."

"And doesn't this unit investigate and ferret out radical activities in Jersey City?"

"It does, sir."

"So this is why you dispatched Officer Crehan to investigate a killing at Ryerson Steel where a nasty strike was in progress."

"Yes. I sent Officer Crehan there when I received a verbal report of the killing. After receiving his preliminary report, all three of us moved the investigation forward."

"And what more did you uncover?"

"Well, first we went over all the information collected earlier and corroborated it. We learned that a worker in a nearby boxcar heard someone shout 'Scab.' Then we learned from the union's picket captain that a man answering the defendant's description had been on the picket line. That man used the nickname 'Em.'

"That led us to canvass the rooming and boardinghouses nearby on Westside Avenue. We found one where the landlady said the description fit one of her boarders. She showed us a register signed with the name 'E. Jackson' and giving Tenafly, NJ, as his previous address."

The prosecutor offered the rooming house register as Exhibit B.

"The coroner, who examined the victim's body, came to headquarters and discussed his report with us."

The prosecutor entered the coroner's report as Exhibit C.

He asked McGurk, "Did his report change the way you looked at the investigation?"

"Completely," said McGurk. "The wounds on the victim's chin and the angle of penetration of the blade into his chest indicated that he had been killed by a short man wielding a trench knife."

The prosecutor offered a Mark I trench knife as Exhibit D. "Is this the trench knife that Emory Jackson had in his possession when he was apprehended."

McGurk examined the knife and said, "It is, sir. I marked its handle."

"Go on with your testimony, Lieutenant."

"We surmised that we were looking for a soldier or ex-soldier as our killer. The Mark I trench knife, a new model, had been shipped to bases where men were being equipped to embark for France. But it was never distributed to the troops because the war ended first.

"Our investigation took us to Camp Merritt which is next door to Tenafly. We learned that a soldier working in supply had been given a Mark I trench knife by his sergeant."

"Who was that soldier, Lieutenant?"

McGurk said, "The defendant, Emory Jackson."

The prosecutor offered the photograph of Jackson and his sergeant posing with Mark I trench knives as Exhibit D.

"Go on."

"We learned that the soldier was named Emory Jackson and his hometown was in Clifton. The Clifton police uncovered his address but when we went there we found that he had just fled. We thought he might be headed for New York City, so our detective sergeant along with police from Jersey City and Hoboken staked out the Lackawanna Railroad Terminal and apprehended the fugitive when he arrived on a train."

The prosecutor pointed to Exhibit D. "Once again. Did Emory Jackson have that trench knife on him when your people caught up with him?"

"Yes, sir."

"No more questions for this witness."

Schor cross-examined McGurk. "Lieutenant, when you first sent Officer Crehan to investigate the killing, did you think it was the act of a radical unionist?"

"No, sir. The first report from the scene indicated that it was the result of a common brawl. I sent Officer Crehan because we were interested in anything unusual that occurs at a plant on strike."

"Did that first report suggest who might have been involved in such a brawl and why?"

McGurk answered, "The sergeant at the scene thought two Negroes might have been fighting over a bottle of whiskey. But first impressions are often wrong."

"Are they?" asked Schor. "No more questions for this witness, your honor. I ask for the usual admonishment."

O'Flanagan rose. "Re-direct, your honor?"

"Lieutenant McGurk, when did you abandon any thought of a brawl between blackamoors?"

"When Officer Crehan told us about the white man the foreman had seen and the bloody overalls he had found."

"So the Bomb Squad never really considered this murder to be the result of a common brawl?

"No, sir."

"Did you suspect that it was a radical supporter of the union who killed the strikebreaker?"

"Yes, sir."

Punch and Counterpunch

The prosecutor was questioning the picket captain. "Did you see the defendant on the picket line, sir?"

"Yes. A number of times."

"What did he call himself?"

"Em."

"Did you know he didn't work at Ryerson's?"

"No, sir. All of us just assumed he worked in a different department than we did."

"Did Em habitually wear bib overalls on the picket line?"

"Yes."

The prosecutor said, "Now I want a 'yes' or 'no' answer to this question. Did Em—did Emory Jackson, the defendant — threaten to kill men who were crossing the picket line?'

The picket captain took a few moments. "Yes, he did but..."

"No more questions for this witness, your honor," said the prosecutor.

"I have some questions for him," said Schor.

"You testified that Emory Jackson threatened to kill men who crossed the picket line. Did any other pickets make the same threats?"

The picket captain looked relieved. "Yes. We all did."

"Did you think Emory Jackson or any other picket actually meant to carry out that threat?"

"No, sir. We were just trying to intimidate them. Scare them so they won't cross the line."

"No more questions, your honor," said Schor.

The Negro who was on the stand next was visibly nervous.

The prosecutor asked, "What did you hear that seemed unusual on the morning of the murder?"

"Not much, sir. Just the word 'scab.'"

"What does that word mean to you?" asked O'Flanagan.

"That's what they calls us when we go to work, sir."

"Who are 'they'?"

"You know, sir. Them men that's on strike. Them."

Schor cross-examined him. "You say you thought you heard the word 'scab.' Is it possible the word was 'scared'?"

"Could be, sir."

"No more questions, your honor."

"Re-direct, your honor."

"Go ahead, Mr. O'Flanagan.

"How about 'cab,' 'dab,' 'gab,' 'jab,' 'nab,' 'stab' or 'tab'?"

The courtroom erupted in laughter. The witness seemed confused.

"Let me re-phrase the question. Was the word you heard 'scab'?"

"Yes, sir."

The foreman was next. The prosecutor took him step by step on what he had seen on the day of the murder.

O'Flanagan's last question was, "Mister Bramhall, do you see the man who was wearing bib overalls and moving away from the scene of the murder anywhere in this courtroom?"

Bramhall pointed at Jackson. "Yes, sir. That's him. The defendant."

There was an audible gasp among the spectators. O'Flanagan looked at the jury and said, "No more questions, your honor."

Schor approached the witness stand. Bramhall seemed tense.

"Mr. Bramhall, how far away was this man who was walking — not running — when you saw him?"

"Oh, about a hundred yards or so."

"Did you see him clearly?" asked Schor.

"Yes, sir. I did."

"Did he turn around and look at you?"

Bramhall said, "No. But I got a good look at him."

"Isn't it true, Mr. Bramhall that you had never seen my client's face until today?"

"His face? No. But I still saw him."

"How can you identify him if you didn't see his face?" Schor demanded.

"I saw him. I saw that he was white. I saw that he was short. I saw that he was wearing bib overalls. I saw the back of his head."

"You saw the back of his head? What are you, a phrenologist?"

"A phren—what? I don't understand," said Bramhall.

"A phrenologist. Someone who can tell a criminal by the shape of his head."

That drew laughter from the spectators and thump of a gavel by the judge who admonished them.

"No more questions, your honor."

O'Flanagan rose. "Re-direct?"

"Mr. Bramhall. Could you have identified the defendant in a lineup where all the men were facing away from you?"

A triumphant, "Yes!"

Schor rose now. "One more question, your Honor?"

"Mr. Bramhall, was such a lineup ever held?"

A defeated "no."

O'Flanagan hated to end his case on that note but he had no more witnesses.

"The state rests, your honor."

It was now the defense attorney's turn.

Schor had five witnesses. He re-called Vince Crehan first.

"Officer Crehan, did you bag that shattered whiskey bottle

you found as evidence and bring it back to headquarters?"

"Yes, sir."

Schor picked up a paper bag off the defense table. "Is this it?"

"Yes, sir."

Schor offered the shards as defense exhibit A.

"Were there any fingerprints on the broken pieces?" Schor was sure they wouldn't be Jackson's. That would have put him at the murder scene. That the state would never neglect.

"No, sir. Just smudges."

"Smudges from more than one person?" Schor asked.

"We couldn't tell, sir. Just smudges."

Schor called Detective Sergeant Anthony Aiello who had not been on the state's list of witnesses.

"Detective, I understand that you questioned the Negro strikebreakers during the investigation into the killing at Ryerson's. Is that true?"

"Yes, sir."

"What did you learn, Detective?"

"Nothing of value, unfortunately," said Aiello.

"Really? You mean that none of the men you questioned had any thoughts on what had happened in that boxcar?"

"Well, yes, they did but our investigation quickly zeroed in on Emory Jackson."

Schor asked, "As a matter of curiosity, Detective, just what did those colored men think happened? What did they tell you?"

"Some of them thought Williams was killed in a fight over a bottle of whiskey. But they were wrong."

"Were they?" asked Schor. "Did you or any other member of the Bomb Squad follow up on this logical explanation?"

"Objection. Leading the witness, your honor," said O'Flanagan.

"Sustained. Rephrase the question, counselor."

"Did the Bomb Squad investigate the possibility that the

victim was killed in a fight with another black strikebreaker?"

"No, we concentrated on capturing Emory Jackson."

Schor asked, "Did the Bomb Squad even consider the possibility that someone other than the defendant might have killed George Williams?"

"No, sir."

"So if Emory Jackson didn't kill the victim, then the murderer of George Williams is still out there?"

"Objection, your honor."

"Sustained."

"No more questions," said Schor as he looked at the jury.

O'Flanagan asked on cross-examination, "Did any of these Negro workers suggest a name of someone who might have fought with George Williams?"

"No, sir."

Schor called the police sergeant who had phoned in the first report of the killing.

"Sergeant what did you see when you entered that boxcar?"

"A dead body and a broken whiskey bottle," he answered.

Schor asked, "What did this evidence suggest?"

"Well, it looked like a couple of colored fellows had got into it over some whiskey and one of them ended up dead."

"Why not a colored man and a white man brawling?"

The sergeant said, "Sir, white folks and colored people don't drink together."

Schor asked, "Did you inform Officer Crehan of your suspicions when he arrived?"

"I did."

"No more questions."

O'Flanagan asked, "Sergeant, did you know for a fact that one Negro had killed another over a bottle of whiskey?"

"No, sir. I just thought that's what happened."

"Why didn't you pursue that line of inquiry yourself,

Sergeant?"

"I'm not a detective. I really wouldn't know where to begin. The Bomb Squad knew what it was doing," said the sergeant.

Jackson's old supply sergeant took the stand next. "Was Emory Jackson a good soldier, Sergeant?"

"Yes, sir, he was." He smiled at Jackson who returned the smile.

"Did you ever know him to be violent?" asked Schor.

"Absolutely not. He's a quiet young man. Minds his own business. Em is pleasant to everybody. Always a smile on his face."

Schor pointed to the trench knife. "Did you give Emory Jackson this trench knife, Sergeant?"

"I did. As a souvenir."

Schor paused and looked at the jury. "Did you give similar trench knives to any other soldiers, Sergeant?"

"I did. I gave three of them to our company mess sergeant and two to the transportation sergeant and I kept one for myself."

"Were either of these men a Negro?"

"Yes. The mess sergeant is colored. All his cooks and mess men are Negroes too. But they're good boys. I liked them."

"Do you know where these men are now?"

"I do not," said the supply sergeant.

In turn, O'Flanagan asked, "Have you any reason to believe that any of these mess men came to Jersey City, Sergeant?"

"I do not, sir."

Schor called Regimental Supply Sergeant Harry Harmon as an expert witness. He established the sergeant's bona fides by quizzing him on his twenty-five years of service.

"Were you always in 'supply,' Sergeant?"

"No, sir. I started out in the infantry but after I got shot at in Cuba and later in the Philippines, I decided I should put in for a less hazardous job." That drew chuckles from the spectators and the jury. They liked Sergeant Harmon.

"Did you know the defendant, Emory Jackson?"

"Not to speak to. I saw him in formations, of course. He brought reports to me but that was it." The sergeant looked at the jury. "If you've been in the Army, y'all know that senior non-commissioned officers are not chummy with privates." That drew more laughter. The judge raised his gavel but did not bring it down.

"Was Jackson ever brought before you on a disciplinary charge?"

"No, sir. Never. He was a good soldier."

Schor continued, "A subordinate of yours has testified that he gave six trench knives to other soldiers and kept one for himself. Isn't that unusual? Isn't that a court-martial offense?"

"Hardly," said the sergeant. "If it was, y'all wouldn't have any people left in supply. The Army knows 'wastage' exists and it ignores what it can't control."

"Do you have any idea how many trench knifes fell prey to 'wastage' at Camp Merritt?"

"Yes. One hundred cases of trench knives were shipped to us. One case—fifty trench knives—was lost in transit, if y'all know what I mean."

"As an expert in supply, can you estimate how many of those fifty knives ended up in the hands of soldiers at Camp Merritt?"

"Fifty."

"Might the same thing have happened at other embarkation camps?" Schor asked.

"No 'might' about it. A case was lost on transit at Camp Upshur and another case at Camp Mills. Both of them are on Long Island. All the paperwork for these camps is funneled through me. I have the original invoices with me if you'd like to see them."

"Please," said Schor who looked at them briefly and offered

them as defense exhibit B.

O'Flanagan said, "I object to these papers being placed into evidence. The state hasn't had a chance to examine them."

Judge Barkley said, "Let me have a look at them."

He examined them. "They look pretty straightforward to me, I'll allow it."

Schor continued, "So, is it your expert opinion, Sergeant, that 150 of these trench knives ended up in the hands of soldiers— most of them now discharged—within, say, twenty miles of Jersey City?"

"It is."

"Your subordinate said he gave three to a Negro mess sergeant. Are there any other Negro units at these camps?"

"All the cooks and mess men at these camps are Negroes, sir."

"No more questions."

O'Flanagan asked, "Do you know of any Negro cooks or mess men who came to Jersey City?"

"No, sir."

The next defense witness was the Hudson County coroner.

O'Flanagan had read the coroner's report time and time again and had even interviewed the pathologist but still couldn't puzzle out why the defense wanted to call him as an expert witness. He would soon find out.

Schor led the coroner in establishing his credentials as an expert witness and then began to question him.

"Doctor, how much whiskey did George Williams drink the morning of his death?"

"I don't know if he had drunk any alcohol."

"Didn't you examine the contents of his stomach during the autopsy?"

"No. In cases like this, all I do is examine the body until I find the cause of death which, in this case, was very obvious."

"I see. So Williams could have been drinking that morning?"

"Sir, I simply don't know."

"Doctor, your examination of the victim showed that the victim had no abrasions on his knuckles or hands that would indicate that he was in a fight. Does the absence of such abrasions also prove that the victim had not been in an argument with someone?"

"Of course not," said the doctor.

"Thank you. Let's move on to how the victim was killed. If the killer stood in front of his victim, as in a confrontation, and threw a punch where would the brass knuckles land?" Schor illustrated by punching forward with his right hand.

"On the left side of the victim's jaw where, indeed, they did land."

"What happened next?"

"The victim's jaw was broken by the force and he would have staggered back. Then the assailant would have plunged the knife upwards into his chest."

"Like this?" asked Schor as he mimicked the move with his right hand.

The doctor didn't answer. He was staring at Emory Jackson as was the jury. The defendant was sipping from a glass of water as Schor knew he would.

"I see you are looking at my client, Doctor," said Schor. "What do you notice about him?"

The pathologist returned his gaze to Schor. "Your client is left handed."

Shit! thought O'Flanagan. The spectators erupted into a babble of noise. The judge had to bang his gavel three times before order was restored.

"One more outburst like that and I will clear the court," he warned.

Schor continued, "Do you think it likely that a left-handed man inflicted those wounds on George Williams?"

"No, sir, I do not," said the coroner.

On cross-examination, O'Flanagan demanded, "Doctor, isn't it possible that a left-handed man could have inflicted those wounds?"

"Possible, but not probable."

O'Flanagan was desperate. "Isn't it possible that Emory Jackson is ambidextrous, capable of inflicting those wounds with either hand?"

"Yes. That's possible."

"No more questions," said O'Flanagan.

Schor said, "Re-direct, your honor."

"Doctor, do you know what percentage of the population is ambidextrous?"

"I believe it is somewhat less than one percent, counselor."

"No more questions, your honor."

"The witness may step down."

Schor waited until the coroner passed the rail, the jury's eyes following him, his testimony sinking in.

Then he looked at the judge and said, "The defense rests, your honor."

"Very well, counselor. Would you like the court to adjourn before you present your closing argument?"

"No, your honor. The defense is prepared to proceed."

The jury got as comfortable as they could in their chairs as Schor approached.

"Gentlemen, this has been an unusual trial with much confusing testimony but one thing is clear—Emory Jackson did not commit murder.

"Emory Jackson did not kill George Williams yet he is sitting in this courtroom accused of that horrible crime. How did that happen?

"Did the police frame an innocent man like you might read in a cheap novel?

"No. He wasn't framed. Our Bomb Squad would never stoop to such nonsense. They are honorable men doing a very difficult job. If he wasn't framed, then what went wrong?

"No matter how good one is at his job, one will still make mistakes. The men of the Bomb Squad made a mistake early on and it was monumental. They went after and captured the wrong man.

"The groundwork for the mistake was laid when Lieutenant McGurk sent Officer Crehan—an inexperienced plainclothesman, not a detective—to what was reported as a deadly brawl between two colored strikebreakers over a bottle of whiskey.

"Crehan abandoned that theory as soon as the foreman said he saw a short, white man, wearing bib overalls, walking off in the distance. Suddenly this became a case of a radical—maybe a Bolshevik agent—murdering a strikebreaker.

"The Bomb Squad never abandoned that theory. Those experienced detectives never investigated the possibility of a drunken brawl.

"That was the great mistake that led to the arrest and indictment of Emory Jackson.

"The prosecution's case against him is ingenious but erroneous.

"Step by step it leads to a soldier and to a trench knife. But Emory is not the soldier nor is his trench knife the one that killed George Williams.

"The judge will tell you the state must prove Emory Jackson is guilty beyond a reasonable doubt. Every aspect of the state's case screams doubt.

"You are right to doubt that Emory Jackson was some sort of Bolshevik agent sent to Ryerson's to cause trouble. Jackson has no police record. The state could not link him to any radical organization because he is not a radical. He is a loyal American who honorably served his country in the United States Army.

"You are right to doubt that Emory Jackson is the man the

foreman saw. The back of a man's head at a couple of hundred yards? Come on!

"You are right to doubt that the overalls the police found belonged to Emory Jackson. Hundreds of those bib overalls were sold in Jersey City alone.

"You were right to doubt that the trench knife that the police found was unique. You now know that 150 of them are loose somewhere within a few miles' radius of the scene of the crime.

"And, perhaps most important, you were right to doubt that a left-handed man, such as the defendant, could have inflicted the injuries suffered by the victim. Even the coroner didn't think that likely.

"I won't waste any more time listing the many other doubts about the prosecution's case. You know what they are. You can recall them as easily as I can.

"Now, just let me recite some facts. The very ones I cited in my opening statement when this trial started.

"Emory Jackson is an honorably discharged veteran of the Great War.

"Emory Jackson came to Jersey City straight from Camp Merritt.

"Emory Jackson walked the picket line even though he didn't work at Ryerson Steel because he sympathized with the men that did, as many of us do.

"Emory Jackson was never seen in or near the boxcar where the murder was committed.

"Emory Jackson was never seen on Ryerson Steel property at any time by anyone. Period.

"Emory Jackson was not on the picket line the day poor Mr. Williams was killed.

"Emory Jackson was not fleeing the state when he was surprised by the police and arrested. He was off to see friends. Looking for work.

"Emory Jackson had no motive to kill George Williams who

was a stranger to him.

"Emory Jackson had no opportunity to kill George Williams.

"In short, Emory Jackson didn't kill George Williams. You must acquit him. Do not let this cascade of errors go any further. Do your duty. Acquit Emory Jackson."

Just a minute later, O'Flanagan approached the jury box to make his closing argument.

"Wow! Wasn't that something? My learned colleague is an expert at rhetorical tap dancing. He can make the flimsiest of conjectures seem like a concrete fact. But look closely. It's still hot air.

"I know you won't be fooled. The prosecution has presented the actual facts of the case to you. Irrefutable facts. Look at state exhibits A, B, C and D too.

"The Bomb Squad didn't do shoddy police work as the defense would have you believe. The police work that ended in the apprehension of Emory Jackson was brilliant. Worthy of the Bomb Squad's well-deserved reputation. I commend them and so should you.

"Let me run through those facts again. Briefly.

"Emory Jackson had no business on the picket line at Ryerson's but he was there yelling, screaming and threatening to kill anyone who dared to report for work. That's what a Red provocateur would do.

"The foreman set George Williams to work unloading a boxcar.

"A worker in nearby boxcar heard someone shout 'Scab.' That's the epithet radicals scream at loyal workers.

"The foreman saw Emory Jackson moving away from the scene of the crime. He gave the police a solid description of the killer. A description of Emory Jackson.

"A Bomb Squad policeman found Jackson's blood-soaked bib overalls near the fence around Ryerson's plant.

"Emory Jackson fled from his boardinghouse the day he killed George Williams.

"The coroner declared the victim was killed with a hard to obtain trench knife.

"The police traced Emory Jackson to Camp Merritt where he got such a wicked trench knife.

"Emory Jackson fled his mother's home intent on escaping to New York City and anonymity. Maybe he was headed back to his Bolshevik pals.

"Emory Jackson was flushed out of that railroad car toilet before he could board the ferry.

"The police found that horrible trench knife still strapped to Emory Jackson's leg when he was cornered. The trench knife Jackson used to kill the victim.

"Those are the facts, gentlemen of the jury, there can be no doubt about them.

"Don't be fooled by the smoke and mirrors conjured up by the defense. George Williams was not killed by another colored worker over a bottle of whiskey. The murder was not committed by some will-of-the-wisp Negro mess man who came from some Army camp, a million miles away, just to kill George Williams. Preposterous.

"Stick to the facts, gentlemen, and you will have no alternative but to convict Emory Jackson of murdering George Williams. Jackson is a dangerous radical who should be put behind bars before he kills someone else. Thank you."

Judge Barkley instructed the jury, defining for them exactly what second-degree murder meant. He reminded them that the defendant was presumed innocent until the state proved him guilty beyond a reasonable doubt.

Judge Barkley cautioned the jury not to make anything of the fact that the defendant did not take the stand to testify. "The defendant does not have to prove his innocence. It is the state that must prove him guilty."

The jurymen left the courtroom to deliberate.

The Majesty of the Law

Jack Farrell sat in the pressroom in the bowels of the Hudson County Courthouse typing yet another story on the Jackson murder trial.

He used two index fingers to type and had been timed at forty-two words a minute. He never bothered to learn to use all ten. Two were enough.

That was in keeping with the way local reporters operated in 1919 and for two more generations after that. They were not perfectionists. Their copy was triple spaced to leave room for their own corrections, the copy desk's corrections and the final review by a printer. Still typos appeared every day.

Farrell would have laughed if you called him a "journalist." He was a newspaperman and proud of his craft. He was smart, he was curious and he was fast.

A reporter's pay was poor but his reward was great. He avoided the pre-ordained backbreaking labor visited on his brothers, cousins and peers. It was the most glamorous job a working-class kid could get.

All reporters were prisoners of their daily deadlines. It was exceedingly rare for a newspaper to hold the press while waiting on a story. The assassination of a president fell into that category but little else.

Farrell had learned early to "go with what you got." Any serious errors or omissions could be cleaned up in the next edition. Maybe.

The Jackson murder trial was a godsend to Farrell who dealt with such boring daily stuff as club meetings, burglaries, obituaries, accidents, church services, dead horses and one-alarm fires.

Usually, the regular courthouse reporter would cover such a trial but the city editor yanked him off the story. "You're covering the hottest trial we've had in years like it's a meeting of the 'Old Maids' Quilting Guild.' Farrell! Get over to the courthouse and cover the Jackson trial. Put some pep into your goddamn copy."

Farrell did. The most mundane motion or questioning was dripping with light purple prose by the time it saw print.

He was getting his second story ready for the messenger today in case the jury finally came back with a verdict.

His first told of Jackson being found "guilty." This one would find him "not guilty." This is how newspapers hedged their bets in the face of an inexorable deadline. A practice the *Chicago Tribune* would regret in 1948.

The bulk of both stories was the same. It was just the lead and a few subsequent paragraphs that differed. Since judgment had not been pronounced yet, Farrell had to use his imagination. Most reporters had one.

When the messenger from *The Jersey Journal* picked up his copy, Farrell returned to the courtroom and sat down next to Abie Ashansky.

Abie and his boss, Charlie Schor, were very pleased with Farrell's coverage but so was their prosecutorial opponent, Jeremiah O'Flanagan.

In Farrell's colorful copy, both men came off as intelligent and shrewd knights of the law battling it out in the best adversarial traditions of American jurisprudence. They liked that. They liked Farrell.

But the jury had been out a long time. Farrell's last story had screamed off the front page in 72-point bold type, "Jackson Jury Still Out."

"What do you think, Abie?" asked Farrell.

"Honestly, Jack. I have no idea. Neither does Charlie and I'll bet that O'Flanagan doesn't either. Who ever heard of a jury out for two days without asking the judge anything about the evidence?"

An hour later the jury returned to the courtroom amid much muttering from the assemblage. The foreman handed the bailiff a note for the judge.

The judge read it and looked grim. He addressed the foreman who was still standing, looking just as grim, "Mr. Foreman, I take it the jury has not reached a verdict."

"We have not, your honor,' said the foreman amidst groans, laughter, shouts and the banging gavel of the judge. Farrell said, "Holy shit!" and ran for the pressroom telephone.

The courtroom now quiet, the Judge said, "A trial drains the emotions of all involved and it is costly to the taxpayers. I want the jury to go back, discuss the case and then take a secret ballot. If there if some progress, continue to deliberate. If not, then return to the courtroom."

The foreman looked skeptical but said, "Yes, your honor." The jury left.

The judge said to the opposing lawyers, "Gentlemen, in my chambers, please."

When they had settled in, Judge Barkley said, "We've got a hung jury. I'm afraid we're in for a mistrial." He looked at the foreman's note. "The vote is six for conviction and six for acquittal and that's the way it's been since they first voted two days ago. No one would budge.

"And I don't think anyone will budge. I just sent the jury back so I could talk to you in private.

"Mr. O'Flanagan, will the state seek a re-trial?"

"No, your honor. I have discussed this possibility thoroughly with the county prosecutor. In view of six votes against conviction, I doubt that we could prove the case against Jackson by presenting the same evidence to a different jury. And, of course, there's that other reason."

All three men understood. The state had exposed its entire case during the trial. The defense would shoot even more holes in it during a re-trial.

"I think that's very prudent, Mr. O'Flanagan," said Judge Barkley. "We best be ready to get back. I don't think the jury will be out long. If I was on that jury, I'm not sure how I would have voted either."

I do, thought Schor, *I'd find him guilty.*

The foreman reported a continuing deadlock and the judge declared a mistrial. O'Flanagan said the state wouldn't demand a re-trial.

Judge Barkley said, "The case against Emory Jackson for second-degree murder is dismissed. Mr. Jackson you are free to go." Pandemonium broke out in the courtroom as Schor and Ashansky hustled Jackson out a side door that led to the holding pen in the basement.

"What did the judge mean when he said I can go?" asked Jackson.

"Just that," answered Schor.

"You mean I can get on the Tubes and go to Manhattan right now?"

"Yes."

"Will I get my suitcase of clothes back?"

"It's been with the property clerk here since the trial started," Schor said.

"What about my trench knife?" asked Jackson.

"You'll get it back. But as your attorney, I have to warn you that New York City has a very tough law against carrying concealed weapons— the Sullivan Law. You and your trench knife wouldn't get past the first cop who saw you."

"Too bad. I guess I'll have to sell it," said Jackson.

Schor had planned on giving Jackson twenty bucks since he knew his "client" was dead broke.

"How much do you want for that trench knife, Emory?"

The greed showed in the man's eyes but Jackson was grateful to his attorney so he said, "I'd take thirty-five." That was how much Jackson paid Schor to defend him.

You little son-of-a-bitch, thought Schor. "I'll give you twenty. No more."

Jackson said, "I'll take it." With that he walked out of the lives of Charlie Schor and Abie Ashansky. Neither would miss him.

But Schor was right. In the weeks during and after the trial, business boomed. Ironically, most of the cases were civil, not criminal.

The extra work was almost more than Schor could handle. He said to Ashansky, "We've got to get help. What say we hire Esther Katz to run the back shop? You know her, the rabbi's niece?"

Abie asked, "Do you think she's up to it?"

"Can't do much worse than you," said Schor. "And she can take shorthand.

"You did a terrific job preparing the Jackson case. Uncovering those 150 missing trench knives turned the case around. Let's stick with it. You prepare cases, I'll try them."

"Will I get a raise?" asked Abie.

Schor answered, "As soon as the fees and retainers start rolling in."

"I'll open the transom," said Abie Ashansky.

Comes the Revolution

Attorney General A. Palmer Mitchell wanted to be president of the United States and J. Edgar Hoover was going to help him get there.

They were convinced that not only were radicals menacing the country but that the Reds were actually plotting to bring the government down on May 1, 1920.

Mitchell would destroy that conspiracy and would be rewarded with the Democratic nomination for president. Whoever the Republicans picked wouldn't have a chance.

Mitchell put J. Edgar Hoover in charge of his counterattack against the Bolsheviks and their allies. Mitchell had tapped Hoover in August as the head of the General Intelligence Bureau. It soon became known as the Radical Bureau. Mitchell and Hoover would work off their list of sixty thousand so-called radicals.

No doubt, the nation had a rough year in 1919.

Seattle had a turbulent general strike led by radicals in February. Anarchists mailed thirty bombs in April to government officials and businessmen including Mitchell.

Eight more, larger bombs went off in eight cities in June killing one man and blowing off the hands of a senator's housekeeper. One virtually destroyed Mitchell's house in Washington.

More than two hundred incidents ranging from lynchings to lethal race riots in thirty cities marred a sizzling summer.

The Justice Department raided an anarchist group in Buffalo, NY, in July and arrested some. But a Federal judge dismissed the charges against them. Taking the radicals to court wasn't working. The department turned to the deportation of alien radicals instead. The Constitution can be a nuisance.

The Boston Police Department went on strike in September terrifying city governments.

The steelworkers went out on strike nationwide that month too.

The Chicago White Sox were accused of being bribed by gamblers to throw the World Series to the underdog Cincinnati Reds in October.

The United Mine Workers struck the coal mines in November distracting Mitchell but not Hoover.

The first of the Palmer Raids, orchestrated and led by Hoover, scooped up 1,400 putative radicals in cities all over America with 650 arrested in New York alone.

It was launched on November 7, the second anniversary of the Bolshevik Revolution in Russia and targeted radical aliens from that country. Hoover's exploits were reported in the press in big, black headlines above the fold on page one. Mitchell was basking in editorial page praise.

On December 21, the "Soviet Ark," an old Army troopship, sailed out of New York under sealed orders with 249 deported radicals on board bound for Mother Russia.

The press howled for more.

Mitchell's machinations alarmed Mayor Frank Hague. He summoned Lieutenant Mickey McGurk.

"It's the Reds, Mickey. All over the country. Where there's trouble, you'll find a goddamn Bolshevik. Even at Ryerson's. Get your ass in gear, boy. Go talk to your friend, Tunney. I don't want one fucking Red stinking up my city."

McGurk found Inspector Thomas Tunney in his office.

"Well, well, look who's here. The boy lieutenant, back from the wars. I haven't seen you since Jersey City blew up."

"Good to see you too, Inspector."

Tunney laughed. "I'll not be an inspector much longer."

"What do you mean, sir?"

"Politics, my boy, politics. I'm reverting to my permanent rank of captain. 'Reverting.' That's another word for 'demotion.'

I'm finished with the Bomb Squad. They're putting me in charge of ferreting out pickpockets."

"Dear lord, that's awful," said Mickey who meant it.

"Ach! There's no use crying in my beer. I've had a good run."

"What will you do now, Inspector?"

"You mean besides hanging around the Staten Island ferry terminal looking for mutts with long fingers?" Both men laughed.

"I guess I'll pull the pin. Take my pension. Maybe open my own detective agency. Write a book."

"You know, sir, practically any town in the country would hire you as their police chief," said McGurk.

"Maybe. But I'm a New Yorker, born and bred. I couldn't live anywhere else," said Tunney. "I'll stick it out here."

"Who's going to replace you, sir?"

"Who the hell knows or cares. I hope it's someone with more political savvy than me."

Finally, Mickey got around to asking Tunney if he knew of any radical activity going on across the river. Tunney knew of nothing happening in Jersey City.

"Why should they fool around there when all they have to do is take the Tubes and they'll find all the action they want here in the city?

"We've had bombs going off all over the place. A bit of a race riot. Strikes. Protests. Everything.

"We had plenty of radicals here before the war, but we have more now. Lots of them are bad guys who would rather destroy things than sit around all night arguing about Karl Marx. We could fill the Polo Grounds with them. That J. Edgar What's-His-Name has his work cut out for him.

"But I don't think too many of them are pickpockets so they are somebody else's problem."

Mickey reassured Hague. The Bomb Squad was still keeping its eye on the strikers at Ryerson's looking for radical activity. There was none. The number of men on the picket line was dwindling as some found work elsewhere. Their ward leaders helped.

Then came the holidays. "How can we celebrate the birth of Christ?" asked Rachel. "We are Jews."

"We're not celebrating that," answered her husband, "we are celebrating the happiness of people we love."

"What the hell is Hanukah?" asked Antonio Aiello.

"Who knows? Something to do with candles," said his wife, Carmella. "But if it is important to the Ashanskys, it is important to us. Keep your mouth shut and look like you know what is going on."

Christmas Day dinner at the Aiellos threatened to surpass the boatload of mouthwatering food that had covered Carmella's table at Thanksgiving.

First came a full Italian meal complete from antipasto to cannoli. Then a rest of less than an hour ensued so the dishes could be washed. What followed was a huge turkey accompanied by a squad of vegetables. Ice cream and black coffee signaled an end to the orgy of eating.

No one slept comfortably that night. More than one lay there contemplating the deadly sin of gluttony.

The New Year's Eve celebration was lighter on eating and heavier on drinking. It was the last before Prohibition would be enforced so beer, wine and liquor all but drowned the nation.

The McGurks' New Year's Eve party was a loud success. The guests were mostly Irish and German with the Italian and Jewish contingents drinking lightly and leaving early.

Many revelers all but passed out after their celebration and awakened certain to regret their excesses.

Hoover, who preferred Edgar over John, had celebrated his twenty-fifth birthday on New Year's Day with his mother in Washington, D.C. A bachelor, he lived with her until he was forty.

The holidays over, it was back to work for everyone on Friday, January 2. Especially, Hoover. He wasn't finished. On that day, his minions struck again arresting the first of the ten thousand people nailed over the next six weeks. Three thousand were held and ultimately 556 were deported.

Lieutenant McGurk was in his office with Tony Aiello when they were interrupted by a knock on the doorframe. McGurk didn't recognize the caller.

"Lieutenant McGurk? I'm J. Edgar Hoover. I head the General Intelligence Bureau of the Justice Department."

"I've heard of you, Mr. Hoover. That's the Radical Bureau. Isn't it?" asked McGurk.

"Yes. I've heard it called that."

McGurk looked at the young man in front of him. Not tall, maybe five foot seven inches, trim, hair combed straight back. Looked a bit German.

"What can I do for you, Mr. Hoover?" McGurk asked.

"This is just a courtesy call, Lieutenant. My superior, the Attorney General, values Mayor Hague as an ally in the fight against the Communists. I understand your Bomb Squad investigates radical activity in Jersey City."

McGurk said, "We would if we had any, Mr. Hoover." McGurk didn't like the young agent who radiated arrogance.

"You may have more than you think. I'm here to suggest that you keep an eye on a longtime radical who is back in your city. Unfortunately, he is an American citizen and we can't deport him. But if breaks the law we can move on him."

"What's his name?" asked McGurk.

"Abram Ashansky."

McGurk and Aiello laughed.

"I fail to see what is funny, gentlemen," said Hoover. "Do you know this man?"

"Indeed, we do," said McGurk. "Abram Ashansky worked with us as a confidante before the war. We were worried about the munitions depot at Black Tom. Ashansky kept an eye out for radicals hereabouts for us. Abie joined the Army and became a lieutenant. He served on General Pershing's staff and was decorated for bravery."

"Some radical," said Aiello. Hoover ignored him.

"I'm glad to hear this. I'll have to update Mr. Ashansky's file," said Hoover who took out a small notebook and made notes.

McGurk thought, *Do you have a file on everybody, you little turd?*

Hoover continued. "Yes, Black Tom. That was a terrible accident."

"Bullshit," said McGurk.

"I beg your pardon," said Hoover.

"I said 'bullshit.' Black Tom was destroyed by German saboteurs. I couldn't prove it by myself and you people couldn't be bothered to try for some reason."

Hoover smiled. "I'm afraid I can't intelligently discuss Black Tom with you, Lieutenant. I joined the bureau a few weeks before the explosions and I wasn't assigned to the case."

By now, Hoover had come to dislike McGurk.

He put the knife in. "While you may not have been able to uncover any dangerous radicals in Jersey City, Lieutenant, we have. We have a man under arrest and he will be deported back to Russia soon."

"What did he do?" asked Aiello.

"I understand he was a member of a Communist militia back in Kiev and then lied about it on his immigration questionnaire when he came here. Probably a sleeper agent."

Aiello felt sick. He changed his tone and said, "You know, sir, we have a lot to learn from you Federal agents. How did you learn about this Red in Jersey City?"

That's better, thought Hoover. "From one of our many confidential informants."

"Was it the same one that told you about Ashansky?" asked Aiello.

"As a matter of fact, it was," said Hoover.

That bastard, Capparelli, thought Aiello.

"What's this Red bozo's name, Mr. Hoover?" asked McGurk who had come to the same unnerving conclusion as Aiello.

"I'm afraid I can't say. Confidential until his hearing, you know."

"Where do you keep vermin like that?" asked Aiello.

"Over in New York City. I believe you call it 'The Tombs.'"

As Hoover was talking to the Bomb Squad, Abram Ashansky was being grilled by a Federal agent at the law office on Newark Avenue. Schor was in court.

"We know you were active in radical circles before the war, Ashansky."

"Really? That's news to me. What do you mean by radical circles?"

The agent looked at his notes, "You were a member of the Industrial Workers of the World. You were or are a Wobbly."

"That's rank nonsense," said Ashansky. "I defy you to produce one bit of proof of that idiotic accusation. I always found their methods repugnant and their politics asinine."

The agent ignored him. "We also have it on good authority that you just returned from the Bolshevik controlled Ukraine. If you are not a Red, what were you doing there?"

Ashansky was quietly fuming. "That, of course, is none of your business. But I have a letter which should put an end to this foolishness."

The agent read General Pershing's letter.

"Oh, my," he said. "It seems we were misinformed."

"Indeed," said Ashansky.

"We are simply trying to protect the country from dangerous radicals," said the agent, "We have to check out every report we get. Some of them, obviously, are incorrect. I apologize, sir."

"Look, I have seen the Bolsheviks at work firsthand and they are vile. Killers not saviors. But we should be careful not to adopt their methods in our struggle against them. They thrive on unfounded accusations. We should cling to the rule of law as guaranteed by our constitution."

The agent, who was annoyed at being lectured by someone who wasn't even born in this country, said, "I've taken up enough of your time, Mr. Ashansky. But just for the record, how did you vote in the 1916 election?"

"For the record? I voted by secret ballot," said Abram Ashansky, an annoyed American citizen.

The agent left.

Ashansky, still fuming, complained to Charlie Schor.

"What the hell kind of stunt is that stupid attorney general pulling? I just was interrogated by one of his insipid goons. Accused me of being a dangerous radical. What kind of country is this anyway?"

Schor answered, "Well, it's still a country where you can call the attorney general 'stupid" and describe a federal agent as an 'insipid goon.'"

Ashansky laughed, "There is that."

Schor said, "Mitchell's got the press all fired up. They all expect the country to explode on May 1. You know more about the Bolsheviks than I do. Do you think that threat is real?"

"No. I don't. We had our revolution in 1776 and almost all Americans, except for a few loons, think that worked out pretty well. This country is not perfect. But there is none better. People know that. America is a work in progress."

Ashansky was still at his office cooling down and drawing up a will when the phone rang. It was Terry Lynch. "Abie, your brother-in-law has been arrested at work by some Federal agents. Sam's boss had the sense to call me. It's probably one of those alien raids. He'll end up in New York, most likely in the Tombs. Jack is already making some phone calls."

Fat Jack Lynch was not only a prominent Jersey City politician, he was secretly the head of the Clan na Gael in Jersey City. He had excellent contacts in New York.

"Son of a bitch," said Ashansky. "I had one of those idiots in my office quizzing me this morning."

"Good Lord," said Lynch, "What happened?"

"Nothing. I showed that letter from Pershing and he went away. He had the audacity to ask me how I voted in the presidential election."

"Not a local boy, or he'd know. Everybody in Jersey City votes Democratic," said Lynch.

"But that's not helping Sam. Any idea why they would arrest Sam?"

"No," said Abie who did remember those Red armbands in Kiev.

"Obviously somebody ratted on him," said Lynch, "maybe you'll find out at Sam's deportation hearing. You and your lawyer boss better get over to the Tombs for that hearing."

"Jack is working hard on it. I'll let you know the time and place."

"Would taking Mickey McGurk with us help?"

"Nah. This has nothing to do with law enforcement. It's politics."

Tony Aiello and Abie then exchanged information before Abie went home. Abie knew he had to tell Rachel the truth since there was no way to explain Sam being out all night. Sam had never done that.

"Rachel, honey. Let me say this first. Everything will be all right."

"Abie, you are scaring me. Is Shemuel hurt? It is eight o'clock at night. Where is he?"

"No, he hasn't been hurt. He's been arrested."

"Oh, my God!"

"Rachel, trust me," said Abie. "It's all a misunderstanding.

Charlie Schor and I will clear it up in the morning."

"Why did they arrest him? Where is he?"

"Sam's in New York City. Some Federal agents think he is a Communist."

Rachel would have laughed had she not been so frightened.

"What silliness. Shemuel is not a Communist. What kind of country is this? You told me we would be safe here. Now this."

Abie tried to soothe Rachel but he could sense her crying through much of the night.

The man who was the immigration hearing officer that would determine Sam Zeidman's fate was an affable Irishman. He got the job because he consistently produced satisfying majorities for Tammany Hall in a precinct in Hell's Kitchen on Manhattan's West Side. He was also a member of Clan na Gael.

'So you're here to represent this— Shemuel Zeidman?"

Schor said, "I am, your honor."

"Don't call me that. I'm not a judge. I'm only a hearing officer," he said. He turned to his aide and said, "Get Zeidman up here." The aide left.

The Irishman said, "Now that we're alone and all cozy, tell me how you know Jack Lynch."

Abie answered, "I served with his brother, Terry, in France and I am a member of the John J. Lynch Association. Can I show you a letter, sir?"

"Sure."

Ashansky handed him the letter from General Pershing.

"Very impressive, Lieutenant. So you were in the Ukraine with this Zeidman?"

"Yes, sir."

The hearing officer looked at a file, "You know he is accused of being a member of a Communist militia and then lying about it when he came to this country?"

"I do. But those charges are false. Zeidman was hired to help guard the electric company's coal pile in Kiev. The city changed hands several times. When the Communists were there, the guards wore a Red armband, when the Whites were there, they wore White armbands."

The Irishman laughed. "Sounds like something I would do. But how do I know that this Zeidman wasn't really a Red trying to fool the Whites?"

"May I have you read another letter, sir?"

This one, from an Army colonel in Constantinople, told of how Shemuel Zeidman had assisted Ashansky in the Ukraine.

"Hmm. What did Zeidman do to help you, Mr. Ashansky?"

Abie felt he had no alternative but to tell a slightly edited version of the truth. "Zeidman and I were fleeing the Ukraine. My mission was over but I hadn't made my report yet. We were holed up in a country house when a Communist soldier discovered us. Zeidman killed that Red and we escaped."

The Irishman was curious. "How did he kill him?"

"Shemuel Zeidman slit his throat with a straight razor."

"Jesus," said the Irishman who went back to studying the file. The aide arrived with Zeidman who looked relieved. He nodded to Abie and stood next to Schor.

The hearing judge looked up. He said, "What the hell! What's one more cutthroat over in Jersey? He can stay."

The Rhythm of Life and Death

Otto Ganz had barely gone up a dozen of the Hundred Steps when he had to stop to catch his breath.

It's this verdamnt cold. It's getting worse, he thought. A minute later, he again started the climb to the top of the Palisades from Hoboken to Jersey City. This time he managed twenty more steps but he was gasping when he stopped.

Mein Gott, it will take me all night to get home. It was February and Ganz was feeling cold despite his heavy wool coat. By the time he pushed up another twenty stairs, he was shivering.

Something is very wrong. This is not just a cold. Ganz was a tough man and he was determined to get home. Two more stubborn efforts, pulling himself up by the handrail, and he was at the top of the Hundred Steps—exhausted.

Otto Ganz was panting now but home was just a couple blocks up Ogden Avenue.

His wife, Sophia, heard the front door open and then slam shut. She was ready to serve supper. Their son, Billy, was finishing his homework on the empty side of the kitchen table.

His wife, Sophia, called out, "Otto? You are late. Supper is ready," She received no answer.

"Otto?"

Sophia walked to the front door and saw her husband sitting on the floor, his back against the door, his head between his legs.

"Good Lord! What's the matter, Otto? Are you sick?"

She reached for him and felt his forehead. "You are burning up, Otto."

Her husband answered, "No, I'm not, my love. I'm freezing."

"Let me help you. We'll get you upstairs to bed and get you warm."

"I will never make it up those stairs." Otto pointed to the parlor. "The sofa."

He pushed, she pulled, and after staggering into the parlor, he dropped onto the couch. He had walked across Sophia's good parlor rug in his dirty work shoes and she had not said a word. Otto sat upright, his arms folded across the chest. It was easier to breathe that way.

Sophia cried, "Billy! Billy! Get on your bicycle and go get Doctor Marrone. Now! Tell him your father is very sick."

Doctor Marrone arrived in less than a half hour and found Otto on the sofa, still in his coat with a blanket wrapped around him. He took the man's temperature. It was 104.7 degrees. He listened to Otto's chest with a stethoscope and didn't like what he heard. "Do you have a phone?'

He called Christ Hospital and, since it was not a busy night, an ambulance arrived within minutes. Two husky attendants carried Otto out on a stretcher to the motorized war surplus ambulance.

Billy was back. "Can I go to the hospital with my father?" he asked.

"No. I'm sorry, Billy, but you can't," said Dr. Marrone. He told Sophia her husband probably had pneumococcal pneumonia. "Can I visit him?" she asked.

"Yes. But you will have to wear a mask. I don't think Billy or Hannah should come with you." Hannah was now visibly pregnant and Marrone was caring for her.

"Oh, my God," said Sophia. "Is it that serious?"

"I'm afraid it is," said Dr. Marrone.

Otto Ganz was deteriorating, slipping towards death. His wife was there every day, mask on, chatting with him and holding his hand. Otto's responses grew weaker and less frequent.

On the fourth day, Billy said, "I don't care what anyone says, I'm going to see my father. I'm eighteen and that's final."

Billy was instructed to wear a thick gauze mask and not to touch his father.

The young man had refused to speak German once the United

States entered the war. He would say, "I'm an American. I don't speak German." And he would not answer to "Wilhelm" either. Billy was an American.

He spoke in German to his father, "Vati, don't you worry about Mama. I will take care of her. You concentrate on getting better. I am sorry, Vati, if I ever caused you pain. I never meant it, I love you, Vati."

Otto Ganz squeezed his son's hand and murmured, "No one ever had a better son, Wilhelm. I love you too."

Hannah was beside herself. She knew her father was dying and she felt she must see him. Both her mother and Mickey argued incessantly against it.

Hannah stopped pushing when Mickey said, "Hannah. You can't go. Remember what happened to Peggy when she got the flu? You can't risk it."

Poor Peggy delivered a stillborn girl. Hannah remembered. "I can't go. You're right. But my father is dying and I can't even say goodbye."

"I'll say goodbye for you," said Mickey

McGurk loved and respected his father-in-law. He knew that if the old man hadn't given his permission—no matter how reluctantly—Hannah wouldn't have married him.

He said, "Poppa, rest easy. I'll take care of your family. We all love you," Otto squeezed Mickey's hand, too drained to speak.

Otto Ganz died the next day with his wife holding his hand. He had mouthed his last words, "Ich liebe dich." Then he was gone.

Sophia took off her mask and kissed his forehead. "I love you too, my Otto. I will not love another. Wait for me."

Mickey McGurk made the arrangements for his father-in-law's funeral with a young German undertaker on Central Avenue, Otto Mack.

Otto Ganz's casket stood in the parlor where his sofa had been. Lutherans do not pray for the souls of the dead. You either go at once to heaven or you are instantly condemned to hell. No one doubted where Otto Ganz went.

Frank Hague arrived with a small entourage. He took the widow's hand and said, "I admired Otto. He was a good man and a loyal Democrat."

Then he added, "I even understand why he always stood with Wittpen."

"You are wrong, Mr. Mayor," said Sophia, "My Otto thought you were a good mayor. He voted for you last time and he was going to vote for you next year too. It is said women are going to get the vote. If we do, Mr. Hague, I'll vote for you."

"Thank you, Mrs. Ganz," said Hague as he thought, *Lose one, win one.*

Hague passed on the shot of schnapps the men were drinking in the kitchen "just to ward off the cold." He didn't drink but didn't object to others imbibing. He had no intention of enforcing prohibition in Jersey City.

The wake at home, the funeral service at Grace Lutheran Church on Summit Avenue and Pastor Schoenfelder's eulogy graveside were meant to comfort the family and their friends. But nothing could dull the pain of losing Otto Ganz. He was fifty-five, not that old, but not young either. Many of his friends were long gone.

Back at the church hall after the burial, the church ladies prepared to feed the bereaved throng. Pastor Schoenfelder was talking to Mickey McGurk. "I haven't seen much of you since I married you and Hannah."

"I know, Pastor. I'm sorry. I do miss your sermons."

"Ha! The Irish. Charming liars." The minister looked at the now obviously pregnant Hannah. "Do I get to baptize this one?" he asked.

Mickey shook his head. "I'm afraid not, Pastor. I'm sorry."

"No you're not," said Pastor Schoenfelder. "But I forgive you. You Catholics don't know any better."

The rough edges of the Reformation and Counter-Reformation had been rubbed somewhat smoother over the past century or so. At least Catholics and Protestants weren't killing each other anymore, except in Ireland which is always the exception.

Mickey and Hannah decided they would stay permanently at the Ganz house.

Hannah had said, "That way my mother and I can look out for each other. Who knows what could happen when you're at work. Or worse, what would happen if my water broke when I was home alone with Francis? I don't need that."

The move back was uneventful.

Francis was delighted to stay in his Oma's house and even happier to be sharing a bedroom with his Uncle Billy.

"I'm a big boy now," said Francis. "We can still do our homework together at the kitchen table, can't we, Uncle Billy?"

Billy, who was graduating from Dickinson High School in a few months, said, "I can't wait."

A week or so after the funeral, McGurk decided to visit an old haunt of his, Hogan's Saloon. He wanted to see if there were any changes now that Prohibition was the law of the land.

The sign on the saloon door was different. It said, "Emerald Isle Social Club. No Admittance. Members Only."

He opened the door and was greeted by an old friend, Al English, the bartender. "Mickey, it's great to see you."

"What do I have to do to become a member, Al?"

"Buy a beer."

English said, "You know Hogan's dead?"

"I heard."

"Well, I run the place now. Me and Mrs. Hogan have come to an understanding," said English looking directly into Mickey's eyes. The widow Hogan was a handsome woman ten years senior to Al English. She thought trading Hogan for English was wonderful. Hogan was a skinflint and now she was a rich widow with a good-looking, younger boyfriend. Such is life.

"Good for you, Al," said McGurk.

Prohibition was not causing any troubles in Jersey City where people were drinking what they liked or could afford. Though, good beer was hard to get.

Across the river in New York, business was even better despite the Federals' best efforts. More than 125 Prohibition agents arrested four thousand people for violations of the Volstead Act during the first two months of Prohibition. But no more than four hundred were indicted and only six were convicted. Everyone got that message.

McGurk got a call from the captain of the 5th Precinct which covered Greenville. "Mickey, Captain Hartnett here. I got a problem. My detective is on vacation. The chief says maybe you can help me out?"

"Of course, Captain. What's up?"

"We had a black bootlegger beaten up pretty bad last night at the Jersey Central's Pamrapo Station. You know where that is?"

"I do. Near Currie's Woods."

"Right. Anyway, our sambo was roughed up good by three or four guys but all he would tell the beat cop was that they were from the 'Clan.'"

McGurk asked, "The Clan? Did he mean the Clan na Gael? A Highland clan? Or what?"

"Damned if I know. Sounds like some radical outfit to me so I figured you Bomb Squad people might take charge. He's over at the German Hospital. Could you go over there and talk to him, Mickey?"

"Sure thing, Captain."

McGurk and Vince Crehan walked towards the hospital entrance. Crehan said, "I thought you said it was the German Hospital? The sign says 'Greenville Hospital.'"

"Yeah. They changed the name during the war when the Germans hereabouts weren't too popular," said McGurk.

The man's dark skin color couldn't hide the bruises on his face. A cut on his forehead had been sewn and bandaged. The doctors thought he might have suffered a concussion as well.

He spoke, "I ain't talking to no policemen. I ain't testifying against nobody. All I is going to do is get out of the likker business. It ain't healthy. No, sir."

McGurk said, "Okay, I understand what you're saying. All we want is some information so we can stop these guys. If you don't want to press charges, that's your business."

"Damn straight. Ask your questions, Mr. Policeman."

"So, do you think it was the competition that beat you up? Does someone else want to take over selling rotgut at the train station?"

The black man was miffed, "I don't sell no rotgut. I sells quality stuff. Them commuters won't buy no rotgut. But you police ain't paying attention. Those bad boys was the Klan."

"The Clan?"

The Negro sighed, "The Klu Klux Klan, man."

McGurk was shocked. "Were they wearing sheets or something?"

"Hell, no. But they said they was the Klan and they said they was going to kill me if I kept selling likker there. I'm from Alabama and I believe them. That's all you're going to get out of me, Mr. Policeman. I don't need no trouble with the Klan."

The Pamrapo station was near the Bayonne line. The investigation in Jersey City was at a dead end, so McGurk called the Bayonne Police. He talked to an old friend, Captain John Rigney, and told him what he knew.

"The Klu Klux Klan? I'll be damned. I heard a rumor that there was something like that going on at the Baptist church over on Forty-Third Street. The Klan. I'll be damned. You know the Klan's added Catholics, Jews and foreigners to their lynching list. They're big-time supporters of Prohibition too."

McGurk said, "I knew the Klan had been revived down South

and in the Midwest but I didn't know they were up here."

"Bound to happen," said Rigney. "Look. I know you don't have a case now, but we'll keep an eye on those birds over at First Baptist for you. Most of them are decent people but you always get a few assholes."

Mickey reported back to the 5th Precinct captain and to Frank Hague.

Hague said, "Any stupid bastard that puts on a sheet and parades around in my city, just might end up using it as a shroud."

Hannah gave birth to a blue-eyed baby boy at Christ Hospital without any complications. The tribe rejoiced.

The McGurks had already picked out a name for him. He would be Anthony, named for Mickey's best friend and colleague, Detective Sergeant Tony Aiello.

Aiello was married to McGurk's second cousin, Peggy McCann, and she would be the infant's godmother.

The identity of the godfather came as a bit of a surprise. It was Vince Crehan, the young plainclothesman who was bucking for detective on Mickey's Bomb Squad.

This would add Crehan to the growing "family" of Irish, Sicilians, Germans and Jews who were bound together by blood, marriage and close friendship. It was a New World phenomenon forged by many who had left their Old World families behind.

The child was baptized in Mickey's home parish, St. Anne's, on the boulevard.

The christening party was held in the Ganz house with relatives and well-wishers wandering in and out all day. Frank Hague, Mickey's "uncle" by marriage, made his token appearance accompanied by several 12th Ward pooh-bahs.

Hague gave six-year-old Francis a silver dollar. He was the boy's godfather.

The next Sunday, Hannah and her mother took Anthony to

Grace Lutheran Church to show him off. As expected, he was declared to be one of the most beautiful children born in recent centuries.

Pastor Schoenfelder, his thumb dripping with water, caressed the infant's forehead and silently said the words of baptism — just in case the Papists got it wrong. The boy's mother and grandmother knew what he was doing and were content.

At first, Francis wasn't sure he liked the idea of a baby brother. It seemed Mommy paid much, too much attention to that little thing who couldn't even talk.

But his Oma showered Francis with love, attention and cookies, constantly praising him for being a "wonderful, big brother."

His father took him out every evening to play catch and his mother was careful not to ignore him.

Francis didn't like that baby Anthony slept in his parents' room but at least he could hardly hear him crying in the room where he and Uncle Billy slept. That was good.

Francis was reconciled with his fate especially when his Uncle Billy said, "Little Tony is lucky to have a big brother like you. I wish I had one."

Peggy McCann, tall as tree and big as a house, gave birth to a girl. The entire tribe was thrilled but none more so than her mother-in-law, Carmella.

"I told you it would be a girl," she said. "I have the perfect name for her."

Peggy braced herself.

Her mother-in-law continued, "Agnes. Agnes Aiello. Don't that sound good?"

Peggy McCann Aiello started to cry. Agnes was the name of her aunt who became her surrogate mother when her father died and her mother was committed to an insane asylum.

Peggy had a secret. She pushed her father off a roof. Only

Tony and her confessor knew why.

"Mama," said Peggy, "I don't think I could love you more than I do now. How sweet of you to think of 'Agnes'."

"It's only right. She's your mother. Me, I'll have lots of grandchildren named after me. But her— maybe this is her only chance."

"Mama, I love you!"

"Of course you do," said Carmella.

Abie Ashansky was not much of a beer drinker. He preferred wine. After a glass with supper, his wife, Rachel, brought up a subject she didn't want to discus in front of her brother.

Sam was attending an English class at night at Temple Beth-el taught by Esther Katz. That's where he met Mordechai "Frenchie" Adler.

Frenchie was from Quebec and had come to the United States simply by walking across the unmarked border. He made his way south and landed in Jersey City.

Sam and Frenchie became fast friends. They spoke in a combination of Yiddish and English with a word of French thrown in now and again.

Before long they were talking about setting up their own trucking business. They had great fun coming up with a name for it. Sam offered "A to Z Trucking" playing off their last names.

They planned to buy a war surplus truck and find a garage somewhere to store and service it. They had a problem though. They had no money. But this was America and though it might take months, or even years, they would find the money and start their business.

"Dearest," Rachel said to Abie, "You know Shemuel wants to buy a truck with that friend of his and they want to start their own business?"

"I know and I wish I could lend him the money he needs. But I can't spare it," said Abie.

"I can," said Rachel. "My dowry. He'd pay it back."

Thus was born A to Z Trucking. Sam and Frenchie worked sixteen hours a day and thought nothing of it.

The two friends were good, hard workers who were scrupulously honest and fair with their customers. Even Al Smith, the moving man, threw a few jobs to them when he had too much to handle. He thought Terry Lynch would like that.

Doreen Aiello was enjoying her studies at the New Jersey Normal School in Montclair. Waiting on her fellow students at breakfast was not taxing although some of them treated her like hired help. But Doreen was noticed. "She's not bad looking, for a wop," said one admirer.

Even happier was her older sister Theresa who worked on the line at the Dixon Pencil Company. One of the mechanics, a young Italian man, had asked if he could take her to Mass on Sunday. This might be the start of something.

Her mother approved but reluctantly. Ever the Sicilian, she cautioned her husband, "He's Neapolitan. You know what they're like."

"Mama, this is America," said Antonio. "You love the Irish girl. Tolerate that guinea boy."

The pride of Jersey City was the William L. Dickinson High School. The huge building was designed by John T. Rowland in the Beaux-Arts style and was completed in 1906. It was designed to accommodate five thousand students although that many were never enrolled.

One of the men who addressed Dickinson's graduating class of 1920 had not graduated from high school. Nor did he possess an elementary school diploma either, having been expelled from the sixth grade.

But there he was—Frank Hague, mayor of Jersey City, undisputed Democratic leader of New Jersey and soon to be vice-chairman of the National Democratic Committee, a post he would hold for a generation.

The auditorium, which held two thousand, was packed with parents, relatives and friends of the graduates, and with members of Hague's organization who hoped he would notice them and remember their zeal.

Hague, a notoriously bad speaker, kept his remarks short. It really didn't matter, since like every other high school commencement address ever given in America, it was instantly forgotten by the graduates.

Billy Ganz was handsome in his cap and gown and held the attention of the assorted Ganzes, McGurks, Aiellos, Lynches, Ashanskys and their friends. They applauded loudly as he walked across the stage to receive his diploma.

Not two weeks later, Billy Ganz had landed a job as a messenger with J.P. Morgan & Company on Wall Street, two hundred feet from the New York Stock Exchange.

"I'm either going to be a banker or a stockbroker someday," said Billy proudly.

"What's a stockbroker?" asked his mother.

Blood in the Streets

Billy Ganz had a delightful summer. He had a job and had money in his pocket. Real money, dollars not dimes.

Every morning he was up and dressed—long pants, no more knickers for him—and boarded the number 17 streetcar making the dizzying drop down the trestle from the Palisades to Hoboken where he would catch the ferry. Then a subway ride and a walk of a few blocks to the J.P. Morgan & Company at 23 Wall Street.

Ganz loved to ride the subways. There were always pretty girls to look at even if they never looked back at him.

Billy was thinking a lot about girls these days and the beach was the best place to get a good look at them.

Coney Island, across two rivers and at the edge of Brooklyn, was not easy to get to from Jersey City but Billy and a buddy had managed it three times this summer. They spent time at each of the three amusement parks—Steeplechase, Luna Park and Wonderland—but first it was to the beach to ogle the girls.

There was a lot to see—faces, legs, arms, shoulders—and what delights you couldn't actually see were there in undisguised profile. Of course, one had to be careful not to stare too long or think too hard. A highly embarrassing reaction could be subdued only by a plunge into the Atlantic Ocean.

Billy even got to take a girl from church—not the prettiest one—on a moonlight cruise up the Hudson on an excursion boat. Billy had been rewarded with a few short kisses, more pecks than passion, and he was looking forward to a long "goodnight" on her stoop.

When they arrived home, her father and two brothers were there waiting. All Billy got was a handshake—from her father.

His job as a messenger took him frequently to the New York

Stock Exchange. He loved the bustle there. It looked like someone had kicked open an anthill on the floor but Billy knew there was purpose behind all the frantic shouting and waving. Money was being made and lost.

That'll be me down there. Real soon, dreamed Billy Ganz.

Lunchtime was Billy's favorite time at work. If the weather was nice, the street would be full of people visiting and eating their lunch. Stenographers, clerks, receptionists and secretaries strolling, sitting, laughing and all of them approachable.

Not that Billy did much of that. He was still a bit shy. Still it was great fun to watch. But not today. Rain was in the forecast for Thursday, September 16, 1920.

The weather was of no concern to Abie Ashansky as he conferred with Charles Schor at their law office.

"I have to be in court all day today," said Schor. "But if you're free, you could run over to Manhattan and pick up a check at the Equitable for a client of ours."

"Pick up a check? Why don't they just mail it?"

Schor laughed. "Those thieving bastards say they don't trust the mail with such a large check. It's for $6,000."

"Wow! What's the story?"

"The usual. Our client's restaurant burned down and the insurance company refused to pay. You know the insurance business. Collect premiums, deny claims."

"What was their excuse?" asked Abie.

"They said their adjustors suspected arson and they wouldn't pay while the case was being investigated. A year later the case was still open. I checked with our fire department people and they said they never considered arson. The fire was caused by faulty electrical wiring. So we sued.

"Our client got his $5,000 insurance money plus an extra $1,000 the jury tacked on as punitive damages."

"So what's our cut?"

"Twenty percent. $1,200."

"Let me get my hat. That's Esther's salary for a year."

The insurance company passed Ashansky from office to office for about a half hour, but he finally signed a receipt and put an envelope with the check into his inside jacket pocket.

As he emerged onto the street, he looked at his pocket watch. It was almost noon. Ashansky knew Billy Ganz worked as a messenger at J.P. Morgan which was close by.

I'll surprise the kid and take him to lunch, he thought.

As he started to walk to J.P. Morgan, Ashansky was one of hundreds on the street who failed to notice a horse and wagon pulling up in front of the U.S. Assay Office across the street.

The teamster fiddled with something under a tarpaulin and then dismounted. He walked towards the corner.

He looked like any other workman although he was quite short. No girl looked at him. No one noticed him.

In his wagon was a quarter of a ton of cast iron window sash weights perched on top of a hundred pounds of dynamite.

As the little man rounded the corner, Abie bent down by a mailbox to tie a loose shoelace.

Billy was walking through the gate in the stone railing that separated offices from the public area in the lobby.

The dynamite exploded.

The ear-splitting blast flattened Abie and tore the mailbox's bolts out of the concrete. The mailbox tumbled end over end, spewing letters and packages for thirty yards.

It was followed a nanosecond later by a scythe of shrapnel that cut its bloody way through the young people in its path. Thirty of them died in that instant.

All was still for a moment. Then an eruption of screams and cries from the hundreds of wounded echoed off the damaged facades of nearby buildings.

A streetcar two blocks away was de-railed and smoke and

debris reached the thirty-fourth floor of the Equitable Building and then rained down. Bloody bits and pieces of the obliterated horse fell adding to the horror.

A bruised and dazed Abie rose to his knees and looked around at the carnage.

My God! What happened? Am I back in France? Where am I?

Abie's head cleared and he was on his feet. So were others, battered but alive.

Billy!

Abie ran towards the entrance of J.P. Morgan. Its long metal grill and glass windows were gone as were all the windows in sight, shattered by the immense pressure wave.

He crunched his way through broken glass and misshapen metal in the lobby and saw Billy Ganz by the stone railing, bleeding and unconscious. Two other messengers were sitting up moaning.

Billy had a nasty cut on his face and Abie could see a sliver of glass sticking out between the eyelids of the boy's left eye. Abie gently rolled up the upper eyelid. The glass was imbedded in Billy's eye.

Abie did not pull the glass out. He looked around and saw Dixie cups lying by a shattered water cooler. He cut the bottom half off two paper cups and put them over both eyes fixing them to Billy's head with paper tape. Rolls of tape were on the floor amid the glass.

Abie searched Billy's limbs for arterial bleeding and found none. The lacerations on his left arm and leg wouldn't kill Billy. Abie cut the sleeves off Billy's shirt with his clasp knife and used them as bandages held down with paper tape. The boy was still unconscious.

I've got to get him out of here. To a hospital.

Abie, a very strong man, grunted as he lifted Billy into his arms and carried him out into the bloody street.

Another young messenger was standing next to an open car door. "Bring him over here, mister. Over here," he yelled waving his arm.

Abie placed Billy upright in the back seat next to another bleeding but conscious man.

"Don't bump those paper cups, buddy. Don't let him touch them if he wakes up. Tell him he's not blind but hurt and tell the doctors he has glass in his eye."

"You bet," said the man putting his arm around Billy.

A girl, her face bloodied, was helped into the front seat and the automobile picked its way through overturned cars, flaming wrecks, clusters of people helping the injured and lifeless bodies. It turned at the corner.

"Where are they going?" Abie asked the messenger who had called to him.

"St. Vincent's," said the boy. "Who was that?"

"Billy Ganz."

"Oh shit! Well, thank God he's alive."

"I certainly do, son. Thank you."

The boy's quick thinking in commandeering private cars to take casualties to the hospital was being emulated by policemen who had arrived on the scene.

Abie's side hurt where the mailbox had glanced off him and he was beginning to stiffen up.

Well, I'm here. I might as well try to make myself useful.

He was splinting the arm of a sobbing young woman with a rolled-up newspaper and a couple of shoelaces when a man holding a big Speed Graphic camera said, "Say, pal, what's your name?"

Taking unawares, Abie answered, "Abram Ashansky. Why?"

"Where you from?"

"Jersey City. Why?"

The man was writing on some copy paper. He pointed to the

lapel pin on Abie's alpaca jacket and asked, "Is that the Croix de Guerre?"

"Yes, but what business is it of yours, mister?"

"You'll see," said the obviously uninjured man who touched two fingers to his fedora in salute and said, "See you in the funny papers, pal."

A puzzled Ashansky watched as the man moved off, stopping to take more pictures.

Less than a half hour later, Lieutenant McGurk got a telephone call from his counterpart on the New York Police Department's Bomb Squad.

"Mickey, some mokes just tried to blow up the Stock Exchange. We got a lot of people dead and a hell of lot more hurt. We don't know who did it, but could you people keep an eye on the Tubes stations and the ferries?"

"Who are we looking for?" asked McGurk.

"Who knows? Maybe you'll know 'em when you see 'em."

The second he heard the words "Stock Exchange" Mickey pumped adrenalin. His young brother-in-law worked near there.

His wife and mother-in-law were at the door minutes after McGurk got home.

"Have you heard anything?" asked Hannah.

"No. Let's see if Billy calls home." He didn't.

McGurk sped directly to St. Vincent's Hospital, the one nearest to Wall Street. The place was in chaos. He flashed his badge here, there and everywhere and finally found someone who had a list of the known dead.

"Let's see—Gallagher, Gannon, Harris… Nope. No Ganz."

McGurk went through the wards one by one catching and quizzing annoyed nurses.

Finally. "Billy Ganz? We've got a Wilhelm Ganz. Do you think it might be him?" McGurk stopped at the bed. It was Billy.

He could sense it rather than see it.

The slender young man was unrecognizable under a swath of immaculate, perfectly wrapped bandages that covered his eyes, face and most of his head. Only his nose and mouth and a tuft of brown hair protruded.

It was Billy all right. He was not conscious.

McGurk grabbed a passing intern by the arm. "How's he doing, Doctor?"

"Not too bad," said the intern. "We saved the left eye. Just barely. Someone on the scene knew what he was doing. This boy showed up here with glass in his eye. That someone put a Dixie cup over the eye to protect it. Gave us a fighting chance. We did the rest.

"He has a deep laceration on his left cheek, and cuts on his left arm and left thigh. All from glass. He didn't get hit by the metal. He's lost a lot of blood. But he'll be okay."

"How come you bandaged both eyes?" McGurk asked.

"If we leave the good eye uncovered, he'll move it and the bad eye will move with it. We don't want that right now."

"Is he in a coma?"

The doctor answered, "No. Just sedated. He should come to pretty soon. He's had a concussion too. He won't be happy. We're going to keep him for a while."

McGurk stood there looking at that sweet, innocent, mutilated boy. He shook his head and thought, *Sweet Jesus. There is no end to it.*

More than 140 people felled by the explosion were seriously injured and hospitalized. Eight of them died. Hundreds more were cut or battered.

Trading was immediately halted on the New York Stock Exchange to prevent a panicky sell-off.

Suspicion immediately fell on the Bolsheviks, Communists, anarchists and others who viscerally hared capitalism. The massive investigation into the bombing, led by J. Edgar Hoover, was launched immediately. It would last three years and produce nothing.

Once hundreds of policemen, nurses, doctors and ambulances— with interns aboard— inundated the street, Abie realized he wasn't needed any longer. He reached into his bloodstained jacket's inner pocket. The check was a bit crumpled but still there.

Good thing. It probably would have taken the damn insurance company another year to cut a new check.

It was an exhausted Abie that opened the door to his flat an hour or so later.

Rachel, her back to him, said, "Hello, my love. How was your day?"

The freelance photographer was bargaining with the city editor of *The Jersey Journal.*

"It's worth twenty bucks. That guy is from Jersey City. Look at his jacket. That's the Croix de Guerre."

Curious, Jackie Farrell wandered over and looked at the photograph. "I know him," he said. "That's Abie Ashansky. Charlie Schor's law clerk."

"You mean from the Jackson trial?" asked the city editor.

"Yep."

The photographer smiled. *Cha-ching!*

The city editor spoke to the photographer, "Okay, twenty dollars. But I want a guarantee that nobody else gets this picture."

"Twenty-five dollars and it's guaranteed."

"You son-of-a-bitch." The photographer didn't take offense. He just smiled.

"All right, you bloodsucker. I'll go get your money."

He pointed to Farrell. "You. Sit down and start writing a sidebar and it better be good. The comptroller is going to faint when I ask him for twenty-five dollars."

Farrell was typing furiously when the city editor returned and looked over his shoulder.

A decorated veteran from Jersey City proved his mettle once again yesterday when he was quick to help the injured at the horrific explosion that took the lives of 40 people on Wall Street in Manhattan.

"Jesus Christ, Jackie. You're writing like an old biddy. That lead's awful. Who the hell would bother to read it?"

"Okay. Okay. I was going to re-write it anyway." Farrell took the page from his typewriter and inserted a fresh sheet of copy paper.

A Jersey City war hero, narrowly escaping death, rose and used his hard earned battlefield skills to save the lives of innocent people cut down by an anarchist's bomb that cold-bloodedly killed 40 men and women yesterday on Wall Street in Manhattan.

"That's a bit better," said the city editor. "Change 'anarchist' to 'Bolshevik'."

The city editor added, "I'm a little nervous about that direct quote too. You haven't talked to the guy."

"Don't worry," said Farrell. "I know Ashansky. That's what he would say."

"Good enough. By the way who are the 'medical authorities' you're quoting?"

"The photographer," said Jackie Farrell.

Abie didn't awake until almost nine o'clock. He ate a bagel, kissed Rachel goodbye and headed for police headquarters.

McGurk, Aiello and Crehan were plotting their day. Abie stuck his head in their small office.

"How's Billy?"

"Okay," said McGurk. "He's on the mend. But he'll be in the hospital for a while."

"How's the eye?"

"They saved it," said McGurk. "How'd you know about Billy's eye?

"I was there, Mickey. I patched Billy up and put him in a car headed for St. Vincent's."

"Good God!"

Abie walked into the law office and handed the Equitable check to Esther Katz. "Jeez, this envelope looks like it went through a war."

"It did," said Abie. Esther then coaxed the whole story from him.

Charlie Schor had been in court all morning and didn't return until one o'clock. He walked in waving a copy of *The Jersey Journal.* "Have you seen the newspaper?"

"No. Why?"

He passed the paper to Abie who was startled to see his picture spread over four columns on the front page.

Abie read the story with growing embarrassment.

Medical authorities on the scene said Ashansky probably saved the lives of a half-dozen people. "He's a hero," said one. Ashansky demurred and said, "I'm no hero. I just did what had to be done. The doctors, nurses and policemen are the heroes."

"When did you talk to Farrell," Schor asked.

Abie laughed. "I didn't. But that's pretty much what I would have said." He read on.

Ashansky is a law clerk associated with Attorney Charles Schor at 600 Newark Avenue and was prominent in the recent murder trial of Emory Jackson that ended with a hung jury.

Ashansky was trained as a lawyer at Russia's most prestigious law school, St. Vladimir's, but might have to put in the better part of three years as a law clerk before taking the bar examination here unless the New Jersey Bar Association intervenes.

"Don't you love Farrell? When you finish reading the story, there's an editorial on page six," said Schor.

The editorial recounted Ashansky's war service and bravery in France, mentioned his budding legal career in Jersey City, commended him for his actions at the Wall Street disaster and then concluded:

Abram Ashansky has proven to be a distinguished citizen of Jersey City. Our people hope that the New Jersey Bar Association quickly clears any obstacles to his taking the bar examination so that he can become an equally distinguished member of the legal profession.

"How about that?" asked Schor.

A red-faced Abie said, "It was just luck that I was there to help."

"Fortune favors the bold," said Charlie Schor.

Billy was released from the hospital as soon as his stitches were removed.

The first time Abie and Rachel visited, Sophia Ganz hugged and kissed Abie while Hannah waited her turn.

Billy shook hands with him and said, "Thank you, Uncle Abie."

Abie ran his finger over the scar on Billy's left cheek. "Looks pretty good. Not bad at all. Do you remember anything, Billy?"

"No. All I remember is a loud bang and then I woke up in the hospital with my eyes covered. That scared me. I thought I was blind."

Abie laughed. "God forbid."

It seemed everyone Billy knew, family and friend, came to visit him on Ogden Avenue. Aunt Carmella brought him a dish of his favorite manicotti. Sam Zeidman, who worked nearby on Bowers Street, brought a quart of ice cream.

His nephew was happy to help him eat it. Francis Otto McGurk was now a second grader at St. Nicholas School and told everyone he met, "The Reds tried to kill my Uncle Billy but my Uncle Abie saved him."

Even the girl from church and her mother came. To Billy's surprise, the older women left him and Betty alone in the living room. The conversation was awkward at first but soon grew animated. Bill thought Betty was quite beautiful when she laughed and she laughed a lot.

Several times, she put her hand on his arm and her touch was electric. The mothers, who saw this, nodded to each other.

When they were leaving, the girl said, "I think you are very brave, Billy." She kissed him on his unscarred cheek and then on the lips. She lingered but a moment and when she backed away her smile was as bright as the future. They would marry someday.

Charlie Schor put down the telephone and called out to Abram Ashansky, "Abe, I've got good news for you."

"What?"

"That was the Bar Association. The credentials committee is going to interview you in two weeks and determine how much credit to give you for your legal education in Russia."

"Terrific," said Abie.

"I'll bet you get to take the bar exam by this time next year. Congratulations, partner."

"What a great country!" said Abram Ashansky.

Abie and his cobbled together American family were destined to spend many years enjoying a peaceful, ordinary life but that wouldn't last. The times would get worse. The 20th century still had almost eighty years to go. But the "family" endured.

Sam Zeidman would marry Esther Katz. Rachel Ashansky would give birth to a son named Dennis. Major General Dennis Nolan would command the Army's 2nd Corps. Billy Ganz would become a stockbroker. Charlie Schor would be a magistrate. Theresa Aiello would wed her mechanic. Abie Ashansky would become a respected lawyer. Doreen Aiello would teach at Dickinson High. Terry Lynch would become a state senator. Carmella Aiello would die happy, surrounded by her grandchildren. Frank Hague would be mayor for another twenty-five years.

Emory Jackson would die alone.

Through it all Lady Liberty stood on her pedestal in the river, touching Jersey City with her morning shadow, her torch beckoning beside the golden door.

And still they come.

Acknowledgments

This book wouldn't have been written if the late Warren Murphy, my friend and colleague of almost sixty years, had not persuaded me to sit down and write my first novel with him. This was an act of incredible generosity when you consider that I had never written anything more complex than a feature story for a newspaper while Murphy was the bestselling author of more than a hundred books.

Her Morning Shadow owes much to the early and ongoing critiques and suggestions of Richard S. Wheeler, winner of the Owen Wister Award for Lifetime Achievement and holder of six Silver Spur Awards for his Western novels.

Leslie Wilbur, emeritus professor at the University of Southern California and the author—at age ninety-three—of *Destination USC: Via Luck, Pluck and the GI Bill*, was a constant source of advice and encouragement.

Special acknowledgments go to the talented folks at John Hunt Publishing. John Hunt gave me my first publishing break, Dominic James my second, and Sarah-Beth Watkins, Krystina Kellingsley and Maria Barry who read the first draft suggested changes which make this, the author hopes, a better book.

Special thanks go to my lovely and longsuffering wife who had to put up with me during the months of writing *Her Morning Shadow* and the agonizing, interminable months of rewriting and editing it. Her thirty-five years of experience helped.

TOP HAT BOOKS

Top Hat Books

Historical fiction that lives

We publish fiction that captures the contrasts, the achievements, the optimism and the radicalism of ordinary and extraordinary times across the world.

We're open to all time periods and we strive to go beyond the narrow, foggy slums of Victorian London. Where are the tales of the people of fifteenth century Australasia? The stories of eighth century India? The voices from Africa, Arabia, cities and forests, deserts and towns? Our books thrill, excite, delight and inspire.

The genres will be broad but clear. Whether we're publishing romance, thrillers, crime, or something else entirely, the unifying themes are timescale and enthusiasm. These books will be a celebration of the chaotic power of the human spirit in difficult times. The reader, when they finish, will snap the book closed with a satisfied smile.

If you have enjoyed this book, why not tell other readers by posting a review on your preferred book site.

Recent bestsellers from Tops Hat Books are:

Grendel's Mother
The Saga of the Wyrd-Wife
Susan Signe Morrison
Grendel's mother, a queen from Beowulf, threatens the fragile
political stability on this windswept land.
Paperback: 978-1-78535-009-2 ebook: 978-1-78535-010-8

Queen of Sparta
A Novel of Ancient Greece
T.S. Chaudhry
History has relegated her to the role of bystander, what if Gorgo,
Queen of Sparta, had played a central role in the Greek resistance
to the Persian invasion?
Paperback: 978-1-78279-750-0 ebook: 978-1-78279-749-4

Mercenary
R.J. Connor
Richard Longsword is a mercenary, but this time it's not for
money, this time it's for revenge…
Paperback: 978-1-78279-236-9 ebook: 978-1-78279-198-0

Black Tom
Terror on the Hudson
Ron Semple
A tale of sabotage, subterfuge and political shenanigans
in Jersey City in 1916; America is on the cusp of war and the fate of
the nation hinges on the decision of one young policeman.
Paperback: 978-1-78535-110-5 ebook: 978-1-78535-111-2

Destiny Between Two Worlds
A Novel about Okinawa
Jacques L. Fuqua, Jr.
A fateful October 1944 morning offered no inkling that the lives of
thousands of Okinawans would be profoundly changed—forever.
Paperback: 978-1-78279-892-7 ebook: 978-1-78279-893-4

Cowards
Trent Portigal
A family's life falls into turmoil when the parents' timid political
dissidence is discovered by their far more enterprising children.
Paperback: 978-1-78535-070-2 ebook: 978-1-78535-071-9

Godwine Kingmaker
Part One of The Last Great Saxon Earls
Mercedes Rochelle
The life of Earl Godwine is one of the enduring enigmas of English
history. Who was this Godwine, first Earl of Wessex;
unscrupulous schemer or protector of the English? The answer
depends on whom you ask...
Paperback: 978-1-78279-801-9 ebook: 978-1-78279-800-2

The Last Stork Summer
Mary Brigid Surber
Eva, a young Polish child, battles to survive the designation of
"racially worthless" under Hitler's Germanization Program.
Paperback: 978-1-78279-934-4 ebook: 978-1-78279-935-1 $4.99 £2.99

Messiah Love
Music and Malice at a Time of Handel
Sheena Vernon
The tale of Harry Walsh's faltering steps on his journey to success
and happiness, performing in the playhouses of Georgian London.
Paperback: 978-1-78279-768-5 ebook: 978-1-78279-761-6

A Terrible Unrest
Philip Duke
A young immigrant family must confront the horrors of the
Colorado Coalfield War to live the American Dream.
Paperback: 978-1-78279-437-0 ebook: 978-1-78279-436-3

Readers of ebooks can buy or view any of these bestsellers by
clicking on the live link in the title. Most titles are published
in paperback and as an ebook. Paperbacks are available in
traditional bookshops. Both print and ebook formats are
available online.

Find more titles and sign up to our readers' newsletter at
http://www.johnhuntpublishing.com/fiction

Follow us on Facebook at https://www.facebook.com/JHPfiction
and Twitter at https://twitter.com/JHPFiction